BY DANIEL KALLA
FROM TOM DOHERTY ASSOCIATES

Blood Lies

Cold Plague

Of Flesh and Blood

Pandemic

Rage Therapy

Resistance

The Far Side of the Sky

The Far Side of the Sky

DANIEL KALLA

A TOM DOHERTY AND ASSOCIATES BOOK | NEW YORK

This is a work of fiction. All of the characters, organizations, and events portrayed in this novel are either products of the author's imagination or are used fictitiously.

THE FAR SIDE OF THE SKY

Copyright © 2012 by Daniel Kalla

All rights reserved.

A Forge Book
Published by Tom Doherty Associates, LLC
175 Fifth Avenue
New York, NY 10010

www.tor-forge.com

Forge® is a registered trademark of Tom Doherty Associates, LLC.

ISBN 978-0-7653-6890-4

Forge books may be purchased for educational, business, or promotional use. For information on bulk purchases, please contact Macmillan Corporate and Premium Sales Department at 1-800-221-7945 extension 5442 or write specialmarkets@macmillan.com.

First Edition: June 2012
First Mass Market Edition: August 2013

Printed in the United States of America

0 9 8 7 6 5 4 3 2 1

ACKNOWLEDGMENTS

While this story does not reflect my specific family history, it does parallel their desperate struggle to escape the Holocaust. I'm comforted to know that my father, who, as a Jewish teenager in Budapest, survived World War II largely on his wits, had the chance to read the manuscript before he died. I am so thankful for the love and support of my family. My wife, Cheryl, my mother, Judy, and my two daughters, Chelsea and Ashley, help to keep me even-keeled through the ups and downs of writing, medicine, and life.

I'm so grateful to Kit Schindell, an invaluable freelance editor whose insights and feedback always improve my work. Also, I want to acknowledge my agents, Henry Morrison and Danny Baror, for their guidance and wisdom.

I consider myself fortunate for my longstanding relationship with the world-class team at Tor-Forge, including such esteemed professionals as Tom Doherty and Linda Quinton. I am most appreciative for all of Paul Stevens's hard work and feedback. And I am thrilled to collaborate again with Natalia Aponte, a friend and top-notch editor who has helped me to hone this story.

Finally, I would like to acknowledge the people who lived and died in Shanghai during World War II. As I researched this novel, I was struck time and time again by the dignity, bravery, and sense of community among the indigenous Chinese and the transplanted German Jews—two oppressed peoples who lived side by side with remarkable tolerance and mutual respect, in an age of neither.

PART I

Chapter 1

The shadow still swayed over the pavement. Franz Adler tried to blink away the memory of his brother's dangling corpse and the silhouette it cast across the sidewalk, but the image looped over and over in his head.

A pane of glass erupted somewhere at street level, startling Franz. His hand slipped and he pierced Esther's skin at the wrong angle. "*Verdammt!*" he swore under his breath as he yanked back the needle's tip.

Three more windows shattered. The mob was so close. Its drunken cheers and raucous laughter infected the room. Franz could almost smell the stench of stale beer and body odor that must have wafted after it.

Concentrate, Adler! Finish suturing and go collect your daughter!

Eyes open or closed, the mental image persisted. As a surgeon, Franz had witnessed numerous deaths, but none compared with the memory of his own brother's.

A damp November chill permeated the spacious apartment. Fearing a fire, the caretaker had shut off the boiler. The windows were draped and the lights off, save for the flickering flame of three candles that projected long writhing shadows against the walls.

Franz had to squint through the weak light to study Esther's blood-caked arm before him.

Another pane shattered three stories below. Franz heard a fresh wave of cheers as though it were some kind of feat to deface a city. But the voices grew more distant as the bulk of the mob stomped farther down Liechtenstein Strasse.

Esther Adler huddled for warmth under the blanket that Franz had wrapped around her shoulders. His sister-in-law's complexion was ashen. Abrasions criss-crossed her face. But amazingly, her gray eyes still possessed a remnant of their usual calm. "Your hands, Franz," Esther said in a hushed voice.

Franz glanced down at his shaky fingers. "Not enough light," he muttered.

"We will manage." A tremulous smile flitted across Esther's lips. "With God's help."

"God?" Franz nodded to the curtains, which glowed red from the fires consuming Vienna. "Essie, how could it be any clearer that there is no God?" he snapped.

She closed her eyes for a moment. "I can't believe that. I won't."

Franz took a slow breath and mentally aligned the edges of Esther's jagged wound, estimating the number of stitches it would require. Twenty, possibly more. He hoped he had enough catgut to close the laceration, which snaked almost the entire length of Esther's forearm but, remarkably, spared the largest nerves and blood vessels.

Hannah needs you, he reminded himself as he ran a fourth stitch through Esther's flesh. She barcly flinched, despite the lack of local anesthetic. Franz always carried his suture kit in his medical bag, but he silently cursed himself for not having brought the rest of his supplies upstairs sooner. From the moment he first heard the wireless broadcasts—Goebbels's shrill shrieks of "*Juden*" this and "*Juden*" that—Franz had expected the worst. But he had not foreseen just how blood-thirsty the backlash would become. *Who could have predicted this?*

Earlier, Franz had tried to rush downstairs to get lo-cal anesthetic and bandages, but Esther grabbed his arm and, dripping blood onto his sleeve, begged him to proceed without freezing. She claimed to be more afraid of the injection than the stitches, but they both knew what she really feared: if the Brownshirts or other thugs caught Franz rummaging through his ground-floor surgery, he would never return. And his daughter, Hannah, was waiting.

"It's fine, Franz," Esther whispered. "Just continue. Please."

Franz looked into her kind eyes. Narrow-faced with sharp features, Esther had deep-set gray eyes that made her look older than her thirty-two years. Though not conventionally pretty, she radiated intelligence, humor, and, especially, compassion. Her empathy was bound-less. Even now, with her arm splayed open in the wake of her husband's lynching, little more than an hour ear-lier, she seemed as concerned for her niece's welfare as her own. But her trembling shoulders belied her com-posed expression.

"All right, Essie," he said as he looped another stitch through her arm, bringing the ragged edges a little closer together.

"We must get Hannah away from here, Franz." Es-ther motioned toward the silhouettes of flames danc-ing against the curtains. "Our time has run out, *ja?*"

Franz nodded, ashamed of having resisted for so long. Until the Nazis set Vienna ablaze, he had clung to his naive belief that their reign of terror was a dark but passing phase in history. That his countrymen would come to their collective senses. But his brother, Karl, had been right from the outset. Nothing, not even blood, would appease these crazed animals.

Franz gazed into Esther's glistening eyes. Even though Karl was his only sibling and the best friend he had ever known, his loss paled compared with hers. Esther had no brothers or sisters, her parents were long dead, and Karl and she had been unable to conceive a child. Esther and Karl had only each other, but that had always been enough. Franz had never known a couple more deeply in love. He racked his brain for some consoling words, but none came to mind. His brother, the lawyer, had been the verbally gifted one. So Franz finished stitching in torturous silence. He was reaching for strips of a torn shirt to use as a bandage when he heard a plaintive scream. He froze, then rushed to the window.

"*Vorsicht!*" Esther cautioned. "Be careful! Don't let them see you!"

Franz gently peeled back the edge of the drape, exposing only enough of a gap to peek out to the street below.

A group of stragglers—some were dressed in civilian clothing, others wore the brown shirts, matching caps, and bloodred swastika armbands of the storm troopers—milled about on the road like wolves circling their kill. In the center of them, an older woman lay sprawled on her back, flailing wildly. A blond woman in a long leather coat stood over her, pinning the fallen woman down with a foot to the chest.

Franz spotted a balding old man lying ten or so feet away. His torso was twisted unnaturally, with his knees facing in almost the opposite direction to his scrawny chest. A fat storm trooper hovered over him, holding a thick wooden club in his pudgy fingers. The trooper raised the club high over his head and let it hang suspended in the air for a long moment.

"*No, no, no . . .* ," Franz muttered.

The storm trooper swung the bat down like an ax into the victim's midsection. Unconscious, possibly dead, the man didn't respond. The woman shrieked again and was rewarded with a heavy kick.

The hair on Franz's neck stood as he recognized the victims. "It's the Yacobsens!"

Hannah loved visiting the Yacobsens' bakery, at the end of their block. The kind old couple—"Tante Frieda" and "Onkel Moshe," as his daughter called them—would shower the girl with delicious treats of strudel, *pfitzauf,* and linzer cake.

"*Gott in Himmel!*" Esther breathed from across the room. "What have they done?"

The fat storm trooper motioned to the blond woman. She grabbed Frieda by the wrist. The older woman resisted as best she could, but a second storm trooper sauntered over and jerked Frieda's other arm back. She howled as though her shoulder had been dislocated. The two Nazis dragged the thrashing woman toward the fat storm trooper, who stood over her motionless husband, tapping his club against his open palm.

"How can they?" Franz croaked. "To an old woman? It's madness!"

He watched the fat storm trooper cock his arm again. He pictured Karl's swollen face and helpless eyes imploring him to act. Franz had never felt as impotent. Unable to stomach another moment, he spun from the window.

I must get Hannah!

Earlier, Franz had left his daughter at the neighboring apartment with the widowed Frau Lieberman before rushing out to retrieve Esther. After ushering his sister-in-law home through minefield-like streets, Franz had no choice but to suture her arm before she bled out. Now that he had closed the wound, he could not bear another minute apart from his daughter, who, though less than a hundred feet from him, felt worlds away.

Franz bolted for the door.

"No, Franz!" Esther cried after him. "Don't go out now!"

"I can't leave Hannah next door while the city burns."

"Hannah is safe with Frau Lieberman!" Esther whispered. "We must not move right now. What if they are already inside the building? What if they hear you?"

"I will be quiet."

"Franz, it's too dangerous. Hannah is safer where she is."

"I have to get her, Essie."

"Just a little longer, Franz." Her voice cracked. "For God's sake, not now, of all times!"

Ignoring her protests, he opened the door. The dark hallway beyond was empty and silent. Holding his breath, Franz took a tentative step out the door. He glanced to either side and then took another.

"Papa?" a little voice mewed.

His heart almost stopped as he spied Hannah tiptoeing down the hall toward him. "*Hannah!*"

Behind his daughter, Franz saw a faint light emanating from a crack beneath the doorway to the neighboring apartment, and he sensed Frau Lieberman's terrified presence. Franz padded toward Hannah, swept her up in his arms, and darted back into his flat. He pushed the door shut and gently clicked the dead bolt behind him.

Franz leaned over and smothered Hannah's head in kisses. "Oh, *liebchen*."

Esther threw her uninjured arm around Hannah as well.

Wriggling free of both of them, Hannah glimpsed her aunt's bloodied arm. She stared at it, wide-eyed. "Tante Essie, what happened?"

Esther tucked her arm in like a wing and turned that side of her body away from her niece. "Your clumsy aunt." She forced a smile. "This is my idea of how to clean up broken glass."

The eight-year-old viewed Esther skeptically but did not comment. Earlier, Franz had told Hannah about the rioting, downplaying the violence and the intended targets. But Hannah had immediately seen through his explanation. In the six months since Nazi Germany had swallowed Austria, in the so-called Anschluss, Hannah had already suffered more than her share of state-mandated anti-Semitism. Though only half Jewish by birth, she had been expelled from school and teased, bullied, or shunned by her Gentile friends. Franz would never forget the day she came home from the park with a bloodied nose and swollen lip at the hands of one of her former best friends.

"Where is Onkel Karl?" Hannah demanded.

Franz glanced over at Esther. Their eyes locked, and they wordlessly agreed: *Not tonight.*

"He has gone . . . gone home," Esther said softly.

"Is he all right?" Hannah asked.

Esther summoned a smile. "They can't hurt him now, darling."

Lips quivering, Hannah looked to Franz. "I'm afraid, Papa. The breaking glass and the shouting."

"Everything will be all right," he soothed. "As soon as I finish bandaging Essie, we will make cocoa."

"I'm not thirsty." Hannah flashed a shy little smile.

"Besides, there is no gas to heat the cocoa. I just want to stay with you."

Franz cleared the lump from his throat. "Of course, *liebchen*. Is Frau Lieberman all right?"

Hannah nodded. With her curly brown hair and darker coloring, she bore far more resemblance to Franz than she ever did to her blond, blue-eyed mother, Hilde. But she shared so many of Hilde's expressions. And like her mother, Hannah could convey so much without uttering a word.

They returned to the sitting room, Hannah still clutching Franz's hand. The girl carried herself with such poise that, much of the time, Franz was oblivious to her slight limp and other handicaps. Hannah's head had been wedged too tightly in her mother's birth canal, depriving her brain of oxygen for precious minutes. She'd had to be delivered by an emergency Caesarean section that left her with spastic weakness of her left arm and leg. Her relatively mild cerebral palsy was not the only birth trauma. Within days of the delivery, Hilde succumbed to an overwhelming postoperative infection, leaving Hannah motherless and Franz a widower.

Franz gently wrapped his arms around Hannah again, cradling her head against his chest and rocking her on the spot. Her soapy childlike fragrance only intensified his guilt. *How will I keep you safe?*

"Vienna—Austria—is no longer our home, *liebchen*," Franz said. Six months earlier, uttering those same words would have been unimaginable. Before the rise of the Nazis, Franz had not even considered himself Jewish. He was an Austrian and a surgeon. Nothing more.

"Your father means that we have to leave the country," Esther added gently.

Tears welled in Hannah's eyes, but her lips broke

into the most genuine smile Franz had seen in ages. "I so want to go, Papa."

"We will go, little one." Suddenly, nothing aside from Hannah's safety mattered anymore. "We will."

⁓ *Chapter 2*

Hannah finally drifted to sleep in Franz's arms. She didn't stir when he carried her into his room and laid her on his bed. He tucked Hannah's favorite doll, Schweizer Fräulein—the Swiss country girl–style rag doll that she had slept with since the age of two—under her arm and then covered her with a second wool blanket. He sat on the edge of the bed and watched his daughter sleep. Brushing his fingertips over her brow, he combed a few fallen strands of hair away from her eyes.

By the time Franz returned to the sitting room, Esther had already slipped into Hannah's bedroom and closed the door behind her. He could hear his sister-in-law's soft sobs drifting out under the door. Tasting acid, he wondered if the Nazis had just left his brother's corpse to rot on the lamppost. He doubted it; they tended to hide the evidence of their barbarism, as they had with all the Communists and other political opponents who had simply vanished overnight following the Anschluss.

Forcing the thoughts from his mind, Franz reached for the telephone. He swallowed his dread and slowly dialed his father's number.

"*Guten tag . . . Hier spricht Herr Adler,*" Jakob Adler answered in his typical solicitor's tone.

"*Papa, wie geht's?*" Franz asked.

"I am fine. They did not . . . reach my street. There are not enough Jews here . . . to make it worth their while," his father wheezed. Jakob had been afflicted by tuberculosis in his youth, and his lungs had steadily deteriorated in recent years. Nowadays, he fought for almost every breath. "And you, Franz?"

"I am all right."

"And your brother and the girls?"

"Hannah and Esther are safe."

"Not Karl?" Jakob asked in barely more than a whisper.

"No, Papa. Karl is . . ." Franz's voice faltered. "The storm troopers found him . . . Karl is dead."

Jakob went quiet. Only his wheezing filled the agonizing hush.

"Papa, there was nothing to be done," Franz muttered. "I was . . . I was too late."

"No, of course. Too late, indeed," Jakob breathed. He sniffled a few times.

The sound of Jakob's soft breathless sobs pushed Franz to the verge of tears. He had never before seen nor heard his father cry. Feeling totally impotent and isolated, Franz held the receiver to his ear and silently waited for his father to say something.

Finally, Jakob cleared his throat. "Franz, you must get Esther and Hannah out of the country. Now."

"And you too, Father."

"No."

"You cannot stay here."

"It is not your decision to make, Franz."

"I will not leave without you."

"You most certainly will! Listen to me, Franz. We both know that my lungs are ruined." As though to prove the point, Jakob paused to pant for three or four breaths. "They will undo me long before Herr Hitler has the opportunity."

Franz winced at the memory of the flabby storm trooper beating the Yacobsens. The Nazis would show his father no more mercy, regardless of his poor health. "You cannot—"

"Son, have I ever asked anything of you?"

"No. Never."

"So please indulge me this one request." Jakob gulped a few breaths of air. "Allow me to spend my final days at home. I want to die here in Vienna, just as your mother and . . ." His voice quavered but this time his lungs weren't to blame. "And your brother have."

Franz recognized the futility in arguing the point over the telephone. "I understand."

"Franz, I would like you to visit the British consulate."

"Papa, everyone knows the British are not issuing new visas."

"I have done legal work for the consulate," Jakob said. "I know the vice-consul, a Mr. Howard Edgewood. A reasonable man. I would like you to speak to him."

"Of course."

"I will telephone Mr. Edgewood in the morning to arrange an appointment."

"Thank you." Franz paused, groping for the right words, but all he could muster was, "Papa, I am so sorry."

Jakob was quiet for another long moment. "I only wish I had not been so horribly short-sighted." He exhaled so heavily that the receiver whistled. "Do not make the same foolish mistake, Franz. Never underestimate the Nazis again. Their hatred is beyond rational, beyond human. They will never stop."

Sleep was out of the question. Franz sat at the table agonizing over possible escape options. He berated himself again for having turned down a French colleague's offer to fill the position of visiting surgical professor at the University of Paris. Franz had reasoned that Jakob was too frail to be uprooted or left behind. Now, with Karl dead and his father facing the same fate, Franz found the irony of his own flawed rationale painful to remember.

Franz was still awake as the dawn broke, but the daylight brought no renewed sense of security. On the contrary, it left him feeling even more exposed.

A gentle rap at the door froze Franz in mid-breath. Ever since the rioting began, he had half expected the authorities to come for him too. After a moment, he relaxed, realizing that if it were the dreaded Sicherheitspolizei or the SS, the door would be shaking from the heavy fists and the orders shrieked through it.

Still, Franz approached warily. He opened the dead bolt and opened the door a crack. As soon as he recognized Ernst Muhler, he opened it wider.

Ernst held a full grocery bag in either arm, a fragrant loaf of fresh bread poking out from one. Tall and gaunt with a blond widow's peak, the flamboyant artist dressed unconventionally, favoring all-black ensembles, but fashion had nothing to do with his current appearance. Ernst's nose was swollen and bloodied. His lips were scabbed and crusted, and he had raccoon-pattern bruising around both eyes. But his smile remained as undaunted as ever. "I thought you could use a little sustenance," Ernst said in his distinctive lilt as he raised the bags in his arms.

Franz glanced down the hallway to ensure that they were alone. "You shouldn't have come, Ernst," he whispered. "It's too dangerous."

"Rumor has it that Vienna has become somewhat volatile of late," Ernst said as he strode past Franz and into the apartment.

Franz slid the dead bolt back into place and followed his Gentile friend into the sitting room. He had known Ernst for over ten years, ever since his wife had dragged him to one of the painter's exhibitions. The eccentric marriage of eroticism and frailty in Ernst's avant-garde work had unexpectedly moved Franz. He wound up buying three paintings and, despite—or perhaps because of—their diametrically opposed lifestyles, the two men had formed a tight friendship. Ernst had since become a rising star on the Vienna art scene, until the Nazis came to power and banned his artwork as "pornographic."

Ernst placed the grocery bags on the kitchen table. "Where's my little puffin?" he asked.

"Hannah is still asleep."

"She must have been scared witless last night." He sauntered over and flopped down on the couch, throwing an arm over the backrest. "You know, Franz, I found these Nazis a bit tiresome even before last night's tempest, but they've truly outdone themselves. Such brave, virile men, aren't they just? Assaulting the helpless, vandalizing property, and burning down temples." He snorted and then clutched his chest. "Ah, but the artist in me cannot help but admire their sense of aesthetics. They truly excel at making ugly things look and sound pretty, don't they? Have you heard what they're calling last night's rampage?" Franz said nothing, but Ernst, who was accustomed to carrying on one-sided conversations, continued. "Kristallnacht. Isn't that lovely?—'the night of crystal.'" He grunted again. "Only the Nazis could make a night of national disgrace and hateful violence sound like an opera that Mozart might have penned!"

Franz pointed to his friend's face. "What happened to you?"

"This?" Ernst ran a finger delicately over his swollen cheeks. "I'm afraid my little Gestapo captain got a touch frisky." He dug a pack of cigarettes out of his jacket pocket as he spoke and effortlessly slid one out. "It won't leave a scar, will it, Herr Doktor? Now that they no longer allow me to paint, my face is my life, you know."

Ernst heaved an exaggerated sigh. He lit his cigarette and took two long drags, leaning forward to bring his lips to the butt in his raised hand. "There's no pleasing the Nazis, is there? First, they deem my artwork degenerate. Now, the little devils have decided my lifestyle is too." Ernst took another puff. "These days I see a lot of my Gestapo friend, *Captain* Erhard Langenbrunner." He sat up straighter, mock saluted, and clicked his heels together. "Erhard is a blue-eyed, broad-shouldered Norseman—the embodiment of Hitler's homoerotic Aryan fantasy, really. Erhard keeps telling me that the Third Reich will not tolerate homosexuals among their ranks. Yesterday, he threatened to send me to Dachau concentration camp with 'the rest of the faggots.'" He sighed again. "Honestly, Franz, only the Nazis could believe they could cure my *proclivity* by locking me up in a camp full of men just like me."

Even Franz chuckled at the absurdity of it.

"Erhard and his friends knocked me around a bit," Ernst went on. "Truly, the attention he pays me makes me suspect Erhard could use a stint in Dachau too. It's always the ones who protest the loudest who secretly harbor the same desire, isn't it?" He touched his bruised cheeks again. "Regardless, I promised the captain I would dedicate myself to exclusively depraving women in the future. And that was that. Besides, it's really nothing compared with what you Jews have been through. So appalling."

A new worry struck Franz. "How do you know the Gestapo didn't follow you here?"

Ernst flicked away Franz's concern along with the ash from the tip of his cigarette. "I've been followed by my attentive little fascists for months, on and off. They are about as subtle as a herd of stampeding elephants. Trust me, Franz, no one followed."

Franz nodded. "Thank you for bringing us the food, Ernst. I will, of course, pay you back."

"Nonsense. You have overpaid for my paintings these last ten years." Ernst winked. "So tell me, how are Karl and Esther coping?"

Franz looked down at his feet. "Of course, you haven't heard."

"Heard what, Franz?"

"Karl is dead. They killed him last night." Franz's voice was deadpan but he could barely believe his own words.

"*No! The bastards!*" Ernst leapt to his feet. "Oh, Franz. I am so sorry!"

Franz brought a finger to his lips and nodded toward Hannah's bedroom, where his sister-in-law was staying. "Esther," he mouthed.

"How?" Ernst asked in a low, plaintive tone. "*Why?*"

Franz shook his head. "They knew Karl had been helping other Jews with their documents. They went to his office to find him."

"Those savages!" Ernst muttered.

"Karl managed to save Esther," Franz said. "She was at the office with him when the troopers arrived. He broke a small window in the back and pushed her out into the lane behind the building. That was where I found her."

Ernst squeezed the bridge of his nose and shook his head. "Franz, I know a man at the Dutch consulate. A dear friend. I will speak to him about urgent visas. We have to get your family the hell out of Austria."

"You are a good person, Ernst. And a better friend."

Ernst grunted a humorless chuckle and reached for his cigarettes again. "What I am is ashamed. Ashamed to call myself Austrian—or German—or whatever the hell it is we are supposed to be these days."

Franz walked Ernst to the door. He paused a moment to study his friend's battered face. Angst, and even a glint of fear, had replaced Ernst's usual flippancy.

"We Jews have no choice," Franz said. "But you, Ernst? Why do you choose to stay?"

"Oh, the same stupid sentimental reasons. Vienna is home. After all, how can I leave the city where Gustav Klimt and Egon Schiele helped to define twentieth-century art?" Ernst sighed. "And, of course, I'm in love." He blew out his lips. "But we have to keep *that* a secret, since my beloved works for city hall. He is not ready to leave his wife and join me in Paris. And lovesick fool that I am, I can't bear to live without him."

With little left to say, they shared a solemn handshake at the door.

Minutes after Ernst left, Jakob telephoned to announce that he had arranged an interview for Franz at eleven o'clock that morning at the British consulate. His father's voice was ragged with exhaustion and grief, but Jakob never once mentioned Karl.

Franz waited fifteen more minutes, but neither Esther nor Hannah emerged from their rooms. Deciding he could not wait any longer, he jotted a quick note to his sister-in-law and left it on the table. As Franz lifted his hat and coat off the peg, he was overcome by the intense memory of the night before. He winced at the recollection of his brother's panicky voice over the telephone. *"Franz, they're here!"*

"Where are you?" Franz demanded.

"My office," Karl whispered. "God help me, Franz! *Essie is here too!*"

"I'm coming, Karl."

"It's so dangerous. I would never have called if Essie weren't—" The line went dead.

Franz dropped Hannah off at Frau Lieberman's with a hasty explanation. The old widow begged him not to leave the building but Franz ignored her. Heart in his throat, he raced the ten blocks over to his brother's office building, though twice he had to suddenly divert to avoid one of the roaming mobs.

Franz ducked into the lane behind Karl's office and found Esther sitting amid shards of glass, propped up against the rear wall of the building. She stared into her lap while the blood dripped freely from her lacerated forearm. "Essie, your arm!" Franz cried, but she didn't even look up at him.

He threw off his jacket and struggled to tear his shirt sleeve. Buttons flew in the air as the cloth ripped. Franz wrapped the makeshift tourniquet tightly above her elbow, and the hemorrhage slowed.

"Is Karl still inside?" Franz asked.

Esther slowly raised her gaze to meet his. In one glance, she confirmed his worst fears. His knees buckled, and he shot a hand out to support himself against the wall. "Oh, Essie, no! Please, no."

"I didn't want to leave him," she said in a monotone voice. "He pushed me out through the back window. I could hear the shouting and then . . ."

They waited in terrible silence for ten or fifteen

minutes until their breathing settled and Franz convinced himself that the street in front of the building had emptied. Esther said nothing as they inched down the lane toward the side street. At the corner, Franz poked his head around the edge of the building. Across the street, under the beam of a streetlamp, a swaying shadow caught his eye. He was filled with dread as he looked up to see the body dangling from the lamppost. Along the front of the dead man's shirt one of the Nazis had splashed a Star of David in red paint. The victim's face was swollen and bloodied, but there was no doubt. *Karl!* He groaned.

Esther followed his gaze across the street. Before Franz could stop her, she leapt out from behind him and dashed toward the lamppost. She flung her arms around her husband's legs and pulled his whole body toward her.

Just as Franz reached her, he heard the nearby sound of shouts and shattering glass. He grabbed Esther by the arm, inadvertently digging his fingers through the warm gash. She gasped in pain but said nothing.

Franz pried Esther's hands free of Karl's legs and dragged her away. After a few strides, she stopped resisting and let him lead her.

Once on the other side of the street, Franz slowed for a final glance at his brother. Karl's waxy face held a neutral expression, but his brown eyes—which in life had brimmed with such compassion and amusement—seemed to find Franz's.

I will take care of Essie. I swear it, Karl.

Chapter 3

Sweat dampened his armpits as Franz stepped out of his building and into the bright but chilly November morning. He yanked his hat even lower on his head and stared down at his feet, reassuring himself that he could easily pass for a Gentile. With his straight nose, hazel eyes, and strong jaw, he didn't possess a particularly Jewish look—at least, not in terms of the hook-nosed, beady-eyed caricatures that filled the newspapers and schoolbooks. His real risk lay in being spotted by a Gentile acquaintance, neighbor, or even patient. From those awful final days at the Vienna General Hospital, before being stripped of his title as chief of surgery and professor, Franz had learned how willing, even eager, some people were to point Jews out to the nearest Nazi official.

Franz would never forget the day his protégé, Dr. Johan Grasser, turned on him. He had once seen so much of his younger self in the promising twenty-seven-year-old surgeon. Up until that spring morning, March 13, the day after the Anschluss, Grasser had shown Franz only deference and loyalty. However, as Franz stepped onto the surgical ward, Grasser's folded-arms stance suggested a monumental shift in attitude. "Have you not heard, Herr Doktor?" The junior surgeon smirked. "We are part of the Reich now. And Jews have no place in German hospitals."

The ambush had left Franz speechless and humiliated in front of a cluster of gawking nurses and orderlies. Despite all the affronts he had faced in the months since, the memory of Grasser's betrayal still stung the most.

On the pavement, Franz's feet crunched with every

step. The ground glinted from the layer of broken glass. Through the shattered window of his ground-floor surgery, he saw upturned furniture and papers strewn across the waiting room. His sense of loss was minimal. Six months earlier, after his summary discharge from the hospital, he had been forced into basic private practice, performing only minor excisions under local anesthetic; the work of a surgical intern.

Franz turned the corner at the end of the block and was stunned to see the street writhing. Moving in complete silence, men and women of all ages, and even children, were kneeling down, using small brushes or their own hands to gather up the broken glass. Armed guards, spaced in regular intervals, hovered over them. Dressed in gleaming black SS uniforms, the guards barked insults and orders while holding horsewhips menacingly at the ready.

A younger man rose up from his knees to stretch his back. Immediately, one of the guards cracked a whip across his neck, hurling the man back to the ground with a groan.

"Schweinhund!" the trooper bellowed. He turned to another SS man with a laugh and snapped his whip triumphantly in the air.

Franz scanned the terrified faces near the pavement. He made eye contact with a middle-aged woman on her knees, recognizing her as Dalia Gruben, a patient whose gallbladder he had removed a few years before. Wide-eyed, Gruben mouthed *Go!* to him.

Franz could barely move. Aside from the taunts of a few schoolyard bullies, he had hardly known anti-Semitism before the Nazis descended. Like most of the city's Jews, he was assimilated; as proud an Austrian as any other. After the Anschluss, seemingly overnight Franz had lost many of his Gentile friends and colleagues. But in the wake of Kristallnacht, the Nazis were elevating persecution and terror to a level he would have never imagined possible.

One of the nearest SS troopers, young enough to still be in his teens, swiveled his head toward Franz. His hand reached for the pistol clipped on his belt, while his pale eyes ran up and down Franz as though assessing a dung heap. *"Juden?"* he growled.

Stunned, Franz shook his head. *"Nein."*

The young man's hand fell away from his weapon and his face lit with an apologetic smile. At that moment, he could have passed for any polite Austrian youth performing a civic duty. "I am terribly sorry for any inconvenience, sir," he said. "We will make sure these filthy Jews clean up their mess. Won't take any time at all, but it is best not to loiter."

Franz nodded and trudged away. He felt like a cowardly fraud as he imagined the eyes of his former patient burning into his back.

The Gentiles of Vienna appeared to have awoken to a typical autumn day. Non-Jewish businesses, their windows pristine, welcomed customers as usual. The scent of baking bread and brewing coffee filled the air. People bustled along the sidewalks past the broken windows, vandalized storefronts, and Jews scrubbing the roads under armed guard as though it were a morning like any other.

Franz resisted the urge to grab passersby by the shoulders and shake them out of their indifference. *Can you not see what is happening to your former colleagues, neighbors, and friends?* He could have screamed. *Has the whole country gone mad?*

Franz kept his head low as he walked along Reisnerstrasse toward the British consulate. Like the other consulates in Vienna, it had been an embassy up until the day of the Anschluss, when Vienna lost its designation as a capital city.

As he rounded the corner onto Jauresgasse, Franz spotted a Union Jack flying from the quaint baroque building on the corner. For months, he had witnessed lineups outside the consulates as Jews scoured the city searching indiscriminately and, for the most part, in futility for any foreign power willing to offer haven. Franz had expected another line in front of the British consulate, but the size of this one stunned him. It snaked on for as far as he could see. Whole families huddled together. A sea of faces—some old and sickly, others fresh-faced but bewildered—caught Franz's eye. Most appeared stunned or petrified. They were so silent that Franz imagined he might have heard a coin falling out of a pocket at the far end of the line. Even though a British visa would represent a new lease on life for entire families, Franz saw no one jostle or shove anyone else. Their orderliness and compliance were ingrained Germanic and Jewish traits.

Franz tucked his gloved hands into his coat pockets, crossed the street, and walked alongside the queue toward the entrance. Halfway down the block, he heard the howl of approaching sirens. Suddenly, a black canvas–covered transport truck turned the corner and roared down the street. It hopped the curb, screeching to a halt in the middle of the crowd. A mother swung her young son out of its path in the nick of time, but she was still bowled forward by the truck's bumper. She managed to scramble away, as did the others near her.

Six or seven SS troopers brandishing machine guns jumped out of the truck and rushed the crowd. More trucks thundered down the road. They skidded noisily to a stop in a long row behind the first one. Men in black poured out of them. Franz spotted a trooper who raised a megaphone to his mouth and shrieked, "All male Jews over the age of fourteen step forward! *Now! Macht schnell!*"

Another trooper unleashed a round of machine gun fire into the air. Startled, Franz stopped dead. Several people dropped to the ground in terror. Others leaned back against the building's windows and walls as though trying to melt into them.

More screams, shouts, and gunfire. And then Jewish men, their faces clouded with fear and despair, began to step forward. With punches and kicks, the SS men herded them—often by the scruff of their necks— toward the backs of the trucks without a word of explanation.

Franz dropped his gaze and carried on. Despite the urge to flee, he was careful not to move so fast as to draw attention. Without even looking up, he passed the consulate's entrance, turned the corner, and walked away from the building.

Legs wooden with dread, Franz trotted three or four blocks before he slowed to glance at his watch. It read 10:55. The eleven o'clock appointment with the British vice-consul might have represented his family's final chance for a visa, but he also knew that the SS would stop him outside the consulate. His only identification— the passport he carried in his pocket—was stamped with an incriminating large red *J*. He could not risk being arrested, not before he had gotten Hannah and Esther out of the country.

Franz spent the next hour wandering the streets, never straying far from the consulate. Strolling the City of Music, his beloved Zeiss Ikon plate camera in tow, had once been his favorite pastime.

Franz had originally taken up photography to appease his wife, who had given him a camera as a birthday present. Hilde soon became his primary subject; he snapped countless photos of her. After her sudden death, Franz found it too painful to view the photos. Even lifting the camera stirred too many memories, so he abandoned the hobby. A few years later, he came across the camera, dusted it off and, on a whim, took it outside to snap photos of buildings that had caught his eye. The initially random pursuit grew into a passion. He began photographing buildings all over Vienna, ignoring the famous landmarks to focus on quaint, often run-down structures whose shapes or settings had struck him as quintessentially Viennese. To Franz, it was never about art so much as precision. He found the challenge of capturing the exact light, focal point, and angle akin to surgery.

But light and angles were the least of his concerns. Every moment he spent exposed on the street compounded his worry. His surroundings, once such a source of pride and comfort, struck him as more than just hostile. His birth city—the only place he had ever lived—felt foreign to him.

After covering at least two more miles, and witnessing more broken glass and vandalized property than he imagined possible, Franz finally looped back toward Jauresgasse. As he reached the British consulate, he was desperately relieved not to see any sign of SS men or their trucks. The lineup had thinned considerably but still ran at least two blocks long and consisted almost exclusively of frightened women and bewildered children.

Franz headed straight for the front of the queue, where two British soldiers in combat fatigues and berets guarded the door with rifles held across their chests. He shouldered his way past a group of women at the front too traumatized to object to the intrusion.

He approached the taller soldier, a chunky redhead. With an embarrassed shake of his head, the guard pointed to a sign posted above him that read in large-print German, *The consulate regrets to announce that His Majesty's Government will not process new immigration visas until further notice.*

"I have an appointment with Mr. Edgewood," Franz said in English. In 1933, Franz and Hannah—a toddler at the time—had spent six months in London at St. Mary's Hospital, where he completed a surgical fellowship while honing his English skills.

"Your name, sir?" the soldier asked.

"Dr. Franz Adler," he said. "I apologize for my lateness."

The second soldier scanned his clipboard and then nodded to his colleague. The redhead showed Franz a slight smile. "No matter, Dr. Adler. With all that broken glass, they're not making it particularly easy to navigate the city today."

The soldier led Franz inside the building, along a corridor, and up two wide flights of stairs. A polite, middle-aged man, who appeared to be a secretary, took his coat and then led him into a brightly lit office. Two large bookcases stood against the wall, their shelves piled high with books bearing only German titles. A painting of King George VI and his queen consort, Elizabeth, hung prominently on the wall behind an oak desk.

Franz had to wait only a few minutes before a squat balding man, who wore a navy blazer and argyle tie, bustled into the room. *"Ein vergnügen, Sie zu treffen, Herr Doktor Adler,"* Howard Edgewood said in accent-free German as he hurried toward Franz with an extended hand.

Franz squeezed the man's chubby hand, noting its

dampness. He deliberately responded in English. "I appreciate you seeing me on such short notice, Mr. Edgewood."

"Of course, of course," Edgewood said as he rushed around the desk and sank into the chair across from Franz. "I admire your father. An excellent lawyer and a true gentleman." His flushed face creased into a frown. "If I may say so, Herr Adler did not sound at all well on the telephone."

His son was just murdered. How did you expect him to sound?

"These are difficult times for him," Franz said.

"Yes, of course. Trying times. Trying times, indeed," Edgewood chirped as he raised a thin file from the top of a stack. "Mr. Adler explained some of the circumstances of your, um, predicament."

Franz looked down at the desktop. "My wife is dead, Mr. Edgewood. I have an eight-year-old daughter. Hannah is a very brave girl, but Vienna is no longer a city that is kind to children of even partly Jewish origin. I have to find her safe asylum. Britain, of course, would be our very first choice."

"Of course, of course." Edgewood nodded sympathetically as he opened the file. "And I would so dearly love to help."

Franz's heart sank, but he said nothing.

"Our quota for refugee visas has been completely filled for the next year. And, Dr. Adler, we are absolutely prohibited from making exceptions." Edgewood shrugged helplessly. "You must understand, there are nearly two hundred thousand Jewish people living in Austria alone. If we were to set such a precedent . . . well, it would be a slippery slope with no end."

Franz swallowed his crushing disappointment. "That

same argument is convenient for all nations which have chosen to shut their doors to us," he muttered.

Edgewood raised a finger. "However, Dr. Adler, I have made several inquiries this morning. And I am hopeful in your case that there might be a way."

Franz sat up a little straighter. "How so, Mr. Edgewood?"

"In light of your distinguished university standing, I believe we might be able to offer you an educational visa. It would be open-ended, of course." Edgewood flashed a shy grin. "And we would concern ourselves with the specifics of your university appointment and location at a later date."

Franz's sense of relief bordered on ecstasy. He laughed joyously. "Mr. Edgewood, there is no place in your great country, from the Isle of Wight to the tip of Scotland, to which we wouldn't be willing to relocate."

Edgewood guffawed as he reached for the papers on his desk. "Yes, well, I do not imagine we will have to banish you to the Shetland Islands just yet." He flipped through a few pages. "And as your daughter is still a minor, we can include her on the same visa."

"And Esther, of course," Franz said.

"Oh, have you remarried, Dr. Adler?" Edgewood asked.

"Esther is my sister-in-law. My brother, her husband . . ." Franz's voice cracked. "He recently died."

Edgewood's smile seeped away. "Oh, I am sorry."

"It will not be a problem, will it, Mr. Edgewood?"

Edgewood shut the file in his hand. "I am afraid it will, Dr. Adler. We cannot possibly include your sister-in-law on an educational visa granted to you. It is simply not legal."

Franz's stomach plummeted. He would have willingly

married Esther to get her name on that visa, but he also knew that, as Jews, they no longer had any legal standing. They would never be able to secure an official marriage license. "And my father?" he asked mechanically.

Edgewood frowned. "Mr. Adler made it clear to me that he had no intention of leaving Vienna." Franz didn't reply. "Dr. Adler, if you and your daughter were to travel ahead, perhaps once you had settled in you would be able to find alternate arrangements for the others. And by then undoubtedly the political climate here would have stabilized somewhat—"

"I will not leave them here." Franz shook his head adamantly. "I cannot."

Edgewood dropped his chin and spoke to the file. "I do not see what else I can offer."

"I am not certain where else to turn, Mr. Edgewood." Franz clasped his forehead between his thumb and forefinger. "I must get my daughter out of Vienna. If anything were to happen to her . . ."

A bleak moment passed in silence before Edgewood's round head suddenly snapped up. "Hold on, Dr. Adler. There might be one other option."

"Yes?"

"My government is about to unveil a new program entitled Kindertransport."

"The 'children transport'?" Franz echoed.

"Yes. We intend to offer several thousand emergency visas to Jewish children in Germany and Czechoslovakia."

Franz frowned. "Only the children?"

"For the time being, yes." Edgewood cleared his throat. "We intend to place the children in emergency foster care until such time as they can be safely repatriated with their parents."

"And you could find Hannah a spot in this Kinder-transport program?"

"I believe so, yes."

Franz wavered. His heart ached as he tried to imagine his handicapped daughter adjusting to life in England without family or friends around her. As awful as the idea seemed, he realized it might also be the only practical solution. "Mr. Edgewood, may I take a little time to consider this?"

"Of course, of course. Take a day or two." He smiled kindly. "And please do reconsider the offer of the educational visa as well."

"Thank you, Mr. Edgewood. I appreciate your kindness."

As Edgewood walked Franz to the door, the diplomat heaved a sigh. "Dr. Adler, I am a huge admirer of this country." He nodded to his bookcase. "Particularly Vienna. Perhaps my favorite city in the world. Or, at least, it used to be. Recent events, especially these last few days, have absolutely appalled me. How a civilized nation could brutalize her own citizens in such a manner is simply beyond me." His face went blotchy with indignation. "It is a ghastly business as far I am concerned."

Franz recognized Edgewood's sincerity. He was aware the diplomat had done everything within his power to help. But something suddenly snapped inside him, and he could not hold his tongue. "Mr. Edgewood, your sympathy and outrage is of no use whatsoever to me." He pointed to the window. "Or any of those other blameless people outside."

"Well, yes—"

"I have given up trying to make sense of the Nazis or even my own countrymen." Franz eyed Edgewood steadily, desperate for an outlet—even one as undeserving as the well-intentioned diplomat—for his outrage. "What I fail to understand is how a civilized world that claims to be so appalled by such brutality can simply turn its back on the victims."

～ Chapter 4

With his clinic looted and left in shambles, Franz had no hydrogen peroxide to soak off the bandages covering Esther's forearm. Instead, he had to make do with tap water. The dried scabs stuck tenaciously to the cloth, and Franz had to tease, pull, and even rip the dressing away. Aside from an occasional wince, Esther registered no reaction to the painful procedure.

"How would Hannah possibly cope in England without you?" she asked.

Franz could only shake his head.

"As well as she compensates for her handicap, it will not be the same for her as the other children." Esther spoke in a hushed voice, partly because Hannah was reading in her bedroom with the door open, but mainly because she had taken to speaking in whispers in the tense aftermath of Kristallnacht.

"She already speaks some English. That will help," Franz said with little conviction.

"It's not right, Franz," Esther murmured. "The girl needs to be with her family."

"But how, Essie? I visited so many consulates this afternoon."

"There are other places still," she said.

"Where? I went everywhere! America, Canada,

France, Belgium, Czechoslovakia, Portugal, Australia, Argentina . . . Huge queues in front of every consulate, despite the mass arrests." He rubbed his temples, trying to block out the nightmarish memory of those panicky women and children. "All of them posted signs stating that their refugee quota had been met or exceeded, and they would offer no more visas. I haven't heard from Ernst regarding his Dutch contact, but I'm beginning to think it's hopeless, Essie."

"We cannot afford to think like that!"

Esther said it with so much self-assurance that, for a moment, Franz wondered if she knew about the British offer of an educational visa for Hannah and him. He had not told her, because he knew she would have insisted they leave without her. And for Franz, that was not an option.

Esther continued to speak, but Franz could not concentrate on her words. His mind kept wandering back to his last face-to-face conversation with Karl at Café Altman, two days earlier.

At his brother's insistence, they used to meet at least once a week at the Jewish-owned café, where the smell of espresso, perfume, and smoke blended into a familiar mélange. Before the Anschluss, Karl would have to arrive early to secure coveted seats at one of the closely clustered tables. The brothers had to raise their voices to be heard over the cacophony of conversations and the Jewish radio station that blared nonstop music and news programs.

This time, sitting at the corner table at dusk, they were the last customers left inside. Like all Jewish businesses, the shop's trade had eroded after the Anschluss, but it was the breaking news out of Paris earlier in the morning that had emptied the café and chased most Viennese Jews into seclusion.

"He has not done the rest of us any favors," Franz said, referring to Herschel Grynszpan, the distraught seventeen-year-old youth who had walked into the German embassy in Paris and shot the first Nazi official he saw, a diplomat named Ernst vom Rath.

"Can you blame the boy?" Karl asked. "His parents were rounded up and dumped at the Polish border without food or shelter. Left there to starve or freeze to death."

"They did the same to thousands of other Polish-born Jews." Franz thumbed at the window. "Besides, Grynszpan is hardly the only Jew with a legitimate grievance against the Nazis."

Karl stared disbelievingly at his older brother. "But, Franz, he's one of the very few to actually *do* something about it."

"By killing a low-level diplomat? *That's retribution?*" Franz slammed his empty cup down on the table. "Now we will all have to pay for his impulsiveness."

"No doubt we will," Karl agreed grimly. "Perhaps if more of us had stood up to them earlier . . . It's too late now, of course, but I still can't blame the boy."

Franz sighed. "That's always been your weakness, Karl. You are too forgiving."

"So are you. You're just too proud to admit it."

"Nonsense. You're the idealist. I've always been the practical one."

"Practical or Machiavellian?" Karl said with a small chuckle.

"I can't help it," Franz said. "I think like a surgeon."

Karl pantomimed a cutting motion.

"Exactly. No beating around the bush. If I see a problem, I prefer to just excise it."

"If only someone could excise the Nazis from Austria." Karl sighed. "Remember, Franz? We were going to take Vienna by storm. You, her greatest surgeon, and me, her leading solicitor. Look at us now."

Franz held up a hand. "Hitler had other plans."

Karl flashed a wistful grin as he toyed with the uneaten strudel on his plate. "Franz, I have not even told Esther this." He glanced over either shoulder. Only the withered proprietor stood, despondently, behind the counter, wiping his coffee press, but Karl still spoke in a whisper. "Last week, the Sicherheitspolizei arrested me."

Franz gripped the table. "*Arrested?* Where?"

"They picked me up on my way to work." Karl shrugged. "I spent the day at their headquarters at the old Hotel Metropole."

"What did they want?"

"They accused me of every crime imaginable, from personally undermining the Führer to having single-handedly brought Bolshevism to Europe." Karl laughed bitterly. "I suspect they are short on proof, though. Otherwise I would not be sitting here now."

"Karl, they must be watching you!"

"Apparently so. I've been helping people file their new securities' registration forms. Not that it's any real help. The Nazis are only using the forms to confiscate—in truth, to steal—their assets." He exhaled heavily. "But Jews can be arrested, or worse, for not filing them. And they're terribly complicated for some, especially older folks."

"This is no time to be risking your life!" Franz snapped. "We must focus on getting the family to safety."

Karl smiled kindly. "I can't simply turn my back on people in need, Franz. It's part of what makes us different from the Nazis."

"*Everything* makes us different from those animals! And if they've already arrested you . . ."

Karl leaned forward, eyeing Franz with a burning intensity that silenced his brother's protests. "Listen, Franz. You must promise me something."

"What is it?"

"If they take me away or . . . you know . . ." Karl cleared his throat. "You will—promise me, Franz— ensure that Essie is safe."

"You're my little brother. I am always supposed to look out for you."

"And you always have." Karl smiled. "Remember that bully, Chaim Greenberg, in grade school? You taught him the price of picking on your little brother."

"This is real life."

Karl's eyes glistened. "You cannot protect me from them, Franz. No one can." He gently clutched Franz's wrist. "Promise me that if anything happens to me, you will take care of Essie. Franz, please. I need that peace of mind."

"Of course I will," Franz said, his voice thick. "Always. You have my word."

Esther snapped her fingers, drawing Franz from the memory. "What do you think, Franz?" she asked.

He busied himself with the bandage. "I'm sorry, Essie. What do I think of what?"

"Shanghai."

He dropped the bandage in surprise. "Shanghai? *For us?*"

"Why not?"

"Aside from the fact that it's on the far side of the world and we have no way of reaching it?"

Esther laughed softly. "Aside from those inconveniences, yes."

"I thought the Japanese invaded Shanghai last year."

"Which is precisely why we would be allowed in!"

She sat up, pulling her arm away from Franz in her excitement. "No one is checking passports. So you don't need a visa to enter the city. I heard the Klinebergs are going. And I spoke to Frau Weiss on the street, who whispered that her son had already left for there. On a luxury liner, no less!" She held her hands skyward. The last strip of her bandage unfurled like a banner. "Apparently, with only proof of transit, the Nazis will allow us to leave. For them this is the ideal solution: banishing Jews to the other side of the planet."

"Stay still, Essie, please," Franz said as he removed the final remnant of her dressing. "The last place we should go is somewhere other Jews are heading."

"Franz!" Her jaw fell open. "How can you say that?"

"Because I'm practical," Franz said. "The Germans have persecuted us with total impunity. The rest of the world has responded by closing their borders to us. Remember the Evian Conference last summer? No country wants the Jews. We are targets wherever we go. Our religion is a curse."

Esther eyed him stone-faced for a moment, then her lips cracked into a faint smile. "Perhaps the Orientals will have more trouble telling us apart from the goyim? We must all look the same to them."

"Shanghai." Franz shook his head as he lifted a fresh strip of cloth and began to rebandage Esther's wound. "Even if we could find a ship with space, how could we afford to pay the passage? And what would we live off once we got there?"

Unperturbed, Esther shrugged. "You find the ship, and let me worry about the cost."

Franz raised an eyebrow. "Essie, what are you not telling me?"

She glanced over in the direction of Hannah's room before whispering, "My mother's jewelry."

"It's illegal, Essie," he breathed. "If they caught you trying to pawn jewelry or smuggle it out of the country . . ."

Esther rose from the table and took a step back. She pulled up the hem of her sweater to reveal the large leather buckle on her gray belt. "I have a friend. A jeweler. He melts the precious metals down and recasts them as buckles, buttons, and other clothing accessories. He covers them with cloth to make them less noticeable." She ran her thumb and fingers over the base of her sweater, squeezing it in places. "And the finest pieces, like my diamond earrings and ruby ring, I sewed into the hem."

"Very clever, Essie." Franz nodded. "But if they were to catch you . . ."

She stared back defiantly. "What alternative is there? Tell me that."

Franz shrugged helplessly.

Her face reddened, and she gazed down at her feet. "I never told Karl. I worried he would have insisted on giving it all away to the neediest of his clients."

"You were right to stay silent. Karl's generosity was his undoing."

The blush left her cheeks, but when she tried to speak her voice cracked. "It isn't much of a nest egg, but I had hoped it would help tide us over."

"You have done well, Essie. But Shanghai?" Franz sighed. "You really think it could be better than London for Hannah?"

"As long as Hannah is somewhere where they can't touch her, then I think it's best for the girl to be with her father. No matter where."

"I wonder." As a surgeon, Franz had long been accustomed to making difficult decisions in critical situations. He rarely second-guessed himself. But as he stared into Esther's resolute eyes, he felt crippled by uncertainty.

The front door suddenly reverberated with three crisp raps. "*Adler!* Franz Adler!" a harsh voice roared.

Ice ran through Franz's veins. He turned to Esther, whose pupils had widened with fear. Hannah came scurrying into the room, moving as fast as her weakened leg could carry her. She threw her arms around him. "Papa!" she cried.

Franz knelt down and kissed her forehead. "Shh, *liebchen*. It will be all right."

The door shook with another hammering. "*Franz Adler!*"

"Just a moment," Franz called over his shoulder. Still holding Hannah tightly in his arms, he looked up at Esther. "Call my father!" he whispered urgently. "Tell him to get in touch with Mr. Edgewood at the British consulate to enroll Hannah in the Kindertransport, straightaway!"

Esther's face crumpled with worry, but she only nodded.

"*Adler!*" the voice bellowed. "*Open this door immediately or we will break it down!*"

Franz gently pried Hannah's arms off his neck. "Hannah, whatever happens, you must do as your tante says." He kissed her on both cheeks. "Everything will be all right, my darling."

Chapter 5

Two young men stood rigidly at the door. One had dark hair and the other was fair, but with their matching scowls and jet-black SS uniforms, they looked interchangeable to Franz.

"Franz Adler?" the darker one snapped.

Franz's throat turned to sandpaper. "Yes. What is the—"

"*Identification!*"

Franz dug his passport out of his jacket pocket and handed it to the man, who flipped it open and examined the photo as though studying a counterfeit banknote.

Don't make a sound! Franz silently implored Esther and Hannah, who had run into Hannah's bedroom.

Finally, the man snapped the passport closed and tossed it back to Franz. "You will come with us!"

"I will just get my coat," Franz said, loud enough for Esther to hear.

As Franz turned back toward the apartment, the darker one grabbed him by the shoulder and spun him around. The men clamped crushing grips around each of his upper arms. They jerked him forward and marched him down the hallway to the waiting elevator, leaving the apartment door wide open behind them.

Even inside the elevator, neither man loosened his hold. The cloyingly sweet hair oil worn by one of them turned Franz's stomach. He hoped they couldn't hear his heartbeat, which slammed like cymbals in his ears.

The Nazis ushered him out of the building and past his ransacked office, pulling him toward a long black sedan, its antenna-mounted swastika flapping ominously in the frosty breeze. A driver sat behind the steering wheel, the engine running. The blond man shoved Franz through the backseat door, while his partner hurried around to the other side.

The car sped off before the doors had even fully closed. As Franz sat sandwiched in the backseat between the two SS men, his concern for Hannah mushroomed. He imagined his daughter, frightened and alone, struggling to carry her luggage aboard a train bound for England.

Dreadful scenarios tumbled around his head as the car roared along Vienna's unusually quiet main roads. From time to time, the tires crunched over glass, but the hordes of frightened Jews scrubbing the pavement were nowhere to be seen. The men on either side of him stared dead ahead, as though at attention. No one spoke. The jerky driving and overpowering odor of hair grease nauseated Franz.

They sped past a burned-out building that had been reduced to a few stone columns rising from rubble. A stooped old man was picking through the debris. It wasn't until they had already passed by that Franz recognized it as the remains of the Leopoldstädter Tempel, the city's largest synagogue, where Karl and Esther had been married.

A mile or so later, the car turned onto Prinz Eugen Strasse and slowed to a stop beside the curb. Franz noticed the long swastika flags draped between the Corinthian columns of what used to be Palais Rothschild, the former residence of Vienna's preeminent Jewish family. His heart leapt into his throat. All of Vienna's Jews had heard of the Central Office for Jewish Emigration and the fearsome SS lieutenant who ran it. Jews who wanted to leave the country—even those in possession of legitimate visas—had to first report to this office, where they were stripped of the last remnants of their citizenship and what little money or valuables they had left. Rumor had it that they were the lucky ones.

Fingers dug into Franz's biceps as the men jerked him up the staircase that led to a set of wide, ornamental doors. As they mounted the last step, the doors flew open and a middle-aged man stumbled out backwards, staggered, and collapsed onto the cement. Blood gushed from his nose, down his chin, and onto his shirt. He glanced at Franz with the panicked eyes of a trapped animal. Scrambling to his feet, the man scurried past them and almost tripped down the staircase in his rush to flee.

The guards pushed Franz through the doorway into an ornate atrium. A long line of haggard men, interspersed with a few women, queued in front of a desk. The man at the head of the line, about thirty feet away, was trembling violently. A burly SS soldier stood behind the desk, berating the man so loudly that his voice echoed through the atrium. "*You Jew-scum!* How dare you come here without proper papers? I should shoot you on the spot."

Franz's pulse quickened with each step, but his guards seemed oblivious to the tirade as they marched him alongside the lineup toward the shouting man. As they neared, the trooper unleashed a vicious backhanded slap across the trembling man's face. "Get out of my sight, *you Jew-pig!* You're making me sick."

The man grabbed his cheek, swiveled, and rushed for the door.

Franz's jaw dropped as he recognized the Nazi behind the desk. He had worked at least three years with Horst Schmidt at Vienna General. He had always considered Schmidt a polite and respectful orderly. Franz had even performed surgery on his then-four-year-old daughter, Gisela, draining a large abscess on her thigh. Afterward, in gratitude, Schmidt's wife had brought him several baskets of baked goods.

"Horst?" Franz murmured with a flicker of hope.

Surprised recognition creased Schmidt's coarse features but was replaced in a heartbeat by a contemptuous glare. Ignoring Franz altogether, he turned to the dark-haired guard. "What is this Jew doing here?"

Franz's innards turned to stone. Years of friendly professional relationship had been reduced to just "this Jew."

"The lieutenant wanted to see him, Hauptscharführer Schmidt," the guard said, using the SS title for the equivalent of sergeant major.

Schmidt turned to the closed door behind him and rapped three times.

"Yes?" a man replied so softly that it was barely audible.

"Obersturmführer, the men have brought you the Jew Adler."

"Send him in."

Schmidt turned back to Franz and eyed him, showing not an iota of familiarity. He opened the door to the office and snarled, "Go!"

Franz braced himself, expecting to be kicked in the back or clapped on the neck as he passed Schmidt. But no blow fell as he walked past him and into the spacious office.

As the door clicked closed behind him, Franz gingerly approached the man seated at a desk against the far wall. A huge framed photograph of the unsmiling Führer, his arm extended in the distinctive "Sieg Heil" salute, hung directly above the desk.

The lieutenant did not look up from the large ledger in which he was writing. His dark hair was short and thinning, and he wore a perfectly pressed SS uniform. His hat rested beside the ledger facing forward, its central insignia so polished that the skull and crossbones shone.

Franz stood in front of the desk and watched as the lieutenant continued to write in the ledger, line after line in precise penmanship. Finally, after five or more minutes, the man lowered the pen onto the desk and raised his gaze. With smooth complexion, high cheekbones, and chiseled features, the lieutenant verged on handsome. He assessed Franz with an icy gaze, as though appraising livestock.

"Herr Doktor Adler," the man said in a soft-spoken tone. "I am Obersturmführer Adolf Eichmann. Thank you for coming to see me," he said without the least trace of irony. "As you might have heard, I have been charged with the task of centralizing Jewish emigration from Austria." Eichmann touched a finger to his lower lip, as though searching for diplomatic words. "My job has taken on new urgency in the wake of the cowardly assassination of the Reich's hero, Ernst vom Rath, by the Jew Grynszpan. As you might have witnessed, our security forces have struggled to contain the exuberance of the very understandable outrage of ordinary German citizens. And, after Kristallnacht, we fear for the safety of the Jewish residents here in Vienna."

Franz wondered if Eichmann was making a cruel joke, but he remained silent.

"Today, we went to the effort of rounding up thousands of Jewish men to put into protective custody. It is not a sustainable solution to the Jewish question." Eichmann shrugged helplessly. "Of course, that is my problem, not yours." He sighed. "I understand that you once held quite a distinguished position at the university. True?"

"Yes, before—" He stopped himself from mentioning the Anschluss. "I was professor of surgery and chief of the department at the university hospital, Obersturmführer Eichmann."

"You Jews certainly excel in medicine and law, don't you? Not to mention banking and moneylending." He laughed quietly to himself. "Dr. Adler, I have made it a priority to take a personal interest in the plight of Vienna's most prominent Jews, such as yourself. But in light of the happenings last night, I am not sure we can continue to guarantee your safety. Do you understand?"

"Yes," Franz said, though he was more baffled than ever.

"Good." Eichmann nodded. "That is why it is of the utmost urgency that you make arrangements to leave the German Reich. The sooner, the better."

"Obersturmführer, I spent most of today at various consulates, trying to secure a visa for my family."

Eichmann's face broke into a smile devoid of empathy. "It never fails to amaze me how the rest of the world decries our legitimate racial policies, and yet they could not make it more clear that they don't want Jews in their midst any more than we do. Would you not agree, Dr. Adler?"

"The rest of the world has not gone out of its way to help the Jews, Obersturmführer."

"That is one way of putting it," Eichmann grunted. "What progress did you make at the consulates?"

Franz considered his answer carefully. He did not want to endanger any of his options by sharing them with Eichmann, but he wasn't sure what the lieutenant might already know regarding his visit with Edgewood. "It is possible that my daughter might qualify for the Kindertransport program."

"Yes, of course." Eichmann wrinkled his nose. "Seeding England with more young Jews."

"She is only half Jewish," Franz said. "My wife was Catholic."

Eichmann scoffed. "In our eyes—as established by the Nuremburg Laws—that makes her a Jew. Nothing more."

"She is much more," Franz blurted, regretting the words as soon as they left his lips.

Eichmann stiffened. His face went blank, and his eyes froze over. "How is that?" he asked in a soft voice more frightening than all of Schmidt's screeching.

"I meant no disrespect, Obersturmführer," Franz said, desperate for a way to placate the man. "It's only that . . . my family has lived in Vienna for generations. We have lived a secular life. I always saw myself as an Austrian first and foremost. I never even raised Hannah as Jewish."

Eichmann eyed him for several seconds without moving a muscle. "And yet, that's all either of you are," he finally said. "Please don't imagine for one moment that I care a whit for your university standing. We have rid ourselves of far more famous Jews than the likes of you—Einstein, Freud, and Mahler, to name only a few."

Franz dropped his gaze to the desk. "Of course, Obersturmführer."

Eichmann leaned back slightly in his seat. His tone turned philosophical. "I am forever astounded at the total lack of appreciation among you Jews for just how deep-seated anti-Semitism is in society and the very legitimate reasons behind it."

Franz continued to stare at the desk without replying.

"If you will excuse the medical analogy, Dr. Adler," Eichmann went on, almost speaking more to himself than to Franz, "Jews remind me of microscopic parasites. As I understand it, those germs invade a healthy body with the sole purpose of multiplying and spreading. All they care about is continuing their line. They mean no harm to the host. In fact, if the host dies, then they will be lost as well. Nonetheless, these tiny leeches do weaken their host and, if left unchecked, they will destroy it." He looked up at Franz, clearly proud of his analogy. "You see, the same is true of Jews and Germany. It isn't personal, but it is imperative we rid the fatherland of this dangerous parasite, and soon." He paused. "Do you understand, Dr. Adler?"

Franz understood more clearly than ever. Kristallnacht was only the beginning. If the Eichmanns of the world had their way, countless more Jews would suffer the same fate as Karl and the Yacobsens. Emotions raged inside his chest, and Franz did not trust himself to speak. Keeping his expression as neutral as possible, he looked up at Eichmann and nodded.

"I'm glad we agree. And if you ask my advice, I suggest that you drag your family to somewhere far away. I doubt the rest of Europe will be much more welcoming to Jews in the near future." Eichmann lifted the top sheet from a stack of papers. He slowly filled in the blanks and then signed the bottom with a flourish. "Consider this your notice. Once you have proof of an accepting destination, bring me the paperwork and I will sign your exit visa. You have two weeks to leave."

Franz swallowed. "I see."

Eichmann studied him with his frigid eyes. "If you cannot find an acceptable destination within two weeks, I will be forced to relocate you to the concentration camp at Dachau." He shook his head, and his voice dropped even lower. "And once there, Dr. Adler, I can no longer guarantee your well-being."

Chapter 6

Franz's head throbbed. He doubted he had slept a moment all night. Upon returning home, he had postponed plans to enroll Hannah in Kindertransport, but he knew that, barring some amazing stroke of luck, he would still have to send his daughter away.

Franz had spent much of the night huddled close to Hannah, whispering stories to her to try to distract her from the raucous mob rampaging on the streets in a second night of anti-Semitic violence. Even after the rioters stomped away and Hannah finally drifted off, sleep eluded Franz. He tossed and turned, haunted by memories of Karl's dangling corpse, Frieda Yacobsen's plaintive screams and, most of all, Eichmann's soft-spoken malevolence.

In the morning, Franz awoke to find Hannah still asleep, curled up on her side and cradling—almost as though shielding—Schweizer Fräulein, her doll. Franz brushed his lips over her forehead and then tiptoed to the bedroom door. He was relieved that Esther had not yet risen either. The evening before, he had downplayed the significance of the SS interrogation. But after coming face-to-face with Eichmann, Franz's time frame for getting Hannah out of Austria had accelerated from weeks to hours.

Money would be pivotal. Esther's hidden jewelry would help if they managed to escape, but now they needed cash. The time had come to access his emergency funds. Karl had persuaded him to hide the money only days before the government froze all Jewish bank accounts.

Franz dressed for the cold and then headed to the

bathroom with a paring knife. He crouched behind the toilet and ran his fingers over the floorboards until he found the gap. He dug the blade between the boards and gently pried one loose, then reached inside the hidden compartment and pulled out the stack of banknotes.

"Thank you, Karl," he whispered as he wedged the floorboard back into place.

The six thousand Reichsmarks—four thousand more than the legal limit for a Jew in Austria to possess—represented a lifeline. He slid the wad of bills inside his coat pocket and patted the front. After convincing himself that there were no bulges, he headed for the door.

Outside, cloud cover and a light morning drizzle had warmed the city. Shards of glass still glittered on the pavement and anti-Semitic graffiti covered the vandalized storefronts, but some of the smashed windows were already boarded up. The streets were quieter than they had been the day before. Franz spied only a few uniformed Nazis, and he saw no forced Jewish work gangs.

Despite the relative calm, he was more on edge than ever. He wore his hat low and kept his eyes glued to the sidewalk as he hurried along Liechtenstein Strasse toward the Rolf Travel Agency. The aged owner, Julius Rolf, had always been courteous and helpful in booking vacations for him. Franz prayed that the Viennese gentleman had not transformed into an ardent Nazi overnight, like Horst Schmidt and so many others had.

Franz arrived well before nine o'clock and was not surprised to see the CLOSED sign still hanging in the travel agency's window. He regretted never having photographed the charming old brick building before. He was certain now that he would not get another opportunity.

Franz decided to wait in the café across the street. Inside the boisterous, smoky coffee shop, he spotted a table being vacated by a young couple. He wove his way over and dropped into a still-warm chair. Anxious to blend in, he picked up the copy of the official Nazi newspaper, the *Völkischer Beobachter*, which the couple had left behind.

A heavyset waitress sidled up to the table. *"Ja?"*

Franz looked up and caught sight of the shiny swastika pin stuck in her lapel. Dropping his gaze back to the newspaper, he mumbled his order for an espresso and *krapfen*.

The coffee was not as good as Willi Altman's, but its bitter bite was still vaguely comforting. Biding his time, Franz turned back to the newspaper. More numb than outraged, he read article after article espousing the glory of Kristallnacht. An editorial characterized the torching of synagogues and vandalizing of Jewish businesses as bold acts of German nationalism. And Hermann Göring was quoted as saying that the government intended to levy a one-billion-Reichsmark fine against the Jews for "instigating events."

Through the window, Franz spotted Julius Rolf entering the travel agency with a younger man. One of them flipped the sign in the window to OPEN. Franz dropped a few marks beside his unfinished *krapfen* and leapt to his feet. He hurried across the street and into the office. The walls were lined with posters of ocean liners and alpine châteaux. A middle-aged man with greased hair, spectacles, and the nondescript face of a low-level bureaucrat rose from his desk and welcomed Franz with a stiff smile. Franz recognized him as Julius's son, Stephan.

"Good morning, sir," Stephan said. "May I be of service?"

"Thank you, but I am accustomed to dealing with Mr. Julius Rolf. Is he in today?"

The man looked over his shoulder and called out, "Father!"

After a moment, Julius Rolf hobbled out from the back room. More hunched than Franz remembered, Julius moved with a shuffling, unsteady gait. "Ah, Herr Doktor Adler! How very pleasant to see you again," he said with a slight slur. "My son, Stephan, runs the business now." He smiled, but only the right side of his face cooperated. "I am merely his assistant."

"Of course, Mr. Rolf, but as you and I have a long history, I was hoping you still might be able to assist me with my travel," Franz said, wondering if the old man knew he was Jewish.

"Yes, yes. One should never turn his back on history. Soon, history is all one has. Please." Julius pointed a shaky hand to the desk at the far side of the office.

"My apologies, Herr Doktor," Julius said as they sat down across the desk from one another. "I am still recovering from a stroke. Your colleagues at the hospital assure me that it can take quite some time to get one's strength back."

Franz nodded sympathetically, doubtful the man would ever get much stronger.

"Never mind all that," Julius said. "Where would you and your darling daughter like to voyage to now?"

"Shanghai."

"Ah. A very popular destination all of a sudden." A knowing look darted across Julius's face. He glanced over to where his son sat and then lowered his voice. "When do you intend to depart?"

"As soon as possible, Mr. Rolf," Franz stressed.

"I see." Julius didn't appear the least surprised by the answer.

"Aside from Hannah and me, I need to book passage for two other adults. My father, Jakob, and my sister-in-law, Esther."

"I know from experience that liners heading to China are heavily booked these days, Dr. Adler." Julius exhaled noisily. "However, I will telephone the booking offices in Trieste and see what is possible." He labored to his feet. "Please excuse me a moment."

The old man shuffled toward the back room. Franz glanced over and caught Stephan glaring at him. Breaking off eye contact, the younger Rolf jumped up and marched into the back room after his father.

Franz tried to eavesdrop on the Rolfs' conversation, but they were talking in low voices, and he caught only snippets. At one point, Stephan raised his voice loud enough for Franz to hear him say, "Bump the Schillings? *You must be joking!* It will be the absolute ruin of us if word ever gets out that we are aiding Jews. Especially at the expense of *real* clients!"

Moments later, Stephan stomped sullenly back to his desk.

Franz could hear Julius talking on the telephone, but he was speaking Italian, and Franz understood only a smattering. From the inflection, he could tell the old man was struggling to persuade the person on the other end of the line. Twice he heard Julius repeat the phrase "*di vita o di morte,*" which Franz understood as "life or death."

Ten minutes later, Julius reappeared and lowered himself slowly into his seat. His cheeks were flushed but his timbre was even. "I am sorry for the delay. My agent in Trieste tells me that space is at a premium on all ships heading to Shanghai."

"No space at all, Mr. Rolf?" Franz gulped.

"Precious little. However, I was able to secure passage for all four of you on a magnificent Japanese liner, the *Bingo Maru*. It is just that the cost is . . . well . . ." Julius shook his head. "Three thousand Reichsmarks per person. Even your daughter is required to pay full passage."

Though it was twice as much as Franz possessed, he felt a glimmer of hope. "The ship is departing soon?" he asked.

"Very," Julius said, raising Franz's hopes even higher.

"When?"

"The fifteenth of December, to be precise."

"Not for a month?" Franz's heart sank as he thought of Eichmann's two-week ultimatum.

"That might seem like a long time to you, Dr. Adler," Julius soothed. "However, typically, we have been booking people six to twelve months in advance."

"Of course, Mr. Rolf. Thank you. Do you happen to know if there is a waiting list for cancelations on earlier sailings?"

Julius nodded, though skepticism was etched into his wrinkled face. "We can always try."

Perhaps proof of a departure date will placate Eichmann? Though Franz doubted anything would. Having run out of other options, he decided he could not afford to pass up this one. "Mr. Rolf, I have only six thousand marks on me."

Julius viewed Franz with another kindly, lopsided smile. "Providing that the tickets are paid in full at least two weeks prior to departure—"

"*Father!*" Stephan protested.

Julius swiveled his head and shot Stephan a look that silenced him. He turned back to Franz. "As I was saying, Dr. Adler . . . as long as you pay the balance at least two weeks prior to departure, I can hold all four places on the ship with your down payment." His face sagged with defeat. "However, if we were forced to rebook for a later date, I doubt I would have anywhere near as much luck as I had today."

Franz reached into his coat pocket, withdrew the stack of bills, and passed them to Julius. The old man did not bother to count the money. Instead, he left the pile on the table and turned to his son. "Stephan, will you be kind enough to draw up a receipt of sale for Dr. Adler?"

Franz shook Julius's hand gratefully. "Herr Rolf, you have no idea how much I appreciate your decency."

"And we appreciate your loyal business." Julius held the grip for an extra moment as he glanced at his son again. "Not all Austrians have changed as much as you might be led to believe, Dr. Adler."

His thoughts weighing heavily, Franz hurried home. He stepped inside the apartment to find Ernst Muhler and Esther seated on the sofa. The artist must have dropped off fresh supplies for Esther, because she now wore the traditional black dress of shiva, Judaism's prescribed seven-day period of mourning.

As usual, Ernst was puffing away on a cigarette. Franz was surprised to also see one in Esther's hand; he could not remember the last time he had seen her smoking. The bruises around Ernst's eyes had begun to yellow but they were no less prominent, especially with the dried tears crusted to them. Franz saw that Esther had been crying too.

Ernst rose to his feet. He walked over and shook Franz's hand. "No chance the Nazis up and decamped while Essie and I were busy chatting?" he joked in a thick voice.

Franz patted his friend's back. "How are you managing, Ernst?"

"It's not exactly the golden age for queer vanguard artists in Hitler's new Germany, but I have no new complaints." He sighed. "Listen, Franz, I heard from my friend at the Dutch consulate. They are so overwhelmed with applicants . . ."

Franz had expected nothing more, but he still could not suppress his disappointment. "Thank you for trying."

"He didn't say no, either," Ernst stressed. "It will just take more time."

"Of course." Franz turned to his sister-in-law. "How does the arm feel, Essie?"

"Fine. Good." She waved away the inquiry. "Where have you been, Franz?"

"The Rolf Travel Agency." Franz withdrew the receipt from his coat pocket. "I have secured four berths on a Japanese liner."

"*Gott zu danken!*" Esther cried with relief as she hopped to her feet.

"The ship isn't sailing for almost five weeks," Franz said quietly.

"We've lasted six months." Esther's voice cracked, and Franz suspected she was thinking of Karl. "We can make it five more weeks."

Ernst pulled the cigarette from his lips. "Sailing where?"

"Shanghai."

"Shanghai!" Ernst whistled. "You really do intend to put some distance between you and the Nazis. You know, I hear Shanghai is marvelous. Full of life and culture. And it's reputed to be a city of debauchery and excess." He raised an eyebrow. "Come to think of it, it sounds like just the place for me."

Esther touched his face. "Why don't you come with us?"

"Perhaps if circumstances were different . . ." Ernst shook his head. "My heart won't let me leave Vienna."

Esther stroked his cheek. "Of course," she said softly.

"Esther, you and I have to wait, but Hannah does not," Franz said solemnly.

"It's only five weeks," Esther said.

Franz shook his head. "I will not expose Hannah to this nightmare for another month," he said, without adding that he expected to be imprisoned in Dachau by the time the *Bingo Maru* cast off. "I am enrolling her in Kindertransport. That is final."

Hannah's bedroom door opened and she limped out, holding a book in her good hand. "Papa, what is Kindertransport?" she asked.

Franz swept her up in his arms. "It's a program run by the English. You're going to go to London, *liebchen*. One of the greatest cities in the world."

Hannah's eyes clouded with concern. "Without you, Papa?"

Franz kissed her cheek. "Only for a short while. I will come and find you soon." He mustered a grin. "Think of it, Hannah. Once I arrive, you can be my tour guide. Show me Big Ben, Buckingham Palace, and all the other wonderful sights! Do you even remember them from our last visit? You were only three."

Hannah stared at him for a long moment. "Why won't you come with me?"

"It's complicated, *liebchen*. I have to stay here for a few more weeks to sort out our papers. I will be there before you know it."

"I can wait," she said, her tone verging on pleading.

"This is for the best," Franz said. "You will be with lots of other children."

"Jewish children," Esther added.

"I don't even know how to be Jewish," Hannah said.

"Not to worry, darling," Franz reassured. "The others will be traveling without their parents too. You will make lots of new friends. They will be just like you, you'll see."

Hannah raised her stiff left arm. "I am not like other children."

A lump formed in Franz's throat.

"I don't mind, Papa," Hannah continued. "Let me stay with you."

Franz felt his resolve slipping. Hannah and he had not been separated for more than three days in her entire life. And the prospect suddenly seemed torturously final.

"Hannah," Esther said in a loving but firm tone. "You must listen to your father."

"Please, Papa," Hannah whimpered.

Eichmann's words—*It is imperative we rid the fatherland of this dangerous parasite*—flashed into his mind. Franz shook off the doubt. "It is decided, Hannah. You will go."

Hannah buried her face in his shoulder and began to weep quietly. Franz cradled her in his arms and kissed her on the top of the head. No one spoke a word.

The telephone rang harshly. Esther hurried over to answer it. "Adler residence." She listened a moment and then called over her shoulder. "Franz. It's Herr Rolf."

"Dr. Adler, I have news," Julius Rolf said once Franz had picked up the phone.

Franz held his breath, anticipating the worst, but Julius went on excitedly. "I have made further enquiries with other booking agents. I was having no luck at all with the other shipping lines. However, one of the agents telephoned me back only moments ago. They have an opening at short notice. A couple who had booked a family cabin on the Italian liner *Conte Biancamano . . .*" He lowered his voice. "They . . . er . . . canceled at the very last moment." Franz picked up on

Rolf's inference, aware that the suicide rate among distraught Austrian Jews had skyrocketed in recent days. "It would be snug, but the cabin could house all four travelers in your family."

"How soon does it depart, Mr. Rolf?" Franz demanded.

"It is terribly last minute. I would understand completely if you were unable to—"

"When does it leave, Mr. Rolf? *How soon?*"

"Sunday."

⌐ *Chapter 7*

The walls of Karl and Esther's home were plastered with framed photos of the family from happier times. The nostalgia almost overwhelmed Franz. Fighting back tears, he located Karl's hiding place behind the bedroom radiator and found the envelope containing eight thousand Reichsmarks.

He took the money directly to the Rolf Travel Agency. While his son glared at Franz, Julius issued the new tickets. From there, Franz headed straight to Palais Rothschild.

Reaching for the handle, Franz could hear, through the thick wooden front doors, Horst Schmidt yelling. Steeling his nerves, he paused to feel for the boarding passes in his pocket.

Inside the cavernous atrium, Schmidt's shouting was intensified. Franz dutifully took his spot at the end of the line. He counted nineteen people in front of him. The silent line inched forward as Schmidt took his time berating and degrading each person who reached his desk. He struck several. One woman fainted. Everyone approached Schmidt tentatively, their eyes to the floor and heads hung low. Franz sensed trouble when the elegantly dressed, middle-aged woman four people ahead of him stepped forward with head straight and shoulders high.

Schmidt leapt up from his chair and leaned over his desk. "Who the hell do you think you are, Jew? Parading up here like you're the Queen of bloody Sheba!"

"I am Stella Kaufman, sir," she said coolly. "I have come to see Lieutenant Eichmann regarding my exit visa. Just as I was requested to do."

"*You are nothing, Jew!* And no one sees the lieutenant without my say-so."

Franz silently prayed that Frau Kaufman would submit to Schmidt's authority, but she continued to hold his stare defiantly.

"Kaufman, is it?" Schmidt said menacingly. "Any relation to the Jew thieves from that department store?"

She sighed. "My grandfather established Kaufman's, yes."

"To cheat and chisel good Austrians out of their hard-earned money with their overpriced rubbish and non-German goods. *Correct?*"

Frau Kaufman didn't answer immediately. The entire lobby went dead silent. Everyone, including the SS guards, had stopped to listen to the exchange. "No, sir," she said. "My grandfather established Kaufman's to provide quality goods to Viennese citizens at reasonable prices. And we have maintained that tradition ever since."

The terrible silence was broken only by a soft snicker from one of the guards near the door. Schmidt's face reddened. He circled the desk in three long paces and lunged at the woman. She leaned back and raised her hands to protect herself, but Schmidt punched her full force in the belly. The woman groaned as she clasped her abdomen. He punched her in the face. She gasped and buckled over. Struck again, she crumpled to the ground. Blood pooled around her head and her howls of protest died away, but Schmidt continued to kick her.

Franz could not stomach another second of the brutality. Unable to stop himself, he stepped out of the line. "Hauptscharführer Schmidt!"

Schmidt's head snapped up. His blazing eyes scanned the room before locking onto Franz.

Another taut silence seized the atrium. No one else in the line dared so much as to breathe.

Schmidt jumped over Frau Kaufman's prone body and stormed over to Franz. He stopped a foot away and stood nose to nose as sweat dripped off his brow. "*How dare you interrupt me, Jew?*" he panted.

Franz stared at the floor, desperate for the right words. "My deepest apologies, Hauptscharführer. It is only that Obersturmführer Eichmann asked me to return with papers. It is already late. I'm worried that I might miss my opportunity to see him today."

"That is what you're worried about right now? *Missing 'Lieutenant' Eichmann?*" Schmidt scoffed, and a few of the other SS men laughed. He raised his bloody hand and cuffed Franz backhanded across the cheek. The stinging blow was hard enough to swivel Franz's head, but he suspected that Schmidt had restrained himself. "Get back in line, you stupid Jew!"

Schmidt turned and marched back to his desk. He deliberately stepped on the fallen woman, eliciting a heavy groan from her, but he did not strike her again. Instead, he flopped back into his seat and snapped his fingers impatiently to the two nearest guards.

They hurried over and grabbed Frau Kaufman—one

by her feet, the other by her hands—and slung her toward the door. On their way past, Franz saw from her pained expression that she had regained consciousness. The guards opened the door and threw her out as though tossing a sack of flour. Another guard dropped a stained towel at Schmidt's feet and quickly swept up the pool of blood. Franz recognized the cleanup for a well-practiced procedure.

Schmidt called out "Next!" as though he were only a passport office clerk processing routine applications. The petrified man at the head of the line had to be nudged forward by the person behind him.

After a cursory interrogation, Schmidt allowed the trembling man in to see Eichmann. He turned away the next two in line—a full-figured young woman and her scrawny husband—with a tirade of profanities and insults, but, possibly exhausted from the effort of pummeling Frau Kaufman, he did not rise from his seat to strike either of them.

As Franz stepped forward with his head bowed low, he saw the man scurry out of Eichmann's office. "What is it, kike?" Schmidt barked at Franz.

"Sir, I have brought proof of my departure as Obersturmführer Eichmann requested."

Schmidt eyed him for a long moment. Finally, he stood up and turned to knock at Eichmann's door. "Obersturmführer, the Jew Adler is back."

Franz couldn't make out the reply from inside, but Schmidt opened the door and grunted for him to enter the office.

Adolf Eichmann sat at his desk, looking as immaculate as before in his pressed black uniform. His short hair was slicked back, not a strand out of place. Again, the lieutenant made Franz stand and wait while he filled in form after form. Franz didn't dare glance at his watch, but he guessed that almost ten minutes passed before Eichmann put down his pen and looked up at him. "Back so soon, Adler?" he said softly. "You must have enjoyed our conversation yesterday more than I did."

"Obersturmführer, I believe I have secured the correct paperwork to prove departure for my family."

"Is that so?" Eichmann leaned back in his chair. "And where does the good doctor and his family intend to go?"

"Shanghai, Obersturmführer."

"Shanghai?" Eichmann let out a small laugh. "I should have guessed. The only place accepting Jews without visas. Which, I'm afraid, is about as welcoming as the world gets for your kind." He sighed. "Still, so many Jews scuttling like rats off to that poor city. It's doomed to become a Chinese Jerusalem. Or worse, another New York." Eichmann flicked his fingers impatiently. "I do not have all day. Show me your passport and proof of passage."

Hand steady but heart racing, Franz withdrew the handwritten boarding passes along with the passports. He passed them to the lieutenant, who scrutinized each ticket.

Eichmann finally lowered the tickets to his desk. "Hannah is the Jew child, yes?"

Franz nodded.

Eichmann looked around the room theatrically. "And where are Jakob and Esther Adler?"

"At home, Obersturmführer. I didn't realize they also needed to attend."

"You clearly didn't get legal advice from your brother, did you?" Eichmann's malicious grin told Franz that he knew exactly what had happened to Karl. "Then again, I suppose I have no shortage of your kind to face in person."

Franz looked away, afraid his expression would betray his feelings. "Thank you, sir," he mumbled.

Eichmann grabbed another sheet of paper off his desk and slowly filled in the blanks. He picked it up and waved it in front of Franz. "You will sign this declaration on behalf of yourself and the others in your family. In it, you renounce claim to all property, assets, and citizenship in the Reich, and you swear that you will never again return."

Eichmann slid the sheet across the desk to Franz. Without hesitation, or even reading the page, Franz signed his name and dated it beside the two places marked with an X. Eichmann laughed. "You people really would sell your own mothers to save yourselves, wouldn't you?"

Eichmann snatched back the declaration and reached for another form that Franz recognized as the Führungszeugnis, or certificate of good conduct, which any person emigrating from Germany also required. The lieutenant signed and stamped it in red with the official eagle-clutching-a-swastika seal. He then stamped the passports and boarding passes. He bundled the documents together and held them out. Before Franz could take hold of them, Eichmann yanked his hand back. "Tell me something, Adler. Do you really think you can outrun destiny?"

"No, Obersturmführer." Then, without thinking, he blurted, "I don't believe anyone can."

Eichmann glared at him. "I would be careful with your tongue, Jew," he said quietly. "My destiny—like all good Germans—is to bask in the glory of the Third Reich. Your destiny, like that of your entire miserable race, is annihilation." He tossed the passport, boarding passes, and the exit visa over the desk and onto the floor at Franz's feet.

Franz dropped to his knees and scooped up the documents. He stuffed them in his pocket, then turned and hurried out of the office without a word. He raced past Schmidt and the line of terrified faces behind the desk.

Out in the moist air, Franz almost laughed with relief. But as he walked the two miles from the Prinz Eugen Strasse to his father's home on Robert-Hamerling Strasse, a new thought darkened his mood. *Father. How will I possibly persuade him to accompany us?*

Franz walked up the steps of the brownstone to the main-floor suite. He knocked on Jakob's door, gently enough so as not to alarm him into thinking it might be the authorities.

His father's appearance stunned Franz. Normally, Jakob lived in a suit and tie, even on bank holidays, but now he wore slacks, an open shirt, a cardigan, and slippers, all black. His gray hair was disheveled and, for the first time in Franz's memory, his father had thick stubble on his cheeks and chin.

Franz considered hugging his father but instead shook his outstretched hand. "I'm sorry, Father," he said, still at a loss for more meaningful words.

Jakob nodded and turned back for the sitting room. Franz followed his father, who moved slowly and had to stop twice to catch his breath on the way to the couches, which were no more than twenty feet from the door. Franz was surprised to see unlit Sabbath candles on the table behind Jakob and a prayer book lying open beside them. His father had lived a secular existence, and Franz had not seen any religious items in his parents' home since his mother died, fourteen years earlier. "Papa, are you sitting shiva?" he asked, bewildered.

Jakob shrugged. "You and I may have long ago given up on Jewish customs." He stopped to gulp a few breaths. "However, your brother never did. I feel I owe this to him."

Franz summoned a grin. "I suppose it's never too late to find God."

"Oh, Franz, in my case, it is far too late." Jakob wheezed. "Besides, at this time, I think we Jews should be far more concerned with God finding *us* rather than vice versa."

Franz noticed an ominous bluish tinge to his father's lips. "Papa, are you still taking the theophylline pills?" he asked, referring to the latest treatment for emphysema.

"I will need a few more," Jakob said.

Franz dug a pill bottle out of his pants pocket. "This is the last of my stock."

Jakob accepted it with a shaky hand. "It will do."

"I will find a new supply as soon as we reach Shanghai."

Jakob tilted his head but said nothing.

"Papa, I have good news." Franz went on to explain about the last-minute berths he had secured on the *Conte Biancamano*. He locked eyes with his father and repeated the lines he had rehearsed on the way over. "I understand your desire to stay in Vienna until the end, Papa. But Vienna has become an ugly place. Mama and Karl might have died here, but it's unfair to their memories to mistake the Vienna of today for the same wonderful city in which they lived. This is no longer our home."

Jakob nodded. "I agree, son."

"All we have left is each other. Now, of all times, we must stay together as a family. Hannah needs her Opa. Esther needs you too." He paused. "And I refuse to leave without you, Papa."

Jakob, the consummate lawyer, measured Franz with unreadable eyes. "Son, I intend to join you in Shanghai."

"You . . . you will?" Franz exclaimed, shocked by the unexpected capitulation.

"Yes."

"That's wonderful." Franz beamed. "I expected you to put up more of a fight."

Jakob shrugged. "You are surprisingly persuasive for a doctor."

"I must have absorbed a little something from all the great legal minds in the family."

"Of course, I cannot leave with you this Sunday." Jakob stopped to catch his breath. "No. I think I will follow you on that Japanese ocean liner next month."

"But, Papa—"

Jakob held up his hand. "I cannot walk any distance. Once you land, you will need to find somewhere to live. By the time . . . . I arrive you will have had a chance to establish a home." He paused again for a few more breaths. "Franz, it is for the best for all of us."

Jakob's impeccable logic left Franz speechless. He recognized that he had just been outmaneuvered. And in that moment, he realized that he would likely never see his father again.

Chapter 8

The temperature had tumbled overnight. A centimeter of wet snow blanketed Vienna, turning the streets slick. Franz and Hannah sat in the backseat of the taxi, silently holding hands as the cab wormed its way through traffic, forced to bypass cars and trucks that had slid into each other or onto the sidewalk.

Hannah stared out the window. Franz sensed his daughter's homesickness growing by the minute but did not share the sentiment. He carried his losses in his heart. Even as they passed landmarks such as the Imperial Palace, which he had known his entire life, he was far too preoccupied for nostalgia. He only wished the taxi would move faster. And he worried Esther might have trouble reaching the railway station with the roads in such poor condition.

Esther had insisted on spending her final night in Vienna in her own home to organize her belongings. Franz understood. Packing his whole life into one suitcase had proved far tougher than he anticipated. Never much of a clotheshorse, he picked his two least-worn suits, opting to wear one on the trip and throw the other in his bag along with a few sweaters, slacks, and short-sleeved shirts, since he had heard that Shanghai sweltered in the summer. But he struggled with the rest of his possessions. Eventually, he chose his most precious surgical tools—the set that his mentor, Dr. Ignaz Malkin, had left him. He also tucked his Zeiss Ikon plate camera into the bag. He pored through his wedding album and pared down the photos. He could not face another photo of Hilde's luminous smile or Karl's laughing eyes. Eventually, he gave up and just blindly tore out pages.

The taxi skidded to a stop in front of Vienna's oldest and largest railway station, the Südbahnhof. As a child, Franz had always arrived at the grand old station giddy with anticipation. For the Adler brothers, the Südbahnhof, with its nineteenth-century classical facade, was synonymous with adventure.

Concerned about his dwindling cash reserve, Franz waved off the approaching porters. Instead, he lugged their cases toward the platform himself. Hannah, who wore two shirts and a sweater beneath her summer jacket and winter coat, carried a small sack with books and snacks slung over her shoulder and clasped Schweizer Fräulein in her good arm.

Though their overnight express train to Trieste wasn't scheduled to depart for another three hours, Franz was glad to arrive early. The lineup already ran beyond Platform Five. Franz scanned the faces in line but saw no sign of Esther.

The howling wind blew intermittent gusts of wet snow into the station. Franz knelt down and retucked Hannah's scarf snugly into her collar.

The Jews on the platform were easy to distinguish from Gentiles, because they invariably carried bulkier cases and were surrounded by clusters of distraught loved ones. Few, if any, had dry eyes. Jakob had been too unwell to see them off. Franz was almost relieved. As guilty as he already felt about decamping from Vienna without his father, to have to watch while the train pulled away, leaving Jakob behind on the platform, would have been too much to bear.

Hannah let go of his hand and rushed off in her slightly lopsided gait toward the main terminal. Franz was about to chase after when he noticed Esther, dressed in a long black coat, gloves, and hat, approaching with a porter wheeling her trunk behind her.

Hannah threw her arms around Esther's midsection. "Tante!" she cried.

Esther walked hand in hand with Hannah toward Franz. "Where's Onkel Karl?" Hannah demanded.

"He's not coming with us," Esther replied.

Hannah looked crestfallen. "Is he staying with Opa?"

"I suppose he is, darling," Esther said.

Hannah turned wide-eyed to her father for clarification. Franz smiled and mussed her hair. "Just think of it, *liebchen*. You get your auntie to yourself for the whole ocean voyage."

Hannah nodded weakly. Franz turned to his sister-in-law. "Is everything all right, Essie?"

"Nothing is all right," she sighed. "But everything is in order, I hope."

The express train rolled to a halt at the platform. After the arriving passengers noisily disembarked, guards and customs officials began separating out the Gentiles, who merely had to flash proof of not being Jewish to board. The line for the Jews moved forward in fits and starts. After ninety minutes, the Adlers' turn finally came.

A pale, fleshy customs inspector sat at the desk on the platform. He bore such a striking resemblance to the storm trooper who had clubbed the Yacobsens that Franz's heart was sent racing. "Your passports and certificates of good conduct," he grumbled.

Franz and Esther dug out their documents and passed them to the official. He examined each piece languidly. "Are either of you carrying valuables or cash beyond the permitted one hundred Reichsmarks?"

"No, sir," Esther said, and Franz shook his head.

"Time to inspect your bags."

The official made Franz lift each case onto the table, beginning with Hannah's. She watched expressionlessly as the man rifled through, leaving a disheveled heap of tangled clothes. He pushed it away for Franz to reassemble. "Next piece."

Franz heaved Esther's trunk onto the desk. The inspector pawed through her belongings with the same disregard that he had shown Hannah's. Suddenly, he stopped and looked up at them, his arm buried deep in the pile of Esther's clothes. "What do we have here?"

Franz feared that the inspector might have found her camouflaged gold or jewelry. He glanced over to Esther, who had paled noticeably.

The inspector pulled out a rolled canvas. "A Monet? Or perhaps a Rembrandt?" he snickered as he began to unroll it. "You do realize the penalty for trying to smuggle valuable artwork out of the Reich?"

"It is not valuable," Esther rushed to explain. "The painter is a friend. It has sentimental value. Nothing more."

The official stared at Ernst's charcoal sketch. It depicted an emaciated woman, her flat chest crisscrossed with scars, sitting in an empty bathtub with an unlit cigarette clamped between her teeth. Ernst had never explained its meaning, but the raw angst on the woman's face had always moved Franz.

"Worthless degenerate filth," the official huffed as he carelessly rerolled it. Rather than return the sketch, he tossed it into a large wooden box at his feet. Esther opened her mouth to protest but said nothing.

The inspector dug through Franz's bag and pulled out the leather case holding the surgical tools. He spread it open, picked up a bronze-handled needle driver and studied it in the light. "Explain these," he said.

"I am a surgeon," Franz said. "These are my tools."

The man continued to play with the equipment, clicking clamps open and closed, before eventually losing interest. He stuffed them back into the pouch and haphazardly tossed the case into the box at his feet.

"I need those!" Franz exclaimed.

"They are the Reich's property now."

Franz felt as though he had just been stripped naked. "But why? They have no value to anyone but me."

The inspector shrugged. "Jews are not allowed to board trains carrying weapons."

Franz's jaw fell open. "*Weapons?*"

"If you would prefer not to part with your tools, you could just as easily stay here with them."

Esther nudged Franz gently in the ribs. "Yes, of course," he muttered. "I understand, sir. Thank you."

Defeated, Franz did not bother to utter a word of protest when the official pulled his camera from the bag and confiscated it, too.

After reassembling their belongings, the Adlers climbed aboard the rear car of the train, claiming two benches facing each other near the luggage rack. Franz's pulse did not begin to settle until he felt the train vibrate under his feet and rattle away from the Südbahnhof. Hannah laid her head on his shoulder and, moments later, the gentle rocking of the car lulled her to sleep.

Esther, wide awake, stared at her brother-in-law. "When will we tell her?"

"Once we are settled in Shanghai."

Esther's lip began to tremble, but Franz couldn't tell if she was closer to laughter or tears. "My God, Franz. We're actually going to China, aren't we?"

He forced a smile. "Just as we always planned," he joked.

"Your brother always did want to visit Asia. He even suggested Bombay for our honeymoon."

"India? *Karl?*"

"He loved those Rudyard Kipling stories." She sighed. "Such a hopeless romantic."

"So why didn't you go?"

"I convinced him the skiing was better at Innsbruck."

Franz's smile evolved into another yawn. With the train's hypnotic motion, he was having trouble keeping his eyes open. He had hardly slept in four days and welcomed the enveloping drowsiness. Esther was saying something to him, but her words sounded as though spoken under water. Moments later, his chin dropped to his chest and her voice disappeared altogether.

"Franz!"

"Not now," he murmured, wondering why Hilde was shaking his shoulder so roughly.

"Franz!" Esther cried.

He opened his eyes, disoriented by the flashlight's beam that swung through the compartment. "Where are we?" He wiped his lip as Hannah stirred to life beside him.

"Maglern. The Austrian side of the border," Esther whispered urgently. "They say all Jews have to get off here!"

"Who says?"

She pointed toward the light source. "Border guards. *The SS.*"

"Not again," Franz muttered to himself. "Not when we're so close."

Esther guided the sleepy Hannah off the train, while Franz made two trips to lug all the bags into the small terminal. Fear gripped him as he heard their train chug away without them.

Inside the terminal, they faced another line and a new official: a broad-shouldered man wearing the dreaded black SS uniform. By the time the Adlers reached the desk, Franz's nerves were raw, and he saw that Esther was also struggling to maintain her calm. The guard had hollow cheeks and a scar that ran from the corner of his left eye toward his ear. His open-mouthed smile was more disconcerting than the scowls Franz had come to expect from the SS.

"Papers, please," the guard said with insincere politeness.

They handed over their documents.

"We're sorry for the inconvenience," the guard said with another ugly smile. "But you Jews are notoriously sneaky at smuggling valuables out of the country. This is your final opportunity. Do you have anything you would like to declare?"

Franz hesitated, waiting to hear Esther's response. "No, sir," she said forcefully.

"Us neither," Franz said.

"So be it," the Nazi sighed.

Franz barely breathed as he watched the man search the suitcases far more diligently than the inspector at the Südbahnhof had. At one point, the guard pulled a hunting knife from his belt and, without a word of explanation, sliced open the lining of Esther's trunk. He dug his hand inside, searching for hidden compartments.

Franz exhaled as the guard shut the last of their suitcases. But his relief was short-lived. The Nazi turned to Hannah. "Little girl, your doll, please."

Hannah glanced up at Franz with huge eyes. "Papa?"

Before Franz could respond, the official snatched Schweizer Fräulein from Hannah's arms. He dug the knife's blade into the seam along the doll's back.

"Papa, *no*!" Hannah squealed.

"Please, sir," Esther pleaded. "She has had that doll since she was a baby."

The SS official looked directly at Hannah. "I'm

sorry, little one," he said with a crocodilian grin. "I have no choice. There's no level your parents would not stoop to."

"You can see that no one has touched the stitching—" Franz began, but it was too late.

The man jabbed his blade farther into the doll's back and ripped open the seam. Stuffing popped out. Hannah clutched her face and moaned. The official shot Franz a can't-be-helped shrug. Listening to Hannah's plaintive sobs, Franz trembled with rage. He had to fight the urge to gouge the Nazi's eyes.

Franz was still so preoccupied with his daughter's distress that he numbly endured the humiliating strip search he had to submit to in the men's room. But his worry skyrocketed again when Hannah and Esther failed to emerge from the restroom where the female guard was searching them.

Franz paced up and down in front of the bathroom. After twelve agonizing minutes, the door finally opened and the guard walked out, followed by Esther, who had an arm around Hannah. His sister-in-law's expression was blank but her eyes reassured him that the guard had not found anything.

Hannah broke free of Esther and hurried over to Franz, holding out her disfigured doll for him to see. "Papa, she's dead!" she cried. "The man killed her."

Franz knelt down to his daughter's level. "No, *liebchen*," he murmured. "She is not dead at all. We will fix her better than new."

"You can't," Hannah said miserably.

"It's what I do, Hannah." He wiped the tears away from her face with his thumb and index finger. "I am a doctor. I sew people together."

"But they took away all your tools," she pointed out.

"No matter." He smiled. "I will find new tools. You'll see."

She wrapped her arms around him and hugged him fiercely. He could feel her trembling through her coat.

They sat on their luggage in the chilly station waiting for the next train to Trieste—the milk runner, so called because it stopped at every village it passed to drop off dairy products. Hours passed before the old train finally chugged into the station. The cars were more cramped than on the express train, but Franz managed to stack their bags and find two seats together.

The train lurched away from the station and slowly gathered speed. Hannah snoozed on Franz's lap. After ten or fifteen minutes of traveling through the darkness, a man up front stood and shouted, "We have just crossed the border into Italy!"

Spontaneous cheers erupted among the trainload of mainly Jewish passengers. Couples kissed each other and families hugged. Someone began singing the Yiddish folk song *"Hobn Mir a Nigndl."* Others joined in, and soon the singing reached a raucous pitch.

The song was one of the ditties Franz's mother used to sing in her sweet contralto while ironing shirts. Though he remembered only a few words, he hummed along with the tune.

Franz looked over at Esther. She was staring out the window at the pitch-blackness. Her shoulders shook and her head bobbed.

PART II

Chapter 9

NOVEMBER 12, 1938, SHANGHAI

Mah Soon Yi hesitated at the walkway leading onto the Garden Bridge.

The steel double-truss bridge marked Shanghai's geographical center, spanning Soochow Creek where it intersected the Whangpoo River. The city was built along the west bank of the Whangpoo as it snaked southward in a lazy S-shape. The Garden Bridge connected Shanghai's most vital districts: the International Settlement and the French Concession to the south of Soochow Creek, and Hongkew to the north. To Soon Yi, the bridge also spanned the divide between West and East, providing a link between the skyscraper-crowned International Settlement and the traditional charm of Hongkew. Or at least it had before the bombs began to fall.

All of this to cross a bridge that would hardly span a rice paddy. Soon Yi sighed to herself.

Still, her chest tightened the moment she set foot onto the bridge. A few feet ahead of her, a soldier leaned against the side of the guard hut that was built onto the walkway, his rifle slung loosely over his shoulder. Soon Yi recognized him as American by his deportment alone. Her pulse slowed with relief even though she knew it didn't really matter who—the Fourth American

Marines, the British Seaforth Highlanders, or the Shanghai Volunteer Corp—guarded the south end of the Garden Bridge. The problem stood fifteen yards to the north, where the opposing guards were always Japanese.

The baby-faced Marine greeted Soon Yi with a toothy grin. Despite the soldier's encouraging nod, Soon Yi stood immobile in front of his hut. "Long as you don't forget to bow, ma'am," he said with a wink, "you'll be just fine."

Soon Yi—or Sunny, as her mother had nicknamed her—knew the drill only too well, but she still smiled at the young soldier's kindness. "I will remember to bow, thank you."

Sunny felt comfortable around Americans. They rarely carried the Old World airs or prejudices that clung so tightly to the French and British Shanghai-landers and even many of the native Shanghainese. Born to an American mother, Sunny had attended the prestigious Shanghai American School, but she had never left Asia and her mother had died when she was only eight years old.

The Marine repositioned his rifle over the front of his chest. He tilted his head, indicating his Japanese counterpart across the bridge. "I'll keep a close watch on that one," he said.

Sunny nodded her gratitude, despite the emptiness of the promise. For months, the guards on the south-ern end had stood by helplessly as Japanese soldiers inflicted vicious physical and verbal abuse on unlucky Chinese pedestrians, whose offenses ranged from im-proper eye contact to not having bowed long or deep enough to the new masters of Shanghai. At the hospi-tal the week before, Sunny had cared for a man dying from an infected bayonet wound incurred at the same checkpoint; apparently, he had flashed a grin that had been perceived as a smirk.

The International Settlement's soldiers were powerless to intervene. They were under orders not to, for fear of inciting an international incident. The political balance in Shanghai teetered more precariously than ever. And Sunny knew that once she stepped beyond the guard hut, the Marine could offer her no real protection.

Up until the previous autumn, Sunny had enjoyed crossing the Garden Bridge, often lingering to peer down at the junks and sampans crowding Soochow Creek. She had once worked at the Shanghai General Hospital in Hongkew, whose streets and lanes were as familiar to her as the medical texts lining her father's library. But since the short bridge had come to represent an armed border within the city, she avoided Hongkew whenever possible. At twenty-four, Sunny was worldly enough to recognize the threat the Japanese soldiers posed, especially when drunk. She had already attended enough Chinese women and girls with unwanted pregnancies, vaginal tears, broken limbs, and other traumas to know that the leers from Japanese soldiers were anything but harmless.

But today Sunny had no choice; her friend needed her. So she tucked her bag over her shoulder, clamped her arms to her sides, and stepped forward. Keeping her head bowed and her gaze low, she approached the Japanese guard hut and stopped ten or so feet before it. An infantryman—wearing a classic khaki uniform, brimmed and pointed cap, and leather puttees covering his pants below the knees—stood erect outside his hut. He held his bayoneted rifle across his chest at the ready, as though he expected the bored American Marine to spring an ambush at any moment.

Legs straight, Sunny bowed fully forward at the waist in the Japanese manner. She felt the eyes of the soldier on her, but he said nothing. Two long minutes passed. Her hamstrings stiffened and her back began to ache, yet the soldier remained silent. Another minute went by. *You beast! You're even more sadistic than the others!*

Uncharacteristic anger simmered inside Sunny. As a Chinese city built and still partly ruled by Europeans, Shanghai was home to thousands of Eurasians. But unlike other ethnicities, as mixed bloods, they could never be born into a community of their own. Sunny was long accustomed to the sense of being a perpetual outsider even, to a certain extent, within her own Chinese family. She managed to ignore most of the bigotry she faced, but this shameful ritual—having to kowtow before the Japanese soldiers while Caucasians walked past unmolested—infuriated her.

Finally, the guard grunted as though scolding a disobedient dog. Without glancing in his direction, Sunny straightened up, squared her shoulders, and made her way off the bridge and onto Broadway, Hongkew's busiest thoroughfare, which hugged the west bank of the Whangpoo.

The previous summer, the Japanese had terrorized Hongkew with indiscriminate aerial bombardment and brutal house-to-house street fighting. Sunny was fortunate to live in the French Concession, on the "safe side" to the south of Soochow Creek, but images of the hospitalized victims—people burned beyond recognition, children blinded by flying glass, and the endless stream of bloodied and broken bodies—were imprinted on her brain. After the Chinese government had capitulated and the gunfire and explosions had lessened from constant to intermittent, life had returned to a semblance of normality for the almost one million people, mainly Shanghainese, still crammed inside the borough. Sunny slipped through the throngs of people. The cool air was heavy with smoke, body odor, and the stench of cooking oil and sundry river smells. The sidewalk writhed with the usual mix of street kitchens, beggars, and vendors, their noisy peddling merging with the rest of the street's cacophony.

Hongkew's shops, bars, temples, and brothels continued to thrive after the invasion, albeit now under the unblinking eye of the Japanese military. Its presence was constant and palpable in the form of marching soldiers, sentries, and, most feared, the Kempeitai—the military policemen who wore white armbands. Sunny had only glimpsed the Kempeitai from a distance and hoped to never get any closer. She had heard enough horror stories to know that a visit from the men in the white armbands was synonymous with internment, torture, and, as often as not, death.

Keeping her canvas bag tucked close to her side, Sunny wove her way seven or eight blocks through the hordes of bustling humanity and turned north. Approaching the busy intersection of Kung Ping and Tong Shan roads, she slowed to pass an open bazaar. As commonplace as street markets were throughout Shanghai, especially in Hongkew, Sunny had never seen one like this. The vendors were all formally dressed European men in trench coats or furs worn over suits. Most wore hats and leather gloves as they stood on the sidewalk selling an array of secondhand clothing, jewelry, watches, and even typewriters. The men ranged in appearance from young and spry to old and decrepit. None were nearly as aggressive as Chinese street merchants. Some stood forlornly behind their own booths, while others clustered in small groups and chatted quietly among themselves. Their dazed and lost expressions reminded Sunny of the shipwreck survivors she had read about in an old novel.

Slowing to study a brass fob watch that might interest her father, Sunny overheard the two vendors behind the table conversing in German. She assumed the men must be part of the contingent of Jewish refugees who had descended upon the city. She had seen the ships in the harbor unloading their human cargo but had not yet met any of them.

While Sunny examined the watch, the two men spoke freely, never suspecting that she might understand German. The slender man, who had a long, distinguished face, was trying to reassure his shorter companion. "What else could you possibly do, Isaac?" he asked. "Miriam does not want the children to go hungry any more than you do."

The other man shook his head miserably. "But her wedding ring? It has been in the family for over sixty years. Miriam's grandmother wore that same ring, Albert."

"It was a decent price, Isaac. The money will go far."

"Still, how can I go home to my Miriam now?"

Albert laid his hand on Isaac's shoulder. "You did what you had to."

But Isaac was inconsolable. "I wish we had just stayed in Berlin."

Isaac glanced in Sunny's direction and met her gaze. Embarrassed to be caught eavesdropping, Sunny broke off the eye contact and hurried away. But even as she crossed the intersection, the naked despair in Isaac's eyes lingered in her memory.

A half mile farther, she entered the heart of Hongkew. Like the rest of Shanghai, the architecture bore minimal resemblance to traditional Chinese style. Most of the buildings had been hastily constructed at the turn of the nineteenth century to house the merchants and lower middle classes servicing the affluent Westerners living to the south of Soochow Creek. Unlike the *hutongs*—traditional homes built around a central courtyard—of other Chinese cities, most buildings in Hongkew were cheaply constructed from brick and crammed tightly around a network of lanes. These *longtangs*, or "lane-houses," were unique to Shanghai.

Before the invasion, the *longtangs* in the neighborhood were so plain and interchangeable that Sunny sometimes had difficulty telling one block from the next. But the Japanese bombardment had permanently disrupted the monotony of the design. Now, heaps of rubble marked the remnants of numerous structures. Some buildings that had withstood the bombing were missing walls or parts of their roofs. Everywhere Sunny looked, she saw boarded or taped windows.

Passing one collapsed building, Sunny spied four little boys in stained shirts and frayed pants, the oldest of whom appeared to be no more than eight, racing each other over and around precariously balanced heaps of brick and stone. *"Xiǎo xīn!"* she warned them.

The boys stopped and stared. "We are always careful, *fū ren,*" the tallest one announced, referring to her with the respectful title of "lady."

Another boy, wearing a torn shirt and frayed pants, pointed to the wreckage. "I used to live here," he said with an almost stunned bravado.

Sunny wondered if any or all of the boy's family had been trapped inside when the building crumpled. "You are very brave boys. I see that. But please, little ones, take care playing among these piles of rocks. They could fall and hurt you."

"We are too fast for these rocks," the smallest one chirped, kicking the stones at his feet.

"And too fast for the dwarf bandits too," the older one added, using the local epithet for the Japanese. The others laughed and then ran off together, disappearing behind a mound of rubble.

Sunny walked another two blocks before turning into a lane that was not much wider than the span of a man's arms. Cars could not navigate Hongkew's constricted lanes, but a steady traffic of bicycles, rickshaws, and peddlers' wagons more than compensated.

Sunny arrived at the fourth brick building. Bullet holes pocked the corner pillar and a portion of its lower archway was missing, but it had otherwise escaped the fighting. She stopped at the second door and rapped gently. The door opened a crack, and a pair of eyes peered out before it swung wider.

Ko Lo-Shen stood on the other side, wringing her hands and bobbing from foot to foot, appearing even more flustered than usual. As long as Sunny could remember, Lo-Shen had worn the same style of *aoqun*—a traditional quilted cotton jacket and long black skirt. Stooped and frail, she looked much older than her forty-five years. But Sunny was well aware of the hardships, disappointments, and tragedies that had conspired to break Lo-Shen's spirit.

Sunny bowed her head. "*Nǎ hǎo, shěn shen,*" she said in a familiar greeting that loosely translated as "hello, Auntie."

"It is good to see you again too, Soon Yi," Lo-Shen sputtered in her nasal provincial Mandarin. She extended her arm. Sunny slipped off her coat and handed it to Lo-Shen, who hung it from the wooden peg on the wall. Lo-Shen turned back to Sunny. Never much one for small talk, she eyed the younger woman anxiously.

"Is Jia-Li in the bedroom, *shěn shen*?" Sunny asked.

Lo-Shen spun and hurried across the colorless room,

with its low ceiling and oppressively small windows, hobbling as fast as her tiny feet, which had been bound during childhood, would carry her. Sunny followed her to the bedroom. Through the door, she heard the sound of violent retching. She took a deep breath and mentally braced herself for a scene she had already faced too many times before.

Inside the dimly lit room, a mattress lay on the floor, a damp wadded cloth and a half-full glass of water beside it. Most of the covers had been kicked off and were huddled in a heap at the foot of the bed. A single beige sheet, soaked in patches, covered the writhing figure on the mattress.

"Hello, Jia-Li," Sunny said calmly in English before switching to Mandarin for Lo-Shen's benefit. "It's good to see you, *bǎo bèi*." She used Jia-Li's familiar childhood nickname of "precious."

Jia-Li whipped off the sheet and sprang up in the bed, looking as pale as the white negligee that hung loosely off her thin frame. Sweat poured down her brow. Her shoulder-length hair was tousled and wild. Flecks of vomit clung to the corner of her lips. Yet, despite her harsh appearance, she was still striking. With sculpted cheeks and full lips that set off her porcelain skin, Jia-Li was the most beautiful person Sunny had ever known.

Jia-Li shuddered violently. "This is the worst one ever, *xiǎo hè*!" she said, referring to Sunny by her Chinese nickname, "little lotus."

Jia-Li claimed the same every episode. "It will be over soon," Sunny said softly. "They always are."

Jia-Li shot a hand out for the bucket beside the bed. She brought it to her lips and retched again but only spat a few drops into the bucket.

Sunny's nostrils filled with the intermingled stench

of sweat and vomit. She grabbed the glass of water and damp washcloth as she knelt down beside Jia-Li. She gently ran the cloth across her friend's mouth, wiping away the remains of vomit. She folded the stained cloth inward and then sponged Jia-Li's dripping brow.

"You brought me something, *xiǎo hè*?" Jia-Li's voice quivered.

"Yes, I did, *bǎo bèi*."

Jia-Li exhaled with relief. "Pills? If not, I have my pipe. I do not like to smoke in Mother's home but—"

"Not this time." Sunny shook her head. "I brought you real medicine."

Jia-Li's face crumpled. She yanked the bucket to her lips and gagged again. "Sunny, *please*, I need something! Opium . . . morphine . . . anything!"

"Look what it is doing to you, *bǎo bèi*!"

Jia-Li's trembling intensified and she began to sob. "What has become of me?"

"Shh," Sunny soothed as she wrapped an arm around her friend. She hugged her tightly enough to feel the shivering. "We will get you through this. Everything will be all right. You will see."

"Why do you waste your time? I'm just another opium-addicted wild pheasant," Jia-Li whimpered, using the derogatory term for the lowest class of Shanghai's prostitutes.

Lo-Shen gasped at her daughter's double admission, though neither would have been a revelation to her. Without a word, the small woman backpedaled out of the room and silently closed the door behind her.

Jia-Li might have been addicted to opium, but Sunny knew she was hardly a wild pheasant. In a city reputed to be home to more than a hundred thousand prostitutes, Jia-Li was among the most sought-after singsong girls in what arguably was the French Concession's leading brothel. Outside of work, Jia-Li lived affluently, residing in an airy suite in the Cathay Building, one of the most upscale addresses in the city. Yet she could never persuade her mother to abandon the apartment in Hongkew and move in with her. During fits of opium withdrawal, Jia-Li inevitably slunk back to her mother's humble flat to suffer the shame of her lifestyle as acutely as anyone possibly could.

Sunny released Jia-Li from her grip and dug a pill bottle out of her handbag. She gently tapped out two pills into her palm. They weighed nothing, but the sight of them conjured a wave of guilt. Sunny had taken the pills from her father's medication supply at home without permission. She knew he would have willingly given them to her. Her father loved Jia-Li like a daughter and had provided morphine in the past to treat her withdrawal. But Sunny did not have the heart to tell her father about her friend's latest relapse. Irrational as it was, Sunny felt somehow responsible. And she hated the thought of disappointing her father.

Jia-Li stared wide-eyed at the pills. "Morphine?" she asked hopefully.

Sunny shook her head. "Cannabis and atropine."

"How will they help?" Jia-Li muttered.

Sunny pointed from one pill to the other. "The cannabis will settle your stomach, and the atropine will stop the cramps."

A frown crossed Jia-Li's lips as she extended her trembling fingers toward the pills. It took her three tries to fish them out of Sunny's palm and pop them into her mouth. Sunny brought the water glass to Jia-Li's lips, tilting it just enough to dribble a small sip into her mouth. Jia-Li swallowed the pills in one loud gulp. Shakily, she lowered the glass, then pursed her lips as she fought off another gag.

Sunny viewed her best friend affectionately. At such times, words were unnecessary between them.

They had grown up on the same cherry tree–lined street that ran through the heart of the French Concession where Sunny and her father still lived. The Kos lived two doors down. Sunny and Jia-Li became friends before they could talk. After her mother's sudden death from a brain hemorrhage, Sunny spent so much time with the Kos that she felt a part of their family too. The girls were inseparable, closer than most sisters. But, at the age of thirteen, everything changed for them when Jia-Li's father's gambling debt finally caught up to him. In the tradition of other overextended gamblers, he jumped to his death from the top deck of the city's notorious nightclub and casino, The Great World. Too proud to accept money from Sunny's father, Kingsley, to pay off her husband's debts, Lo-Shen sold her house, relocated her family to a poorer area of Hongkew, and took on work as a seamstress.

Confused and lonely, Jia-Li fell for an eighteen-year-old boy in the neighborhood. Sunny distrusted him the instant she glimpsed his reptilian smile, but Jia-Li was too smitten to heed her warnings. The boyfriend exerted a hypnotic influence, introducing Jia-Li to the opium pipe and then selling her off as one of Shanghai's most precious commodities—a "first-night virgin"—long after he had already deflowered her. Soon after, he abandoned Jia-Li altogether, leaving her brokenhearted, opium addicted, and reliant on her income as a prostitute. Ashamed, Jia-Li tried to sever all ties with her past life, but Sunny worked her way back into her friend's heart. In turn, Jia-Li proved to be a dedicated and streetwise companion, introducing Sunny to aspects of Shanghai that she never knew existed, while fiercely protecting her from the same pitfalls to which Jia-Li had fallen victim.

Jia-Li's retching finally settled. "Why, Sunny?" she croaked. "Why do you come back after I keep breaking my promises to you?"

Sunny did not answer right away. Instead, she smoothed down the spears of hair that stuck out the side of Jia-Li's head. "I would do anything for you."

⌒ *Chapter 10*

"What is Virchow's triad?" Her father sprung the question before Sunny had even set foot inside the den that served as his office.

"'Virchow's triad' refers to the three factors that contribute to the formation of blood clots or deep-vein thrombosis of the legs," Sunny replied without having to consider the answer.

Mah Kun Li—"Kingsley" to his English-speaking friends and medical colleagues—sat behind his prized redwood desk, a hundred-year-old hand-carved relic from the late Qing dynasty. A chart lay open in front of the doctor, while others were piled neatly in two stacks on either side of the desk. Kingsley saw his patients at his clinic in the International Settlement or, for those too ill to travel, in their own beds, but he often brought charts home to complete in the evening. Though it was well past ten o'clock, he still wore the top button of his navy blazer fastened and his tie perfectly knotted.

"Which three factors?" her father demanded,

speaking English as he almost always did in Sunny's presence.

Sunny listed them with her fingers. "Immobility, injury, and hypercoagulability."

"Correct."

Kingsley had been devastated when his old alma mater, Hong Kong University, and the other reputable medical schools in East Asia had all declined Sunny's applications, based (he was convinced) on her gender and mixed race rather than merit. He committed himself to personally training his daughter as a physician, even while she attended nursing school. She had since spent most of her spare moments studying his medical texts or shadowing him at work. Three years after Sunny's graduation from nursing school, Kingsley continued to quiz her relentlessly, to the point where she could recite whole passages from texts such as *Gray's Anatomy* or the *Merck Manual*.

"So tell me, Sunny," he said. "What is the single greatest risk factor for developing a venous thrombosis?"

Sunny bit back a smile, recognizing the question as a trick that she might have fallen for a year or two earlier. "The person most at risk for developing a thrombosis is someone who has had a previous blood clot," she said as she reached his desk.

"Precisely so," Kingsley said with a satisfied nod.

Sunny circled the desk, wrapped her arms around her father, and hugged him tightly, feeling his bony frame through his suit jacket. She kissed his smooth cheek and inhaled his spicy cologne. The scent grounded her, conjuring the warm sense of security it always had.

Many Chinese, especially her highly traditional aunt, would have frowned upon such a show of physical affection by a daughter for a parent, but Sunny never let that stop her. She was her mother's daughter, born with a fiery streak of independence that, while often landing her in trouble with both Western and Eastern cultures, defined her as much as her Eurasian heritage or her passion for medicine.

Sunny released her father from the embrace. He viewed her intently, and she braced herself for another medical question. Instead, he asked, "How is Jia-Li faring?"

"Jia-Li is ... doing ... better," Sunny sputtered, wondering how he could have known about her friend's relapse.

"Ko Lo-Shen came to see me earlier. She brought me a *yuèbǎng*." The traditional moon cakes were his favorite. "To thank me for sending you to look after her daughter." He raised an eyebrow. "And for providing medicine to Jia-Li."

Sunny's face began to burn, but she said nothing.

"Soon Yi, you only had to ask."

His tone was impassive but Sunny could sense his disappointment. She looked down, too ashamed to meet his eyes. "I know, Father. I should have told you. You have been so generous to Jia-Li. I had hoped that the previous episode would be her last."

"There will be a next time, Sunny," Kingsley said gravely. "And more times after that."

Sunny only nodded.

Kingsley laughed softly. "Did I not teach you the one truism about opium? It is the worst lover to try to leave, and the most difficult relationship to end."

"You did."

"In my experience, the addict has to lose absolutely everything before she will leave the pipe behind." He cleared his throat. "If she ever will."

"Jia-Li will," Sunny said, aware her voice lacked conviction.

"I hope so, Sunny," Kingsley said. "Between her . . . circumstances . . . and living in a city where the opium is as plentiful as rice, she will have a long and difficult battle ahead."

Sunny looked up and met his gaze. "None of this excuses my behavior, Father."

He shrugged his narrow shoulders, and his lips broke into the wisp of a smile. "Tell me, Sunny. What is a Sister Mary Joseph's nodule?" he quizzed.

"A hardened lymph node found under the umbilicus." And then, anticipating his next question, she added, "It indicates an underlying abdominal cancer, commonly of the stomach or large bowel, which has already spread to the point of being inoperable."

Kingsley continued to grill Sunny. She knew he was trying to distract her from her nagging guilt, and she loved him even more for the effort, but she could not shake the shame of her deception or her worry for Jia-Li. Though her friend's stomach had settled and her sweats had broken, Sunny had left Jia-Li still curled up clutching her belly and whimpering for her pipe.

After finishing her father's evening quiz, Sunny kissed him good night and headed to her bedroom. Three of her favorite poems, penned in ornate Chinese calligraphy, hung like banners on one of the walls. She glanced past them to the room's only artwork, a charcoal portrait of her mother, Ida Hudson Mah. In the sketch, Ida's shoulders were turned slightly from the painter and she offered him an enigmatic grin. Sunny remembered the Mona Lisa smile, but in her recollection, her mother's eyes always brimmed with more warmth than the artist had captured.

As Sunny lay under the blanket, the memories blurred and she drifted to sleep, her dreams a jumble of childhood scenes, military checkpoints, bombing victims, and opium dens.

Sunny awoke to the smell of brewing coffee. In the kitchen, the housekeeper, Yang, stood over the stove, boiling eggs to accompany vegetable dumplings. The tiny, tireless woman had been with the Mahs since Sunny was born. Yang had begun as Sunny's amah and evolved into their housekeeper. She understood English perfectly but never spoke a word of it. At times, Yang could be so quiet that she seemed to blend into the walls, but she could also be as protective as a tigress of her cubs if she sensed the slightest threat to Sunny. "Oh, Soon Yi, what were you doing in Hongkew?" Yang demanded as she placed a full plate and a cup of tea in front of her.

Sunny glanced at her father, who shrugged helplessly. She turned back to Yang. "Jia-Li needed my help," she said in Shanghainese.

"No one can help Jia-Li," Yang said with a trace of sadness. "You must stay away from Hongkew, *xiǎo hè*. The Japanese soldiers . . ."

Yang had not set foot in Hongkew since the Japanese invasion. On the second day of the occupation, soldiers had gunned down her youngest brother and his wife on the street without incitation or warning. Ever since, Yang had harbored a loathing and fear of the Japanese that bordered on phobic. "Hongkew is not good anymore, not good at all," she muttered, turning her attention back to the boiling eggs.

As Sunny and her father ate, they traded pages of the *Shanghai Morning Post*. Flipping to the back pages, an article near the bottom caught her eye. The headline read, "No End to Flood of Jewish Refugees."

Sunny had heard the talk, much of it disparaging,

among Shanghailanders about the influx of refugees. She thought of the distressed man she had overheard at the street market. Reading on, she learned that even the Jewish relief organizations were being overwhelmed by the steady flow of impoverished arrivals. Some wealthier Jewish Shanghailanders had donated money to establish homes and schools for the refugees but, according to the article, those same Jews were also supporting a motion before the Shanghai Municipal Council calling for a moratorium on more arrivals.

Sunny held up the page to show her father. "Did you see this?" He nodded. "Father, they're establishing a refugee hospital to help care for German Jews."

"So I understand."

"Perhaps they need help?" Sunny said.

He shook his head. "I have heard of several renowned specialists arriving among the refugees. I doubt they require the assistance of a simple Chinese doctor."

Sunny sighed, frustrated by her father's self-deprecation. Kingsley was one of the first physicians in Shanghai to prescribe insulin and had become a leading diabetes specialist. However, he had never shed his sense of professional humility, ingrained after so many years of schooling and practicing with the British doctors who, even while seeking his guidance and expertise, still looked down their noses at him.

"I am reasonably fluent in German." Sunny did not have to remind her father that she had won the languages prize at her school. "Perhaps they need nurses?"

"As I see it, there is only one way to find out."

Sunny noted the address of the refugee hospital. She wondered if she would have time to drop in after her shift. It would mean traveling to Hongkew after dusk, an unsettling prospect, but the memory of those distraught Jewish men in the market cemented her resolve.

Kingsley lowered the newspaper. "Sunny, you realize that Fai is still visiting his mother in the country? The poor woman is dying, so we will have to make do without a driver for another few days."

She nodded, almost reconsidering her trip to Hongkew. "I will ride the cable car to work."

Sunny gathered her bag, kissed her father on the forehead, and headed out. It was unseasonably warm for November, so she decided to forgo the cable car and walk the almost two miles to the Country Hospital on Great Western Road.

Her route took her through the heart of the French Concession, the wedge-shaped residential district that ran west from the Whangpoo River along the southern border of the International Settlement. The concession, known by many locals as simply "Frenchtown," had been under French sovereignty since the mid-nineteenth century, and the Gallic imprint was everywhere, from its street names, architecture, and parks to the police officers dressed in the style of Parisian gendarmes. Only the French themselves were missing. They were outnumbered almost a hundred to one by the Chinese. Even the British and Russian populations were larger. So many Russians had poured into the French Concession after fleeing the Bolshevik Revolution that a section of Frenchtown had been nicknamed "Little Russia." Sunny reveled in the cultural diversity of her neighborhood, where on one block alone she might pass a patisserie, a Siberian fur store, and a traditional tea shop.

Sunny arrived at the Country Hospital half an hour early for her shift. Enjoying the sunshine, she strolled around the hospital's perimeter, stopping to admire the building where she had worked since the Japanese invaded Hongkew. The neoclassical Renaissance design was striking enough to compete with any of the grand edifices lining the city's famous riverfront Bund. Rumors continued to swirl that the hospital's anonymous benefactor was Sir Victor Sassoon, an Iraqi Jew and the city's most influential tycoon.

Passing under the hospital's central stone arcade, Sunny entered the marble-floored foyer. The matron, Mrs. Gwendolyn Bathurst, stood at the bottom of the stairs in her starched white uniform with her hands at her hips as she waited for the arrival of her next shift of nurses.

"Good morning, Matron," Sunny said.

"Hello, Nurse Mah," the plump British woman said coolly.

Matron was as old-fashioned as they came, but, despite her frosty demeanor and lofty expectations, Sunny was fond of Bathurst. The woman was fair to a fault and never showed a flicker of racism or favoritism toward her staff.

"I believe Dr. Reuben is looking for you this morning," Bathurst announced.

Sunny nodded, detecting a note of warning in the woman's tone.

"I think you had best attend to your ward now," Bathurst said.

"Yes, of course, Matron."

Sunny headed to the nurses' room, changed into her uniform, and pinned her hair under her cap before climbing the two flights of stairs to the surgical ward. On the spacious floor, twenty steel-framed beds lined the walls, separated from one another by translucent free-standing dividers. Sunlight poured through the large windows.

Meredith Blythe and Stacy Chan stood at the central desk. Blythe had a square face, broad shoulders, and narrow hips that always made her uniform appear ill-fitting, whereas Chan was as diminutive as an adolescent girl. The two friends lived together and, as much as possible, worked the same schedule. Earlier in the year, a rumor had circulated that the pair had been seen kissing in the park across from the hospital. Sunny never paid heed to the gossip.

Transcultural friendships were common at the Country Hospital. The racial demographics of the staff and patients reflected the city it serviced and consisted of a mix of Western Shanghailanders and native Shanghainese. However, Sunny was the only Eurasian employee, and the outsider stigma still clung to her even within the hospital's relatively tolerant milieu.

Sunny had a quick glance around the ward. With a sinking feeling, she noticed that the third bed along the near wall was empty. "Mr. Chum?" she asked the other two nurses.

Blythe shook her head. "He passed on yesterday aft."

"Probably for the best." A pit formed in her stomach as Sunny spoke. She had grown attached to the old man, who, even as he withered away from colon cancer, fed her a steady diet of homespun wisdom on life and marriage while encouraging dalliances with almost every unattached male who passed through the ward.

Sunny was relieved to see that Stanley Wheelman still occupied the bed in the far corner. As soon as she looked his way, the young American beckoned her with a weak flicker of his fingers. She hurried to the bedside. "Good morning, Mr. Wheelman," she said with a bright smile. "How are you feeling today?"

"No worse, Nurse Mah," the emaciated man croaked. "That's for sure."

"May I examine your wound?" Sunny asked.

His head bobbed slightly. Sunny pulled the sheet

down from his chest and peeled back the loose cotton bandages covering his abdomen. The stink of decay assaulted her nose and nearly made her eyes water. She spotted a few loops of bowel poking through the gaping vertical wound. But the angry red skin around the edges had faded to a calmer salmon pink—the first sign of improvement she had seen in him.

"I wouldn't let them cut me open a third time," Wheelman said hoarsely. "Just like we discussed."

Sunny nodded. "Did the doctor start you on the sulfonamides?"

He frowned. "If you mean those new horse pills, then yes."

"Good." Sunny was pleased to hear that his surgeon had finally acquiesced and begun treating him with antibiotics, Western medicine's latest wonder weapon against infections.

"Nurse Mah, I wanted to thank you for helping to convince—" Wheelman began.

"Nurse, may I have a moment of your time?" The frigid words, spoken in a clipped English accent, came from behind her.

Sunny turned to see Dr. Samuel Reuben glaring at her from the ward's entrance. "I will return shortly, Mr. Wheelman." She headed toward Reuben, who pivoted and glided out of the ward without waiting.

Sunny followed Reuben out into the corridor, where he stood with arms folded over his chest. His navy bow tie sat perfectly horizontal and his lab coat was as crisp and spotless as ever, but his long thin face, usually pale in complexion, had reddened to the point of crimson. His dark eyes burned behind his tortoiseshell glasses. "Is it true that you persuaded Mr. Wheelman to decline surgery?" Reuben demanded.

She met his eyes. "I suggested that Mr. Wheelman consider all options before deciding, sir."

"What other options?" Reuben snapped. "The man has an infected intestinal wound that requires resection and drainage!"

"I thought he was too weak and frail to survive another operation, Dr. Reuben."

"*You* thought, did you?" he scoffed. "Based on all your experience as a surgeon?"

Sunny considered her words carefully. She knew how resistant surgeons, and Reuben in particular, were to unsolicited opinions. "Despite the first-class care you have provided, Mr. Wheelman has not shown significant improvement after two surgeries."

"The man suffered from a perforated appendix and an abscess. I assumed he would have a difficult course after surgery."

"Of course, sir." Sunny nodded contritely. "But his wounds have been so slow to heal, Dr. Reuben. I thought his condition might be complicated by terminal ileitis. I heard that the sulfonamides had been proven somewhat effective in reversing the course of ileitis."

"And where had you heard that?"

Sunny cleared her throat. "I read it in an article in *The Lancet.*"

"Really? Are they distributing *The Lancet* to nurses now?"

"My father sometimes lends me his copy."

"Borrowing your father's medical journals does not qualify you as a doctor, Miss Mah!"

"Of course not, sir, I realize that."

"Do you really?" he huffed. "Sometimes I wonder."

Sunny bowed her head again, mainly to conceal the anger that was burning in her eyes. "I am sorry I overstepped my bounds, Dr. Reuben. But the patient thinks he has improved on the medication."

"Yes, well, never underestimate the effect of a placebo or a sympathetic face," he grumbled. "Regardless, I have little choice now but to continue the medication and dressing changes. To effectively leave his care in the hands of Providence."

"Thank you, Dr. Reuben."

"Oh, there is no reason to thank me." Reuben uncrossed his arms and pointed at Sunny. "Miss Mah, I do not care whether or not your father is a physician. If you ever again sabotage my treatment plans, as the chief of surgery, I will ensure that you no longer work at the Country Hospital or any reputable facility in this city. Am I clear?"

"Yes, sir," she said through clenched teeth.

Without another word, Reuben swiveled and stormed off down the hallway. As soon as he had left, Stacy Chan poked her head through the doorway, concern etched in her small features. "Soon Yi, are you all right?" she asked in Shanghainese.

Sunny adjusted her cap. "I am fine, Stacy. Thank you."

"I have never seen Dr. Reuben so upset."

"I suppose not." In fact, Sunny had seen him in a similar state the last time they had disagreed over a diagnosis, but he had never threatened her job before.

"Can I get you a cup of tea?" Chan offered.

"No." Sunny mustered a reassuring smile for the meek girl. "It's time for you to go home and for me to get to work."

Sunny inhaled slowly. The clash with Reuben had shaken her more than she let on. His self-serving words had struck a chord. In spite of all her father's teaching, she was not a doctor and never would be. *What business do I have interfering in vital medical decisions?*

Another voice called to her. "Miss Mah, may I speak to you? Please."

No. Not now, of all times.

Sunny turned to see Dr. Wen-Cheng Huang striding toward her. She watched impassively, but her chest thumped harder as he approached. Clean-shaven and hair slicked fashionably to the side, Wen-Cheng wore a navy double-breasted suit and patterned tie, looking every bit the dashing young doctor who could turn a woman's head or earn a patient's confidence in a handshake. Only his unusually pale brown eyes contradicted the facade. They held the same wounded puppy expression as the last time she had seen him.

"Dr. Huang, I must return to my ward now," she said.

Wen-Cheng reached out as if to grab her wrist but stopped short of touching her. "Why have you not replied to my letters?"

Finding it painful to look into his plaintive eyes, she focused on the panel of black-and-white photographs of the hospital's directors behind him. "There is nothing more to say."

"Nothing?" Wen-Cheng frowned. "I poured my heart out to you."

"They are only words," she murmured.

Three months earlier, Sunny had been willing to sacrifice everything for Wen-Cheng. She believed the married physician when he told her that she was the love of his life and that only family and circumstance had trapped him in a loveless arranged marriage. Sunny was even prepared to shoulder her father's crushing disappointment and to lose face—a grievous fate in Chinese society. However, when the time had come to commit, Wen-Cheng was unwilling to stare down his own father. He begged Sunny for more time, promising her that in another year or two he would find a way to leave his wife. Heartsick as she had been, Sunny realized that Wen-Cheng would never divorce her. And Sunny decided it would be better to live with the heartbreak than the incompleteness of being his mistress.

But now, gazing into his adoring eyes, the desire flooded back. Desperate to throw her arms around him and to feel his skin against hers, she sensed her resolve weakening.

Wen-Cheng gently caressed her hand. The contact was electric. "I have made so many mistakes with you." He switched from English to Mandarin. "Without you in my life, there is no light. I love you, Sunny. I always will."

But Sunny knew that nothing had changed between them. She slipped her hand free of his. "Please do not write me any more letters, Dr. Huang." She turned for the door. "I will not answer them."

～ Chapter 11

Sunny crossed the Garden Bridge lost in a haze of emotions. She was so preoccupied with Jia-Li's relapse, Dr. Reuben's threat, and, especially, her conflicted feelings for Wen-Cheng that it took her a moment to register the Japanese guard's expectant stare.

Her stomach plummeted as she realized that she had forgotten to bow. Hastily, she thrust herself forward at the waist and bowed deeply, hoping it was not already too late. Her heart beat in her throat, but she did not dare look up at the guard.

"*Qù!*" The soldier uttered the Chinese word for "go" in a surprisingly even tone.

Sunny hurried on, grateful that the sentry was not the same malicious guard as the day before, who might have beaten her—or worse—for her oversight.

Electric streetlights and neon signs lit Broadway. The street bustled with even more commotion at eight in the evening than it had the previous noon. Young Chinese men wandered about in search of nightlife but, cognizant of the danger, kept in tight packs. Loose clusters of Japanese soldiers and sailors littered the sidewalks, several of them drunk to the point of staggering. Young, heavily rouged prostitutes in tight dresses—the true "wild pheasants"—stood under almost every streetlight. They beckoned to nearby men, regardless of uniform or race.

Sunny neared two Japanese sailors who wore their white jackets unbuttoned and shirts untucked. They loitered near a streetlamp while warbling an unrecognizable tune. The shorter one tapped his mate on the shoulder. The other sailor's head whipped in her direction so quickly that the tail of his bandana flapped. His dark eyes widened and his lips twisted into an ugly grin. Pointing unsteadily at her midsection, he slurred some Japanese words to her.

Sunny lowered her gaze and stepped off the sidewalk, trying to give the sailors as wide a berth as possible. But moments after she passed them, she heard heavy footsteps behind her. The bandana-clad sailor uttered another catcall at her back. Heartbeat drumming in her ears, Sunny stole a quick peek over her shoulder and saw that the two men were gaining. She considered ducking into a store or hurrying down one of the nearby alleys but realized it might only leave her more isolated and vulnerable.

Steeling her nerves, she spun to face the drunken sailors. Expression blank, she shook her head and pointed to the girls standing beneath nearby street-lights. The sailor in the bandana grunted and continued to lurch toward her, close enough for Sunny to pick up the stink of stale sake on his breath. His mouth twisted into a lascivious smile that accentuated the jagged scar running between his nose and lip.

He pawed at her chest. Sunny backed away, almost stumbling off the sidewalk. Steadying herself, she crossed her arms over her chest. "Do not touch me!" she snarled in English.

The sailor's cheeks reddened and his nostrils flared. He spat a stream of Japanese words.

Sunny's legs tensed, bracing for an attack. An image flashed to mind of an older woman who had been raped so viciously that she arrived at the hospital hemorrhaging. "It is better not to resist," the woman had murmured to Sunny as she was rushed to the operating room.

Dismissing the woman's advice, Sunny dropped her arms to her side, trying to decide whether to poke her fingers in his eyes or launch a knee into his groin.

Eyes locked on his, she waited. The feverish moment of stillness seemed to last forever.

The shorter sailor threw an arm over his mate's shoulder and muttered a few words. The man jerked free of his friend's grip. Then, just as suddenly, he broke into uproarious laughter.

Sunny's breathing eased as she watched the shorter sailor guide his drunken friend away. Even as he wobbled off, the man repeatedly glanced over his shoulder and leered at her menacingly.

She wheeled back toward the sanctuary of the International Settlement but slowed after a block and tried to calm her nerves. She thought of the others—soldiers, resistance fighters, and civilians caught in the middle—

who had faced worse without shirking their duty. She could not allow one drunken sailor to break her will. Reluctantly, she turned back toward her original destination.

Anxious to escape the thoroughfare that teemed with intoxicated soldiers, pickpockets, and prostitutes, Sunny veered off Broadway at the first intersection. Reaching Tong Shan Road, she spotted one of the city's distinctive green trolleys. It rolled to a stop ahead of her and she jumped aboard. The bus was crowded with Chinese in outfits ranging from traditional country robes to short Western dresses and three-piece suits. Some spoke Shanghainese, the local dialect, while others conversed in Mandarin, Wu, or Gan. The tonal sounds of her native tongue helped to soothe her raw nerves.

Three stops later, Sunny stepped off the bus. The chilly breeze carried a hint of fried fish, reminding her that she had missed dinner. Sunny wasn't concerned, as she knew one of Yang's meals would be packed and waiting in the icebox for her. As she neared the address of the refugee hospital on Ward Road, she wondered if she had confused the numbers. The decrepit building, an abandoned schoolhouse, had lost a chunk of its side wall and a portion of its roof from bomb damage. She could not imagine it functioning as a shelter, let alone a hospital.

Sunny noticed lights burning through the few windows that weren't boarded. She rounded the corner and saw a flatbed truck parked at the side entrance. Two Chinese laborers unloaded mattresses from the back with the aid of a lean man in a trench coat and fedora. The man in the hat glanced over to her. "Can I help you, lady?" he asked in English.

"No . . . well, yes . . ." Sunny said. "I have come to see the refugee hospital."

The man stepped closer. Sunny saw that his lips had broken into an amused grin. "You don't look particularly Jewish to me."

"I am a nurse."

"A nurse?" The man pulled off his hat, held it over his chest, and tipped his head in a slight bow. "Welcome to our world-famous, as yet unnamed, refugee hospital. Simon Lehrer at your service."

The young man possessed intelligent brown eyes, curly black hair, and thick eyebrows that converged above his prominent nose. Sunny found his looks intriguing if not quite handsome. "You are American," she said.

He nodded. "From the Bronx. Just like the Yankees."

"Which Yankees?" she asked.

Simon laughed. "The baseball team, of course. And you? You sound British."

"Not exactly. I was born here in Shanghai. My name is Soon Yi. Mah Soon Yi."

Simon tipped his head again. "A pleasure to meet you, Miss Mah. What brings a not-exactly-British nurse from Shanghai to our little hospital?"

Sunny fought back a smile. "Employment."

He sighed. "I would love to offer you work, Miss Mah. God knows we could use all the nurses we could dig up and then some, but we're on a bare-bones budget."

Embarrassed, Sunny looked to the ground. "I intended to volunteer."

"Ah, that's a whole different ball game." Simon whistled. "You do understand that most of the patients and the doctor are German? Only a few speak English."

"Ich spreche ein bisschen Deutsch," she said.

"Well, aren't you just full of surprises?" he said with

unconcealed admiration. "How would you like the grand tour of our facility, Miss Mah?"

"I would, Mr. Lehrer. Or is it 'Dr. Lehrer'?"

"I wish! My mother could die happy." He chuckled. "No, I'm nowhere near brainy enough to be a doctor. It's just plain Simon."

Sunny felt an immediate rapport with the New Yorker. "Pardon me for prying, but what brings you to Shanghai?" she asked.

Simon shrugged. "Nepotism."

Sunny tilted her head, waiting for more of an explanation.

"My family owns a furniture factory in New York. After I graduated from college, I was supposed to go back and help run the outfit, but I wasn't ready to devote my life to coffee tables and recliners." He laughed again. "My granddad had done business with Sir Victor Sassoon's family. They pulled a few strings and got me the job—well, more like internship—with Sir Victor. They sent me over here to learn all about high-stakes real estate and financing." He winked. "But I came to see a little of the world beyond Coney Island. Besides, it wasn't until the refugees started to pile into the city that Sir Victor found any real use for me."

"You speak German, I assume."

"As a tyke, I learned German and Yiddish from my nana. She's lived in the Bronx forever but wouldn't speak English if you held a gun to her head."

Sunny studied Simon's face, deciding that he was no older than thirty. "Pardon me for saying so, but you seem very young to run a hospital."

"Run it? Hardly." Simon waved the suggestion away. "That would be the CFA—the local charity struck up by established Jewish families like the Sassoons, Herdoons, and Kadoories to help out the refugees." He gestured to the two Chinese men lifting a mattress from the truck, one of whom held a cigarette between his lips. "The boys and I just do some of the CFA's legwork. Truth be told, it's my first job that I haven't wanted to quit in a week. I've already stayed in Shanghai half a year longer than I planned to. Come on. I'll show you around."

Simon turned to his two helpers. "Missy and my wantchee walkee." He spoke to them in the local dialect of pidgin English—a curious hybrid of English, Chinese, and Portuguese words used for basic but effective communication between the Chinese and Shanghailanders.

The man with the smoke squealed with laughter. "All right, we'll wait here, boss," he replied in English.

Sunny laughed too, realizing that Simon was joking with the men. She found it impossible not to warm to him.

Approaching the front entrance, Simon pointed up to the missing section of wall. "With a little brickwork and a coat of paint, you won't even recognize it. Try to imagine it. Why, it will be a . . ." He winked again. "A dump with a makeshift wall and a fresh coat of paint."

Inside, they walked down a narrow hallway that opened onto a modest-sized ward. The cement floor and white walls were spotless. Only the mismatched beds, some wood and others steel-framed, hinted at the improvised nature of the hospital.

Half of the beds were empty. Some patients were asleep. A few peered back at Sunny but none stirred or spoke. No one seemed to be paying any attention to the steady sobs coming from behind a curtain in the corner. Sunny motioned toward it. "That woman sounds terribly upset."

Simon nodded. "Her husband died earlier this afternoon."

"This afternoon?" Sunny frowned. "Why is the wife still here?"

"Jews believe that the soul stays near the body after death. We never leave a corpse unattended until the burial. Normally, a *shomer,* a male Jew, volunteers to sit with the body." Simon shrugged. "But the widow insisted on staying at her husband's side too."

A balding, middle-aged man stepped out from behind the curtain, shaking his head. Sunny would have recognized him as a doctor even without the lab coat or stethoscope. "This is still no hospital, Mr. Lehrer," he grumbled in German.

"I'm pretty sure it took a few days to build Rome, Max," Simon said agreeably. He motioned to the doctor and then to Sunny. "Dr. Feinstein, allow me to introduce Miss Mah, a nurse from right here in Shanghai who has come to volunteer."

"Nurses are helpful," Maxwell Feinstein said with a small smile. "X-ray and laboratory facilities would be too. And fluid solutions to administer intravenously. Now, those would be most helpful of all, Mr. Lehrer."

Simon began to translate his German into English, but Sunny stopped him. *"Ich verstehe."* She turned to the doctor. "You need fluids to run through the veins."

"Exactly so," Max stammered, shocked to hear an Asian woman speaking in his tongue. "Pardon my abruptness, Miss . . . ah . . . Miss Mah." He nodded in the direction of the sobs, which had grown even louder. "That young man over there died from dysentery acquired from drinking the contaminated water that runs through all the pipes here."

"Surely everyone knows that the drinking water always has to be boiled?" Sunny said.

Simon ran his hand through his thick hair. "We warn all the new arrivals."

"People forget. At home, it was never a concern." Max groaned. "Regardless, in Hamburg, I could have easily managed his illness. He would be going home soon to his own bed, instead of into the ground. And his poor wife knows it too." He held up his palms. "At my old hospital, the challenge was in making the right diagnosis. Here, a correct diagnosis does not help because I rarely have much to offer in the way of treatment."

"We're working on that, Dr. Feinstein," Simon said patiently. "You got to give us just a little more time."

"I can give you all the time you want." Max pointed toward the curtain. "He is the one who ran out of time."

On their way out, Simon said, "You have to excuse Max. From what I hear, he was a top-drawer doctor back in Germany. He's not used to working under these stringent conditions."

Sunny nodded. "Still, I don't imagine he will be returning to Germany any time soon."

"The same goes for our other five or six doctors: They're bright, well trained, and full of good intentions, but they're like a school of fish on land. We'll get this hospital better stocked, but in the meantime we need some good old-fashioned commonsense care. I get a feeling you know a thing or two about that."

Outside, the two assistants had cleared the truck of the mattresses and were standing on the empty flatbed sharing a cigarette.

Sunny's stomach knotted at the thought of having to navigate the drunken Japanese soldiers on Broadway on her way home. She wished that her father's driver, Fai, was in town. Anxious to get going, Sunny edged toward the road. "When would you like me to begin?"

"Is now too soon?"

Sunny smiled. "Tomorrow would be a little more practical."

Simon put his fedora back on and adjusted it carefully. "Where do you live, Miss Mah?"

"Frenchtown." She turned for the street. "Good night, Mr. Lehrer."

"You don't think I'd let you walk home alone in the dark at this time, do you?"

Sunny was too proud to show her relief. "I have been doing so since I was a child."

"I'm not surprised." Simon applied one final bend to the brim of his hat. "But if I have my history straight, Shanghai wasn't under an enemy's foot when you were a kid." His smile faded. "Can I ask you something, Miss Mah?"

"Please, Mr. Lehrer. My name is Soon Yi, but my friends call me Sunny."

"Sunny. Suits you!" He laughed. "And I am Simon. No more of this 'mister' stuff."

She smiled. "Simon, you had a question?"

"Forgive my curiosity, Sunny, but you're only half Chinese, right?"

She nodded. "My mother was American. She came from Chicago."

"Do the Japanese make a distinction?"

"Between someone of pure Chinese descent and me?" She exhaled. "No."

His face clouded with disgust. "I have seen how they treat the locals."

"So have I," Sunny murmured.

Simon shook his head. "The Nazis in Germany . . . the Japanese here in Shanghai . . . Treating people as less than human because of the shape of their faces or the sound of their names. Sometimes it feels like the whole damn world is unraveling."

PART III

Chapter 12

NOVEMBER 13, 1938, TRIESTE, ITALY

A temperate briny breeze wafted in from the harbor. Franz looked over at his daughter, who stood beside him at the wharf's railing. Eyes wide with wonder, she drank in the sights and smells of the sleepy coastal town.

Franz thought back to his first visit to Trieste. He'd been around the same age as Hannah was now, there to take a one-day Adriatic cruise with the rest of his family. The small ship had barely steamed out of sight of land, but to Franz—whose nautical experience was limited to sailboats, toys or real ones, that never strayed far from the lakeshore—it was as though they had ventured into the stratosphere on a hot air balloon.

Inhaling the fresh sea air, Franz realized he had only once before traveled on an ocean liner. For their honeymoon, Hilde and Franz had cruised the Adriatic coast aboard the aptly named *Rapsodia*. Curious and brimming with desire, they had spent most of their time secluded in their cabin. The ports of call and the open sea had served as pleasant backdrops—a chance to stretch their legs or fill their stomachs—for a mutual and fiery sexual awakening. Franz could recall the minutest details, from the cream-colored linens at the dining table to the sleekness of Hilde's black stockings as he slid them off her thighs, but their days of love-making seemed somehow surreal, more like a favorite dream than an actual memory.

Hilde had so effortlessly nurtured his passions in three years of marriage, but that side of him withered after her death. Focused on raising Hannah and building a surgical career, Franz never found time to pursue another romance, despite the well-intentioned meddling of friends and family. And, for reasons he did not fully understand, nor did he ever feel the need to seek out a new wife.

Franz glanced over to Esther. He wondered if, in the wake of Karl's death, she was destined to fall into the same romantic void as he had.

Esther motioned to the *Conte Biancamano*. "She's a gorgeous ship, isn't she, Hannah?"

"It's so huge," Hannah murmured.

Franz shared his daughter's awe. By far the largest of the vessels moored at the wharf, the *Conte Biancamano*'s white hull cut an imposing figure as her bow nosed out into the harbor like a skyscraper flipped on its side. Hannah pointed to people crossing the gangplank onto the ship. "Are we allowed to go on now, Papa?"

"I think so." Franz mussed her hair. "But you probably don't want to go aboard so soon," he teased.

"I do. *I do!*" she cried as she spun from the railing.

Franz and Esther fell in line after her, but a familiar voice stopped them. "Adlers, ahoy!"

Ernst Muhler strutted toward them in a black beret that matched his blazer. Hannah reached him first and leapt into his arms. "Onkel Ernst, what are you doing here?"

"You didn't actually believe I would let you go to China without me, puffin?" Ernst laughed and swung her around in the air before lowering her.

Franz shook Ernst's hand, and Esther leaned over Hannah to kiss him on the cheek. "Are you really joining us?" she asked.

"You talked me into it." Ernst chuckled. "Actually, with all my prattle about art and excess in Shanghai, I suppose I talked myself into it."

"*Wunderbar!*" Esther laughed. "How did you possibly manage it?"

"Your agent, Mr. Rolf, secured me a spot in your cabin. I hope it's all right."

"It's perfect," Esther said, and Franz nodded his encouragement.

"The rest was easy." Ernst touched a fresh abrasion on his cheek. "My Gestapo shadow, Captain Erhard, expedited the paperwork. Short of packing my bag and driving me to the station, the little fascist couldn't have been more eager to see me off."

Esther frowned. "And what of your . . . your friend?"

Ernst's eyes flickered with sadness. "My friend decided it would be advantageous to his career to embrace Nazism, with all its lofty principles." His expression hardened and his lip curled into a hint of a sneer. "Needless to say our friendship is kaput."

Esther wrapped Ernst in another hug. "Then it's for the best."

"No question. I will miss Vienna, though." Ernst turned to Hannah and grabbed her by the shoulders. "*Ach,* no more of this sentimental nonsense. We're embarking on a wonderful new adventure, aren't we, puffin?"

The smile slid from Hannah's lips as she held up her rag doll to show Ernst the torn seam and the cloth Franz had tied around it to hold in the stuffing. "The soldier at the station stabbed Schweizer Fräulein. Papa is going to do surgery on her later."

Ernst examined the doll before passing it back to Hannah. "Ah, not to worry, Hannah. There is no one your father cannot put back together."

They headed together for the short queue at the gangplank. They had waited only moments when a handsome young officer approached, clipboard in hand. He wore a starched white uniform with one and a half bars on each epaulette. "*Buon giorno!*" The officer beamed and fired off several Italian words Franz did not understand.

"*Mio italiano è* . . ." Franz faltered.

"Pardon me." The man switched seamlessly to German. He stroked Hannah's cheek. "The *signorina* is so beautiful. I just assumed she had to be Roman." He winked at her and then straightened. "Ensign Luigi Comparelli at your service."

Franz introduced himself and the others. Luigi scanned the manifest in his hand. "Of course, Dr. Adler and family. And Signor Muhler. *Bene.*" He ticked off their names. "It is my pleasure to welcome you aboard the *Conte Biancamano.*"

Luigi guided them across the gangplank. On the other side, a waiter in a white dinner jacket stood offering glasses of champagne and a selection of warm hors d'oeuvres. They hungrily sampled the savory puff pastries and smoked salmon crackers. Franz and Esther declined the drinks, but Ernst grabbed a glass and downed it in a single gulp.

Luigi led them farther along the shining deck, past tidy rows of deck chairs and tables. Officers, waiters, and porters bustled about offering food, blankets, books, newspapers, and sundry other distractions. More than the pampered excess, the warm hospitality overwhelmed Franz. In the past six months, he had come to expect only indifference or cruelty from strangers. With a pang of guilt, he thought of his father and the other Jews left in Vienna.

The moment Hannah spied the swimming pool near mid-ship, her face lit up. "Papa, *look*!" But the smile vanished as fast as it had appeared. "Will I be . . . allowed?"

The Nazis had banned Jews from the recreational club in Vienna where Hannah had been learning to swim in the indoor pool. She missed swimming more than any other pastime. "Of course you will, *liebchen*!" Franz said. "We can catch up on our lessons."

Hannah's smile resurfaced. Luigi chuckled. "I know where I will be able to find *signorina* for the rest of our voyage."

Ernst cupped his hand over his cigarette as he lit it. "But if you happen to be in search of this *signore* any time soon, you're best advised to check the bar."

"I will keep that in mind, Herr Muhler," Luigi laughed as he led them inside the ship and into the main dining room. A high ceiling supported the most elaborate chandelier Franz had ever seen. The servers had laid out a sprawling lunch buffet stacked with foods to appeal to every sense, including fruit baskets, roasted chickens, pyramids of cheese, and multilayered cakes that stood two feet high. The irresistible mélange of aromas set Franz's stomach growling. But his appetite was tempered by the thought of the deprivation and hunger among those left behind.

Luigi gestured to the buffet. "I am happy to show you to your cabin after lunch."

Hannah tugged at Franz's sleeve. "I want to see our room first, Papa, please."

Luigi led them out of the dining room and down a wide hallway on the ship's starboard. He stopped at the second-to-last door, slipped a key in the lock, and pushed the door open. "Your home for the next four weeks," he said with a sweep of his hand.

Sunlight poured in through a wide porthole. A double bed stood below the window, and a set of bunk beds lined the near wall. Their suitcases were neatly stacked beside the closet. A vase of fragrant, fresh-cut flowers stood on a table in the middle of the room. One ice bucket held a bottle of sparkling water, a second chilled a bottle of champagne.

Hannah flopped onto the double bed. Franz tested the firm mattress beside her, while Esther claimed the lower bunk, leaving the top one for Ernst.

In the hallway, Franz tipped the grateful ensign a five-mark note and requested a needle and thread. As he was leaving, Luigi said, "Oh, and Dr. Adler, the bursar wanted me to remind you that you are able to bill directly to your on-board account."

Franz shook his head. "I do not require an account."

"But you already have one." Luigi frowned. "With the funds wired ahead from Vienna."

"You must be confusing me with another guest."

Luigi withdrew a sheet from his inside coat pocket and consulted it. "According to the bursar, Dr. Franz Adler holds an on-board account with a balance of eight thousand Reichsmarks."

Father! It had to be. "Oh, yes, of course, I remember now," Franz mumbled, realizing the substantial deposit must have represented the last of Jakob's savings. The gesture only confirmed that his father did not intend to leave Vienna.

⌒

At sunset, they gathered on the aft deck for the liner's castoff. The ship's orchestra played a medley of Verdi and Puccini tunes. Hannah happily tossed streamers over the railing. Esther joined in, but Franz sensed the sorrow behind her brave face. He shared in it too as the finality of their departure sank in.

Hannah nodded off at the dinner table before dessert arrived. Franz carried her back to their cabin and laid her down on the bed. Ernst headed off to explore the ship's nightlife. Esther climbed into the bottom bunk and soon read herself to sleep.

Franz picked up the needle and thread that the steward had left on the table. He gently pried Schweizer Fräulein free of Hannah's grip and began to repair the seam. The predictable rhythm of his fingers felt natural, and reminded him how much he missed performing surgery. Life always made the most sense to him inside the operating room. He wondered again if he would be able to perform surgery, or even practice medicine, in Shanghai. *What use would I be, if not as a doctor?*

Franz examined the doll. Satisfied with the repair, he tucked it back into Hannah's arms. Despite his fatigue, he was too stimulated to sleep. He donned his coat and shoes and slipped out of the room.

The shops, lounges, and casino were abuzz, but he headed straight for the doors to the upper deck. Outside, an eruption of stars, along with the three-quarter moon, lit up the cloudless sky. He had to bundle up tight to fight off the chill from the icy wind, but he enjoyed the solace of the deserted deck.

The sweet scent of tobacco drifted to him. He turned to see a man striding toward him, a pipe between his teeth. He wore an overcoat and a felt homburg that he held on to in the brisk breeze. As he neared, he pulled his pipe from his lips. *"Deutsche?"*

"Nein, Österreicher," Franz replied.

"Aren't we all German now?" the man said with a north German lilt. He indicated the sky with the bowl of his pipe. "The night is a whole different beast on the Adriatic."

"Not quite the same as the city, is it?"

"Wait until we reach the Indian Ocean." The man pointed to the heavens again. "It's as though you're experiencing an entirely different sky. Then it all changes again in the South Pacific."

"You have been to Shanghai before?" Franz asked.

"I have lived there. And you?"

"First time."

The man chuckled softly as he held out a hand. "Schwartzmann. Hermann Schwartzmann."

Franz viewed his new companion in the weak light. He had a thick mustache and a hooked nose, but his age was difficult to discern. He met the small man's surprisingly strong grip. "Franz Adler."

"Do you know much about Shanghai, Herr Adler?"

"Almost nothing."

Schwartzmann flashed an enigmatic smile. "The Paris of the East. Or, if you prefer, the New York of the Orient."

"Inside China?"

Schwartzmann laughed again. "Geographically speaking, I suppose it is. In fact, it is the gateway to the country." He paused almost theatrically. "But Shanghai is governed by three separate powers, none of which happens to be Chinese." Franz's escape from Vienna had unfolded so swiftly that he had ended up on the boat knowing next to nothing about his destination. Schwartzmann dragged on his pipe. "To appreciate Shanghai, you must understand that it has never really been a Chinese city per se."

"I am not following you, Herr Schwartzmann."

"Shanghai is the world's sixth-largest city—over three million residents. However, a hundred years ago it was little more than a mud flat anchorage for fishing boats."

"So what transformed it?" Franz asked.

Schwartzmann swung his pipe triumphantly. "Opium!"

He went on to explain how in the early nineteenth century the British mass-produced the narcotic in India. They traded it up and down the Yangtze in exchange for silk and spices, while nurturing whole communities of opium addicts all along the river. The practice incurred the wrath of the Chinese emperor, inciting the Opium Wars. The English navy quickly crushed the feudal Chinese. The emperor capitulated and, in the Treaty of Nanking, conceded the British access to Chinese rivers and control of the five ports, including Shanghai. The Chinese believed that they were hoodwinking the British by giving them the low-level, ever-flooding flatlands of Shanghai, but the British recognized Shanghai for the geographical gem that it was: "The cork in the bottle that is China." The English wanted to establish Shanghai as a hub of international trade, so they designated only a small section of the city to fall under British rule. Other countries followed suit. Soon Shanghai boasted several sovereign regions, called concessions. Later, most of them merged into one greater area, known as the International Settlement. The French refused to cooperate, opting instead to maintain an autonomous concession.

"You see, Dr. Adler?" Schwartzmann concluded. "Up until last summer, Shanghai consisted of the larger International Settlement and the smaller French Concession, surrounded by the Chinese-controlled Greater Shanghai."

"And then the Japanese invaded," Franz said.

"Exactly." Schwartzmann drew an imaginary circle in the air with his pipe. "In their bid to conquer northern

China, the Japanese overran the city's Chinese-controlled area, including the harbor. Thus, of Shanghai's three sovereign governments, none are Chinese."

"What is Shanghai like now, Herr Schwartzmann?" Franz asked.

"Like nothing else in the world." Schwartzmann puffed pensively on his pipe for a few moments. "No description does it justice. You simply have to experience it." Another gust of wind blew across the deck and he had to fight to hang on to his hat. After the wind settled, he said, "I suppose if I were forced to choose one word to describe Shanghai, it would be 'contradiction.'"

"Why so?"

"Contradiction," Schwartzmann repeated. "Especially since the invasion. Neighborhoods as opulent as the finest in Paris are next to others that lie in rubble. The most modern automobiles, trucks, and cable cars share the streets with primitive rickshaws and wheelbarrows. The summers can be as hot and sticky as the jungle, while the winters are often as cold as the Alps. And the *people* are even more incongruous. White, yellow, brown, black, and every color in between. The wealthiest and most sophisticated ladies and gentlemen share sidewalks and promenades with some of the poorest peasants you will ever find." He held up a finger. "There is only one constant in Shanghai."

"Which is?"

"Money." Schwartzmann rubbed his thumb and index finger together. "There is nothing and no one you cannot buy. And absolutely *everything*—including love, life, and death—carries a price tag in Shanghai."

"Too bad, money is something not many of us managed to bring out of Germany."

Schwartzmann frowned at Franz. "What do you mean?"

"Well, obviously I cannot speak for you, but after Kristallnacht, we were lucky to—"

"Oh." Schwartzmann waved his pipe. "I am not a Jew."

"You're not? But—"

"I am a senior attaché with the German High Commission. There are no Jews left in the Foreign Service." He nodded to himself. "Ah, Adler, of course. I should have seen it. A Jewish name."

Even though the wind had died down, Franz went ice cold, feeling suddenly betrayed by the friendly little man. His anger with all Nazis boiled to the surface. He thought about how easy it would be to lift Schwartzmann and toss him over the railing into the black sea below.

Reading Franz's mood, Schwartzmann cleared his throat. "You must understand. I am a diplomat. By definition that makes me apolitical. Nothing more."

Struggling to keep his arms at his side, Franz squeezed his fists so tightly that his fingernails dug into his palms. He glared at Schwartzmann. "No, *you* must understand. You work for the German government. *That makes you a Nazi.* Nothing less."

⌒ *Chapter 13*

The water turned from navy to azure and the days grew longer and warmer as the *Conte Biancamano* rounded the Greek mainland into the Mediterranean, heading for North Africa.

Despite the uncertainty ahead and heartbreak behind, Franz found it impossible not to relax aboard.

The ship was a floating resort where their needs were not only met but often anticipated. After five days of grazing at bottomless buffets, Franz's clothes hung less loosely than they had in those final days in Vienna, when he had barely eaten. A deepening bronze tan replaced his winter pallor. And he could feel his muscles strengthening and endurance growing from his long strolls around the deck in the warm salty air.

From time to time, Franz spotted Hermann Schwartzmann in the company of his lean, pointy-faced wife. The diplomat had waved faintly at their first passing, but Franz did not acknowledge the gesture and, from then on, they ignored each other.

Esther never strayed too far from Hannah but otherwise kept to herself, consuming a steady diet of books that she borrowed from the ship's library. Since her fair skin was prone to sunburn, Esther sat in the shade and covered herself with a hat and long, loose clothes. She continued to wear only black, and at night after Hannah had fallen asleep, Franz would hear her quiet sobs as she whispered Kaddish, the Hebrew prayer of mourning.

Ernst joined the Adlers for most meals but disappeared for long stretches during the day and evening. Franz never knew if the artist was back in the cabin, "planted at the bar" as he jokingly claimed, or somewhere else altogether.

Hannah spent most of her time in or around the swimming pool. She had formed fast friendships with some similarly aged children, most of whom were also Austrian Jews. She frolicked one afternoon away with a boy, Otto Goldstein, who was on board with his mother and grandparents. A year older and considerably taller than Hannah, Otto was a gentle soul and so sensitive to her handicap that she accused him of not trying in their games of water tag. That evening, Hannah asked, "What is Buchenwald, Papa?"

"A prison of sorts," Franz replied, taken aback by her interest in the concentration camp. The Nazis had originally built Buchenwald, Dachau, and the other camps to intern Communists and political prisoners, but Franz had heard that lately, especially following Kristallnacht, thousands of Jewish men had been imprisoned there. Several of the men aboard had been released from concentration camps, but only after their loved ones had secured proof of emigration. At the dining table the evening before, Franz had witnessed a passenger turn ghostly pale at the mention of Buchenwald. His silence said more than all the rumors of torture, starvation, and executions.

Franz frowned. "Why do you ask, Hannah?"

"Otto told me that the soldiers took his father there."

"It does not mean he did anything wrong, *liebchen*."

"Otto's mother says his father will meet them in Shanghai." Hannah paused. "But Otto doesn't believe her."

"Why not?"

"Every night, his mother cries herself to sleep. Otto does not think they will ever see him again." She looked away and added, "Sometimes, at night, I hear Tante Esther crying too."

Franz braced himself for the inevitable question about Karl, but Hannah didn't ask. And he could not bring himself to ruin his daughter's recent cheerfulness by confirming what she clearly suspected.

The next morning, Esther voiced a similar concern. "Your daughter worries about me."

He patted her shoulder. "I do too, Essie."

"You should have far greater worries," Esther said, shrugging. "I think Hannah knows something happened to Karl. She keeps asking when and how he plans to reach Shanghai."

"I want to tell her, Essie, but I haven't seen Hannah this happy in so long."

"It's not the time," she agreed. "But I hate lying to her."

They stared out at the busy harbor. The *Conte Biancamano* had reached Africa. She moored outside the Egyptian city of Port Said at the entrance to the Suez Canal with several other vessels that included passenger liners, freighters, and a couple of cruisers and destroyers flying the Union Jack. Esther and Franz stood at the starboard railing, gazing out at the Old Town of Port Said on one side of the canal and the endless sand of the Sinai Peninsula on the other.

Franz spotted a small cutter motoring toward them. Armed British soldiers sat on either side of two young men whom Franz recognized as fellow passengers. "I wonder what this is about," he said.

"*Ach so.*" Esther nodded to herself. "So they tried it after all."

"Tried what?"

She pointed at the two prisoners, who were huddled in blankets. "The Irving brothers. I had heard a rumor that they were going to swim for shore."

"Why?"

"They're stateless refugees. Like us."

Franz bristled at the term, still unable to wrap his mind around their descent to homeless outcasts. "What does that have to do with anything?"

"Without visas, of course, the Irvings weren't allowed ashore. I had heard they were going to try to swim for land and then make their way across the Sinai."

"To Palestine?"

Esther nodded. "Good for them for trying."

Franz swept a hand toward the sand dunes that

stretched out to the horizon. "You think Palestine would be so preferable to Shanghai?"

"Of course! Palestine is destined to be the Jewish homeland."

"According to the Zionists."

"No, the British. They promised as much in the Balfour Declaration."

"Essie, they're not allowing any more Jews to enter Palestine. They couldn't be clearer about it."

"Someday it won't be up to them."

Franz had long heard the arguments in support of a Jewish nation, but he had always considered himself Austrian and could never imagine another allegiance. "I'm not a Zionist, Esther."

"I never used to be either. But surely recent events have convinced you that we need a nation of our own?" She held up her hand. "If we had one, we never would have reached this terrible point. Maybe Karl would not have . . . If only there was a refuge for Jews fleeing persecution elsewhere."

"Here in the Middle East?"

"Where else?" Esther shrugged. "Clearly, no Gentile nation is willing to protect us."

"Essie, I'm hardly even a Jew."

She turned from the water to view him tenderly. "I think the Nazis have made it abundantly clear that being a Jew is not a matter of choice. You are born one."

"And I will die one, I know," he sighed. "I am sorry, Essie. Perhaps others have seen me as a Jew, but it's not how I see myself. And it's certainly not how I see Hannah."

"You can't change that any more than an African can choose to stop being a Negro."

"Judaism is a religion, not a race."

"It still defines who we are."

"Does it? Would you define a Frenchman by his Catholicism or an Englishman by his Anglicanism? In the Great War, Jews fought and killed other Jews, based on nationality, not religion."

"That's not what God intended for us."

He tapped his temple. "I am a man of science, Essie. I believe in things I can see. And all I've ever seen is havoc wreaked in the name of God."

Esther turned back to the harbor, lapsing into silence. After a few moments, she spoke again without looking at him. "A few days before Karl died, he told me that he had never felt closer to God."

Franz squinted. "Never closer? Really?"

"Your brother believed that faith is at its deepest when most tested."

Franz stroked Essie's shoulder again. "Karl was special," he said by way of apology. "I do not share his faith. And certainly not his decency."

"Believe me, Franz," Esther said quietly. "You do."

⌐ *Chapter 14*

DECEMBER 8, 1938, EAST CHINA SEA

Three more weeks drifted by in lazy luxury. The *Conte Biancamano* sailed unscathed through a few winter storms, but the seas were largely calm and the skies blue as the ship crossed the Indian Ocean, circumnavigated Malaysia via the Strait of Malacca, and entered the South China Sea, heading north for the Chinese mainland.

On the last scheduled day of their voyage, Franz

woke to find Hannah standing by the bed and shaking his shoulder. "Today is the day, Papa!"

He rubbed the sleep from his eyes and sat up. "Are you excited, *liebchen*?"

"I think so." She turned Schweizer Fräulein over, pulled up the gown, and examined the seam again. Hannah had been keeping as close an eye on the doll's stitches as Franz had on Esther's sutured arm. "I'm a little scared too, Papa."

"Me too." Franz stared into Hannah's trusting eyes, wondering again how his eight-year-old would cope with the drastic changes and challenges that awaited them in Shanghai. "Hannah, life is going to be different after today."

"How, Papa?"

He smiled. "To begin with, I don't think we will eat as well as we have on this ship."

Hannah shrugged. "I'm tired of all the food." She arched out her flat belly and patted it, mimicking the adults she had seen onboard. "It would do me good to skip a few meals."

Franz chuckled. "Many of us, yes, darling. But not you."

She tugged at his arm. "Let's go outside, Papa. I want to see China."

On the deck, Hannah chose a viewing perch near the smokestack on the port side. They sat and watched the craggy beaches and low-lying cliffs of the Chinese coastline drift past.

Ernst sauntered up to them with a lit cigarette in hand. Despite the sunshine, a bone-chilling December wind whipped off the ocean. Ernst bundled his light blazer tighter around him. "Some fool steered us away from the tropics."

Hannah giggled. "That was three days ago, Onkel Ernst."

"Doesn't make it any less foolish." Ernst cupped her cheek. "Today our adventure really begins, doesn't it, puffin?"

"Are you scared?" Hannah asked.

"No. I miss land too much." Ernst turned to Franz with a small grin. "Besides, if God had meant for man to live on water, he would have provided a wider selection at the ship's bar."

Hannah pointed ahead to the approaching break in the shoreline, where the sea's color turned from blue to yellowish brown. "What is that?"

"I think that's where the Yangtze meets the ocean," Franz said.

Hannah's eyes widened. "So we're near Shanghai?"

"Shanghai is still about fifty miles upriver," Ernst pointed out.

"That could take forever," Hannah groaned.

Ernst laughed. "We've just traveled ten thousand miles, puffin. You can probably survive another fifty."

She pointed back to the wide estuary. "Why is the river yellow?"

"The Yangtze crisscrosses China," Ernst explained. "It's loaded with soil from its three-thousand-mile journey to the sea. All that silt turns the water yellow."

Franz looked over to his friend, surprised and impressed.

"What?" A sly smile creased Ernst's lips. "You think we only talk about different types of gin cocktails at the bar? I have picked up a few useful tidbits."

The *Conte Biancamano* slowed, swung around, and eased into the Yangtze estuary. The ship came to a stop and dropped anchor in the tawny waters. Moments later, a small boat chugged up beside the hull, and a Chinese official climbed aboard via a lower gangway.

"Who's that man, Papa?" Hannah asked.

"I'm not sure." Franz turned to Ernst. "What does our local expert have to say?"

Ernst clasped his chest in a *mea culpa* gesture. "Sometimes all we *do* discuss are gin cocktails."

An older woman lying on a nearby deck chair stirred. She pulled back the broad white hat covering her eyes and sat up. "My dear child, *he* is our river pilot." She spoke German with a thick English accent.

"What does the pilot do?" Hannah asked.

The woman rose stiffly to her feet and hobbled nearer, leaning heavily on the jade handle of her ornate wooden cane. "He helps guide the ship up the river. The depth is unpredictable and there are all sorts of hazards our captain cannot see. The pilot, on the other hand, knows the Yangtze well enough to steer us blindfolded."

"Why aren't we moving?" Hannah demanded.

"We have to wait for the tide to rise before it is safe to proceed."

"How long will that take?" Hannah groaned again.

"Perhaps an hour or so." The woman laughed and her heavy lids creased so deeply that they almost obscured her eyes. "I assume this is your first visit to Shanghai, my dear?"

"Yes!"

"One of the most common phrases you will hear spoken on the streets of Shanghai is *man zou* or 'walk slowly.' It is similar to our 'good day,' but what the Chinese really mean is, there is never a hurry. *Man zou* is more than just an expression. It's a way of life here. My dear, now that you are in the Orient, I am afraid you will have to get accustomed to waiting."

"Hannah is usually more patient, and generally more polite," Franz said in English. "But as you can see, she's most excited about our arrival."

"No need to explain." The woman smiled. "Her youthful enthusiasm is so appealing. Wonderful. Frankly, it's infectious." Despite her wrinkled skin and sunken cheeks, she had striking green eyes. She held out her knobby arthritic fingers, palm downward, for Franz to shake. "I am Lady Leah Herdoon."

"Dr. Franz Adler," he said with a slight bow.

"A pleasure to meet you, Dr. Adler. Are you a physician?"

"A surgeon, yes." Franz motioned to Ernst. "And this is my friend, Ernst Muhler."

Lady Leah touched her chin. "You are not, by chance, the artist?"

Ernst flicked the ash from his cigarette over the railing. "I have no idea whether it's by chance or not, but yes, I am an artist."

Her weathered face lit with admiration. "What an honor, Mr. Muhler. I am a true admirer of your work. In fact, one of your paintings hangs in my modest collection. Your *Two Women in the Snow*. One of my most prized possessions. So gripping. I shivered the first time I saw it."

"I'm delighted," Ernst said with the same feigned indifference he tended to show anyone who gushed over his work.

"What brings you to Shanghai, Mr. Muhler?" Lady Leah asked. "An exhibition?"

Ernst shook his head. "Adolf Hitler."

Lady Leah eyed him suspiciously for a moment before breaking into a small laugh. "Oh, I see. Your genre is most unlikely to appeal to the Nazis."

"Apparently." Ernst fluttered his hand through the air. "They much prefer their art to mimic their own lives: regressive, *démodé*, and overbearing."

Lady Leah turned to Franz. "And you, Dr. Adler? Forgive me for prying, but do you happen to be part of the German Jewish contingent?"

Franz nodded. "Austrian, actually."

"Yes, of course," she said. "I think you will find Shanghai far more hospitable than Austria. In fact, our Jewish community is thriving."

"Our?" Franz gaped at the aristocratic woman. "My lady, are you Jewish?"

She nodded. "My husband, Sir David—God rest his darling soul—his family has been in Shanghai for almost a hundred years. Iraqi Jews originally. British subjects, of course. My husband's great-grandfather, Edward, was the original baronet."

Lady Leah explained that Sir Edward, along with several other Jewish traders, helped to colonize Shanghai in the mid-nineteenth century. They nourished a vital Jewish community in the city, which grew exponentially in the early 1920s after the Russian Civil War, when five thousand Ashkenazi Jews joined twenty thousand White Russians fleeing to Shanghai.

Lady Leah indicated Franz and Hannah with a sweep of her gnarled fingers. "And now, Shanghai is seeing a third influx—German and Austrian Jews—which promises to be more sizable than the first two communities combined."

"Perhaps the Zionists are wrong," Franz said. "Maybe Shanghai is destined to be the Jewish homeland."

"I doubt there is room. Shanghai is already frightfully crowded. Fortunately, anti-Semitism is a concept foreign to the Chinese." Lady Leah paused pensively. "And thanks to the Japanese, the Chinese understand only too well what it means to be downtrodden."

The anchor's chain rattled noisily as it retracted. The deck vibrated again as the engines powered up. "We're moving!" Hannah said excitedly.

"We are indeed, my dear," Lady Leah said laughingly. "Remember, *man zou!*"

The *Conte Biancamano* nudged ahead and slowly gathered speed as she sailed up the murky Yangtze along its southern bank. The river was so wide that Franz could barely make out the northern bank on the horizon. As they motored westward and inland, Lady Leah explained more about the local history and flavor, including the intricate process of the rice farming that sustained most of the riverside inhabitants. As she spoke, they passed several vessels, including ocean liners, freighters, tugs, and naval ships, flying a wider variety of flags than they had seen in either Trieste or Port Said.

Finally, just before noon, their ship turned south and sailed into the mouth of a tributary. "The Whangpoo," Lady Leah announced. "Only fourteen more miles to Shanghai."

Hannah moaned, eliciting a laugh from the others.

Farms and fields lined both banks of the quarter-mile-wide Whangpoo, which was crowded with even more shipping traffic than the Yangtze. "Look, Papa!" Hannah pointed to the exotic sailboats around them. "What are those?"

The cigar-shaped boats sailed so close that Franz could pick up the smell of fried oil and seafood emanating from them. "That is a sampan," Lady Leah said. "What you and I might call a houseboat. In China, many people live their entire lives from birth to death on the very same sampan."

Franz studied the exotic craft. A patched, dirty triangular sail billowed over the sampan's hull and another flapped like a jib at the front. A Chinese woman knelt on the near side of the boat and, while holding a crying baby in one arm, leaned over and pulled laundry out of the muddy water with the other. At the back of the sampan, a man worked to untangle fishing lines. A boy stood up at the edge of the boat, pulled down his pants, and urinated into the river, indifferent to Franz's and other watching eyes.

Lady Leah pointed out a smaller sail-less boat, no more than twelve feet long, nearer to shore. A man stood at the helm and propelled the boat with a long pole that he planted with slow two-handed strokes. "Those, my dear Hannah, are called junks. Soon, the sight of the junks and sampans will be as familiar to you as bicycles and automobiles were in Vienna."

The skies had turned gray and overcast. As the ship was now protected from the exposed sea, the wind had died and the temperature had warmed slightly, but a damp chill hung in the air. The rank smells of fish and decay grew stronger by the minute.

Lady Leah's crooked finger swung toward the western shore. "Behold, Shanghai."

In the flat light, Franz struggled to make out the dark structures lining the riverbank a mile or so ahead.

"*Oh, mein Gott!*" Ernst exclaimed. "What the hell happened to it?"

The buildings came into focus, and Franz suddenly understood Ernst's reaction. The city had clearly been bombed and shelled. Several buildings had collapsed, while fire and smoke damage had blackened others.

"This is Hongkew, Shanghai's northern district." Lady Leah shook her head. "Poor Hongkew bore the brunt of the Japanese invasion last summer. Many of us Shanghailanders now refer to it as 'the Badlands.'"

As the *Conte Biancamano* neared the wharf, Franz recognized a swarm of activity. People hustled along the waterfront, while others loaded and unloaded ships. The din floated across the water toward them. No one spoke a word as their liner sailed past an imposing naval ship flying the Rising Sun flag from its flagpole. The huge barrels of its polished guns pointed toward them as though warning them to turn back.

A quarter mile upstream, a narrow waterway cut through the urban chaos of Shanghai. "Soochow Creek," Lady Leah said. "Some call it the busiest little river in the world." She indicated the arched bridge spanning the creek. "The Garden Bridge connects the International Settlement and Hongkew. Sadly, it has become an armed border."

Ernst pointed to the International Settlement's approaching shoreline. "Apparently, the two neighborhoods don't share the same architect."

"Nor the same real estate prices, Mr. Muhler." Lady Leah smiled. "That—over there—is the beginning of the Bund. The most famous road in Shanghai. Possibly in all of Asia."

Franz's jaw almost dropped at the night-and-day contrast in the landscape. On the far side of the promenade, the tallest buildings he had ever seen lined the Bund and spanned the waterfront for blocks and blocks. Their neoclassical and art deco facades were as awe-inspiring as any he had seen in Vienna, Paris, or London.

Lady Leah pointed across to a high-rise with a green pyramid roof. Its tall mullioned windows reflected back the *Conte Biancamano*'s smokestack as the ship floated by. "That is the Cathay Hotel. Built by the most famous Jew in Shanghai—possibly the city's best-known inhabitant—Sir Victor Sassoon." She sighed. "A bit too much of a playboy for my taste, but Victor is a decent fellow."

Hannah's eyes were wide with awe. "When do we get to go ashore?"

"Soon, dear. I must head back to my cabin to prepare." From inside her jacket, Lady Leah withdrew a small engraved silver case. She slid out two business cards, passing one to Franz and the other to Ernst. "Dr. Adler, Mr. Muhler, and of course little Hannah, it was such an unexpected pleasure to meet you. I wish you nothing but good health and fortune in Shanghai. My telephone directory is on the card. Once you have settled in, I would be honored to give you a Shanghai-lander's tour of this strange and wonderful city."

Soon after Lady Leah left them, the *Conte Biancamano* dropped anchor across from the teeming Bund.

Luigi Comparelli hurried up to them. "Ah, my most favored guests," he said with a deep bow that barely creased his starched white uniform.

"Luigi!" Hannah hugged him.

He knelt down to her level. "Ah, *principessa,* I cannot tell you how much it saddens me to have to bid you *arrivedérci* today."

"You are a dangerously charming man, Ensign Luigi," Ernst said as he lit a new cigarette.

"A risk for all Italians, I'm afraid." Luigi grinned. "I came to tell you too that lunch will be served only for another half an hour. And then the ship's tender will take guests to shore."

"We should go find your aunt," Franz said to Hannah.

"Dr. Adler, you will have to close your account with our bursar. For Shanghai, I suggest withdrawing American dollars would be most practical." Luigi dug in his inner pocket and withdrew a sealed envelope. "Also, Dr. Adler, this letter came for you."

Even before Luigi handed it over, Franz recognized his father's meticulous penmanship. His heart sank as he sensed only grim news. "I'll read it later," he mumbled as he tucked it inside his coat pocket.

They made their way to the dining room, where they found Esther, wearing a green dress, at their usual table. It was the first time since leaving Vienna that Franz had seen her in anything other than black. She had even applied mascara and lipstick.

Ernst brought both hands to his cheeks. "Hannah, where is your aunt? And who is this *stunning* creature before us?"

Esther blushed slightly. "Nonsense. I thought I should look . . . presentable . . . for arrival."

"Trust me." Ernst pulled his hands from his cheeks and clasped them in front of his chest. "You look more than just presentable."

"You look lovely, Essie," Franz agreed.

They served themselves from the buffet. As they ate, they reviewed their short-term strategy. "So, it's decided?" Franz looked from Ernst to Esther. "We will rent a hotel room?"

Esther nodded. "Only until we can find more affordable accommodations."

After lunch, they returned to their cabin for a final check. Franz was saddened to close the door on the room where he had felt more secure than at any other time in recent memory. Following Luigi's advice, he withdrew the remaining funds in his account in American currency. It amounted to just over sixteen hundred dollars. He wondered how long the nest egg would feed, clothe, and house four people in a city the size of Shanghai. Having been warned about the local pickpockets—who, according to the ship's grapevine, were organized into their own guild—Franz tucked the envelope of money deep into his inner coat pocket, beside his father's letter.

Hannah was giddy with excitement at the prospect of going ashore, but the adults shared looks of melancholy and worry as they loaded into the back of the tender for the short jaunt to the dock. The others aboard were mostly upper-middle-class German Jews. Most were heading for Chinese soil as stateless refugees with little more than the money in their pockets and the clothes on their backs.

At river level, the stench from the Whangpoo's filthy brown waters was intense. Several people on the tender covered their mouths and noses with their hands or collars. Two people even retched over the side of the boat. Hannah kept her nose pinched for the entire trip but said nothing.

As the tender nosed up to the dock, the smell of fried fish and cooked meats overpowered the noxious river odors. The noises of backfiring cars, roaring trucks, and screeching peddlers melded into a thunderous clamor. Clutching Hannah's hand, Franz stepped tentatively onto the wharf. They followed the other passengers up a staircase toward a bland building with a sign that read CUSTOMS HOUSE over its entrance.

The line inside moved quickly. It took little time to reach the Indian man who sat behind the desk wearing a white turban and a beige uniform. "Welcome to Shanghai," he said in his refined British accent. "May I see your identification, please?"

They passed him their passports. He glanced at

them, comparing their faces to the photos, but showed no reaction to the large red *J* stamped inside each passport. After he jotted their names on a piece of paper, he handed back the documents. "What is the total amount of foreign currency you are bringing into Shanghai?"

"Roughly sixteen hundred American dollars," Franz said.

The official nodded. "And tobacco and alcohol?"

"No alcohol. Tobacco . . ." Franz turned to Ernst.

"I have two packs of cigarettes left." Ernst shrugged. "One and a half, actually. It was a long, bumpy ride to shore."

The official eyed them. "No more than two packs? And no alcohol? Are you certain?"

Franz smiled with relief that alcohol and tobacco were the man's primary concern, rather than the jewelry Esther had smuggled out of Austria.

Beyond customs, the terminal teemed with people of every race, busier than even the Südbahnhof at the peak of rush hour. Some Chinese wore Western-style clothing; others were dressed in traditional silk gowns and matching jackets and pants. Franz even noticed a cluster of orange-robed Buddhist monks with shaved heads.

Across the room, Hannah spotted crew members from the *Conte Biancamano* waiting beside piles of luggage. As soon as Ernst and the Adlers claimed their suitcases, a young Chinese man wearing only a light jacket and stained pants rushed up to them pushing a large empty cart as though it were a wheelbarrow. "I porter," he announced in pidgin English. "I catchee suitbags."

Ernst nodded and pointed out their bags. The scrawny man effortlessly hoisted the heavy suitcases onto his cart, expertly balancing them in one tall pile. "Taxi?"

he asked as he began to push the cart toward the street.

Franz nodded, wondering if they could afford the expense.

The Bund was dense with traffic. Cars, trolleys, and double-decker buses crawled along the congested road. Bicycles and yellow rickshaws, pulled by lean young men in short pants, wove between the vehicles. A Sikh policeman stood in the middle of the road, guiding the traffic with hand signals and repeated shrill blows on his whistle.

They walked past a little boy, at least a year or two younger than Hannah, sitting on the pavement. His left foot was mangled and his right arm had been amputated above his elbow. With his left hand, he held up an inverted cap with a few coins inside. "No mama, no papa. No whiskey soda," he squealed in broken English. "No Russian sweetheart. Okay?"

Ernst and Esther kept moving alongside their porter, but Hannah stopped and stared at the boy. She looked up at Franz, her eyes brimming with sympathy. "Papa, do we have any money?"

Franz dug in his pocket and found the last of his German coins. He gave them to Hannah, who dropped them in the boy's hat. The little boy acknowledged the donation with only a nod before he turned to the next passersby and repeated the same "No mama, no papa . . ." chant.

At the curb, they saw several passengers from the ship walk up a plank and onto the back of a weathered flatbed truck. A tall man in a trench coat approached them. "Are you folks Jewish?" he asked in fluid German tinged with an American accent.

"Yes." Esther glanced at Ernst. "Three of us, anyway."

"Welcome to Shanghai." The man flashed a warm smile, holding Esther's eyes for an extra moment. "I am Simon Lehrer. I work with the CFA."

"I am Mrs. Karl Adler," Esther said, and then introduced the others.

Simon grinned. "Will your husband be arriving soon, Mrs. Adler?"

"My husband . . ." Esther glanced over to Hannah, who was still focused on the young beggar behind them. "He has passed," she said quietly.

"Oh . . . I am so sorry," Simon muttered.

Franz was eager to redirect the conversation before Hannah overheard it. "Pardon me, Mr. Lehrer, but what is the CFA?"

"The Committee for Assistance of European Refugees in Shanghai. How's that for a mouthful? Bet you're sorry you asked." Simon chuckled and pointed toward the truck. "Why don't you come with us to the Embankment House? Sir Victor Sassoon has established a hostel there for the new arrivals until more permanent dwellings can be found."

Franz shook his head. "I don't believe that will be necessary, thank you, Mr. Lehrer . . ."

"You're not signing your life away or anything," Simon said. "It's just a place to stop and gather your bearings. We offer hot meals, a roof over your heads, and a few lectures on adjusting to life in Shanghai."

Esther eyed Franz uncertainly. "Maybe we should? Until we do gather our bearings?"

Hannah's fingers dug into Franz's palm and she looked up at him with worry. "Papa, what about the hotel?"

Simon knelt down to Hannah. "This is kind of like a hotel. Except there will be a bunch of other kids around to play with."

Unmoved, Hannah continued to stare at her father, imploring him to decline the offer.

Franz turned back to Simon. "Thank you all the same, Mr. Lehrer. I believe we can manage on our own."

"Okay. Suit yourself." Straightening up, Simon glanced at Esther. "If you change your minds, you can always find me at the Embankment House on North Soochow Road." He laughed again. "Just ask for Simon. The New York busybody. They'll know how to reach me."

They thanked Simon and rejoined the flow of pedestrian traffic, heading toward the lineup of black taxicabs parked at the curb. Franz had only made it a few steps when someone shoved past him so hard that he toppled forward, almost falling over.

Franz regained his balance and looked up to see Simon sprinting away. *"Stop, you!"* Franz shouted after him, but Simon had already disappeared into the throng of people ahead.

"Are you injured, Franz?" Esther asked, pointing frantically at the front of his coat.

Franz looked down and saw that his coat had been slashed open over the right side of his chest. He thrust a hand inside the gap where the inner pocket had been only moments earlier. *Nothing.* "Essie, the money!" he cried. "It's gone!"

"Can't be," Ernst muttered in shock. "Robbed by the man from the CFA?"

Before Franz could answer, Simon emerged from the crowd and made his way toward them, dragging a terrified skeletal Chinese youth by the arm. With his free hand Simon held up the envelope full of American bills and the unopened letter from Jakob.

Passing the papers back to Franz, Simon arched an eyebrow. "Are you still convinced you can get by here on your own?"

Chapter 15

Sunny Mah sometimes followed the long route to the Country Hospital, via Rue Cardinal Mercier, just to pass the Cercle Sportif Français. With its curved portico entrance and detailed relief work, the building was one of her favorites, but she had never before set foot inside the French club. Now, she could hardly believe she was sitting on the glassed-in garden terrace, enjoying afternoon tea and sampling pastries.

Sunny felt acutely underdressed in her simple navy *qipao*—the traditional high-collared Chinese frock—among the mix of Western and Asian women who were dressed to the nines in colorful silk cheongsams or elegant skirts and jackets. Across the table, Ko Jia-Li resembled a Chinese Greta Garbo in her gray silk suit and matching pillbox hat as she smoked a cigarette in a long black holder. Like so many of Shanghai's young Chinese women, Jia-Li revered all things foreign.

As one of the only social clubs to admit Asian members, the Cercle Sportif Français had a reputation as an "open club," but it was still the exclusive domain of the city's upper crust. "I still don't see how you managed to get us a table," Sunny wondered aloud.

Jia-Li waved the cigarette holder casually. "I have a friend . . ."

The answer was her catchphrase. Jia-Li was a star in the stable of the city's most influential madam, Chih-Nii, who reported directly to the undisputed head of Shanghai's underworld, Du Yen Sheng or "Big Ears" Du. She counted some of the most influential men in Shanghai among her clients. Consequently, Jia-Li had access to people and places that few others in the city shared.

Sunny was pleased to see her best friend so carefree. Full of confidence, gossip, and laughter, Jia-Li seemed to be back to her old self. Her dilated pupils, which always constricted under the influence of opium, suggested that Jia-Li had not touched a pipe recently.

Jia-Li blew out a languid stream of smoke. "You cannot keep up this pace, *xiǎo hè*."

Her friend was right. Recently, Sunny had put in almost as many hours at the Jewish refugee hospital as she had at the Country Hospital. As exhilarating as she found the volunteer work, it was exhausting. The day before, she had fallen asleep at the Country Hospital while charting at the nurses' desk. She awoke, mortified to find Dr. Samuel Reuben hovering over her. "It appears, Nurse Mah, that you cannot stay awake long enough to care for your patients," he gloated. "Perhaps you could borrow Mr. Hamilton's bed for a nap while he is still in the operating theater."

Sunny shook off the humiliating memory. "I can't stop now, *bǎo bèi*. They need me."

Jia-Li stroked Sunny's hand across the table. "Everyone always needs you, *xiǎo hè*. You will die of exhaustion if you don't learn to say no."

"To everyone?"

"Never to me, of course!" Jia-Li said with a giggle. "Besides, I haven't touched a pipe in over a month. You have cured me for good this time."

"Is this time truly different, *bǎo bèi*?" Sunny asked.

"I can't put Mother through that again. It would kill her." Jia-Li tapped the ash from her cigarette into the ashtray. "Enough humdrum talk. Tell me more of your handsome doctor."

Sunny felt a blush coming on. "He's not mine at all."

"Please, *xiǎo hè*. It's me."

"It's over." And then Sunny hurried to add, "Not that it ever really began."

"I thought he had a good heart."

"That has nothing to do with it."

Jia-Li sat up straighter, and her affected pose gave way to a more sincere expression. "It has everything to do with it," she said softly.

"Wen-Cheng is married. He does not have the courage to face the consequences of choosing a life with me. Neither of us do."

"Your father would understand."

"I don't believe he would."

Jia-Li waved the cigarette holder in the air. "Your father, of all people, knows what it means to follow his heart in spite of what others think or say. His family is so traditional. Imagine what it must have been like for him to bring home a round-eyed wife. An American, no less!"

Sunny nodded. "Grandmother did not speak to him for five years. Even when they lived under the same roof. And his own sister still has not forgiven him."

"Exactly! Your father would want you to be happy. He loves you that much."

Sunny doubted Kingsley would accept such loss of face so easily. It didn't matter, though; her mind was made up. But Wen-Cheng had never stopped trying to win her back. To prove his dedication, he had helped Sunny stock the refugee hospital with medical supplies. He had rounded up a surprising quantity of equipment, dressings, and medication, and even managed to provide bottles of Ringer's lactate solution. As touched as Sunny was by his commitment, she was determined not to waver in her resolve.

"And you?" Sunny asked, deliberately changing the subject.

"Me?" Jia-Li resumed her starlet pose with cigarette held high above her head. "Darling sister, my romances rarely last longer than an evening."

Despite the pretense, during her fits of narcotic withdrawal, Jia-Li often admitted that she still clung to the fantasy of true love rescuing her from life in a brothel. Several men, including clients, had already auditioned for the role. But Jia-Li invariably fell for penniless musicians and artists who had neither the means nor the will to see her salvation through.

Sunny cocked her head. "So you no longer believe in love, *bǎo bèi*?"

"Oh, it's too late for me." Jia-Li said matter-of-factly. "Not for you though."

"I'm two months older than you."

Jia-Li chuckled and took another drag from her cigarette. "You know, *xiǎo hè*, sometimes I think our problem is that I've lived too much and you've lived too little."

"Maybe," Sunny said, though she was thankful that her life had been so much more sheltered. "Perhaps we should both leave Shanghai?"

A flicker of excitement lit up Jia-Li's eyes. "And go where?"

"Singapore? Paris?" Sunny smiled. "Or even New York. Remember how we always planned to go there when we were little girls?"

"I do," Jia-Li said quietly.

"Why not, then, *bǎo bèi*?"

Jia-Li motioned to the span of bare branches outside the window. "Because you and I are like those birch trees. Far too firmly rooted here to ever leave Shanghai."

"It's true," Sunny sighed.

Jia-Li stubbed out the last of her cigarette. "Let's go shopping, *xiǎo hè*."

Sunny glanced up at the clock and saw that it was already after three o'clock. "I have to go to work now."

Jia-Li rolled her eyes and shook her head. "Which job?"

"The refugee hospital."

"One simple little word: *fǎu. Non.* No."

They left the club together. The doorman hailed a taxi for Jia-Li, but Sunny declined her offer of a ride and instead rode a bus into the International Settlement. She crossed the Garden Bridge on foot, where she faced the usual tense, humiliating bowing ritual. She arrived at the refugee hospital just before four o'clock. The roof of the old structure had been patched and its exterior painted, but, as Simon had predicted, from the outside it still looked more like a derelict building than a hospital.

On the open ward, Sunny saw that the beds were still full after an outbreak of salmonella poisoning had overrun the hospital. The culprit had turned out to be contaminated eggs served four days before at the local synagogue luncheon. The mood of the small hospital was surprisingly upbeat, since none of the sickened patients, even the small children, had died. Dr. Max Feinstein credited Sunny for saving lives with her unorthodox technique of rehydrating patients. Instead of forcing down large amounts of fluid, which the patients invariably vomited up, Sunny had them sip every three to five minutes a few tablespoons of a solution she constituted from water with small amounts of baking soda, salt, and sugar.

Several smiling, grateful faces greeted Sunny on the ward. She could tell from their robust color that many were near ready for discharge.

"Miss Mah!" Dr. Feinstein called from the small laboratory down the hallway.

Sunny found him hunched over his microscope. "Here, quickly!" His bald head gleamed. "Look here."

As Max moved out of her way, she picked up a whiff of iodine cleanser, a scent he carried like aftershave. She peered through the monocular lens and saw the magnified cluster of violet, ovoid cells. "Do you see them?" Max demanded.

Sunny looked up from the microscope. "Are those *Diplococcus pneumoniae*?"

"Exactly so!" Max laughed. "Good for you! Few of my medical students in Hamburg would have been able to recognize the bacteria."

"Is this sample from Mrs. Gimbelmann?" Sunny asked. "The young lady with the fever of unknown origin?"

"Not unknown anymore!" Max trumpeted. "I performed a lumbar puncture this morning. The woman clearly has meningitis."

Sunny nodded. "Do you have enough antibiotics to treat her?"

Max flashed a paternal grin. "Your friend, Dr. Huang, brought me a fresh supply only yesterday." He shook his head. "It's not as though we are working in the Universitätsklinikum Hamburg-Eppendorf here, but this would be no hospital at all without the assistance of Dr. Huang and yourself."

"I couldn't agree more," Simon said from behind them. "Without Sunny, we might as well lock up the doors and turn off the lights."

Sunny turned to see Simon smiling at them from the doorway. "Dr. Feinstein, Sunny." He beckoned them out to the hallway. "I want you to meet someone."

Simon's guest was as tall as him but broader across

the shoulders. The handsome newcomer had a square jaw, dark curly hair, and grave hazel eyes, and appeared to be five or ten years older than Simon. "Allow me to introduce Dr. Franz Adler," Simon said.

The name meant nothing to Sunny, but Max's eyes widened. "You are not *the* surgical professor from Vienna, are you?"

Franz nodded. "I am a surgical professor or, at least, I used to be."

Max pumped his hand. "It's an honor, Dr. Adler. Truly. Your reputation for surgical innovations precedes you. I am Maxwell Feinstein from Hamburg."

"The internist?" Franz said. "I read your fine paper on electrolyte management in patients with shock."

Max shrugged modestly. "So Hitler forced you to flee to Shanghai too?"

"We were very lucky to find passage here."

Max sighed heavily. "Not so lucky as you might think."

Simon chuckled. "Dr. Adler, you'll have to excuse Dr. Feinstein. He is not one of our most optimistic arrivals."

"It is true. In spite of the Nazis, I'm still very homesick." Max cleared his throat. "Our . . . our eldest daughter and her two sons are still in Hamburg."

"They did not accompany you to Shanghai?"

"Her husband was convinced the Americans would open their doors to downtrodden Jews." Max glanced over to Simon, but there was no judgment, only worry, in his expression. "Now they cannot leave."

Franz nodded solemnly. "I know how it feels to leave family behind, Dr. Feinstein."

Simon gestured to Sunny. "Dr. Adler, allow me to introduce our brightest and loveliest nurse, Sunny Mah."

"A pleasure to meet you, Miss Mah," Franz said in English.

"Miss Mah is not merely a good nurse, Dr. Adler," Max said in German, his only tongue. "She is more capable than most junior physicians. Only this past week, she single-handedly managed an outbreak of dysentery that could have proven disastrous."

Sunny's cheeks burned. "My father is a doctor, a diabetes specialist. He has taught me a few approaches for treating dehydration."

Franz viewed her with disconcerting intensity. "Where did you learn to speak German so well?"

Her face heated even further. "I had a terrifying languages teacher at school—Mr. Hinkel. He seemed to be about seven feet tall. When Mr. Hinkel told you that you were going to learn German, you learned German."

"I faced a few Hinkels in my school days." Franz's smile wiped the gravity from his eyes.

"Dr. Adler has agreed to lend his time and talent to our little hospital," Simon announced.

"We are honored to have you." Max raised his shoulders helplessly. "But I fear your prodigious skill will be wasted. Our surgical facilities are so rudimentary."

"Dr. Feinstein, I have been banned from surgery for the past six months. I would be thrilled to offer whatever assistance I can, no matter how basic." Franz looked down at his feet. "I had no idea how much I would miss being a doctor."

Max nodded his understanding. "Of course. I only wish we had better facilities—any, really—to offer you."

Simon glanced from one doctor to the other. "Let me talk to Sir Victor. He might provide some extra funds for surgical tools."

"And, Dr. Adler, I work with the surgeons at the Country Hospital," Sunny added. "It is probably the best-equipped hospital in all of Shanghai. I cannot promise anything—"

"Yes, yes!" Max said with sudden excitement. "Sunny and her friend, Dr. Huang, have been our oasis in this medical desert."

Franz viewed Sunny with a shy smile. "Miss Mah, I am beginning to suspect that you are an important person to know here in Shanghai."

～ Chapter 16

Ernst stopped so suddenly on the sidewalk that the people around him had to lurch out of his way to squeeze and shoulder past. "My God, we're in the midst of some kind of retail orgy!" he cried.

Franz and Ernst had just turned off the Bund, past the green-roofed Cathay Hotel, and were walking down Nanking Road under overcast skies. The guidebook that Simon had loaned Franz described Nanking Road as one of the city's main east-west arteries and the retail heart of Asia. The book had not exaggerated. The rows of specialty shops and department stores extended as far as the eye could see. Shoppers laden with colorful bags thronged the sidewalks. Ernst waved his hand at the beehive of consumerism swarming around them. "This could pass for Mariahilfer Strasse back in Vienna, *ja*?"

Aside from a few traditionally dressed Chinese and the rickshaws interspersed among the Buicks, Chevrolets, and Daimlers, the shopping frenzy could have been playing out in almost any European city. With one difference. "It doesn't smell the same here," Franz pointed out.

"Indeed," Ernst agreed with a wrinkle of his nose. More than the unfamiliar sights and sounds, Shanghai's exotic smells constantly reminded Franz how far they were from home. Not all aromas were as putrid as the reek of the untreated sewage, rancid cooking oils, or body odors wafting from hordes of pedestrians. Franz found the scents of burning incense, exotic perfumes, and roasting meat at the ubiquitous street kitchens appealing but still equally as foreign.

Out of nowhere, a black limousine screeched up to the curb in front of them. Two thick-necked white men in navy pinstripe suits and black fedoras bounded out. The first bodyguard, a giant with a machine gun slung over his shoulder, scanned the crowd. Suddenly, two young Chinese women burst out of the door of a nearby shop, giggling and screeching. Startled, the guard jerked his weapon in their direction. The girls froze. The nozzle of the machine gun twitched.

Heart in his throat, Franz feared a massacre. But the guard slowly lowered his weapon, and the girls scuttled away with another eruption of nervous laughter. The bodyguard surveyed the street again. Satisfied, he signaled to someone in the car. A diminutive Chinese man climbed out of the backseat. The man wore a hat similar to those of his bodyguards, but he also had on dark glasses and a sable coat over a white silk robe that almost touched his white shoes.

Gangsters? Franz wondered. He remembered the previous day's orientation lecture at the Embankment House. A spokesperson from the CFA committee had gone to great lengths to point out all the potential hazards and pitfalls the refugees would face in the city. Ernst had dubbed the speech as the "welcome-to-Shanghai-where-everything-kills-you lecture." The lecturer's admonitions included, but were not limited to, the tap water, raw fruits and vegetables, shellfish, mosquitoes, pickpockets, casinos, brothels, street traffic, and especially kidnappers. He warned that "abduction is so common in this city that the English have turned it into a verb—to be *shanghaied*."

Mouth agape, Ernst watched the two Goliaths and their sable-clad employer disappear into the Sun Sun Co. Department Store. The artist shook his head and heaved an exaggerated sigh. "Getting noticed in *this* city is going to take considerable effort on my part."

"I am confident you will manage," Franz said.

Ernst uttered a small laugh. "And so you should be, my friend."

They continued west along Nanking Road. After a few more blocks, the substantial brick and stone buildings gave way to lower-rise shops with more Asian flavor. Neon signs and brightly colored banners adorned with Chinese calligraphy hung over the entrances. Silks, embroideries, linens, and jewelry filled the windows. The thin wailing of Chinese music tinkled out through open doorways.

Viewing the lantern-filled window of a shop, Franz stumbled over something hard. He looked down and saw a pair of legs jutting across the sidewalk. A gaunt man in frayed pants and a filthy shirt sat slumped against the storefront. Eyes open, the man's head flopped onto his shoulder. He looked like other coolies—the young men who drifted into Shanghai from rural areas to drive the rickshaws and carry much of the city's labor, literally, on their shoulders.

Ernst jumped back a step. "Franz, he's . . ."

"Dead. Yes."

Ernst desperately patted his pockets for a cigarette. "The lecturer warned us about this. He said thousands of people die on the streets of Shanghai every year."

Franz knelt down to take a closer look. The man

stared back, his face pale and lean. Franz doubted that he was much older than twenty.

"Leave him, Franz," Ernst urged, backing farther away. "You can get diseases from the bodies. Remember? Someone regularly comes around to collect them."

Despite his professional familiarity with death, Franz was chilled by the sight of the young man sprawled across the sidewalk while shoppers stepped over his corpse as though it were no more than mislaid trash. "Ernst, what kind of a place have I brought Hannah and Esther to?"

Ernst inhaled from his cigarette and then motioned to the corpse. "Clearly, no one was caring for this poor devil, but nobody was out to kill him either." He pointed his cigarette at Franz. "Remember Kristallnacht? Don't ever forget what you are shielding little Hannah from."

Franz knew Ernst was right, but he still pined for home—the Vienna before the Nazis, where welcome smells wafted from bakeries and cafés at every corner, and where there never was a need for corpse collectors. Franz thought of his father again. The guilt burned. He had yet to open Jakob's letter.

Ernst clapped him on the shoulder. "Come. Let's find a place to call home. That will help."

They reached the corner of Nanking and Thibet Roads, where two massive department stores flanked the intersection, looming like giant sentries. Across the street, a park sprawled in front of them. Franz consulted the guidebook in his pocket. "This must be the Recreation Ground. Apparently, there is a wonderful children's playground. I will have to bring Hannah."

"You see," Ernst said, exhaling a puff of smoke. "Now all we have to do is find an adult playground for yours truly, and we can all live happily."

Franz and Ernst headed west until Nanking turned into Bubbling Well Road. Soaring buildings, as lofty as the ones fronting the Bund, lined the street. Franz nodded to the tallest of the skyscrapers. "The Park Hotel," Ernst said before Franz could even check the guidebook. "They say the bar inside is well worth a visit."

"Have you ever come across a bar that wasn't worth a visit, Ernst?"

"Not really. But I'm absolutely committed to keep searching until I do."

They reached a wide road where a signpost read AVENUE EDWARD VII. Ernst indicated the Chinese man directing traffic. He wore the uniform of a Parisian gendarme. "Either we've arrived at Frenchtown, or the security is not so tight at the local asylum."

As soon as they crossed into the French Concession, the architectural rigor of the International Settlement gave way to the carefree grace of scattered villas and apartment buildings. The sidewalks were sprinkled with cypresses and plane trees, and the manner and style of the people were noticeably more relaxed, more French.

A few streets farther, they turned eastward onto the thoroughfare of Avenue Joffre, where Franz saw Cyrillic lettering on the storefront. The odor of boiled cabbage filled the air, and several people spoke Russian. The deeper they headed into the neighborhood, the more tightly clustered and run-down the buildings became.

Ernst stopped outside one particularly ramshackle apartment block and pointed to the second floor. Hanging laundry obscured the balcony's railing, while cracks ran like a giant cobweb across the window above. "I think we have stumbled into *our* price range."

Simon had recommended Hongkew as offering the most affordable housing, so Franz and Ernst had spent most of their morning wandering the neighborhoods near the refugee hospital. In the narrow lanes, they passed countless plain apartment blocks, many advertising vacancies in German. Placards in the windows promoted tailors, grocers, and even physicians with Jewish-sounding names. They walked by two cafés and a makeshift bakery that exuded the welcome smell of home. German refugees were everywhere—men in suits, women pushing strollers, and old people propped up by canes—all of whom could have just stepped off an Austrian tram. Franz was simultaneously disoriented and moved by the incongruous sight of Vienna replicated in Asia. He would have happily relocated to Hongkew if not for the clusters of Japanese soldiers. Though they seemed utterly indifferent to the refugees, the soldiers reminded Franz too much of the Nazis at home. He would never feel secure settling Hannah among them, so Ernst and he continued on to Little Russia, Simon's alternative recommendation.

Walking along Avenue Joffre, Franz stopped to assess several buildings. They visited two that advertised vacancies. The first flat was oppressively dark, dingy, and grimy. They lasted only minutes at the second, which reeked so much that Franz wondered if something or someone was decomposing behind the walls.

A block farther east, Franz spotted a plain, five-story brick building that also displayed a vacancy sign. Something about the structure caught his eye and he longed for his old camera, mentally aligning the perfect spot from which to photograph it. He looked up and noticed an older Chinese man staring at him from the second-floor window. Franz pointed to the vacancy sign. The man nodded and disappeared from the window.

Moments later, the man opened the front door. A long braid secured his gray hair behind his head, and wire-rimmed glasses covered his watery brown eyes. He wore a collarless, black Sun Yat-sen jacket that was common on the streets, but Franz had never seen anyone else pair it with a shirt of any color, let alone one in lavender. A thin young man in a Western-style collared shirt and khakis stood behind the older man and watched warily.

"Good day, gentlemen. May I help you?" the older man said in impeccable English.

"Are you the landlord?" Franz asked.

The man shook his head. "I am not. However, I help care for the building when he is away. My name is Zhou Heng," he said, stating his family name before his given name, as per Chinese tradition. "And this is my son, Shan."

Franz introduced Ernst and himself. Heng switched unexpectedly to German. "Herr Adler, *möchten Sie ein zimmer mieten?*"

"Indeed, Mr. Zhou, we are searching for a flat," Franz said, surprised by Heng's near-perfect pronunciation. "There are four of us in total."

"Would you gentlemen like a tour?" Heng asked.

Ernst held up his hand. "Where in God's name did you learn your German? You're not from Cologne or Essen, are you?"

Heng chuckled. "Not quite so far west, Herr Muhler. Nanking, in fact. However, I am a professor of languages. Or rather, I used to be."

"Nanking?" Ernst said. "Isn't that the capital of China?"

Shan squinted hard at Ernst, but Heng smiled good-naturedly. "Perhaps in the Japanese's eyes, but it is not our capital, Herr Muhler." Heng exhaled slowly. "In China's five-thousand-year history, Nanking was only the capital for ten forgettable years."

Ernst glanced over to Franz with a raised eyebrow. "I stand corrected."

"Please follow me." Heng spun and headed back into the building. He walked briskly down the narrow corridor and almost bounded up the stairs to the third floor.

Reaching the door to the first apartment, Heng pulled a keychain from his pocket and opened the door. Looking over his shoulder, Franz saw that Shan had not accompanied them.

The room was compact and sparsely furnished with a table and chairs and one worn brown sofa, but it looked relatively clean and was free of unsavory odors. Heng pointed out the galley kitchen with its icebox and single gas-element stove before he guided them to the bedroom. Studying the double bed that barely fit inside, Franz wondered how three unmarried adults and one child might coexist inside such a cramped space.

Heng led them to the tiny bathroom. He pointed to the low toilet. "Please notice the indoor plumbing," he said proudly.

Ernst grimaced. "Are you suggesting that some flats here do not have plumbing?"

"This is China, Herr Muhler," Heng said. "Only the newer buildings have indoor plumbing. The night soil men are still very busy in Shanghai."

"The night soil men?" Ernst pulled his head back as though fearful of the explanation.

"In the early morning, you will see them all over the city," Heng said. "They carry out their loads on bamboo poles to the barrels on carts. The farmers outside the city pay handsomely for the product. There is no finer fertilizer than human waste."

Ernst's face greened slightly, but Franz appreciated the scientific rationale. With a pang of nostalgia, he thought of his great-uncle's farm and the familiar stench from the oddly named "honey wagons" that dumped human excrement on the soil. Still, he realized the lecturer had not exaggerated; washing and cooking all produce would be essential.

Back in the main room, Franz asked, "Have you lived in Shanghai for long, Mr. Zhou?"

"Eleven months. Since January fifteen, actually."

"Just you and your son?" Franz asked, surprised by the exactness of his answer.

Heng turned away, quiet for a moment. "Neither my wife nor our daughter ever reached Shanghai."

"Are they still in Nanking?" Ernst asked.

"No, Herr Muhler, they are not."

Heng's implication was unmistakable. Empathy for the genteel man welled in Franz, and his thoughts turned to his own brother and father.

"I'm sorry," Ernst stammered, embarrassed.

Heng cleared his throat and adjusted his glasses. "The rent for the apartment is one hundred and twenty *mex*—or Chinese dollars—per month. Roughly forty American dollars, depending on the bank and the given moment. The exchange rates in Shanghai fluctuate like the wind."

Franz turned to his friend. "What do you think?"

Ernst nodded his approval. "As far as I am concerned, anywhere we do not have to endure a visit from the night soil man is acceptable to me."

In a hurry to return to Embankment House to share the news, they hailed a rickshaw. While Ernst absorbed the sights and sounds around them, Franz focused on the man pulling them. He appeared to be of a similar age as the dead man on the street and wore similarly tattered clothes. His exposed muscles in his forearms and calves contracted with each stride, and he chanted a steady stream of *"hey-haw, hey-haw"* as he ran.

The runner dropped them off a few feet from the Garden Bridge. The memory of the dead man still haunted Franz and he tipped the runner more than double the cost of the ride, ignoring the lecturer's warning that, in business, the Chinese misinterpreted generosity for stupidity.

On the south side of the bridge, the British soldier waved them past with a stalwart nod. At the opposite guard post, the Japanese guard barely glanced in their direction. Instead, he focused a withering scowl on the old Chinese couple bowing before him. Ernst turned to Franz with a snort. "I am beginning to appreciate why the Nazis and Japanese get on so famously."

Stepping off the bridge, they headed west on North Soochow Road toward Embankment House, where the day before the rickety pickup truck had dropped his family off. While the second floor of the massive art deco building served as a clearinghouse for refugees, it otherwise functioned as an upscale apartment block. At the entrance, Ernst veered across the street to the tobacconist to replenish his supply of cigarettes. Franz had barely stepped into the second-floor gymnasium-sized room, half-filled with rows of steel bunk beds, when he heard Hannah's voice. "Papa!"

Franz spotted her emerging from a group of people clustered near the communal kitchen in the corner. Clutching her doll, Hannah rushed toward him. He knelt down and caught her in open arms. "Did you find a flat for us, Papa?"

"I think so, *liebchen.*"

She hugged him happily. "Can we go now?"

"Is something wrong here?" he asked.

"No. Everyone is nice, but I . . ." She searched for the right words. "I just want to be in our own home, Papa."

"Me too." Franz kissed her on the forehead. "Let's go find your aunt and we can pack up our belongings and go see our flat."

Hannah hugged him again.

"Franz!" Esther called from nearby.

He freed himself from Hannah's embrace and looked up to see Esther approaching alongside a woman he did not recognize. Wearing a fur coat and feather-capped hat, the stout middle-aged woman had a hawklike face and carried herself with an air of solemn importance. Before Esther had a chance to introduce her, the woman thrust out a hand. "Dr. Adler, I am Mrs. Clara Reuben," she announced as though the name should resonate with him.

"A pleasure, Mrs. Reuben."

"I volunteer with the CFA." Clara spoke German with an English accent. "I help to run the refugees' school that the Kadoorie family has established. And, of course, I sit on the board of the Shanghai Jewish School."

"Mrs. Reuben has kindly offered to look for a position at the Jewish school for Hannah," Esther added.

Clara pinched Hannah's cheek. The girl smiled back dutifully, but Franz felt her stiffen in his arms. "Do not worry, we will find somewhere suitable for little Hannah," Clara said. "Of course, I cannot promise the Shanghai Jewish School. We do offer a limited number of scholarships and bursaries, but there is frightful competition for those positions."

"Any help you can provide us would be greatly appreciated," Franz said.

"There is more—" Esther began excitedly.

"I understand you are a surgeon," Clara cut her off. "A professor, no less."

"I was, yes. At the University of Vienna."

"Perhaps you have heard of my husband, Dr. Samuel Reuben?" Clara paused a moment, waiting for Franz to show a glimmer of recognition. "He is the chief of surgery at the Country Hospital. The most reputable hospital in Shanghai, of course."

Franz nodded, though he had never heard of her husband.

"I will speak to my husband. He trained in London, of course," Clara said with a tinge of superiority. "But his grandparents were German. He might be able to find work for you."

Despite her condescending tone, Franz relished the prospect. "I have agreed to help out where I can at the refugee hospital, but I would welcome the—"

"Yes, of course." Clara fluttered her bejeweled hand toward the sky. "I am speaking now of a real hospital, capable of performing major surgeries."

Franz's spirits soared. "That would be wonderful, Mrs. Reuben."

She viewed him intently. "Your sister-in-law tells me that you are widowed."

"For quite some time, yes," Franz said.

Clara nodded with satisfaction. "Perhaps we can discuss this further over dinner at our home. My lovely niece, Charlotte, lives with us." She raised an eyebrow. "I would very much like for you to meet Lotte."

～ Chapter 17

Sunny and Simon sat bundled up on a wooden bench outside the refugee hospital. The December sun had just dipped behind the city's western outskirts, where most of Shanghai's wealthiest foreign executives lived behind walled estates. Sunny had known the outspoken New Yorker for less than two months, but they had fallen into a warm friendship that felt years old to her.

Simon held out a pack of cigarettes, but Sunny waved it away. He tucked the pack back into his pocket without lighting up. "I don't even know how old you are, Sunny," he remarked, apropos of nothing.

"I will be twenty-five in March," she said.

"And no brothers or sisters, huh?"

She shook her head. "My mother died when I was a little girl."

"That can't have been easy."

Sunny shrugged. "I am fortunate to have the father that I do."

"I have a big family," Simon said. "Four brothers and two sisters. I'm second in age, the oldest boy. Growing up, my little brothers drove me crackers. Those brats. Now, I miss them all. Especially Fridays, and our Shabbat—our Sabbath—dinners with the whole family jammed around the table. They're so loud you can't even hear yourself think."

Sunny smiled. "Sounds like a loving family, Simon."

"Yeah, I suppose. My parents have been married thirty-four years." He sighed. "Of course, they argue a lot. Like cats and dogs, sometimes."

She chuckled. "Many of my friends say the same about their parents. Chinese women are supposed to honor, respect, and obey their husbands, but they can make very demanding wives."

"I'm beginning to think the Chinese might be the lost tribe of Israel. Or maybe vice versa?" Simon grinned. "My parents might argue like crazy, but they still go dancing every week." He went quiet for a moment. "That's what I want, Sunny. To find a nice Jewish girl who would still want to go dancing with me after thirty years, despite the bickering."

Sunny realized, for the first time, that her upbeat companion was lonely. "Then go find her, Simon."

He nodded to himself. "I think I might already have."

"Would I know her?"

"Jeez, I don't even know her myself. I've just met her."

"Is she one of the refugees?"

He nodded. "She's not even my usual type. Not flashy or anything. It's just . . . one glimpse and I knew. She is the one."

"You see."

"Ah, I'm just full of hot air, as my pop would tell you." He dug in his pocket and pulled out the cigarette pack again. This time, he slid out a smoke and lit it. "How about you?"

"Me?"

He flashed a grin. "A smart, pretty girl like you. How come you're not already married?"

She felt her face flushing. "I . . . I never . . ."

He viewed her keenly. "You ever been in love, Sunny?"

A vision of Wen-Cheng popped into her head but she brushed it aside. "I am working two jobs. My country is at war. And my city torn apart."

He nudged her gently with his elbow. "Too busy for love, huh?"

She could see that he was fighting back a smile. She was thankful for the weak light, aware that her face had reddened.

Someone cleared his throat behind them. "Good evening, Miss Mah, Mr. Lehrer."

Sunny glanced over her shoulder to see Franz Adler standing a few feet behind them. She looked away, embarrassed that he might have overheard their conversation.

"Excuse me for interrupting," Franz said.

"Not at all." Simon rose unhurriedly to his feet. "We're chitchatting about love and marriage. I was just asking Sunny why no one has snapped her up yet."

Simon! Sunny wanted to crawl out of her skin.

"Oh, I . . . see," Franz said. "Dr. Feinstein is expecting me, so I'd best be on my way—"

Simon held up a hand to stop him. "Esther is your sister-in-law, isn't she, Dr. Adler?"

"She was married to my brother, Karl. Yes."

"So you're both widowed now?"

"Simon, please!" Sunny interjected. "Dr. Adler is in a hurry."

"I apologize, Dr. Adler. Sunny's right. I am being rude." Simon chuckled without a trace of self-consciousness. "But I'm a Jew from the Bronx. They don't come any nosier than us."

"I understand, of course," Franz said with a stiff smile. "I lost my wife just days after our daughter, Hannah, was born. Almost nine years ago. But my brother died during Kristallnacht."

"So . . . so recently?" Simon muttered.

"The storm troopers." Franz folded his arms over his chest and shifted from one foot to the other. "During the night of the riots, they came for Karl. We found him hanging from the streetlamp outside his office."

Sunny forgot about her embarrassment. "To find your brother that way . . . I can't even imagine."

"Karl used to say that for every Nazi brute there are ten decent Gentiles, but most are too scared to act. My faith in people is not as charitable. But, Miss Mah, I know my brother would have admired you for the selfless way you are helping us refugees." He stared at her with disarming sincerity. "I certainly do."

Sunny was about to reply when she saw her father's

sedan pull up to the curb with his driver, Fai, at the wheel. Kingsley had never learned to drive. A passionate walker, he had bought the used car only after it became clear that his patients were scattered too far across the city for him to manage his practice on foot. Sunny never told her father about the run-in with the two drunken Japanese sailors, but he worried about her walking alone, especially after dark, and so came to pick her up after most evening shifts. If Kingsley was too busy, he would usually send his driver ahead to fetch her.

Kingsley hurried up the pathway toward them.

Sunny made the introductions.

"My daughter tells me you are quite a famous surgeon, Dr. Adler," Kingsley commented as they shook hands.

"Only within the walls of my own home, I am afraid, Dr. Mah," Franz said.

Kingsley nodded. "Will you be operating here at the hospital?"

"I would like to," Franz said. "As of now, we do not have the equipment or facilities to perform much more than the most basic of procedures."

"The new operating room is going to be finished any day now," Simon pointed out.

Franz nodded. "And when the equipment arrives, I might be able to offer the patients a little more than simply moral support."

Kingsley touched his chest. "If I can help in any way . . ." Like his daughter, he had become attached to the refugee hospital. He offered his advice on managing the blood sugars of diabetic patients and regularly donated any supplies he could spare, including insulin.

"Dr. Mah, you've already helped a ton." Simon

nodded at Sunny. "And your daughter is nothing short of a godsend. Our own angel of mercy."

"You are too kind, Mr. Lehrer." Despite Kingsley's impassive tone, Sunny sensed his pride and she beamed inwardly. He motioned toward the car. "Please excuse us, gentlemen, but Soon Yi and I really must depart. I am late for a rather urgent house call."

"Don't let us hold you up," Simon said.

"One day, Dr. Mah, I would enjoy learning more about your practice." Franz turned to Sunny with an almost imperceptible smile. "Good night, Miss Mah."

Sunny held Franz's gaze for a moment before turning to follow her father to the car. In the backseat, Sunny was still thinking about the Austrian surgeon when Kingsley asked, "What is a pulsus paradoxus?"

Her mind only half on the question, she replied, "The physical finding whereby a patient's pulse becomes measurably weaker during exhalation than inhalation."

"Is that so?" Kingsley said.

"I mean vice versa."

"Correct. In which diseases does one—"

"It can be seen during cardiac tamponade, emphysema, and pericarditis." She reached out and touched her father's sleeve. "Did you and Mother ever used to go dancing?"

"*Dancing?*"

"Yes, after you were married?"

"How does that expression go?" Kingsley considered for a moment. "I have two left feet."

"So you never danced with Mother?"

"No, we did." He turned to look out the window. "Your mother loved to dance. She would even put up with my graceless stomping." He laughed quietly. "Her poor toes."

Sunny had always sensed that her father adored her

mother, but he rarely spoke of her. She was somehow comforted by the idea of her parents going out dancing.

Kingsley cleared his throat. "How does one distinguish pericarditis from cardiac tamponade?"

Sunny fielded a few more questions before Fai slowed the car to a stop in front of a nondescript lane. Kingsley grabbed his bulky medical bag as they got out. They walked past several *longtangs* before stopping in front of a black door that resembled the others in the lane.

A middle-aged man in navy pajamas met them at the door. His eyes were frantic but his tone was calm and respectful. *"Ni hǎo, yī sheng,"* he said, bowing before Kingsley. "Thank you for taking the time to come, Doctor."

"I am pleased to be here," Kingsley said, matching his politeness. "Mr. Lung, how is the boy?"

Lung shook his head gravely. "Please." He turned and trotted down the corridor into a narrow bedroom, Kingsley and Sunny following.

A young boy, about seven or eight years old, lay on a low bed covered to his chest by a light sheet. He was comatose: his glassy eyes stared up at the ceiling, and dried tears crusted his cheeks. His face was so sunken that ridges of his orbital bones stood out. He was still except for his chest, which pumped up and down like a piston firing.

At the foot of the bed, a little girl sat with legs crossed. Rocking back and forth with quiet worry, she did not take her eyes off the boy to even glance at the visitors.

Kingsley's lips tightened. "Mr. Lung, you told me little Bai was still awake."

"He was when I went out to the neighbor's to telephone you, Doctor," Lung rasped from the doorway. "By the time I returned, he was in this state."

Kingsley lowered his bag to the floor. He removed a

stethoscope and listened to the child's chest while feeling for the pulse at the neck. After a moment, he pulled the stethoscope from his ears and turned back to his bag. As he rummaged inside it, he asked Sunny in English, "Do you smell his breath?"

"Acetone." Sunny named the sickly fruity aroma. "He's in a diabetic coma. That is why he's breathing so deeply."

"Yes, he suffers from diabetic ketoacidosis. His body is attempting to breathe off carbon dioxide to reverse his blood acidity." Kingsley pulled out a vial of insulin and large syringe. "Insulin will help but will not alone suffice. We must rehydrate him urgently, Sunny. Can you search for a suitable vein?"

Sunny hurried to the far side of the bed, across from her father. She knelt down and touched Bai's arm. His skin felt dry to the point of leathery. She barely palpated the thready pulse at his wrist but could not see or feel any veins below the skin. "Father, there's nothing," she murmured.

Kingsley finished drawing up the insulin without comment. He tapped a few air bubbles from the tip of the syringe. Then he pulled the sheet down, pinched the skin around the boy's navel, and injected the insulin. The boy did not register a flicker of a response.

Kingsley turned his attention to Bai's other arm. He ran his fingers up and down the arm, rolling the skin. "I will have to try this blindly," he said as he extracted more supplies from his bag. He attached rubber tubing to a bottle of clear intravenous fluid.

After Sunny snugly tied a tourniquet around Bai's upper arm, Kingsley applied a hollow needle to the skin at the crease of Bai's elbow. He poked it through the skin, sliding the tip slowly back and forth and rotating it at various angles in search of a vein. Sunny watched intently, hoping to see a drop of blood from the hub that would confirm the needle had entered a vein. But it remained as dry as the boy's skin.

Kingsley withdrew the needle. Fingers still steady, he moved the tip farther up the arm and tried another spot, without success. After a third futile attempt, he released the tourniquet and looked up at Sunny with concern.

"Would you like me to try, Father?"

Kingsley shook his head. "The boy's veins have all collapsed. He is too dehydrated."

She glanced over to Bai's little sister, who was still rocking. "What else can we do?"

Kingsley shrugged slightly.

"There must be something," Sunny said.

"There is one other approach." He frowned in thought. "It is entirely experimental. I have only read about it. However, I do carry the necessary equipment."

Sunny viewed Bai again and saw that his skin had mottled, suggesting death from dehydration was near. "There is nothing to lose, Father."

Kingsley turned and dug even deeper in his bag. From inside a cloth-wrapped package, he extracted a massive needle the size of a carpentry nail. For a moment, Sunny wondered if her father intended to jab it directly into the boy's heart.

Kingsley moved a few feet down the bed and tossed the sheet off the boy. He felt along the boy's leg until his fingers came to rest at a prominence just below Bai's knee. "The tibial tuberosity," he said.

Measuring two fingers below the bony prominence, Kingsley applied the needle directly to the skin overlying the tibia. He gripped the dull end of the needle against his palm and leaned down onto it with all his weight. The needle pierced the skin and bone with a nauseating crunch. He let go of the needle and it stayed upright, vibrating like a sword thrust into stone.

Kingsley reached for a glass syringe, attached it to the needle, and slowly pulled back the plunger with his thumb. The syringe filled with a reddish gelatinous and flecked substance. "Bone marrow," he announced. Satisfied, he uncoupled the syringe and secured the tubing to the end of the needle. He lifted up the intravenous bottle and held it high in the air. Fluid began to flow in a steady drip.

"How does the fluid run from the bone marrow to the heart?" Sunny asked.

"It passes through the network of veins lining the marrow," he said. "Or so I have read."

Kingsley insisted on holding the bottle himself as the fluid ran into Bai's bone marrow. No one spoke. Sunny knelt down beside Bai's sister. "What is your name, little one?"

"Hua," the girl said in a shy voice.

"Ah, like the flower. How fitting." Sunny moved a little closer and the girl stopped rocking. "You are a good sister to stay with Bai like this."

"I don't want the ancestors to take him away," Hua said.

Sunny smiled. "Nor do I."

"It will be harder for them to take him if someone watches," Hua said matter-of-factly.

"Yes, it will."

Hua gestured to the needle sticking out of the leg. "Will that nail him to the ground, so the ancestors can't take him?"

Sunny stifled a laugh. "I hope so, yes."

The girl turned her attention back to her motionless brother.

Five or six minutes passed. Sunny became aware of a

new silence that had descended on the room. The boy's respirations had quieted; he was breathing more easily.

The intravenous bottle had emptied. Kingsley disconnected it from the far end of the rubber tubing. As he was reaching for a second full bottle, Hua suddenly yelped. Sunny's eyes darted from the little girl to her brother. Bai blinked a few times and smacked his cracked lips together, as though trying to wet them.

Sunny looked over to Kingsley. With only a trace of a smile, her father turned his attention back to exchanging the old intravenous bottle for a new one.

Sunny touched Hua's shoulder. "The ancestors won't be able to take your brother now."

"I'm glad," Hua said.

"I am too, little one." Sunny glanced at her father again, her heart swollen with pride and affection.

⌒ *Chapter 18*

DECEMBER 16, 1938, SHANGHAI

A week after the Adlers and Ernst had moved into the cramped third-floor quarters on Avenue Joffre, Franz's disorientation had still not cleared. The nonstop street noises and the ubiquitous peddlers, beggars, and corpses abandoned on sidewalks only compounded his sense of alienation. And food tasted different, even familiar delicacies from the French bakeries and cafés.

Hannah and Esther shared the bedroom, while in the main room, Franz slept on the sofa and Ernst on a bed of cushions. As he had on the ship, the artist disappeared for long stretches without explanation. He always returned full of amusing anecdotes—life as a bewildered foreigner in Asia—but Franz sensed the loneliness behind his happy-go-lucky attitude.

Esther busied herself with relentless homemaking and nesting. Some of the local peddlers already called to her by name from the street below. She had stocked the shelves in their little apartment with a set of secondhand dishes, pots, and cutlery, bartered in exchange for a pair of earrings and a small brooch. She had imbued their apartment with a sense of home, down to the dried flowers on the windowsill and a row of German novels lining the shelf, but her efforts only heightened Franz's homesickness.

Hannah was adjusting to her new life better than the adults. She had already befriended Natasha Lazarev, a nine-year-old Russian girl who lived with her parents and two brothers on the top floor of their building.

With Hannah at the Lazarevs' and Ernst gone for the day, Franz sat at the table cradling a cup of tea and watching his sister-in-law scour the rusted sink. A beefy red scar coursed along the inside of her arm, but Franz could see from the way she feverishly scrubbed that her injury no longer impeded her. "Why do you always avoid rest, Essie?" he asked.

"I did nothing but rest on that ship for almost a month." She shrugged. "Besides, for me, rest is no rest at all. You understand, Franz?"

"I do." The smile slid from his lips. "After Hilde died, between the new baby and the hospital, I hardly slept. But it was almost better that way."

She stopped scouring. "I dread the nights. That is when I miss him most."

The image of Karl and Esther snuggling on a couch and laughing quietly at some private joke popped into Franz's mind. "I am not sure that ever changes, Essie."

Esther's shoulders straightened and she began to scrub again. "Have you opened your father's letter yet?"

He shook his head.

"What if his news is good, Franz?"

"Do you think it could be?"

"No."

The loose knob rattled and the door creaked open. Franz looked over as Hannah entered. "*Guten tag, Papa, Tante Essie*," she greeted politely, but Franz saw that she was on the verge of tears.

"*Was ist los, liebchen?*" he demanded.

Hannah shook her head but said nothing. She crawled onto his lap. He wrapped his arms around her and cradled her.

"What happened, Hannah?" Esther asked, drying her hands on her apron as she walked out of the tiny kitchen. "Did you have a fight with Natasha?"

Hannah shook her head again. "Natasha's brother wanted to know if . . ." Her voice faltered. "If I had ever been in the circus."

The anger ripped through Franz. Hannah had faced taunts from insensitive, cruel, or oblivious children most of her life, especially during those final months in Vienna, but rarely had he seen her so hurt. He resisted the urge to rush upstairs to confront the little boy himself, remembering how disastrous the previous interventions had proven.

Esther waved her hand. "*Ach*, Hannah, you don't listen to such nonsense. You are too smart and too special for that."

With her face still buried in Franz's shoulder, Hannah muttered, "Ivan is only six."

"You see," Esther said as she approached. "He doesn't know."

Hannah looked up at her aunt, defeated. "I thought

it would be different here, but nothing changes, Tante Essie."

Esther stroked Hannah's cheek with the back of her hand. "Oh, darling, such ignorance and heartlessness is everywhere. You cannot change those people. What you have to do is rise above them."

"How do I do that, Tante Essie?"

"You ignore them," Esther said. "You don't allow them the satisfaction of a reaction. And know in your heart that they are nothing but narrow-minded. What those people say does not matter. Never ever let them stop you, Hannah. You understand?"

"I will try," Hannah promised.

"That's my girl," Esther said.

Hannah wriggled free of Franz's grip and hopped out of his lap. She threw her arms around Esther and hugged her. "I'm so happy you came with us."

"Me too." Esther kissed the child's head. "Me too."

Hannah let go of her aunt. "I thought Onkel Karl would be here by now."

Esther turned to Franz, her eyes seeking permission to tell Hannah. He hesitated a moment and then, with a sinking heart, nodded.

Esther knelt down in front of the girl. "Onkel Karl is not coming, Hannah."

The girl's eyes widened. "Not ever?"

"No."

Hannah's face scrunched with suspicion. "He is dead, isn't he?"

"Yes, Hannah," Esther breathed.

The tears Hannah had been holding back earlier welled in her eyes as she looked frantically from Esther to Franz. "He was never going to come here, was he?"

"No." Esther ran a finger under her eye and sniffed

once. "He died that night, Hannah. The night of the fires. Kristallnacht."

"I knew it!" Hannah cried. "The Nazis killed him, didn't they?"

"Yes," Franz said softly.

"And Opa Jakob?" Hannah demanded, her face creased with hurt and anguish. "Did they kill him too?"

Franz held up his hands. "I don't know."

"You do. You must!" Hannah backed clumsily away from both adults.

"Your grandfather was supposed to come over on the next ship to Shanghai, but I think his lungs might be too weak for the journey."

"He's never going to come either!" Hannah spat.

Franz shook his head once and dropped his hands to his side. "I don't think he will."

"You were all lying to me!" Hannah spun and rushed to the bedroom.

Franz started after her, but Esther caught him by the forearm. "Give her time."

He knew she was right, but he desperately wanted to comfort his daughter. The betrayal in her eyes pierced his heart.

Ten minutes passed and Hannah had still not emerged. Franz slipped on his coat and hat and then knocked at the bedroom door. "I have to go to an appointment now, Hannah. I will see you at dinner, all right?" He lowered his head. "I am so sorry, *liebchen.*"

Hannah did not reply. With a reassuring smile, Esther gestured for him to leave the child alone. Heavyhearted, Franz turned and trudged out of the apartment.

On his way out of the building, he almost collided with Heng Zhou, who was hunched under the weight of a gray canvas sack that was slung over his shoulder.

"Good day, Dr. Adler." Heng struggled to lower the

sack to the floor. "Amazing how the same bag of rice gets heavier each year."

Franz wondered where Heng had acquired so much rice—and why—but he thought it rude to ask. "Lifting that sack would surely put me in traction."

Heng smiled. "Your family has settled in well, Herr Doktor?"

"We have, Mr. Zhou. Thank you."

"I am so glad." Heng chuckled softly. "To be truthful, I suspected as much when I heard the street peddlers calling out to Mrs. Adler."

Franz nodded. "She will have them speaking German soon."

Heng laughed again. "I would not be surprised. It amazes me how much more capable women are than men. You are lucky to have her."

"Mrs. Adler is my sister-in-law. A widow. My wife is . . . I am a widower myself."

"Ah." Heng fixed his moist red eyes on Franz. "What a wonderful influence on your daughter Mrs. Adler must still be. Our home is sadly lacking a female presence." Franz wondered if he was about to elaborate on the fate of his wife and daughter, but Heng merely offered another benign grin. "Please do not let me delay you any longer, Dr. Adler."

"Perhaps you and your son might join us for dinner one day soon?" Franz suggested.

"We would be delighted." Heng beamed. "Most delighted."

Franz watched Heng stiffly hoist the sack over his shoulder again and totter for the staircase. "Mr. Zhou, are you sure I cannot assist you?"

"No, no, no," Heng called without looking back. "This is good for my old back and legs."

At the street corner, Franz hailed a rickshaw. "The

Country Hospital," Franz said slowly in English. Digging out his frayed guidebook, he was about to point to the spot he had marked on the map but the driver had already turned, lifted up the handles of the rickshaw, and set off.

Franz had not realized how far west the hospital was. Along the way, they passed sumptuous villas and sprawling gated mansions that could have been plucked from the finest neighborhoods in Europe. The driver must have trotted at least two miles before he slowed to a halt in front of a striking building. Again, defying common practice, Franz tipped the driver handsomely. From the driver's ear-to-ear smile, Franz wondered if he had drastically overpaid; he was still bewildered by the local dual currency and the difference between the "big" and "small" money.

The Country Hospital's Renaissance design reminded Franz far more of a hotel or bank in Vienna's upscale Ring Strasse district than a community hospital. Butterflies filled his chest as he stepped through the columned entrance and into the marble foyer, but the subtle smell of septic cleaners grounded him. Hospitals always had that effect, providing a sense of order and purpose that, for Franz, could not be found in the outside world.

Several people, many wearing lab coats or nursing uniforms, circulated through the foyer. A patient in a wheelchair was registering at the admissions desk. Franz scanned the faces but none matched Clara Reuben's description of her husband. Biding his time, he studied the oil portraits of past medical directors lining the wall. Out of the corner of his eye, he saw movement and turned to see Sunny Mah, her slim frame almost lost under the thick starched apron and bib she wore over her heavy uniform.

Franz was pleased to see someone familiar, especially the likeable young nurse. He considered Sunny's oval face the perfect blend of Western and Eastern features: teardrop eyes, straight nose, angular cheeks, and milky white complexion. But, like other women who had caught his eye since Hilde's death, her beauty was appealing in the same detached sense as a lovely piece of art or music might be. "Good afternoon, Miss Mah," he said in English.

She smiled warmly. "Dr. Adler, do you work at two hospitals now as well?"

"No. At least, not yet. I am here to meet a Dr. Reuben about potential opportunities."

Her shoulders stiffened. "You are acquainted with Dr. Reuben?"

"I have only met his wife, but she was kind enough to facilitate introductions." He frowned. "Miss Mah, didn't you work overnight at the refugee hospital?"

"No one else was available. And Dr. Feinstein was particularly concerned about two of the patients."

"What is that English expression about the burning candles?" he asked.

"Burning the candle at both ends."

"Exactly so." He nodded. "Does sleep not interest you?"

"I am terribly fond of it, Dr. Adler." Sunny smiled again. "I did manage two or three hours last night. The cot in the staff room is quite comfortable."

"They must have changed mattresses since I tried to sleep there two nights ago."

Sunny's face lit. "Dr. Adler, the new surgical equipment is supposed to arrive today!"

"I have scheduled a hernia repair for tomorrow." He spoke matter-of-factly, but inside he bordered on euphoric.

Sunny's smile widened. "You must be very pleased at the thought of returning to the operating room."

He sighed happily. "You have no idea, Miss Mah."

She cleared her throat. "Would you mind, Dr. Adler, if I . . . I were to observe?"

"Mind? On the contrary, I would appreciate your assistance."

"Oh, yes, I would like that. Thank you."

"Dr. Adler?" someone called from halfway across the room.

Franz looked over to see a tall man approaching, his lab coat flapping with each step. Franz recognized Dr. Samuel Reuben by his tortoiseshell glasses and bow tie that fit with his wife's description.

Sunny turned for the staircase. "I had best get back to my ward duties. Good-bye, Dr. Adler," she said over her shoulder.

"Dr. Adler, I hope I did not keep you waiting long." Reuben shook Franz's hand firmly. "I was dealing with a particularly scarred gallbladder that was loath to leave the liver bed."

"They can be such a struggle," Franz said.

"Not so much a struggle, Dr. Adler, as simply meticulous time-intensive work." Reuben's eyelids narrowed, and he pointed a long finger toward the staircase. "Do you know Nurse Mah?"

"We recently met at the refugee hospital."

"Then you have probably already experienced how headstrong she can be," Reuben huffed. "She belongs to *that* breed of nurses. Women who fancy themselves as doctors. Deprived by fate of their rightful calling. I'm sure you have seen the same type in Austria."

"Nurse Mah has struck me as nothing other than capable and caring." Franz was surprised by the sudden surge of protectiveness he felt for her.

"Give her time," Reuben scoffed. "As a result of that gallbladder," he continued, as though the organ were the patient, "I am running late this morning. Would you mind if we chatted while I perform my rounds?"

"Of course not. A pleasure, I am sure."

As Reuben bounded up the two flights of stairs, he recited his own résumé, stressing his medical and surgical training at King's College in London and twice mentioning that he was the chief of surgery. He didn't inquire about Franz's background or experience, but at one point he said, "I understand you held a university position in Vienna."

"Until the Nazis dismissed all Jewish faculty."

"Well, you will soon discover that Shanghai is not Vienna."

They arrived at the men's surgical ward. Franz noticed Sunny attending to a patient on the far side of the room. He tried to catch her eye, but she did not glance in his direction. He wondered if he might have said something earlier to offend her.

Reuben walked over to the first bed, where a pale, middle-aged man with hollow cheeks lay. Reuben grabbed for the chart hanging from the foot of the bed. "Good day, Mr. Fife," he said as he studied the chart. "How are you feeling?"

Fife looked at him with frantic eyes. "About the same as yesterday, I think, Doctor."

Reuben turned to Franz and spoke as though the patient were not present. "Mr. Fife came to me with an advanced cancer of the rectum. The tumor obstructed his bowel and adhered to the pelvic wall. I managed to fashion a very workable colostomy despite the bulk of cancer."

From his fellowship six years earlier at St. Mary's Hospital, Franz was familiar with the British tendency to hold frank discussions in front of patients, but he still felt uneasy.

Reuben pulled back the sheet and, without warning, exposed Fife's abdomen. The odor of feces wafted to them. Wrinkling his nose, Reuben studied the half-full rubber colostomy bag. After a moment, he draped the covers back over Fife's chest and turned to leave.

"Dr. Reuben, excuse me," Fife said tentatively. "Does everything look all right?"

"Mr. Fife, you cannot expect to bounce back so rapidly from a surgery as major as yours," Reuben said with a hint of exasperation. He placed the chart back on the bed railing and moved on. "Have a little patience, man. That's the spirit."

Fife looked crestfallen, but he merely nodded and mumbled, "Thank you, Dr. Reuben."

Moving from bed to bed, Reuben assessed his postoperative patients, cataloguing their histories, surgeries, and prognoses but interacting minimally with the people themselves. Franz saw that Reuben belonged to the class of surgeons who tended toward aggressiveness—the "when in doubt, cut it out" approach that was so common in their profession—but Franz also recognized him as an able diagnostician and surgeon.

They stood at the bedside of the last patient, a young redheaded Scot. "A difficult case, Mr. Stewart," Reuben sighed as he retracted the sheet to expose a bulky dressing over Stewart's right groin. "I have repaired his hernia twice, but the abdominal wall defect is too big and the inguinal ligaments too lax to support the stitches. They keep tearing through. And the hernia has relapsed for a third time."

"May I?" Franz asked.

After Reuben and Stewart nodded their consent, Franz peeled the bandage back to reveal a grapefruit-sized bulge over the right groin, blanketed by a row of stitches. "Which approach did you use, Dr. Reuben?"

"The Bassini approach, of course," Reuben said.

Franz smoothed the bandage back into place. As soon as they had stepped out of the patient's earshot, he said, "A colleague of mine in Vienna showed me how the McVay modification can make a huge difference to the outcome in challenging recurrent hernias such as Mr. Stewart's. I have been astounded by the results."

"Have you indeed?" Reuben said coolly.

"Yes, Dr. McVay described it only four years ago but—" Franz stopped in mid-sentence.

Reuben's cheeks had turned splotchy, and his dark eyes burned behind his glasses. "Dr. Adler, I did not invite you here for a second opinion."

"Of course, I was merely—"

"Nor do we require more staff surgeons at the Country Hospital." Reuben clasped his hands together. "I appreciate that you have come from a more established background in Vienna. However, you and your compatriots have arrived in Shanghai as *refugees*."

"Not by our own choice, I assure you," Franz said, swallowing back his rising indignation.

"Regardless, my wife and I are trying to help as best we can," Reuben went on. "However, you must understand that I am seeking only an assistant to help in surgery and with the postoperative care."

You mean your own intern.

"If you are interested," Reuben continued, "I can pay a wage that—while perhaps not what you are accustomed to—will, I am hopeful, help support your family. However, we have to be crystal clear on the scope of your duties and my expectations. There will be only one lead surgeon between us. Do you understand?"

"I do, Dr. Reuben."

"Are you interested in the position as described, Dr. Adler?"

Franz was not, but he also realized he could not afford to turn down the financial security the job might offer his family. "Yes, I am. Thank you, Dr. Reuben."

"Excellent," Reuben said with a wisp of a smile. "I have to visit my clinic now. I will meet you here tomorrow morning at six thirty." He turned to leave. "Oh, and Dr. Adler, if you don't mind, the nurses are terribly busy. Would you please remove Mr. Fife's colostomy bag and clean him up?"

~ Chapter 19

"I will never get used to this," Wen-Cheng commented as he and Sunny strolled down Rue Montauban toward the North Gate of the Old Chinese City.

Sunny's stomach flipped, assuming Wen-Cheng was referring to their ill-defined relationship. "Used to what?" she asked.

"Visiting a 'Chinatown' in my own country." He pointed toward the maze of buildings ahead of them. The once-walled Old Chinese City was the original site of Shanghai but had since become an open market, largely run to overcharge Shanghailanders and Western tourists who came seeking a glimpse of "authentic" Chinese life.

"Yet you find it perfectly natural that two Chinese people should converse in English in their native country," Sunny said, surprised by her own irritability.

Wen-Cheng laughed. "I realize that Shanghai is not and never will be truly Chinese. I am not a rabid nationalist, but I do find the whole idea of this China-town a little condescending."

"Then why are we here?" she said, more sharply than she had intended.

"Because the Old City is still beautiful in its way. Besides, you can find some of the best tea in China here."

They entered through the gate and continued past the Tsung Woo Day temple. As they walked the long street toward the center of the Old City, they passed numerous sidewalk shops selling everything from ivory, sandalwood, jade, and porcelain to Chinese medicines. The pitches and calls from merchants—"let me show you," "you try," "only a dollar"—filled the air, accompanied by the scratchy chords of Chinese music that emanated from gramophones inside the shops. Some artisans stood out front of the stores, sweating over workbenches as they beat gold into jewelry, stitched silk into fans, or engraved grains of rice.

Happy childhood memories flooded back to Sunny, and she smiled to herself. Wen-Cheng raised an eyebrow. "What is it?"

"I used to love to come here, especially in summer."

"Me too," he agreed. "When the blue canopies are all up like one long tent."

"And the street turns into a bazaar with the jugglers, musicians, and magicians. My father used to bring my best friend, Jia-Li, and me here. He would let us each choose one toy to buy from the toy makers. There were too many options. It was the hardest choice imaginable."

"Perhaps for a child." Wen-Cheng nodded knowingly. "I can think of harder ones now."

Sunny broke off the eye contact. "Are we having tea?" She pointed ahead, where the famous Woo Sing Ding teahouse sat on stone pillars in the middle of a man-made lake. The elegant two-floor, eighteenth-century building—connected to land on either side by distinctive zigzag bridges—was one of the most identifiable and visited tourist sites in Shanghai.

"I thought we could walk the gardens first. Unless, of course, you prefer tea now?"

They circled the picturesque teahouse and headed toward the entrance to Yuyuan Garden. The market's noise died away as they stepped inside. The walled gardens consisted of reflecting pools, rockeries, and lacquered pavilions that were connected by bridges and walkways. The tranquility of the place always put Sunny in a pensive, almost spiritual, mood. With no one in sight, they stopped on the terrace of a pavilion overlooking a pond. Across the water stood the garden's celebrated rockery that jutted twenty feet up the north wall, resembling a choir cut of stone figures.

Wen-Cheng pointed to it. "Five hundred years ago, they dragged those rocks here from thousands of miles away. It is supposed to recall the peaks, caves, and gorges of southern China."

"I have never been there," Sunny muttered to herself.

"I have. I don't remember any caves or gorges." He shrugged. "Did you know that these gardens were built in the sixteenth century by a high-ranking official in the Ming dynasty, just so his father could have a quiet place to meditate?"

"I would do the same for my father," Sunny blurted.

Wen-Cheng's brown eyes shone. "He is a lucky man, your father."

"Not necessarily." She broke free of his gaze. "A more dutiful daughter would not dream of coming here with you."

"Now you sound like a traditional girl with bound feet," he said laughingly. "I thought you possessed more of your American mother's 'free spirit.'"

"My mother came to China as a Christian missionary," she snapped. "I doubt she would have accepted *our* circumstances any more than my father might."

He held up his hands. "Sunny, I meant no offense."

Sunny accepted his apology with a single nod. For the next few minutes, they stared wordlessly into the green pond below, watching the carp skim under the water's surface. Wen-Cheng finally broke the silence. "How are things at that refugee hospital?"

"They manage somehow."

"Are you running low on any provisions?"

"We are running low on everything, I am sure. Keeping the apothecary supplied is always a challenge, particularly for the sulfa antibiotics."

Wen-Cheng squinted, deep in thought. "I know where I can borrow some more medications and dressings for you."

"*Borrow?*" Sunny frowned. "You are not risking trouble to get us these supplies?"

Wen-Cheng shook his head. "I want to do this. For you, Sunny. I know how much it means to you." He tilted his head. "There is something I do not quite understand, though."

She braced for another intimate inquiry. "Oh?"

"There is so much poverty and need here among the local Chinese. The coolies, the beggars, the sampan families . . . Why do you choose to work at a Jewish refugee hospital?"

She shrugged. "They are in need too, Wen-Cheng."

"I realize," he said. "Why them in particular? Why cross the bridge every day and face the insults and taunts from the *Rìběn guǎzi*"—he used the Shanghainese pejorative for "Japanese devils"—"for people you do not know and have no connection to?"

She hesitated a moment. "The hospital is so basic and the need so great. And I speak their language. I love my work at the Country Hospital, but I am one of many nurses there. At the refugee hospital, sometimes I am the *only* nurse on duty."

"You must be a huge help to them."

"There is more to it, Wen-Cheng. Those refugees . . . they don't belong here."

"Why not?" he asked. "Shanghai already has an established Jewish population."

"Yes, but the German refugees are not like the other Jews. They don't call Shanghai home. They don't even have a home. They're outcasts." Her voice dropped to near a whisper. "I know a little about how it feels not to belong."

Wen-Cheng stared at her for a long moment. He reached out and laid his hands on her shoulders. Sunny did not resist as he pulled her closer. His warm breath tickled her face as his lips skittered across her cheek. She hungered for the taste of his mouth and the feel of his body pressed against her, but just as his lips touched hers, the cold reality of their circumstances doused her arousal. She stepped back and wriggled free of his grip.

Wen-Cheng looked down at his hands as though he had dropped something. "Sunny?"

"We can't!"

His hands fell to his side. "I love you, and I thought . . ."

"None of that matters," Sunny said, her voice catching in her throat. "Not when you are still married."

"I am trying, Sunny, but it's not easy," he said. "My wife's family has been friends with mine for generations. My father and her father—"

"*Enough!*" She had heard the same rationalization too many times before. Frustrated and disappointed with herself for letting things reach this point again, she wheeled and ran off.

Sunny did not slow down until she reached the gates of the Old City. Burying her cold hands in her coat pockets, she marched along Rue du Consulat and turned north at the Bund. Awash with a contradictory mix of regret and self-reproach, she strode along the riverside promenade, ignoring the Whangpoo's swarming boat traffic on one side of her and the Bund's rumbling automobile congestion on the other.

Sunny finally calmed as she neared the neoclassical Hongkong and Shanghai Bank, which was nicknamed the "Jewel of the Bund." She slowed to watch several Chinese men and women rub the manes of the sculpted bronze lions that guarded its columned entrance in the belief that the contact would bring them luck. Though cynical of such superstition, Sunny was half-tempted to rub the lions herself. But luck was not the issue. What she needed was more restraint and a far less entangled relationship.

Sunny was still mulling over the conversation with Wen-Cheng when she arrived at the doors of the refugee hospital. As soon as she stepped inside, Simon called to her gleefully, "Today's the day, Sunny!"

"Has the ether arrived?" she asked.

"The whole shebang—mask, medicine, everything!" Simon laughed as he caught up to her in the hallway. "You should see Dr. Adler. He's like a kid in a candy store."

"I can imagine."

Simon squinted at her. "Sunny, what is it?"

She shook her head. "Nothing."

"Sunny, it's me." He tapped his chest with both hands. "The nosy Jew from the Bronx. I can tell something is eating at you."

She considered unloading her romantic quandary on Simon, but it felt too fresh and raw to broach. "I didn't sleep well last night."

"A bad sleep? That's why you look like you've just seen a ghost?"

"Can we please just go see Dr. Adler?"

They found Franz and Max Feinstein standing inside the newly built operating room. The room had the same plain walls and cement floor as the rest of the old, converted schoolhouse, but it boasted a new steel gurney and a rolling light with multiple bulbs. A heavy-set middle-aged man lay on the stretcher with a sheet pulled up to his shoulders. Someone had laid out a tray of shiny new surgical tools on the adjacent table.

Max looked uncomfortable in his white gown and surgical cap, while Franz appeared relaxed and authoritative in his. He beamed at Sunny and Simon. "Oh, wonderful, Miss Mah." He turned to the patient with a wave of his hand. "We can begin now, Mr. Kornfeld."

Sunny had never seen Franz as enthused. "Certainly, Dr. Adler. I will go scrub and gown straight away."

Franz nodded. "Miss Mah, it has been a while since Dr. Feinstein was last in the operating theater—"

"*Decades!*" Max corrected, clutching his head in his hands.

Laughing, Franz pointed to the mask and bottle marked ETHER lying on the far end of the table. "I was hoping you might provide the anesthesia. Have you ever done so?"

"Yes." Her heart skipped a beat. Sunny had been trained to administer the anesthetic gas, but at the Country Hospital the junior doctors always assumed the role of anesthetist.

Sunny gowned and scrubbed at the sink outside the operating room. By the time she returned, Max and

Franz were both masked and gloved and the patient draped for surgery. They had been joined by another nurse, Berta Abeldt, who was large-boned, with a ruddy complexion and friendly eyes.

Franz turned to the patient. "Are you ready to begin, Mr. Kornfeld?"

"I was ready a year ago," Kornfeld moaned.

Franz looked at Sunny and nodded; the mask over his mouth couldn't conceal his broad smile. She gently applied the pear-shaped fabric mask over Kornfeld's nose and mouth. She held the can of ether five or six inches from the mask and carefully tipped the spout. The liquid dropped in a steady patter onto the fabric. As soon as the sweet acrid smell of the anesthetic vapor reached her nose, she righted the can.

Kornfeld's eyes remained wide open, but his cheeks began to flush. Sunny dribbled more ether onto the mask. "Deep breaths, Mr. Kornfeld," she encouraged.

The patient's eyelids fluttered and then slowly drifted shut. She counted to ten and then ran her finger across his eyelashes without eliciting a blink. "He is asleep, Dr. Adler."

"Good work, Miss Mah!" Franz turned to the scrub nurse. "Scalpel please, Mrs. Abeldt."

Berta passed Franz the scalpel. He applied the blade to the crease of Kornfeld's groin and, with the precision of a watchmaker, sliced steadily along the skin.

Peering over Franz's shoulder, Max chuckled. "It must feel good to be operating again, does it not, Dr. Adler?"

Franz glanced over at Sunny with another barely contained grin. "Like returning home after a long, hard journey." His smile faded and he looked away. "Of course, I am not really home at all, am I? I wonder if I ever will be."

Chapter 20

Franz sat alone at the kitchen table, a cup of jasmine tea in front of him. Esther had gone to the market, Hannah was visiting Natasha upstairs, and Ernst, as usual, was absent without explanation. Franz was enjoying the rare solitude. As much as he loved his family, the four of them were living in a space not much larger than his old bedroom. Privacy had become a rare and precious commodity.

Franz was still basking in the afterglow of having completed his first surgery in Shanghai. The operation couldn't have been more basic, but he felt revitalized to have his hands busy with the work he loved. He imagined performing all kinds of surgeries, despite the refugee hospital's rudimentary facilities. Perhaps nothing as complex or challenging as his procedures at the Vienna General Hospital, but he would work as a surgeon again. It meant the world to him, particularly in light of the demeaning role he had fallen into at the Country Hospital.

Only three days into his new job as Samuel Reuben's assistant, he dreaded the thought of a fourth. To have landed a medical position with a steady, albeit modest, income within weeks of landing in Shanghai was more than he had expected. However, between his wounded pride and Reuben's determination to turn him into a kowtowing orderly, Franz found it impossible to feel as grateful for their good fortune as his sister-in-law seemed to be.

Esther concealed most of her bereavement behind her usual poise. However, the day before at the refugee hospital, Franz had stumbled upon a rare display of her devastation. Esther had accompanied him to work to help prepare patients' meals after the regular cook, Mrs. Beerman, had fallen ill with a head cold. After finishing rounds, Franz headed into the small kitchen to collect her. As he stepped through the doorway, he spotted Simon and Esther beside the sink. Her back turned to Franz, Esther stood clutching her face, her body trembling with sobs. Simon had one hand lightly draped over her shoulder while he murmured words of encouragement. Franz heard Simon say, "And what about your niece? Seems to me you're as close to a mother as Hannah will ever know."

Esther wiped at her eyes and mumbled something that Franz could not catch.

Simon chuckled. "Ah, it's nothing. I bawl like a hungry newborn when my Yankees are losing."

Esther laughed through her tears. Simon looked over and made eye contact with Franz. Smiling grimly, he silently reassured Franz that he had the situation under control. Franz backed out of the room without Esther ever having been aware of his presence.

A succession of raps on the door pulled Franz from the memory. He was surprised to find Ensign Luigi Comparelli standing at the threshold. After a warm handshake, Franz led the ensign into the apartment. "I assumed you and the *Conte Biancamano* would be well on your way back home by now."

"Not for another week." Luigi swept his hand through the air. "We only just returned from a cruise to Hong Kong."

"How did you find us, Luigi?"

"Ah, Dr. Adler, I am a terrific, how do you say . . . detective!" He seemed proud of himself for producing the word. "I went to see the Jewish organization at the port, where they pick up the new arrivals. I spoke to an American gentleman, who was most helpful." He grinned, amused. "That man . . . he loves to talk even more than most Italians."

"Simon, of course." Franz chuckled.

Luigi looked around the room. "Where is the beautiful little *principessa*?"

"Upstairs playing at a friend's apartment. Shall I go get her?"

Luigi waved his hand in front of him. "No, please, do not disturb her. I have little time." He frowned. "I miss her, your daughter. The ship's pool is not the same without little Hannah. Is she doing all right in Shanghai, you know, with her . . ."

Luigi's concern touched Franz. "She is a tough one. We still have to find her a school in the new year, but she has embraced Shanghai as a whole new adventure."

"*Buono.* I think she will go far, that one."

"I hope so, Luigi. Do you have time for tea?"

"No, *grazie.* I must get back to the ship." Luigi dug inside his coat pocket, withdrawing a small envelope. A sheepish expression crossed his face as he held it out for Franz. "A telegram for you, Dr. Adler."

"For me?" Franz frowned. "From where?"

"It came through the shipping line's central office." Luigi cleared his throat. "I believe it is from Vienna."

Franz could tell from the ensign's uneasy stance alone that it contained bleak news. "Thank you, Luigi," he muttered, "for going to such effort to bring this to me."

"It was my pleasure, really." Luigi edged toward the door. "Please give Mrs. Adler and Mr. Muhler my best wishes. The *signora,* she is well? Not so sad anymore?"

"Mrs. Adler is doing better, thank you," Franz said distractedly.

Luigi smiled again. "And, of course, a big hug for my *principessa*."

After Luigi left, Franz wandered over to the chest of drawers where he had deposited his father's letter, still unopened. He took it back to the table, along with a paring knife, and laid both envelopes side by side. He reached first for the telegram and carefully sliced the top open. He unfolded the single page and saw that the message had been transmitted two days earlier.

Dear Dr. Adler,

I am saddened to advise that your father passed away the night before last. I was able to cancel his berth on the Bingo Maru and am holding the refund in trust for you.

With deepest condolences.
Julius Rolf

Franz lifted Jakob's letter from the table and tore open the envelope. His hand shook as he read his father's familiar handwriting.

Dear Franz,

I realize you doubted my final promise, spoken the day we last met. Please know that I did hope to join you in Shanghai. However, my tired old lungs have stubbornly refused to cooperate. It would be futile for me to attempt the journey now.

To be frank, my son, I do not see myself lasting many more days in this condition. Do not despair. Take solace in knowing that I am prepared, eager might not even be too strong a word, to depart this world. While I refuse to conveniently embrace religion at this late hour, somehow I believe that I will soon be nearer to Karl and my dear daughter-in-law Hilde, and, of course, your beloved mother. The prospect brings me much comfort.

I have lived a full life. Even as I write this letter, I am comforted by so many wonderful memories of us all. I consider myself fortunate to have witnessed this tragic turn in Austrian history at the end of my life. I think of the little ones who have no past and, now, no future. And your brother, cheated out of the rest of the rich life that he and Essie deserved together. However, to know that you have led Esther and Hannah thousands of miles beyond the clutches of these savages provides me relief and peace beyond description.

My son, please remember that the best revenge is to live a long, full, and happy existence. Raise Hannah Ruth to be proud of her heritage. Show them that we can rise above their hatred and their bullying. They will not last, but it is imperative that we endure. Embrace your grandchildren.

I realize that in this current madness, legal considerations are moot. However, I have been a lawyer too long not to tell you that I have drawn up a will. I have given my furniture and clothes to Frau Weiss and her husband. They have taken good care of me since my Elise died. You will understand that I have given my watch to their son Rolf. I fear that you will not be home to collect it for yourself.

The one regret I will take with me is not having told you often or convincingly enough how very proud I am of you. My part in bringing Karl and you into this world so eclipses any other small contributions I might have made that they do not bear mentioning. You have no idea how much respect and affection I hold for you in my heart.

With my love and devotion,
Father

Franz's chest ached as he stared at his father's words. However, he found a sliver of solace in knowing that time and illness had taken Jakob peacefully, and he no longer had to worry that his father might suffer the same brutal fate as the Yacobsens.

My mother, my wife, my brother, and now my father . . .

He was still staring at the letter when the apartment door swung open and Esther entered carrying a canvas bag full of groceries. The moment she saw him, she dropped the bag to the floor. "What is it, Franz?" she breathed.

He stood up and walked over to her with the telegram extended.

Esther took it from his hand and glanced down at it. *"Az och un vai,"* she murmured in Yiddish. Her eyes misted over. "Oh, Franz."

He put his arms around Esther and drew her into a hug. After a long silent moment, he finally said, "It's just us now, Essie."

～ Chapter 21

Franz had spent most of the day at the Country Hospital changing bandages and administering enemas to constipated postoperative patients, but he was numb to Reuben's latest degradations. Three days after learning of Jakob's death, Franz thought of little else. It revived the pain of Karl's loss, and he found himself thinking more of Hilde than he had in a very long time.

As Franz neared home on foot, he spied Ernst standing outside their building, beside another man. Franz slowed to ensure that his friend was aware of his approach. He recognized the lean young man as Heng Zhou's son but struggled to recall his name.

"Franz, you remember Shan?" Ernst rarely spoke English, though he had spent time in Philadelphia and Toronto for exhibitions of his artwork and was more fluent than he let on.

Franz bowed his head. "Good day, Shan."

Shan nodded slightly but said nothing.

"Shan speaks little German, so I am practicing my English." Ernst sighed. "Chinese is optional in this city, but you're absolutely sunk without a firm grasp of English."

Franz turned to Shan. "You are not a linguist like your father?"

"Shan is an electricity engineer," Ernst answered for him.

"Electrical engineer," Shan corrected softly.

Ernst chuckled out a stream of smoke. "Science is lost on me. I have the mathematical capacity of a half-witted chicken."

"Fortunately, you paint," Franz pointed out.

Ernst took another long drag of his cigarette. "Speaking of, Franz, would you mind if I were to set up an easel in our flat?"

Franz had not heard Ernst mention painting since Vienna. "Are you going back to work?"

Ernst shrugged. "I've found a new inspiration."

"Shanghai?" Franz asked.

Ernst made a face. "God, no!"

"What then?"

"Nanking." The flippancy left Ernst's tone, and he lowered his voice. "Were you aware of what happened there last winter?"

"Only vaguely."

Ernst shook his head. "Shan was there. His stories . . . they are beyond belief."

Shan showed no response. "It must have been horrific," Franz mumbled.

"Beyond horrific! Tens of thousands of civilians massacred, including women and children." Ernst shuddered. "They went from door to door. Ravaging and murdering like they were delivering newspapers."

Franz stole another glance at Shan. *Were your mother and sister among the victims?* But Shan's impassive stare seemed welded to his face.

"Tell Franz about that . . . contest," Ernst urged him.

Shan brought his cigarette to his lips. "You tell him."

"Two Japanese soldiers decided to hold a contest," Ernst explained. "To see who could kill a hundred people the fastest with those hideous Japanese swords!"

"Samurai swords," Franz offered.

"*Ja, ja.*" Franz was so inflamed he reverted to German. "They lined up the innocent people and chopped away, like it was . . . I don't know . . . a kind of deranged woodcutters' race. And the Japanese journalists reported the whole macabre spectacle. Like it was all great sport. Both soldiers killed a hundred people. They . . ." He turned to Shan and switched back to English. "What did they call it to break the tie?"

"Extra innings," Shan said softly.

"Extra innings, *ja*!" Ernst cringed. "Some kind of American baseball term. They . . . Franz, they just kept murdering people to see who was better with a blade."

Franz thought of his own brother's senseless murder.

"And the rest of the world didn't even take notice," Ernst continued. "Yet we've all heard about the atrocities committed during the Spanish Civil War, haven't we?"

"That was closer to home," Franz said.

"Perhaps. But I think people remember Spain because of all the writers and artists who flocked to the cause. Art raised awareness about that war. My God, Picasso eternalized the massacre in Guernica with one mural!"

Franz raised an eyebrow. "And you want to do the same for Nanking?"

"Someone has to!"

"We're encircled by the Japanese army, Ernst. Do you think it wise to incite them?"

Ernst grimaced. "Franz, where are your principles? What would Karl have said?"

"I have no idea," Franz snapped. "All I know is that they strung Karl from a lamppost for sticking to his principles."

"Shanghai is not Vienna," Ernst said, unmoved. "Do you see any Japanese soldiers in Frenchtown?"

Franz had heard enough. "The Reubens are expecting us for dinner soon," he said as he cut past them and into the building.

Upstairs, Hannah and Esther were already dressed for the outing. Appearing uneasy in her formal navy jacket and skirt, Esther kept fiddling with the angle of her gray velvet evening hat. Franz's heart melted at the sight of his daughter in a powder blue frock and her hair tied back. She had outgrown her only winter dress; the sleeves were a little short. He could see the muscle wasting in her left wrist, but it only made her more precious in his eyes.

"Such beautiful women!" Franz said, clutching his chest.

"Oh, Papa, you're silly!" Hannah giggled. "This dress is too scratchy."

"Fineries are for show, not for comfort, *liebchen*."

"Will there be other children there, Papa?"

"I am not certain," he said. "The Reubens do not have children of their own."

"Do I have to go, Papa? Mrs. Reuben . . ." Hannah looked down at her scuffed black shoes. "She squeezes my cheek until it hurts."

"Mrs. Reuben is trying to secure you a place in a wonderful new school, Hannah," Esther said. "We should be most grateful to her."

Hannah nodded dutifully. Franz went off to the bedroom to change into his navy suit. By the time he emerged, Ernst had joined them, wearing a black jacket over his open-collared black shirt. The two men exchanged nods, neither acknowledging their earlier disagreement.

Outside, Franz spotted the Reubens' black Daimler idling at the curb and they climbed inside. In the light evening traffic, they made it to Grosvenor House in less than ten minutes. Reuben had once boasted that his apartment building in the heart of the French Concession's most desirable neighborhood was "the epitome of Gothic–art deco union." Even in the darkness, Franz had to concede that Grosvenor House, which resembled a gigantic upright bat with spread wings, was an impressive piece of architecture.

The doorman led them to an elevator, where another Chinese attendant, dressed entirely in white, escorted them to the twentieth floor. A fair-skinned butler, immaculately dressed in tails and white gloves, met them at the door of the Reubens' suite. He took their coats and led them into a parlor that was more than twice the size of the Adlers' apartment.

From his first day at the Country Hospital, Franz had heard Reuben speak of his family's deep roots in the British Shanghailander community. Even Reuben's mother, a German Jew who emigrated to Shanghai with her family in the 1880s, came from privilege. Franz had imagined that the Reubens would have an imposing home, but the spacious flat with its ornate furniture and dramatic city views exceeded even his expectations.

Clara Reuben swept toward them wearing a long, snug black gown that accentuated rather than concealed her fullness. "Ah, the Adler family! And Herr Muhler. How wonderful you could join us on the first evening of Hanukkah."

Franz had almost forgotten that they had come to celebrate the Jewish holiday. "Thank you so very much for inviting us."

"Come, come," Clara said. "I want you to meet the others."

Samuel Reuben stood beside the fireplace with a tumbler of Scotch in hand. He was conversing with a shorter Asian man who had graying hair and a Clark Gable mustache. In his finely tailored black suit, the man exuded an air of quiet authority. Beside him, a slender young woman stood statue-still in an elegant but simple blue dress. With drawn cheeks and a long forehead, she wasn't a classical beauty but neither was she unattractive. Her small, frail features and alert pale eyes gave her a fawn-like presence.

"Excuse me, my dear," Clara said, swooping in and interrupting her husband in mid-sentence. "I was hoping to introduce our guests." She held a hand out to the Asian man. "Colonel Tsutomo Kubota is a senior leader in the new Shanghai government."

Kubota bowed deeply. "With respect, Mrs. Reuben." He spoke in a refined British accent. "I am not a member of the municipal Chinese government at all. I am merely one of my government's advisers to Lord Mayor Fu Xiaoan."

Ernst's lip twitched, and Franz braced for a caustic remark, but none came.

"Colonel Kubota is being as modest as ever. We've all seen the battleships in the harbor. We know who really controls Shanghai." Clara clutched Kubota's arm affectionately. "We befriended the colonel years ago through our mutual club, Cercle Sportif Français." She turned to the woman in the blue dress. "And this, of course, is our lovely niece, Charlotte Weczel. Her parents—my eldest sister and her husband—passed away in an automobile accident when Lotte was only twelve. Lotte is like the daughter Samuel and I never had."

The young woman smiled shyly and made eye contact with Hannah only.

Clara introduced Ernst and the Adlers, stressing Franz's role as her husband's assistant. The butler served drinks: wine for Franz and Esther, a martini for Ernst, and pineapple juice for Hannah. Self-conscious about her limited English and thick accent, Esther hardly spoke. Ernst was also surprisingly subdued, but Franz watched his friend's steady consumption of martinis with growing alarm.

Hannah clung closely to Esther's side while the Reubens carried most of the conversation. Clara went to pains to position her niece near Franz and tried, at every turn, to engage them in conversation, which was awkward since Lotte was so timid. At one point, Clara said, "Dr. Adler, were you aware that Lotte is an accomplished cellist?"

"I was not," Franz said, turning to Lotte. "Do you perform often, Miss Weczel?"

"Very rarely, Dr. Adler," Lotte said in a small voice.

"She was offered a position in the Shanghai Symphony Orchestra," Clara announced. "But our Lotte does not like to appear on stage."

Lotte glanced at Franz but did not maintain eye contact. "I find it difficult to play in front of larger audiences."

Franz smiled. "If I possessed an ounce of musical talent, I'm sure I would feel the same."

"It's a shame about the stage fright." Clara sighed. "All the rehearsals and training we saw her through. Still, it hasn't completely gone to waste. Lotte teaches music at the Shanghai Jewish School." She looked meaningfully at Franz. "If all works out, Lotte might just be teaching your little Hannah."

The butler appeared at the doorway and intoned, "Dinner is served."

Starched white linen covered the long dining table. Each place setting was laid with gold-rimmed china, sparkling crystal, and polished silverware. Name cards dictated the seating arrangements. Clara and Samuel sat at opposite ends of the table and, as Franz expected, he was seated beside Lotte.

A menorah, with two unlit candles, stood in the center of the table as the sole reminder of the religious holiday they had come to celebrate. The sight of the eight-branched candelabra rekindled bittersweet memories for Franz. His father never showed any interest in religious rites, but his mother had insisted on hosting an annual family Hanukkah dinner. The joyous gift-giving affairs were effectively secular substitutes for the Christmas dinners that their Gentile friends held. After their mother's death, Karl and Esther continued the tradition, adding more of a religious flavor, while maintaining the celebratory mood.

Two female Chinese servers materialized and filled glasses with wine or, in Hannah's case, more juice. Everyone stood while Clara used the *shamash,* or lighting candle, to ignite the first candle in the row that symbolized each of Hanukkah's eight nights. She recited a short Hebrew prayer over the candles and then turned expectantly to her husband. Reuben fidgeted with his glass as he muttered the Hebrew prayer of thanks for the wine. "All right then," he announced, indicating with obvious relief that the abbreviated ceremonial portion of the evening had ended. "Shall we eat?"

The two servers reappeared, carrying plates laden with deep-fried potato pancakes. The rich scent of the latkes set Franz's stomach rumbling. Covered in applesauce, the latkes tasted even better than they smelled. Franz would have liked a second helping, but the servers swept away the dishes, refilled the glasses, and soon returned with heaping plates of beef brisket, potatoes, and winter vegetables. After the main course, the attendants served a dessert of surprisingly delicious apple strudel—"in honor of our Austrian guests," Clara declared.

Hannah was excused to the parlor to read her book when the servers brought out port glasses and served the dessert wine. Only Samuel accepted a cigar from the case that was offered by one of the attendants, while Ernst lit one of his own cigarettes.

Kubota turned to the artist. "Mr. Muhler, I once attended an exhibit of Gustav Klimt's work and was most impressed. I am embarrassed to admit that I am not familiar with other Austrian painters. Forgive my ignorance, but is your work at all similar to Klimt's?"

Ernst viewed Kubota for a long moment before answering. "Oh, Colonel, I suspect you're familiar with at least one other Austrian painter. He has never been particularly talented, but your government seems to be fond of his work."

Kubota frowned. "Who would that be?"

Ernst lifted his glass. "Adolf Hitler."

The table went silent. Clara shot Ernst a withering stare. "I would ask, Mr. Muhler, that you never mention *that* man in my home again."

Kubota eyed Ernst with curiosity but did not appear insulted. "Neither his artwork nor his politics intrigue me in the least, Mr. Muhler. I would, however, like to hear about your art."

"Much as I admire Klimt, my work is nothing like his." Ernst considered it for a moment. "If I had to apply a label, I would choose 'spartan realism.'"

"Yes," Franz agreed, hoping to steer his friend away from politics. "Ernst has a gift for capturing the beauty of frailty and vice versa."

"'The beauty of frailty'? Such nonsense, Franz. You sound just like an art dealer now." Ernst guffawed, then turned back to Kubota. "There is no point in trying to describe my art. You have to see it to form an opinion. However, I am most interested to discuss your work."

"Mr. Muhler, my work is painfully mundane compared with yours." Kubota smiled. "Despite my military title, I am simply a bureaucrat. A low-level diplomat, if you will."

"Oh, Tsutomo, enough with the humility," Reuben piped up from the far end of the table, pointing with his lit cigar. "Colonel Kubota here is a very influential man in Shanghai."

"No doubt," Ernst said. "But I am still not entirely clear as to why a Japanese colonel should hold so much sway in a Chinese city."

Esther glanced at Franz, imploring him to intervene. He cleared his throat. "Colonel, my avant-garde friend is a born firebrand." He forced a laugh. "Do not fall into his trap."

"Come now, Franz, let the man speak," Ernst said in German, slurring his words slightly.

Kubota nodded pleasantly. "Mr. Muhler, as you have probably already noticed, the English and French hold a fair degree of sway—as you put it—in Shanghai as well."

"Maybe so, but I have not seen any of the bomb damage their planes left behind."

Reuben began to rise from his seat. "See here, Muhler, I think that's quite enough."

Kubota waved Reuben back into his chair. He turned back to the artist. "Mr. Muhler, it is difficult to boil a thousand years of history down to a single act or incident."

"Please." Ernst held out his hand theatrically. "Enlighten me."

"All right, I will try." Kubota looked as placid as ever. "Are you aware that China has been at war since long before the first Japanese bomb fell? For almost thirty years, to be exact."

Ernst frowned. "At war?"

"Yes, Mr. Muhler, a civil war." Kubota went on to explain that the Republic of China had been established in 1911 after the Qing dynasty imploded under the weight of its own bloated bureaucracy. Weak from the outset, the new republic was, at best, a regional force based in the south, which led to constant skirmishes among the factions. In the 1920s, Generalissimo Chiang Kai-shek and his Kuomintang nationalists consolidated their power base within the republic and made some gains in the north. Chiang then turned violently on his former allies, the Communists, and launched a full-scale civil war.

Ernst tilted his head. "How does any of this concern Japan, Colonel?"

Annoyed, Samuel puffed out rings of smoke, while his wife fussed with her starched napkin. Lotte stared off into space. Esther continued to try to discourage Ernst with disapproving glances, but to no avail.

"China is our closest neighbor," Kubota said. "The stability of our entire region depends on a strong, unified China. Her instability is a great threat to my country." He brought his hands together in front of his chest, fingertips touching as though in prayer. "I greatly admire China and her people. In truth, my career was inspired by the words of one of the greatest Chinese nationalists, Dr. Sun Yat-sen. Are you familiar with him?"

"Only the name."

"Sun was the first president of China. Fifteen years ago, I was fortunate to be in the audience in Kobe when he gave his brilliant speech on pan-Asianism. Sun praised the Japanese resistance to Western imperialism. He lauded Japan for her 'Rule of Right' as opposed to the West's 'Rule of Might.'" Kubota pulled his hands apart. "I was schooled at Cambridge, Mr. Muhler. And while I might be an unrepentant anglophile, I am also a proud Asian. Dr. Sun's vision of a strong, independent Asia—those words he spoke that day—shaped my future."

Ernst smiled pleasantly, but Franz recognized the glint of outrage in his eyes. "I think we have probably covered enough politics—" Franz began.

"Those are lovely sentiments, Colonel," Ernst cut him off. "Poetic, even. But does your nation's desire for a unified China somehow justify the massacre in Nanking?"

Chapter 22

Sunny stood close to the operating table so she could keep an eye on the patient and pass her the bucket as needed. The twenty-seven-year-old woman, Golda Hiltmann, was restless on the gurney, groggy and retching from the ether.

Franz decided to wait another few minutes, until Mrs. Hiltmann had roused more fully, before sending her to the ward. Sunny did not mind. She was enjoying his company and still aglow from the life-saving procedure they had just performed.

Sunny looked over at him. "Dr. Adler, if it were not for this new operating room—and you, of course— Mrs. Hiltmann never would have . . ."

Franz motioned to the pile of blood-encrusted utensils. "Any surgeon could have performed that procedure. But, Miss Mah, *you* are the one who diagnosed the ectopic pregnancy."

"It was terribly obvious." Sunny fought back a grin. "A woman ten weeks pregnant who shows up with left-sided abdominal pain and light-headedness? Only a ruptured pregnancy outside the womb could be responsible."

"You don't give yourself enough credit."

But Sunny was bursting with pride. She could not wait to tell her father how she had made the diagnosis, managed the ether, and even, at Franz's insistence, stitched the abdomen closed. Despite all Kingsley's quizzes, Sunny had never felt closer to being a doctor.

Mrs. Hiltmann stirred and lifted her head off the bed, only to retch again into the bucket before flopping her head back onto the bed.

Sunny reddened, embarrassed at how pleased she was to be confined to the patient's bedside with Franz. "Thank you for letting me be involved, Dr. Adler."

"Nonsense. I relied on your help."

"I appreciate the opportunity to learn from you. You treat me more like a colleague than any doctor ever has before."

Franz looked down at the blood spray on his gown. "It's good to have someone to teach again. It used to be one of the great pleasures of working at the university hospital."

"You must have been a popular teacher."

"You would have to ask my students," he said, shrugging. "Sunny, you are already as capable as most junior doctors. I could teach you to be a surgeon, you know. Of course, only if you were interested."

Overjoyed, she burst out laughing.

"Did I say something funny?" he asked.

"My father has never wanted anything more than for me to be a doctor, but a surgeon?"

"I see." Franz smiled. "Is he one of those physicians who believe surgeons are only one rung higher than trained monkeys?"

"Not quite." She shook her head. "I do think he sees more of a challenge on the internal medicine side."

"Your father reminds me a little of my own," he said.

"Is he a doctor as well?"

"He was a lawyer, but he was always very supportive of my career." Franz began sorting through the soiled instruments. "He died last week. In Vienna."

"Oh, Dr. Adler, I am sorry."

"Thank you," he said without raising his gaze from the tray. "It was for the best, really."

"It must be difficult to be so far away at such a time."

Franz dropped a retractor and looked up at her with

tortured eyes. "Papa wouldn't come with us, Sunny. He couldn't, he was too sick. And I couldn't stay. I had to get my daughter out."

Sunny interlocked her fingers, resisting the urge to reach out and touch him. "I'm sure he understood."

"I think so, but sometimes . . ."

The patient stirred again and tried to sit up. "Is the operation over?" she slurred.

"Yes, Mrs. Hiltmann." Franz squeezed her shoulder lightly. "All went well. You will still be able to have babies."

"*Got sie dank. Danke, danke,* Dr. Adler!" Her voice cracked. "I cannot thank you enough for this mitzvah!"

Franz removed his hand. "Miss Mah is the one who saved your life. She recognized your condition and alerted me."

"Yes, of course." Hiltmann clasped Sunny's hand between her damp, trembling fingers. "Thank you so much, Miss Mah."

"Mrs. Hiltmann, you are most welcome."

Franz and Sunny shared a restrained but warm good-bye on the ward. On her way out, Sunny ran into Simon in the hallway. He was lugging an oxygen tank and whistling a slightly off-key Gershwin tune that she finally recognized as "I Got Rhythm."

As busy as work with the CFA committee kept Simon, he spent his free time at the refugee hospital helping out with maintenance, supplies, and administrative tasks. Despite his endless jokes about the building's dilapidated state, he wore his pride in the hospital as prominently as his favorite fedora.

Simon beamed at her. "The rumor going around is that Dr. Adler and you just stole one right out of the Grim Reaper's catching mitt."

"Catching mitt?" Sunny frowned.

Simon chuckled. "You and the doc just cheated death."

Sunny sighed. "You have a flair for dramatics, Simon."

"Well . . . did you?"

She shrugged. "The patient was in grave condition, but the surgery went well."

Simon threw his hands up. "Jeez, Sunny, you're too Chinese and too American to sound so darned British all the time."

Sunny laughed. "I suppose we did save the patient's life. Then again, so did you."

He grimaced. "*Me?*"

"It would have all been for naught had you not supplied us with new surgical equipment."

"I guess," he said. "Still, we ought to give some credit to Sir Victor too. After all, he coughed up the dough."

"Maybe, but, Simon, you built this hospital with your own sweat and tears."

Simon's smile widened. "Oh, Sunny, if only you were Jewish . . . and a Yankees fan . . ."

Laughing, Sunny glanced at the clock on the wall: 8:35. "I am late to meet my father."

"What's the hurry? He usually drops in when he gets here, anyway."

"Not tonight. We have to go home to decorate the Christmas tree."

"You're Christian? I assumed your father would be . . ."

"My father's family is Taoist," she explained. "But my mother was a Methodist. She came to China as a missionary. My father converted to the same faith before their marriage. We've tried to keep the Christmas celebrations alive in her memory. It was her favorite time of year."

"Ah." Simon nodded knowingly. "Mixed religions. If

it's anything like the States, I am guessing there were four unhappy parents when your mom and dad tied the knot."

"My mother's parents disowned her. They have never even acknowledged me. And then she died and they . . . they did not even attend her funeral. Their own daughter." She swallowed. "My father's father was already dead, but his mother was no more accepting. Mu was always good to me, but she did not speak to my father for almost five years, even while she lived with us. My aunt, his own sister, shunned him too."

"Good old religion," Simon groaned. "It truly is the great divider, huh?"

"Only if people let it be."

"They always do seem to let it be." Simon lifted up the oxygen tank. "I better get this installed before Dr. Feinstein has a fit."

⌒

The winter evening was chilly, but the sky was clear and star-filled. Sunny scanned the street but saw no sign of her father or his driver, Fai. She started for home, knowing that her father would find her somewhere en route. As she walked, she remembered the morning in the Old City when she had bolted from Wen-Cheng's embrace. She had avoided him ever since. But her growing ambivalence concerned more than just his marital status. She thought of Franz again. *You're straying from the unworkable to the impossible,* she scolded herself. *He is Jewish. He is a widower with a child. You are nothing to him.*

Sunny shook her head, trying to dispel Franz from her mind, but it was no use. His handsomeness aside, he possessed a quiet depth that she had encountered in few men aside from her father. She sensed the anguish behind Franz's stoic exterior. And she could no longer deny her growing desire to comfort him.

Still thinking of Franz, Sunny neared downtown Hongkew. She could hear the noisy revelers and the jazz music seeping out of the nightclubs on Broadway. A vague unease gripped her. She glanced over either shoulder. Nothing.

Sunny picked up her pace. She reached the intersection and rounded the corner toward the harbor. Just then, a hand shot out from the darkened doorway and locked onto her arm. Sunny stumbled and slammed shoulder first into the window of a jewelry store, bouncing off the glass. She yelped, more from surprise than pain. The attacker grasped her other arm. Instinctively, she struggled, but her assailant pinned her against the window.

Sunny swung her knee but missed her attacker. He hissed several Japanese words. Her nose filled with the familiar stench of sake and tuna, and she knew he was the sailor from the nearby docks who had accosted her before.

He slapped her twice, and the second blow glanced off her mouth. Her lip stung, and she tasted blood. *"Get off me!"* she screamed as she flailed her legs. Her foot connected with his shin, and the sailor cried out.

Using the distraction, she spun away from the window. She glimpsed the sailor's scarred face, contorted with drunken rage. He yanked a long knife from his belt and jabbed the blade at her chest, stopping only millimeters away. Sunny froze. A malicious smile crossed the sailor's lips and accentuated his ragged scar. He ran his thumb slowly across his own neck.

Sunny's breath caught in her throat and her hands trembled uncontrollably. She imagined it would be better to die than face the pain and shame of acquiescing to the repellent man. Only the thought of her father stopped her from lunging at his knife.

The sailor tore open her coat, sending the buttons rattling on the pavement like pebbles. Then he grabbed for the top of her dress and sliced it open in one motion.

The sudden draft felt like ice on her skin. Sunny had never felt more exposed. She closed her eyes and braced for the unimaginable. The sailor grabbed her breast and squeezed roughly, then dug his blade under her bra and tented the fabric upward.

Sunny heard the noise of tires screeching. The sailor's body obscured her vision, but she screamed out, *"Bāng zhù! Help! Please!"*

A car door opened. Feet scuffled nearer. Then she heard her father's raised voice. "Release her immediately!"

The sailor shoved Sunny hard, and she toppled backwards against the glass again. She cried out desperately, *"Father, the knife! Watch out!"*

She regained her balance and righted herself. A blur caught her eye, and she saw the blade plunge into the right side of Kingsley's chest with a nauseating whoosh.

"Father, no!" she screamed. Dress and coat flapping open, Sunny threw herself at the sailor's back. He fell forward under her weight. She grabbed his hair with one hand and clawed wildly at his face with her other.

Shrieking in outrage, he wrenched free of her grip and elbowed her in the chest, knocking the wind out of her. She tensed her legs, poised to spring again, when his hand shot out.

Sunny watched in disbelief as the blade tore into her abdomen. She heard a ripping noise before the jolt of searing pain rocked her. Out of reflex, her hands clutched her belly. She felt the blade slice through the skin between her thumb and forefinger on its way back.

Her knees gave way and she crumpled to the pavement. Looking up, she saw the sailor turn back on her father, who had propped himself up against the building by his shoulder.

"Leave the girl!" Kingsley panted. "Not my Sunny!"

The world swam around her. Out of the corner of her eye, she saw Fai advancing toward the sailor, a tire iron held high over his head. "Leave them alone!" he screamed in Shanghainese.

The attacker froze, bloodied knife held out in front of him. Suddenly, he thrust the blade at Fai's chest, but the driver stepped to his right and it whizzed inches past him. Fai swung the iron and caught the attacker on the wrist. The sailor howled in agony as the knife flew out of his hand and clattered to the ground.

Fai swung again, but the sailor managed to dodge the iron's arc. Clutching his injured arm to his side, the attacker took off, disappearing into the night.

Fai dropped to his knees beside Sunny. *"Missy? Missy?"*

Kingsley pushed himself upright and staggered a few steps toward her. "Sunny!" he wheezed. "Speak to me!"

Her head spun wildly. She felt a warm trickle running along her frigid belly. She desperately tried to answer, but the words would not form. The streetlight above her dimmed steadily.

Chapter 23

" A re you certain I am not taking you too far out of the way?" Franz asked as Simon shut the door to the refugee hospital behind them.

"Never been more certain in my life, Doc." Simon clapped him on the shoulder. "For a hero like you, Hong Kong wouldn't be too far out of my way."

Franz chuckled. "Hero! Such exaggeration, Simon. If you really—"

The shriek of tires silenced him. Franz squinted into the wobbly light of the car's headlamps as the vehicle hurtled toward them. It hopped the curb and screeched to a stop halfway across the sidewalk. The driver's door flew open and a man jumped out, waving his arms above his head. "Help!" he screamed. *"Chop, chop!"*

"That's Fai! Dr. Mah's driver." Simon sprinted toward the car, and Franz followed.

Fai stooped over and reached through the rear door. *"Riběn guǎzi* cut doctor and missy!" he shouted over his shoulder.

Franz didn't understand but there was no mistaking the man's distress, and Franz's pulse hammered in his temples.

Fai straightened up, pulling Kingsley out of the car by the armpits. With his driver's help, Kingsley was able to rise to his feet. But even with Fai's arm wrapped around him, he swayed like a sapling in a windstorm. His breath came in rapid grunts.

Franz shot his hand out to Kingsley's neck. His fingers stuck on contact with the skin. *Blood!* His hand skittered up and down the man's neck, finally finding the faint racing pulse. "What happened?"

Kingsley weakly waved away the question. "Oh, Dr. Adler . . . thank God . . . please . . . Sunny!"

"*Sunny?* Where is she?"

"Franz, help!" Simon called.

Franz looked over to see Simon dragging Sunny out from the backseat. He lunged forward and caught Sunny in his arms just as Simon pulled her free. Lifting her up, Franz felt warm blood on her exposed abdomen. She lay ominously still in his arms.

"Is she . . ." Simon's voice cracked.

Franz lifted her higher, bringing her mouth to his ear. He heard faint breathing. He wheeled and raced for the hospital entrance, Sunny light in his arms.

The noise from the street had roused Maxwell Feinstein and two of the German nurses, Liese and Berta. They rushed out to the street.

"*Nein!*" Franz stopped them. "Ready two beds!"

"*Ja, ja!*" Max shepherded the women back inside.

"And prepare the operating room!" Franz called after them.

He burst through the open door, bumping Sunny's head against the casing, but she didn't respond. "This way, Herr Doktor!" Berta cried.

Franz followed her voice to the ward, where Max and Berta were hastily dragging partitions around two empty beds. Several patients were sitting upright in their beds, clutching sheets to their chests and murmuring among themselves.

Franz lowered Sunny into the nearest bed. She blinked as she hit the mattress but uttered no sound. Under the light, the extent of her hemorrhage was obvious. Blood was already caked to her left side and continued to ooze from the one-inch gash below her rib cage. He palpated her abdomen. The muscles tightened in response. "I need intravenous supplies! And when will the operating room be ready?"

"Soon, Herr Doktor," Berta answered shakily. "Liese is preparing the equipment."

Franz hurried over to the other bed, where Fai had deposited Kingsley. Someone had stripped off his shirt. He sat up, his legs dangling over the side of the bed, and gasped for air. Franz spotted the wound on his hairless chest just below the right nipple. The edges puckered in and out with each rapid breath. Stethoscope plugged into his ears, Max was trying to examine Kingsley, but he kept struggling to stand. "Sunny . . ." he wheezed. "Sunny . . ."

Max glanced at Franz with worried eyes. He pointed to the stab wound. "The knife has punctured the right lung. It has collapsed, and his chest is filling with blood."

Kingsley tried to rise again, but Max held him gently in place. "Do not . . . worry . . . about . . . me," Kingsley gasped.

But Franz knew that if the blood continued to pool in Kingsley's chest, he would suffocate in his own fluid. "We must drain your chest, Dr. Mah," Franz said.

"No . . . no . . . no." Despite a heroic effort to rise, Kingsley fell back onto the bed.

"Listen to him, Dr. Mah," Max implored. "It has to be done!"

"No!" said Kingsley. "Fix . . . Sunny . . . first."

"I will, I swear," Franz said. "But that will take time in the operating room. I can put a tube in your chest right now in a matter of minutes."

"After," Kingsley gasped. "Not until . . . Sunny . . ."

Franz darted back to Sunny's bed, where she lay still on the stretcher. He ran his fingers along her ice-cold neck. He held his breath until he found the weak pulse.

Berta reappeared, fumbling with coils of rubber tubing and two bottles of Ringer's lactate. Franz snatched the needles out of her hand and dropped to his knees. He ripped open the sleeve of Sunny's dress and touched along the skin of her elbow crease until a stringy vein rolled under his fingers. With his other hand, he pierced the skin over the vein and advanced the needle. *Steady, Adler. You will not have a second chance.*

As soon as a drop of blood formed at the needle's hub, Franz grabbed the tubing from Berta and connected it to the needle. He took the bottle and attached it to the pole beside the bed, mounting it as high as he could to maximize the rate at which it flowed into Sunny's vein.

Franz turned back to Kingsley. "The fluids are running into her, Dr. Mah. The operating room will be ready any minute." He motioned to Kingsley's chest. "Meantime, I am going to drain the blood from around your lung."

Eyes at half-mast, Kingsley stared back without argument.

"Berta, please get me a scalpel and tubing," Franz instructed.

Franz was assessing the best location on Kingsley's chest to insert the drainage tube when Liese appeared at the doorway. "The operating room is prepared, Dr. Adler!"

Franz glanced over to Sunny, who was as white as a sheet and motionless. Kingsley weakly pushed Franz's hand away from his chest. "Take . . . her," he breathed. "Please!"

"Go, Franz!" Max nodded. "I will insert the tube into Dr. Mah's chest."

"I'll help any way I can," Simon added from across the room.

Franz hesitated a moment and then pointed to the bottle of fluid hanging from the pole. "Berta, take the intravenous!"

Once more, he swept Sunny up in his arms. Berta freed the bottle from the pole and held it up as high as she could. Together they rushed Sunny down the hall into the operating room and laid her on the operating table. Franz grabbed a clean gown off the wall and threw it over his suit. He slipped a cap over his hair and tied a mask around his mouth. "Liese, you will have to give the ether," he stated.

Sunny lay on the table with her bloodied abdomen exposed, sterile towels draped over her chest and below her pelvis. Franz saw that her eyes had opened a crack. "Father . . ." she croaked. "Where is Father?"

The sweat dripped into Franz's eyes. "On the ward, with Dr. Feinstein."

"Is he all right?" she gasped.

Franz wiped his brow with the sleeve of his gown. "He's alive, Sunny. We will do all we can for him, but first we must fix you."

Sunny lifted a hand and plucked at the air near Franz. "Please, Dr. Adler. Please . . ." Her hand dropped to the bed and her eyes fluttered shut.

Franz glanced over to the nurse at the head of the bed. "Begin, Liese!"

With a tremulous hand, Liese brought the ether mask to Sunny's face and dripped the anesthetic on it. "Steady . . ." Franz said, watching a few drops miss the mask. After two or three more drops, he said, "All right, enough."

Franz hurriedly wiped Sunny's abdomen with iodine-soaked cotton. He grabbed the scalpel off the tray and touched it to the side of her belly just below the rib cage. More sweat dripped toward his eyes, but he ignored it. He applied pressure and sliced vertically through the abdominal wall in one long motion until he passed below her navel.

He wedged an L-shaped steel retractor through the edges of the incision and yanked back. Bright blood welled and bubbled over the edges of the wound like a fountain switching on. He jabbed a second retractor through the incision and pulled the incision apart. "Retract, please!" He passed the handles to Berta.

Franz jammed a handful of sponges inside Sunny's abdomen, trying to mop up as much of the blood as he could. From the degree of hemorrhage, he assumed the knife must have lacerated her spleen. At least, he hoped so. If the blade had penetrated a major vessel, or even her intestine, he stood practically no chance of saving her. *Stay with us, Sunny. Please.*

Franz dug his left hand through the incision up to the level of his wrist. Warm blood enveloped his hand as he felt his way past the loops of slippery bowel until his fingers touched the base of the deflated spleen. Exploring its surface, his finger slipped into the ragged gash in its center. Engulfing the pear-sized organ in his hand, he ran his fingers over the surface until he found the base where the main blood vessels entered. "Clamp!" he grunted.

Berta passed him a long scissor-shaped clamp. Pooling blood still obscured his sight, so he blindly plunged the instrument deep into Sunny's belly until its tip met his other hand. He ran the clamp's teeth alongside his fingers and then clicked across the splenic artery.

Franz took all the remaining absorbent gauze sponges off the tray and wadded them inside her abdomen. Holding his breath, he slowly withdrew them.

No fresh blood welled in place of the old. "All right," he said to himself, feeling his first glimmer of hope.

He took the long needle driver off the tray and loaded it with catgut. Moving the intestine out of the way, he feathered the needle driver down to the level of the clamp. He encircled the spleen's base with three loops of catgut before tying it off, then added a second ligature for support. "Long scissors."

Franz inserted the scissors and cut across the far side of the clamp, slicing through the splenic artery and freeing Sunny's spleen. He gently pulled it out through the incision and dropped it onto the tray.

Franz and both nurses stared into the gaping incision, watching for any sign of fresh bleeding. "How is she, Liese?" he asked without taking his eyes off the wound.

"Her pulse is weak but she is still breathing, Herr Doktor."

"Good," Franz said. "I'm going to close the wound now."

He removed the clamp and explored the inside of Sunny's abdomen one last time, running his fingers up and down the intestine to ensure he had not missed a second injury. Satisfied, he reached for the needle driver and sewed the layers of the abdominal wall closed.

Franz dropped the tools on the tray. Liese had already pulled the ether mask off Sunny's face. Eyes still closed, she was breathing evenly and on the verge of rousing. "Keep the fluids running in," he told Berta as he rushed for the door. "And clear the operating room as quickly as possible for Dr. Mah!"

Franz broke into a run down the corridor, heading toward the ward. Simon met him at the doorway. "How is she, Franz?" he demanded.

Something caught Franz's eye, and he ignored the

question. Mouth open, he stood at the doorway and gaped at the sight.

Kingsley lay still on the bed. A rubber tube dangled freely from his chest and blood dripped steadily into a pool on the cement floor.

Max was shaking his head continuously as he slowly draped a white sheet over Kingsley. "Even with the tube," he muttered, "he had simply lost too much blood."

PART IV

"U*nglaublich!* Can you believe we have already been in Shanghai for almost a year and a half, Franz?" Esther asked from the armchair where she sat lengthening Hannah's school skirt.

"Feels more like a lifetime and a half," Franz replied.

"*Ja*," Esther sighed. "Quite a lot has happened since, no?"

"You might say so, Essie!" Franz chuckled at her understatement. Europe had gone to war. The Germans had trampled Poland in the fall. While fighting had reached a stalemate over the winter months, with the dawn of spring the Wehrmacht had launched a new blitzkrieg and invaded Scandinavia. Denmark had already surrendered, and now Norwegians shuddered as hostile forces occupied the streets of Oslo. The Adlers kept their wireless tuned to the BBC night and day, hoping and praying to hear word that the British and the French had struck back decisively. But each day brought only bleaker news from Europe. Rumors ran rampant among the refugee community about Jews caught in the Nazis' clutches inside Germany, Czechoslovakia, and especially Poland. Franz had heard frantic stories of walled ghettos, mass arrests, starvation, and torture. With the borders closed and escape routes cut off by the hostilities, the flow of new refugees into Shanghai had stemmed from a flood to a trickle.

Locally, tensions had steadily risen as the Japanese saber-rattling intensified. More and more Shanghailanders and expatriates had packed up and departed for Hong Kong, Singapore, and other safer harbors. Leaving was not an option for the Adlers or the twenty thousand other German Jews. Esther's multiple visa applications and letters to the American, British, Canadian, and Australian authorities had all been politely declined or ignored altogether. Esther remained optimistic, but Franz was more convinced than ever that no one wanted the displaced Jews.

Still, Franz was astounded at how the refugee community had gelled. On his walks and rickshaw rides around the city, he saw that the German Jews had made a home for themselves, ironically, replicating the towns and streets they had escaped. Franz had never felt a strong affiliation to the Viennese Jewish community, but in Shanghai, through his work at the refugee hospital, he had already come to know several families in his same predicament. Many were secular Jews like him; some were only half Jewish, or married to Gentiles. Franz took unexpected pride in how their resourcefulness had largely overcome the poverty to which most of the refugees had arrived. Cafés, restaurants, theaters, bakeries, and sports clubs had sprung up all over, especially in the streets surrounding the refugee hospital—a neighborhood that had come to be known as Little Vienna. All kinds of authentic fare, from matzo, bagels, and smoked meat to nonkosher Austrian delicacies such as Wiener schnitzel, were readily available. In the evenings, Shanghai buzzed with Jewish culture.

The sharp whine of strings drew Franz's attention. Across the room, Lotte Weczel sat beside his daughter. Hannah's face was creased in concentration as she balanced a diminutive cello between her legs. Franz had yet to adjust to the sight of his daughter's lopsided playing style. Her bow hand sawed fluidly across the strings while her contracted left hand fumbled to finger each note. The music emerged in squeaky bursts, but the tune was identifiable and her improvement undeniable.

Lotte had suggested the cello to Hannah, lending her a child-sized instrument and offering to teach her. Despite her handicap and unremarkable musical aptitude, Hannah embraced the instrument with the same ferocity that she tackled every new challenge.

Lotte muttered a few quiet words of encouragement and then glanced to Franz with one of her shy smiles. They had been seeing each other for over a year. They shared an appreciation for music and old-time architecture. Lotte often toured him through the lesser trod areas of the International Settlement, exposing him to eccentric villas and other turn-of-the-nineteenth-century gems that he might never have otherwise found. She also cared deeply for Hannah, and vice versa. However, Franz's relationship with Lotte remained passionless and, aside from a few staid good-night kisses, platonic. Little about Lotte stirred him romantically or sexually. And though she would occasionally reach for his hand while walking or sitting in the cinema, he sensed no more interest on her part than his.

While neither Franz nor Lotte were in any hurry to advance their relationship, Clara Reuben made it her priority. She no longer relied on persuasiveness or guilt alone, but had become even more direct, suggesting that unless Franz married into the family, her husband would have trouble continuing to fund his modest salary at the Country Hospital. She also implied that Hannah's scholarship at the exclusive Shanghai Jewish School would be in jeopardy. For Franz, the latter was a far weightier threat. Hannah was thriving at school, where both the teachers and students seemed sensitive to her handicap. Franz was prepared to do anything to protect his daughter's well-being, even marry a woman he did not love.

He had told Esther as much the week before over tea. His sister-in-law had responded with a pained shake of her head. "Lotte is a sweet woman, but that's not reason enough to marry."

"Her aunt might be reason enough."

"You can't let *that* woman bully you, Franz! It's just not right. For you or Lotte."

"Essie, we are discussing Hannah's future."

"No, Franz. We are discussing *your* future."

"What if they expel Hannah from school?"

She held up her hands. "Because her father refused to marry a board member's niece?"

"For not paying the dues. We both know Clara secured us the grant for Hannah."

"Maybe so, but Hannah is a good student. They would have no cause to withdraw her scholarship now."

"Her mother was not Jewish. So, technically, neither is Hannah."

Esther shook her head. "Did you hide this from the school when she enrolled?"

"No, but Clara says the pressure for spots is greater than ever. And the board feels other, *fully* Jewish children are more deserving of scholarships."

"Oh, Franz, that woman would tell you that the sun will not rise again until you marry her niece. She is bluffing."

"How can you be so sure, Essie?"

She sighed. "*Ach.* I do not trust the old turtle."

"Lotte is a kind soul. She is good to Hannah. It would not be the end of the world."

Esther patted his arm. "You and I have both been blessed to know what it means to marry for love. There is no other reason, certainly not blackmail! What kind of marriage would yours be?"

The music stopped and the momentary lull pulled Franz back to the present. Hannah lowered her bow to the ground.

Franz clapped enthusiastically. "Brava!"

Esther put down her sewing to join in on the applause.

"I am still terrible, Papa," Hannah said with a timid smile.

"Not so, *liebchen.* I hear improvement each time." Franz motioned to her cello. "You remember when you first tried?"

She giggled. "Onkel Ernst said I sounded like a cat trapped beneath the wheel of a cart."

"Wait until he hears you now." He laughed. "No more crushed cats. Only lovely music."

"Is he coming tonight for dinner?" Hannah asked hopefully. "Maybe I can play for him?"

Ernst no longer lived with the Adlers. A few months after their arrival, Lady Leah Herdoon had made good on her shipboard promise and toured them through the city in the back of her Rolls-Royce limousine. After a sumptuous dinner at her mansion on the western outskirts, Lady Leah commissioned Ernst to paint two original pieces. The money was enough for him to rent a suite in a building a few streets over from the Adlers. Lady Leah also introduced Ernst to one of Shanghai's top art dealers, Lawrence Solomon, who invited Ernst to show at his gallery. Ernst produced several large oil canvases that captured the haunting vulnerability of his subjects—female nudes he had chosen from the youngest of the dockside prostitutes. The show was a critical and commercial success. As soon as it closed, Ernst threw himself into his next project and, in the process, had become a relative recluse.

"No, Hannah, Ernst is not coming tonight," Esther said.

"When will we see him again?"

"Soon, *liebchen*," Franz said. "Sometimes artists become consumed by their work."

Hannah giggled. "You mean his paintings are eating him?"

"Something like that." Franz smiled. He treasured such small moments of naivete; they were fewer now. In a month, Hannah would turn ten. Lean and lanky—she was destined to be tall like her mother—her face had already shed most of its childlike roundness. She was maturing into a lovely girl with poise and confidence. *Where did my little child go?*

Lotte gathered up Hannah's sheets of music and rose from the chair. "I am to meet Aunt Clara for lunch. I must be going."

Franz checked his watch, surprised to see that it was almost noon. "Yes, me too. I have to go to the hospital."

"It's Sunday, Papa. I thought we were going to the market."

"Later, *liebchen*, but first I had best check on my patients." And, since Sundays were the only days that Franz didn't have duties at the Country Hospital, he often ran an afternoon clinic for new patients at the refugee hospital.

After good-byes, which included an awkward hug with Lotte in front of Esther and Hannah, Franz headed out. He intended to walk, but the streets were soaked from the latest downpour. He had not seen the sun in weeks. None of the locals could remember a damper spring. Concerned that the passing cars might soak him with sprays of filthy water, Franz opted against taking a rickshaw and splurged instead on a taxi.

As the cab wove through the traffic of Frenchtown, the International Settlement, and finally Hongkew, Franz realized how familiar Shanghai's streets had become. Night soil men balancing loads on bamboo poles, corpses abandoned on the curbs, natives wandering the sidewalks in pajamas, and street dentists extracting teeth in public were all second nature to him. Even the aromas and stenches barely registered. Shanghai was still not home—he doubted it ever could be—but it felt more comfortable than he would have once dreamed possible.

The taxi driver dropped him off in front of the refugee hospital. Franz headed to the staff room. Sunny sat at the small table, using chopsticks to pick at a bowl of rice. "Good afternoon, Franz."

"Oh, hello, Sunny." He cleared his throat. "I didn't expect to see you today."

She smiled in the distant way that she had taken to since her father's murder. "I promised Miriam I would cover her shift. It's her son's birthday."

Franz slipped off his wet coat and hat and hung them on the rack. As casual as he tried to appear, he was aware of his pulse speeding. Though he had seen Sunny often over the past year and a half, she had only recently begun to emerge from the mourning that enshrouded her like a dense mist.

Sunny had returned to work within two months of

her stabbing but, traumatized and heartbroken, she functioned more like an automaton. Almost a year passed before she approached Franz about accepting his offer to apprentice under him. It took months more before the sparks of her former self reappeared. When she emerged, it was like a bud blossoming. His attraction to her was stronger than ever; they were bound by grief now.

Franz shifted his weight from one foot to the other. "How are the patients today?"

"Mr. Irving's wound infection has improved. And I suspect Mrs. Klein could go home today." She continued to list off the status of each of his patients.

"Good," Franz said. "Sunny, on Tuesday Mrs. Kolberg is scheduled to have her gallbladder removed."

"Would you like me to assist you?"

"No."

She jerked her head back. "No? Fr— Dr. Adler? Did I do something to . . ."

Franz fought back a smile. "I intend to assist *you* on this particular operation."

Her face lit up. "Do you think I am ready?"

"It's time," Franz said, drinking in her gratitude.

Sunny stood from the table. "I brought you something from home." She rummaged through the bag at her feet and extracted a square leather box that Franz recognized as a Kodak Brownie box camera. "My father bought this seven or eight years ago. He claimed he never could find the time to use it." She grinned. "Truth is, I don't think he was much of a photographer. The few images I saw of his were almost too dark or blurry to identify."

She held the camera out to Franz, but he waved it away. "Sunny, I couldn't."

Her cheeks flushed but she didn't lower her hand. "I

have no use for it, Franz. I would not even know which end to point. And I thought you used to enjoy photography in Vienna."

He wavered, admiring the Brownie's black-and-burgundy design. "Are you certain?"

"My father hated wastefulness," she encouraged. "He would be very pleased to know that it might bring you some pleasure. So would I."

"It will. Thank you, Sunny." The weight of the camera in his hand filled him with excitement.

Sunny cocked her head. "Have you seen Dr. Feinstein today?"

"No. Is he in the laboratory?"

She bit her lip. "He does not look right, Franz."

"Perhaps I should speak with him."

Franz found Max hunched over his microscope in the cramped laboratory. When the internist looked up, his eyes were red and his face as pale as his lab coat. "What is it, Max?" Franz asked.

"Rachel," Max gulped. "My daughter, Rachel."

Max had not spoken of her in over a year. Rachel's situation—trapped with her family in Germany after her husband had gambled, and lost, on the hope of landing an American visa—was tragically common among the relatives of the refugees in Shanghai. "There is news?" Franz asked.

Max nodded despondently. "We received a letter from a neighbor. A Gentile widow who was . . . was always kind to us. The SS . . . they took them away—Rachel, Erik, and the children, all of them—to a 'relocation camp.' The letter was dated almost six months ago."

"Perhaps . . ." Franz started but he couldn't conjure any words of reassurance. "Oh, Max, I am so sorry."

Max merely nodded and turned back to the microscope.

Franz trudged down the hallway to the makeshift clinic Simon and his men had constructed at the back of the building. Golda Hiltmann was already waiting with files neatly stacked on her desk. Frau Hiltmann had volunteered at the hospital ever since recovering from her ruptured ectopic pregnancy, but she would not be continuing the role for much longer.

"How are you today, Golda?" Franz asked.

"Wonderful." Beaming, she patted the bulge of her abdomen that rose above her desk. "Only four more weeks to go."

"So close." He summoned a smile. "How many patients do we have today?"

"Six." She gestured toward the closed door of the examining room as she handed him a chart. "The first patient is already inside."

Without even glancing at the name, he opened the door and stepped into the room. The man in the navy three-piece suit stopped in mid-pace and turned to face him. The sweet smell of pipe tobacco hit Franz like a slap.

Schwartzmann! Hans? No . . . Hermann. Hermann Schwartzmann!

Franz barely even noticed the slender woman who leaned forward in the chair behind Schwartzmann. The diplomat offered Franz a contrite smile. "You remember me from the *Conte Biancamano*, correct, Dr. Adler?"

"I remember you," Franz said coolly.

Schwartzmann's lip and mustache twitched together. "How have you been?"

Franz's expression was stone. "I am still here."

"Good, good. Yes. I'm glad to see it." Schwartzmann swung an arm to the pale silent woman behind him. "My wife, Edda. We have been in Shanghai all this time too. The longest stint yet." He laughed nervously. "Not even sure whether I would recognize Germany anymore. Especially now, with the war measures at home. All things considered, Shanghai is probably a safer place to be during such uncertain times . . ."

Franz stood silently with arms folded across his chest, allowing the man to trip over his stream of words. "What do you want, Mr. Schwartzmann?" he finally asked.

Schwartzmann looked down at his feet. "I need your help."

"*My help?*" Franz was too stunned for outrage. "Do you have any idea where you are?"

Schwartzmann looked back up at Franz with hands held open. "A hospital."

"A hospital built for and run by the Jews *your* government drove out of Germany."

"That . . . that is not my business," Schwartzmann stammered.

Franz was dumbfounded. Schwartzmann waved a hand in front of his chest. "Please, Dr. Adler. I did not mean it that way. What I meant to say was—"

Franz regained his equilibrium and jerked his finger toward the door behind him. "My colleague has only just learned that his daughter, her husband, and their three children were all dragged away by the SS for who knows where!" He tasted the bile in his mouth. "Do you suppose he will ever see them again?"

Schwartzmann shrugged. "I . . . I don't know."

"And you have the gall to come here to ask for our help?" Franz's voice rose with each word.

Schwartzmann looked up at him with plaintive eyes. "Edda is sick," he said hoarsely.

Franz glanced over to the woman again. She was not so much pale as yellow. She was clearly suffering from jaundice. "That is not my business," Franz said, but the words felt wrong even as he spoke them.

Schwartzmann cleared his throat. "Edda has a tumor in her bile duct. It is obstructing her liver. The doctors call it a 'cholangiocarcinoma.' Without surgery, they say she will not . . ."

Franz looked over to Edda again. Eyes downcast, she remained motionless. He turned back to Schwartzmann. "There are several Gentile surgeons in Shanghai. Even some capable Aryan Germans."

Schwartzmann's shoulders sagged. "They were the ones who told me you were the only surgeon who could give my wife a fighting chance."

Franz had not resected a cholangiocarcinoma in well over two years, but he had once held the reputation as Vienna's best at the procedure. It was a challenging operation under the best of circumstances, and the refugee hospital lacked the delicate tools required. Franz shook his head. "It's impossible."

"Dr. Adler, I have no right to be here. By rights, you should throw me out by my coattails." He motioned to his wife again. "My Edda is a good woman. She has never harmed a soul. For her sake, not mine. I am begging you, as a doctor and a human being . . . please."

Franz stared at the man for a long moment. As he was about to speak, Edda pushed herself up with considerable effort. She smoothed her coat out and then took a halting step toward her husband. "Come, Hermann, we have taken enough of the doctor's time," she said in a gravelly voice. She turned to Franz with a weak but apologetic smile. "Please excuse us, Dr. Adler. I told Hermann it was an ill-conceived idea to come." She glanced over at her husband, and her eyes filled with the kind of disapproving affection that only a life-long spouse could muster. "He wouldn't listen to me."

Schwartzmann's head dropped. "Yes, yes. Of course, dear." Without looking at Franz, he said, "Thank you for your time, Dr. Adler." He took his wife's arm and turned for the door.

Franz looked down and studied his hands as the couple shuffled past him. "Please, Mrs. Schwartzmann," he said, indicating the examining table. "Won't you have a seat?"

⌒ *Chapter 25*

Breakfast time was the hardest. Before her father died, they had eaten together every morning. Sometimes they exchanged only a smattering of words, preoccupied by traded sections of the newspaper and their days ahead, but breakfasts without him were beyond lonely. Sunny had tried skipping them altogether. It didn't help; the anguish would catch up to her later in the morning anyway, along with a headache.

Yang felt the emptiness too. The once quiet housekeeper had taken to filling in the sorrowful silence with incessant chatter. "Look at you, Soon Yi," she said as she piled sticky rice dumplings and steamed fish onto the plate. They both knew Sunny would only peck at the food. "What man would want a skeleton for a wife?"

Sunny had always been slight, but she had not weighed under a hundred pounds since her fifteenth birthday. While she had pulled out of the worst of her grief, her appetite had yet to recover. The scale read ninety-seven pounds. Sunny didn't care, but to appease Yang she forced down a few bites.

"Your auntie sends more letters," Yang muttered.

"Always." Sunny sighed. "Bing-Qing is insisting that I move in with her and her husband."

Bing-Qing's own children were married and long flown from the nest. Kingsley had never had much time for his older sister. Though raised under the same roof, as adults they were night and day in terms of their attitude and lifestyle. As much as Kingsley had embraced science and the Western way, Bing-Qing had veered in the opposite direction, gravitating toward an existence more traditional than even their parents had lived. Bing-Qing had disowned her little brother when he married the *yang guiz*—or "foreign devil," as she referred to Sunny's mother—and reappeared after Ida's death only to meddle in Sunny's upbringing.

Now Bing-Qing was at it again. In her latest missive, she decried it as shameful for an unmarried young woman to live alone in the city. She argued that Sunny's dubious living circumstances brought dishonor to the entire family. Sunny suspected that, behind the indignation, her aunt had her eye on her inheritance, especially the family home in the prosperous neighborhood.

"Do not worry, Yang," Sunny reassured. "The Whangpoo will freeze over before I move in with my aunt and uncle, or let them move here."

Yang nodded, hiding her relief in a flurry of tidying. "Sometimes, *xiǎo hè*, when you were not present, your father would call your auntie 'The Padlock.'"

Sunny frowned. "Padlock?"

"Like the ceremonial ones parents place around their babies' necks to ward off evil spirits." Yang showed a rare smile. "Your father said that your auntie was as protective as a padlock because no evil spirit would ever have the patience to sit through one of her lectures."

Sunny laughed, reminded again how glad she was to still have Yang with her. The tiny woman helped keep her father's memory close. After his death, Sunny and Yang had reached the tacit understanding that she would stay on in her role, though Sunny didn't require a full-time housekeeper. Her inheritance also allowed Sunny to keep Fai on as her driver. She felt indebted to Fai for his devotion to her father and for his bravery on the night of the attack. Besides, she was terrified of the prospect of walking alone through Hongkew after dark, knowing that her father's murderer was still stationed somewhere at the docks. Everywhere Sunny went, especially in Hongkew, she kept an eye peeled for the sailor with the scarred lip, fluctuating between an intense desire to avoid him and a longing to find him. She had no idea how she would respond if they ever did meet, but for the first time in her life, she knew how absolute hatred tasted.

Sunny forced down a few more bites of dumpling and rose from the table. Outside, she spotted Fai standing at the curbside polishing a nonexistent smudge on the hood of the Buick. The street was dry for the first time in weeks, but gray clouds hovered above, threatening to correct their oversight at any moment.

"Hello, Missy," Fai said. "Country Hospital or the other?"

"The refugee hospital. But Fai, first I am going to visit Father."

As they drove, Sunny noticed that the trees had still not blossomed. Most years, by April, the French Concession was at its loveliest, with cherry blossoms bursting out along the boulevards. However, this year, after a month of near-constant rainfall and cool temperatures, the trees were mostly still bare. To Sunny, they reflected the spirit of Frenchtown. The sidewalks bustled as busily as ever, but the collective mood had dampened as much as the blossoms. With Europe at war and the Japanese army surrounding the concessions in an undeclared siege, people wore their worry as plainly as their overcoats.

Fai slowed the car to a halt on the Bund in front of the Cathay Hotel, where Simon stood waiting with a small bouquet of white lilies in his hand.

Sunny had once regularly accompanied her father to visit her mother's graveside. After recovering from her stab wound, she had ventured out to the graveyard once or twice a week. Today, though, was the first time that she would not be going alone.

As Simon climbed into the back of the car, he said, "Hope it's kosher to bring flowers."

"Of course." Sunny smiled. "Thank you for coming, Simon."

"Are you kidding? Thanks for letting me tag along. Your father was a good, good man. I'm honored to go pay my respects."

She touched his elbow. "I'm glad you're here, Simon."

"Anything for you, kid."

Simon treated her as a concerned big brother would, and she loved him for it. However, in the weeks following her stabbing, she had felt smothered by her friends' sympathy and concern. Simon hovered. Jia-Li hardly left her side. And Wen-Cheng and Franz practically tripped over each other on their frequent visits. Though she loved them all, what she craved most in those early months was solitude. Sunny did not want to think about what had happened to her father, let alone discuss it. She just wanted to withdraw from the world and from anything that reminded her of him. But as time passed, more and more, she came to relish the memories and wanted to share them with the people closest to her.

Fai pulled into the driveway of the old cemetery on the outskirts of the International Settlement just as the skies began to drizzle again. Only a few visitors remained, scattered throughout the sprawling grounds. Sunny and Simon walked past rows of crosses, headstones, statues, and a few mausoleums before reaching her parents' side-by-side graves. Simon turned to Sunny, silently seeking permission to place the flowers. She nodded, and he laid the bouquet between the matching black marble markers and then backed away, giving Sunny privacy.

She knelt at the foot of the graves. She hung her head and closed her eyes but did not pray. Instead, she silently spoke to her parents, though she directed most of her words to her father. She summarized Bing-Qing's letters. She also told him about the goings-on at both hospitals and her nervous excitement at the idea of performing as the lead surgeon. She finished by telling both parents how much she loved them.

As she straightened up, she paused to wipe away the tears and to murmur under her breath, "I miss you so much, Father."

She turned and walked toward the car. Neither of them spoke until the car was back on the road. "Does it help?" Simon asked. "Visiting them?"

Sunny looked out the window at the slate gray skies. "I always feel a little better."

"We Jews have a similar ritual," he said. "Then again, I guess all religions must. After all, who wouldn't want to pray for loved ones they had lost?"

Sunny didn't explain that she never went to the graveside to pray. "In the Chinese culture, regardless of religion, respect of ancestors is the cornerstone of all belief systems. Apparently, it's what makes us such a filial society."

He laughed. "You folks really are the lost tribe of Israel."

"We do like our pork, though."

The smile left his lips. "Sunny, can I ask you for some advice?"

"Always."

"It's been a year and a half since I first laid eyes on Esther, and I still feel the same way about her. I can't get her out of my mind." He looked down at his interlocked fingers. "I'm just not sure if I should tell her."

"Why not, Simon?"

"Because she's still so in love with her late husband."

Sunny squeezed his arm again. "That doesn't mean she can't love you too."

"I guess." He chewed his lip. "Sometimes when I'm with Essie, I feel this closeness. And other times, I figure I must be screwy to even think it."

"How will you ever know unless you tell her?"

Simon chuckled. "Holy cow, I knew you were going to say that!"

"Then why did you ask?"

"I guess I wanted to hear it. Helps me get the nerve up. After all, what did that Shakespeare guy say?" He snapped his fingers. "'Better to have loved and lost . . .' and all that jazz."

"He might have a point," she said.

"How about you, Miss Shoot-from-the-hip?" he asked. "Have you told the good doctor?"

For a moment, Sunny wondered which doctor Simon meant—Wen-Cheng or Franz? "You are talking rubbish now, Simon."

He grabbed her hand. "Sunny, I've seen the way Franz looks at you. I *know* that look."

"He has been seeing Dr. Reuben's niece for months." She shook free of Simon's hand and fixed him with a determined stare. "Besides, Dr. Adler looks at me the way a teacher would a favored student. Nothing more."

"Suit yourself." Simon folded his arms over his chest. "Doesn't happen very often, but every once in a while I do get something right."

⌒

Fai dropped Sunny off out front of the refugee hospital, but Simon remained in the backseat, since he was heading to the CFA office. Many refugees, like the Adlers, were already self-sufficient, but with almost twenty thousand displaced German Jews living in the city, the complexities of feeding, housing, schooling, and caring for the others were endless.

As Sunny walked the pathway up to the hospital, her hands went clammy. She was filled with both excitement and apprehension at the prospect of removing a patient's gallbladder. And, after her conversation with Simon, she blushed at the thought of seeing Franz again.

He greeted her at the door to the operating room with a luminous smile. "So, are you ready to perform surgery?"

She grimaced. "I am not at all sure that I am."

He eyed her with certainty. "No one is, their first time."

They scrubbed together at the sink. Franz verbally walked her through the steps of the operation as she visualized them in her head. By the time they returned to the room, the patient, a stocky woman named Rosa Kolberg, lay unconscious on the table as Liese steadied an ether mask over the woman's face. The other nurse, Berta, held out a sterile gown for Sunny. "Here you go, young doctor," she giggled.

Gowned and gloved, Sunny stepped up to the patient's right side while Franz took the usual position of the assistant, across the table. She accepted the scalpel from Berta. It felt heavier than usual. She held the blade up in the air and looked over to Franz, wavering.

Franz grinned behind his mask. "I suppose we could wait, but I doubt Mrs. Kolberg's gallbladder is planning to remove itself."

Sunny took a deep breath, applied the blade to the skin, and sliced horizontally. As she dissected through the layers of flesh toward the gallbladder, Franz offered only the odd word of instruction, maintaining the role of assistant rather than teacher. Sunny was simultaneously exhilarated and terrified. By the time she freed the slippery stone-laden gallbladder and pulled it out of the patient's abdomen, she felt fully in control. As she ran the last few loops of catgut to close the skin, she could not keep the smile from her lips.

After they shed their gowns, Franz motioned for Sunny to follow him outside the hospital. On the front steps, he extracted two cigars from his pocket. He clipped the ends off both and passed one to her. "A tradition with all my students," he said. "Congratulations! Your first surgery. Of many, I believe. *Mazel tov!*"

Sunny tasted the salty tobacco. Franz fired a match and lit both cigars. Predictably, she choked on her first inhalation. Franz also coughed. Soon they were both laughing. "I am a terrible smoker too," he croaked. "Disgusting things. But a tradition is a tradition."

They smoked together in silence for a few moments. She enjoyed his proximity but nearly gagged each time the soggy cigar tip touched her lips. After three or four puffs, her head was spinning.

Franz pulled the cigar from her lips. His forehead creased, and he looked at her with troubled eyes. "Sunny, I am going to perform a surgery more involved than any I have ever attempted at this hospital. The patient has a tumor of her bile duct."

"Are you planning to do a Whipple's procedure?"

"Yes, exactly," he said. "We do not have the necessary equipment here. I will have to borrow it from the Country Hospital. Providing, of course, that Dr. Reuben will lend it to me."

The mention of Reuben's name dampened her mood. She could think of little that was more distasteful than being beholden to him.

"The patient . . ." Franz went on. "She is the wife of a man I know."

"From Vienna?"

"No. They're German, not Austrian. And they're not Jewish. In fact, he is a diplomat who works for the German government." He squeezed the bridge of his nose. "You understand, Sunny? He's a *Nazi*."

"Oh."

He shrugged. "I'm a doctor, and the patient needs my help. It should be very simple."

"And yet it's not simple at all, is it?"

"Her husband works for the people who murdered my brother, tormented my child, and stole our home. He is the last person in the world who I would choose to help."

Sunny nodded to herself. "If I were asked to care for a Japanese soldier now, I'm not sure I could. Especially that sailor with the scarred lip." Her voice dropped to a whisper. "I think I would sooner die than help my father's killer."

"Exactly!"

But as Sunny stared into Franz's compassionate eyes, she knew how he would proceed even if he didn't. Her father would have done the same.

Chapter 26

"Cut here, please, Dr. Adler," Reuben instructed with his usual operating room haughtiness, as he tugged on the two ends of the stitch that held the thyroid gland together.

As Franz snipped the catgut, he considered how much he preferred assisting Sunny over Reuben. But he had little choice; his family relied on his income from the Country Hospital. Still, relative to most of the other refugees, fortune had smiled on Franz. If not for the intervention of a kind old travel agent, his family might have faced the same miserable fate as Max Feinstein's daughter and her children. At least in Shanghai, Jews were free of persecution. Franz had never seen any evidence of anti-Semitism among the Chinese, nor the Japanese.

A few months earlier, at one of the Reubens' dinner parties, he had raised the subject with Colonel Tsutomo Kubota, who was a fixture at the tiresome soirees. "While we might be strategically allied with the Germans," Kubota said, "it does not mean we share their philosophies or bigotries."

"Does anti-Semitism not exist in Japan?" Franz asked.

Kubota considered the question. "For a nation without an indigenous Jewish population, we possess an unusual fascination for your people. Much of it dates back forty years to the Russo-Japanese War. We could not have won without a sizable loan from the Jewish American banker Jacob Schiff. Our nation is still grateful." He held out a hand. "However, our interest goes deeper still. You are familiar with *The Protocols of the Elders of Zion?*"

"A hateful hoax," Franz muttered. Fabricated in turn-of-the-nineteenth-century Russia, the widely circulated document propagated the myth of a worldwide Jewish conspiracy to control governments through economic and political influence.

"All nonsense, I realize." Kubota nodded. "At Cambridge, I roomed with a brilliant fellow named Lionel Reif. I spent school holidays with his family and developed a deep appreciation for the Jewish way of life. However, most Japanese have never met a Jew. They believe the stereotypes of *The Protocols* exist but interpret them in a very different light than the authors intended. To my people, if the Jews control all the banks and governments, it can only mean that they are important and influential people to be respected, not shunned."

"What does that mean, Colonel?" Franz frowned. "That your people display anti-Semitism in reverse?"

"I suppose so, yes." Kubota smiled. "Most Japanese believe that Jews create wealth and success wherever they go. As you know, we are one of the few nations to encourage immigration of the German Jews. My government even once considered populating the province of Manchuria with Jewish refugees to encourage growth and industry."

Samuel Reuben pulled Franz out of the memory. "We are still waiting, Adler," he said tersely as he swung the end of the stitch from side to side.

Franz snipped the suture near the base of the thyroid.

After assisting Reuben for almost eighteen months, Franz had developed grudging respect for his colleague's skill and judgment. He also appreciated that Reuben craved deference. As long as Franz responded accordingly, he was treated more like a junior doctor than an orderly. But the moment Franz disagreed or suggested an alternate approach, Reuben inevitably did the opposite and punished him with some kind of degrading task.

Only weeks after Franz had started at the Country Hospital, after a complicated resection of a colonic tumor, Reuben viewed him with a smug smile and said, "Surely even Vienna's youngest-ever surgical professor must be impressed by such an operation?"

Franz never considered the professorship much of a feat. He had effectively fallen into the role after his mentor, Dr. Ignaz Malkin, was debilitated by a heart attack and insisted that his protégé inherit the role rather than a loathed rival. But Reuben referenced Franz's former title often, calling him "Herr Professor."

As they walked the corridor toward the surgical ward, Franz turned to Reuben and said, "You know that I perform a few operations at the refugee hospital."

Reuben glanced sidelong at him. "Yes. If some poor refugee has a bothersome hernia or gallstone, I hear you are the man to see."

"Exactly." Franz ignored his condescending tone. "Most of the time, we do basic procedures. However, I have a more complex case that I hope to tackle there."

His interest piqued, Reuben stopped and turned to him. "Oh? What procedure is that?"

"A Whipple's."

"A Whipple's," Reuben echoed reverentially. "I have yet to perform one. Just my luck, I hardly ever get cancers of the pancreas. At least, none that are operable. What is the diagnosis?"

"Cholangiocarcinoma."

Reuben's dark eyes widened behind his tortoiseshell glasses. "One of your refugees has a cholangiocarcinoma?" Franz knew better than to correct Reuben's misconception that the patient was a refugee. "How did you possibly make the diagnosis at that little hospital of yours?"

"She came to me diagnosed. She had contrast X-ray studies performed elsewhere."

"Did she?" Reuben's forehead wrinkled. "So I presume the patient can also afford treatment elsewhere?"

"I suppose so. Yes."

Reuben raised an eyebrow. "Then why would she choose to have the surgery at a hospital with such basic capabilities?"

"Someone recommended me." Franz shrugged, eager to move the conversation forward. "However, we do not have the necessary equipment. If I am to perform surgery, I will have to borrow precision tools from a more equipped facility. I was hoping you might lend me—"

"Yes!" Reuben surprised Franz with his sudden willingness. "Yes, of course."

"Thank you. That will be of great help to—"

"I can't lend you the equipment, of course," Reuben cut him off. "But I have a much better idea. A Whipple's is far more involved than simply having the right forceps and clamps. Think of all the postoperative attention required. It should really be undertaken by two experienced surgeons." He nodded to himself. "We will perform the surgery here. At the Country Hospital. Together."

Together? I will end up holding retractors while you hack out the tumor. Franz silently chided himself for not having predicted Reuben's response.

"Well, what do you think, man?"

Staring into Reuben's stubborn eyes, Franz reached a decision. He had agreed to treat Edda Schwartzmann but could not proceed without the right equipment. The Schwartzmanns and Franz were going to have to live with the compromise. "Thank you, yes. We will do it here."

"It's agreed then," Reuben said. "The sooner the better, too. Why don't you have the patient come by my clinic tomorrow for an initial consultation? We can schedule the operation for the end of the week."

"I will inform the patient and her husband."

"I will let my secretary know. What is the patient's name?"

Franz was grateful that Edda's ambiguous surname could pass for Jewish, but he thought it best not to mention her first name. "Mrs. Schwartzmann."

"Schwartzmann. I will tell Mrs. MacMillan." Reuben frowned. "Schwartzmann, is it? I used to play bridge with a Schwartzmann at the French club. Must be six or seven years ago, at least. A diplomat. Full of funny anecdotes. I used to think of him as quite a likeable chap. I later found out the rotter had become a Nazi!" He snorted in disgust. "What was his first name? Herbert . . . Horst . . . No. Hermann! Hermann Schwartzmann."

Franz kept his expression blank, but Reuben still made the connection.

"Hang on! Is this woman related to *that* Schwartzmann?"

Cornered, Franz could only nod. "His wife."

"You must be joking!" Reuben cried. "You would have me operate on a Nazi?"

"I never asked you to."

"Worse!" His pale face went splotchy with indignation. "You wanted to make me complicit—to borrow my equipment!—without revealing what kind of treason I would be a party to." He shook his finger at Franz. "Never mind that my nation is at war with his. Schwartzmann and his lot would wipe us Jews off the face of the earth if they could. And you honestly expect me to help his Nazi wife?"

Franz looked beyond Reuben to see Sunny standing

motionless at the end of the hallway. "I don't know whether she is a Nazi or not," he said calmly. "All I know is that she is suffering and will die without surgery."

"So let her then," Reuben grunted.

"I am no more eager than you are to help Schwartzmann." Franz met Reuben's outraged eyes. "I did not choose his wife as a patient. They came to me."

"What difference does that make? You are *choosing* to operate on her."

"I don't see it as my position to judge them. And I cannot neglect her suffering because I loathe everything her husband stands for."

"Such lofty principles," Reuben snickered. "But I wonder if those are your only motives."

"What else then?" Franz asked, wrestling the exasperation from his tone.

"Perhaps you relish the challenge," Reuben said. "I suspect you would operate on a rabid rat for the thrill and the glory. If the Schwartzmann woman dies, then it was expected. But if she lives, word of the success could only further Herr Professor's reputation."

Franz felt the anger simmering. He realized it would be best to walk away before saying anything he could not take back. "You have made your point," he said with teeth almost touching. "I will not borrow equipment from you or the Country Hospital."

"No. You will most certainly not."

Franz turned away, but Reuben called after him. "Oh, and Adler."

Franz stopped but didn't turn to face him. "Yes?"

"If I hear that you are operating on Nazis *anywhere* in Shanghai, I will not be able to maintain our professional association."

There is little professional about it! Franz wanted to scream.

Reuben's oxfords clicked angrily away on the polished floor. The noise stopped for a moment, and Franz heard him say, "The same applies to you, Nurse Mah. If you assist in the care of Nazis in any way, then you will no longer work here either! Am I clear?"

Franz looked over his shoulder and saw Reuben disappear around the corner. Sunny hurried to him. "Are you all right, Franz?"

He nodded. "You heard all of it?"

"Most of it," she said sheepishly. "I did not intend to eavesdrop. I was just—"

"That man!" His voice cracked with anger.

"What will you do now?"

He rubbed his temples. "I have no idea, Sunny."

"What choice do you have? You cannot operate without proper equipment."

Franz saw her point. Reuben had inadvertently just offered him an easy way out of his dilemma. By rights, his conscience should have been appeased. "Dr. Reuben is not the sole keeper of surgical tools in Shanghai, Sunny. I know people at the Shanghai General and other hospitals."

"But if Dr. Reuben finds out that you went ahead and operated on the patient . . ."

"I might be searching elsewhere for another intern's job."

"And how will you provide for your family?"

More than just his salary was at stake. Franz thought of Clara Reuben's ultimatum concerning Hannah's position at the Jewish School, but he kept it to himself.

"Can you risk so much for one patient?" Sunny asked.

Why did the Schwartzmanns have to come to me?

He ran his hands through his hair, resisting the urge to pull out clumps. "I am a doctor, Sunny. God knows, right now I wish I wasn't. I took an oath. How can I turn my back on a patient because it suits me?"

Her face lit with a sympathetic smile. She laid her hand softly on his shoulder. Her touch stirred him so much more than any of Lotte's kisses. "My father . . ." she said. "My father would have felt the same."

"I knew you would understand."

"So when are we going to perform her surgery?"

"No, Sunny! *If* I were to operate—and I am not saying that I intend to—then I will find someone else to assist me. I could not risk your career, as well."

Her smile held steadfast. "Everything you just said about your sense of duty and obligation applies to me also, Dr. Adler. What kind of nurse would I be if I backed away now?"

Franz didn't have an answer. Partly because she had a point, but mainly because at that moment it took every inch of restraint not to wrap his arms around her.

⌒ *Chapter 27*

Franz and Heng's late-afternoon teas had evolved into a weekly routine. They always met in Heng's flat, where an appealing blend of jasmine, lavender, and incense permeated the room. Though it was the exact same size as the Adlers' apartment, one floor above, the Zhous kept their home so uncluttered that it seemed far more spacious to Franz.

Franz and Heng sat, as usual, on the low wooden chairs in the same spot where Shan's mattress lay at night. Franz had long ago sniffed out his favorite cafés in Frenchtown for his daily espresso—one of the few luxuries he allowed himself—but he drank only tea with Heng, and always the same jasmine blend.

Their visits reminded Franz of his weekly ritual with Karl at Café Altman. His little brother would have liked Heng. Unassuming, gentle, and erudite, the former professor possessed many of the same traits as Karl, even a fatalistic sense of humor. But Franz doubted that his brother, the lawyer, would have ever embraced Communism the way the older man had. Heng had surprised Franz with the admission only a few months before, and he immediately swore Franz to secrecy. Not even Esther knew.

Heng now sipped his tea in silence, mulling over the loaded question Franz had just posed. Finally, he said, "I studied languages, not ethics, Franz."

"Surely you must have an opinion."

Heng lowered his cup. "While I am not familiar with the wording of your Hippocratic oath, I doubt it requires a physician to put his own family in jeopardy for the sake of a patient."

Franz shook his head. "It's not just that."

"What else then, my friend?"

"Perhaps Dr. Reuben is right. Maybe pride is driving me more than any sense of obligation or duty."

Heng studied Franz for a silent moment. "You said you have performed this operation before, correct?"

"I have, yes."

"I assume that regardless of the outcome you will need to be discreet about your involvement."

Franz grimaced. "Operating on a Nazi's wife? I can't imagine anything I would less want to call attention to."

Heng nodded. "Then I think it's safe for us to assume that, in this instance, you are not driven by pride."

Franz stared down at the tea leaves at the bottom of his teacup. "I do not like to see any person suffer."

"Perhaps that is all there is to it?"

Franz sighed. "Isn't it still selfish of me to compromise my family's well-being for the sake of a patient? Especially this woman."

"Because of who her husband is?"

"As far as I'm concerned, he represents the very worst in the world today."

Heng tilted his head. "It seems to me he faces stiff competition for that honor."

"Ah." Franz nodded. "The extremists, like the rabid Nazis who would kill us Jews with their own hands, have always been around. But the complicit moderates! They are the ones who empower the fanatics. People like this diplomat who are too educated to believe Hitler's nonsense about a superior race but happy to benefit from his hostile policies. They have turned a blind eye and allowed the fanatics to spread their poison and terrorize people at will. Ultimately, men like Schwartzmann have done the most damage."

Heng tapped his chin. "You mean through willful neglect?"

"Exactly so! A willful neglect of common decency." Franz raised his shoulders. "Why would I risk so much to help this man? It's not a sacrifice that I'm eager to make. You understand?"

"I understand a little about difficult choices." Heng removed his glasses and rubbed his eyes. "And sacrifices that affect more than one's own self." He wiped his glasses on a cloth handkerchief. "I have never told you what became of my daughter, Chang Jen."

Franz shifted in his seat. "I knew that you and your son escaped Nanking. What I . . . um . . . had heard about the bloodshed there, I always assumed . . ."

"My wife, Lien, yes." Heng put his glasses back on and adjusted their position. "Not my daughter, though.

Chang Jen died two years before the Japanese invaded Nanking. It broke my poor wife's heart and her spirit. I doubt she would have lasted much longer even if the Japanese had never invaded."

At a loss for words, Franz simply nodded.

"Shan and Lien were never political. I sympathized with the socialists but only in an academic's impotent way. But Chang Jen, ah, she was different." He smiled to himself. "When she was still just a child, no more than twelve or thirteen, she read a translation of Marx's *Das Kapital*. It changed her. She devoured everything by socialist writers she could get her hands on. And her passion only deepened as she grew up." His grin faded. "I warned her that Nanking—the capital of Chiang Kai-shek's nationalist China—was a terribly dangerous place to be a Communist. I begged her to go to the countryside, where the Communists at least congregated in the relative protection of the hills and villages. Chang Jen insisted on being at the forefront. 'To spread the word within the heart of the enemy,' as she used to say. She became an editor at the most popular—and therefore dangerous—underground newspaper in Nanking: *Xīn Zhìxù. The New Order*."

Heng was silent for a long moment. "The Japanese were bearing down on China like a hungry dragon, but the generalissimo never concerned himself with that threat. No. While leaving our borders unprotected, Chiang and the Kuomintang concentrated on rooting out every last Communist sympathizer.

"It was a hot August afternoon—1935. Most of the others from the newspaper had gone to the river to cool off." Heng chuckled again, a soft hollow sound. "Not Chang Jen. She was far too dedicated for such frivolities. There were only three others present when the Kuomintang soldiers raided." He held out his small hands. "There were no formalities such as a trial of any kind. They took all four prisoners out to the local quarry . . ." He dropped his hands. "They were dead before sundown."

Franz thought of Karl again. "Oh, Heng . . . I'm so very sorry."

"My wife . . . Lien was devastated. Shan reacted with anger." He stared intently into his cup as though looking through a window into the past. "The terrible irony is that we were only a week away from leaving Nanking when Chang Jen was killed. Since she refused to leave Nanking on her own, I had decided to relocate the whole family. Through an acquaintance in Canada, I had found a position at the University of British Columbia." He paused to collect himself. "After my daughter died, we never left. I joined the Communist Party, primarily in Chang Jen's honor. I threw myself into the movement, willing to do whatever was required to destabilize Chiang's government. I even wrote for *The New Order*."

"Such a terrible waste," Franz muttered.

"Nowadays, I am not even sure why I still belong to the party. I don't really believe in it anymore after Stalin negotiated the nonaggression pact with Hitler. It would have broken Chang Jen's heart to have seen the Soviets betray proletariats everywhere by conspiring with the Nazis." Heng looked up from his teacup as though snapping free of a trance. "Pardon me, Franz. I truly have become an old man the way I ramble on sometimes."

"It is more than understandable."

"There is a point to all of this," Heng said. "My daughter was born a revolutionary. She no more chose Communism than she chose to be Chinese. However, Chang Jen understood the risk of distributing a radical newspaper right under the generalissimo's nose. She once told me that it was a sacrifice she was willing to make. But the sacrifice went far beyond her. My wife, Shan . . . and even me to a lesser degree. We all paid too." He tapped a knobby forefinger to his temple. "Do you understand?"

"I see." Franz nodded. "I cannot make this decision without consulting my family."

Heng reached for his cup, sipped from it, and made a face. He laughed softly. "Please, my good friend, don't ever again permit me to chatter on until my tea goes cold."

∽

Franz trudged back to his apartment, weighed down by pity for his wise friend. He opened the door to find Esther and Simon sitting beside each other on the couch, howling with laughter. Neither of them seemed to even notice him enter.

Simon choked out the end of his story. As best as Franz could tell, it involved a disagreement between a German refugee and a rickshaw driver that was held in a mishmash of languages. "*No chargee, du ganèf!*" Simon repeated three times, impersonating the distraught refugee's shrill cry, in half pidgin English and half Yiddish, of "Don't cheat me, you thief!"

Esther was laughing so hard that she clutched her sides. "Stop, Simon. Please."

Franz's mood lightened at the sight of them so happy and carefree. The American had that effect on Esther. He wore his love for her as prominently as his favorite fedora. Esther was harder to read. While she seemed to revel in Simon's company, she never spoke of him in a romantic sense. And a year and a half after her husband's murder, sometimes late in the evening Franz would still hear the quiet sobs coming from the room she shared with Hannah. In her waking hours, however, Esther never dwelled on the past. She had established a full life for herself in Shanghai, frantic with work and social engagements. Aside from managing the Adlers' home, she walked Hannah to school, volunteered for the CFA, and even ran a small business reselling clothes and jewelry on consignment. She seemed to know everyone in the neighborhood and most refugees by name. The peddlers called to her so often from the street below that the Russian and Jewish boys in the neighborhood had taken to jokingly cry out, "Mrs. Esther, Mrs. Esther!" in mock Chinese accents.

Esther wiped away her tears of laughter. Simon looked over to Franz with a broad smile. "Hi ya, Franz. How goes it?"

Franz shrugged. "I must speak with you two."

Simon and Esther shared an uneasy glance, as though caught by a teacher while up to no good. "What is it, Franz?" Esther said.

He stood in front of them with his arms at his side. "It concerns a patient."

Esther tilted her head in surprise. "At the refugee hospital?"

Franz nodded. "Essie, do you remember on the *Conte Biancamano* I told you I had run into a man who turned out to be a German diplomat?"

"The fellow you originally mistook for Jewish?" she asked. "*He* is the patient?"

"His wife," Franz said. "She requires surgery."

Simon's jaw fell and he straightened in his seat. "You plan to operate on a German official's wife at *our* hospital?"

"Even worse." Franz went on to tell them about Edda Schwartzmann's cancer and Samuel Reuben's threat to fire him if he operated on her anywhere.

"You feel guilty for helping them?" Esther ventured.

"Manners and culture aside, Schwartzmann is still a Nazi to me." Franz swallowed. "How is it right to use a hospital built for Jewish refugees to help such a person?"

Simon and Esther traded concerned looks, but said nothing.

"Essie, if Reuben ever finds out . . ." Franz held out his hands. "How can I risk Hannah's—and your—future that way?"

Esther stared at Franz with the same measured calm she had shown so often in their final days in Vienna. "Franz, you are certain that no Gentile surgeon can offer this woman the same treatment?"

Franz shook his head. "Those surgeons are the ones who sent her to me."

Esther shrugged. "The answer is simple. You must operate."

Franz was stunned by the casualness of her response, but Simon nodded his support. "Look, I don't like this one little bit either," he said. "But Essie's right. You can't just turn your back on the woman."

"What if Reuben or other Jews in the community find out that I operated on her?"

Esther's expression remained placid. "You mentioned that her husband could pass for Jewish. How about his wife?"

Franz had a mental image of the emaciated, jaundiced woman. "She just looks ill."

Esther held up a hand, palm upward. "So where is it written that she has to register at the hospital as the wife of a Nazi diplomat?"

"Brilliant, Essie! It just might work!" Franz exclaimed.

"She could be admitted under any name. Nobody checks. And no one, except those of us in the operating room, even needs to know her real diagnosis!"

Simon nodded his silent endorsement, while Esther offered a tight smile. But Franz's relief was short-lived. An icy chill crept down his neck. So much would be at stake.

⌒ *Chapter 28*

APRIL 21, 1940, SHANGHAI

Sunny's fingers tingled and her back ached. She had hunched over the operating table for more than four hours—longer than any other surgery she had assisted—while Franz calmly excised Edda Schwartzmann's cancerous bile duct, along with the head of the pancreas and sections of her stomach and duodenum. Sunny marveled at his craftsmanship. With the touch of a magician, he merged all the fragmented organs back into some semblance of workable order, before sewing her abdomen closed.

Edda coughed twice on the operating table as she began to rouse. Free of the heavy cotton surgical gown, Sunny stretched her throbbing lower back.

"Now you look like a real surgeon," Franz said as he stretched too. He turned to the other nurse. "Berta, before we move her to the ward, will you please check and, if necessary, change the dressing on Mrs. Schwar—" He cleared his throat. "—Mrs. Silberstein's abdomen."

It was the second time that Sunny had heard Franz stumble over the patient's name, but Berta seemed oblivious to both slipups. "Certainly, Dr. Adler. I will ensure Mrs. Silberstein doesn't bleed through the dressing."

"And please, give her morphine injections as required for the pain."

"Of course I will, Dr. Adler." Berta's tone bordered on offended.

"I'm sorry, Berta." Franz grinned contritely. "You always have everything under control. A surgery of this length—with all that ether floating about—numbs the mind. Mine, at least."

Appeased, the nurse unfolded her plump arms and smiled. "Certainly, Dr. Adler."

Aside from Sunny, the other volunteer nurses at the refugee hospital were all middle-aged or older, married German refugees. They chattered relentlessly about Franz, referring to him behind his back as "Herr Doktor *Attraktiv.*" They were forever hypothetically marrying him off to unattached friends, sisters, or nieces. Sunny's name came up from time to time, but none of the other nurses were aware of how deep her feelings ran. While Simon had a hunch, only Jia-Li recognized how hard Sunny had fallen for the surgeon. The previous day over lunch, Jia-Li had pressed Sunny about him.

"I still do not see the problem, *xiǎo hè.*" Jia-Li exhaled a puff of smoke. "*This* doctor is not married, is he?"

Sunny shook her head. "But he has been involved with another woman for the past year."

Jia-Li arched an eyebrow. "A year, and yet he has not proposed to her?"

"Not that I am aware of."

Jia-Li brought the cigarette holder to her lips. "Sunny, if there is one thing I understand better than you, it is how men think. Trust me, if your widowed doctor loved this woman, he would have asked her to marry him by now."

"Do you really think so?"

"Without a doubt." Jia-Li laid her hand on top of Sunny's. "But he needs to hear how you feel."

Sunny pulled her hand free and waved it vehemently. "No! I can't."

"I know you too well." Jia-Li laughed out another stream of smoke. "Most women would have let him know long ago through gestures and tone of voice. Not you. You keep it all in. I would wager that the good doctor doesn't have an inkling of your feelings for him."

"Good."

Jia-Li's expression hardened. "Not good at all, Sunny. You must tell him!"

"I won't." Sunny folded her arms across her chest. "I will not be the other woman. Not again. I still have not forgiven myself for the last time. With Wen-Cheng."

Sunny had left the restaurant more determined than ever to bury her feelings for Franz. However, now as she walked beside him down the hospital's narrow hallway with their elbows only inches apart, her resolve wavered.

At the end of the corridor, Hermann Schwartzmann paced furiously, a stream of pipe smoke marking his circular route. As soon as the diplomat saw them, he stopped dead in his tracks and yanked the pipe from his lips. He opened his mouth but closed it without a word, as though afraid to inquire about the outcome.

"Your wife is beginning to wake, Herr Silberstein," Franz said in the same cool tone he always adopted with Schwartzmann. "You will be able to visit her soon."

"Oh, good. Wonderful." Schwartzmann nodded gratefully. "And the . . . the surgery?"

"It went as well as can be expected," Franz said. "We found no unpleasant surprises. We were able to remove the tumor. And I could not see or feel any obvious spread of the cancer inside her abdomen."

Schwartzmann's shoulders sagged with relief. His face crumpled for a moment, but he quickly regained his composure. "Oh, thank you, Dr. Adler. Thank you so very much."

Franz held up a finger. "I must remind you that none of this guarantees a cure. As I warned you, cholangiocarcinoma is an aggressive tumor. While I did not feel any masses, it does not mean the cancer has not already spread microscopically beyond the bile duct."

Unperturbed, Schwartzmann slipped the stem of the pipe back between his lips. "You did indeed warn us. Without your intervention, my Edda's fate would have been sealed. You have given us a chance. That is more than I had the right to ask of you."

Franz studied him for a long moment before speaking. "Even if her recovery is uneventful, your wife will have to remain in the hospital for a few weeks, possibly longer."

"I understand," Schwartzmann said.

Franz glanced over either shoulder to make sure no one was within earshot. "I trust you will respect the terms of our agreement. No visitors aside from yourself. And you will tell no one where *Frau Silberstein*"—he stressed her alias—"had her surgery or who performed it."

Schwartzmann laid a hand over his heart. "I swear it—again—on my life."

Franz nodded. "The nurses will let you know when Mrs. Silberstein has awakened enough for you to visit."

Franz began to turn away when Schwartzmann called to him. "Dr. Adler?"

"Yes?"

"You are a fine, fine man, Dr. Adler," Schwartzmann said.

Franz still could not separate the polite diplomat from the regime that he served. The familiar sense of indignation stirred again. "No, Mr. Silberstein. I am just a Jew. Nothing more." He strode off without waiting for a reply.

Schwartzmann stared after the departing surgeon before he turned to Sunny. Their eyes locked for a moment, and she detected a glimmer of shame in them. "Thank you, Miss Mah." He broke off the eye contact. "I understand Dr. Adler would not have been able to perform the operation without your assistance."

Schwartzmann struck Sunny as so civilized. She wanted to ask him how he could work for a government like Hitler's, but instead she simply nodded.

∼

Sunny caught up with Franz outside the changing rooms. He looked grim.

"It's over now, Franz."

"We will see," he muttered.

"It was the right thing to do."

"For whom, Sunny?"

"For them. For you. For everyone."

He nodded slightly. "We will see," he repeated.

She ran out of words to reassure him. Instead, she asked, "Where are you going now?"

"To the Country Hospital. And I had better arrive armed with a flawless excuse for my absence this morning."

"I have little doubt that Dr. Reuben will be enthralled by the details of Mrs. Silberstein's hemorrhoid repair."

Franz showed a fleeting grin. "Are you heading to the Country Hospital as well?"

"Yes, but I planned to stop for lunch along the way."

Without even considering, Sunny blurted, "Would you have time to join me?"

"Not really, no."

She flushed with embarrassment before turning to leave.

"Wait, Sunny," Franz called after her. "I had better eat something."

Outside the hospital, the sun had finally broken through the clouds, bringing with it the first inklings of spring. Inhaling the warm air, Sunny glanced at Franz. Some of the worry had drained away from his features as he blinked in the bright sunlight.

Fai was already waiting at the curb. He drove them back to the International Settlement via the Garden Bridge. As the car idled at the Japanese checkpoint, Sunny's heart thudded hard. As always, she scrutinized the guard's face in search of a scarred lip but saw none.

"Are you all right, Sunny?" Franz asked.

Sunny looked away from the window.

"It can't be easy, Sunny. With so many Japanese soldiers to remind you of that night . . ."

She forced a smile. "I am all right, Franz."

As soon as they reached the International Settlement, Sunny pointed to the curb and said, "Here is fine, thank you, Fai."

They climbed out in front of Public Garden, which jutted out to a point at the southern intersection of the Whangpoo River and Soochow Creek. Many native Chinese resented the colonial English-style greens, which up until the turn of the nineteenth century had bore a sign reading NO DOGS OR CHINESE ALLOWED. But Sunny had always loved the manicured lawns, colorful flower beds, and, especially, the central red-topped gazebo where her father used to bring her to watch brass bands play in the summer.

They walked along the perimeter of Public Garden. The oily aromas from the street kitchens wafted by. Sunny's stomach rumbled as they approached the little stall where the same gnarled old woman who had been there forever made some of the best bamboo-wrapped rice dumplings in the city.

A new concern struck Sunny, and she felt her face reddening again. "I am sorry, Franz. The food here . . . it's not kosher."

Franz shrugged. "Neither am I."

"But I thought . . . oh, good. Do you trust me to order our lunch?"

He bowed his head. "With my life."

She laughed. "Hopefully, it will not come to that."

Sunny ordered four *zongzi*s or dumplings and, out of tradition, haggled with the woman until they agreed on a price. At the next stall, she ordered two other Shanghai delicacies: *cong you bin* or fried chive pancakes, and *you-tia,* fresh Chinese crullers. Sliding the pancakes off the grill, the cook stacked and folded them inside newsprint before passing them to Franz.

They headed inside Public Garden and found an empty bench facing the gazebo. After they spread the food between them, Sunny described each dish, relishing the opportunity to teach Franz for a change. He sniffed the *zongzi* dubiously before taking a small bite. As he chewed, his eyes lit with pleasure. He took a much bigger second bite. "Delicious. And all this time, I was warned to stay clear of the street kitchens."

"You only have to know which ones are safe." Sunny grinned. "I can help there."

They ate in comfortable silence. Sunny was full after finishing a *zongzi* and three slices of *cong you bin,* but Franz kept going until only a few pieces of *you-tia* remained. "I was hungrier than I realized," he said with a sheepish grin as he wiped his lips with a handkerchief.

"It was a long, difficult surgery."

Franz's smile shrank. "I suppose."

"Tell me, Franz. Please."

He paused a moment. "I always love the peacefulness of the operating room. Inside, I can tune out the rest of the world and focus only on the patient and the surgery. But today . . ."

"You performed a flawless operation."

"Today I dragged all the ugliness of the world into the operating room with me."

Sunny touched his hand. "It's over now."

Franz laid his other hand on top of hers. "I hope it gives Mrs. Schwartzmann relief from her symptoms. Perhaps even a cure. But if the Reubens were ever to discover that I went ahead and operated . . ."

"We won't let that happen," Sunny said, distracted. Franz's touch had been spine-tingling. She felt her earlier resolve melting away. For a moment, she lost herself in his troubled hazel eyes.

He squeezed her fingers and leaned closer. "I am not sure where I would be without you."

"At the wrong street kitchen, no doubt."

A faint smile crossed his lips but his gaze grew even more intent. "You have no idea how much you mean to me, Sunny."

She swallowed. "I feel it too, Franz."

"You know, with Lotte . . ."

The mention of the other woman's name broke the mood like an air-raid alarm sounding. Sunny sat up straighter and tried to pull her hand free of his, but Franz held on. "I don't love her, Sunny."

The words were painfully reminiscent of Wen-Cheng's rationalizations. Sunny yanked her hand out of his grip and stood to her feet. "We should be getting to the hospital now."

Franz nodded but made no effort to rise from the bench. He spoke to the ground. "If it were only about my position at the Country Hospital, I would never let that stop me. I could find work elsewhere." He turned to her, his face taut with angst. "But Hannah is so happy at school. She is accepted there. I cannot take that from her. I simply cannot."

Sunny's head spun. "The Country Hospital? Hannah's school?" She squinted. "What do those have to do with us?"

"Mrs. Reuben is desperate for me to marry her niece. She persuaded the school to accept Hannah in the first place. And Clara can just as easily have her removed if she so chooses."

"Mrs. Reuben is blackmailing you?" Sunny dropped back onto the seat beside him. "Franz, I had no idea."

"How could you?" He reached for her hand again but stopped and pulled back before making contact.

⌒ *Chapter 29*

"D r. Reuben has canceled the afternoon surgeries," the Country Hospital's matron, Mrs. Bathurst, announced before Franz even had a chance to remove his jacket.

"Why is that, Matron?" Franz asked, wondering if Reuben had already caught wind of the clandestine surgery on Edda Schwartzmann.

"A dignitary of some kind or another has arrived in town, and Mrs. Reuben has arranged an afternoon tea." Bathurst glanced from side to side before adding, straight-faced, "The Reubens have been known to hobnob now and again, Dr. Adler."

Franz was relieved to not have to face Reuben, but he couldn't shake his despondency over how Sunny and he had left things between them. Anxious to avoid her while the wound was so fresh, he raced through his rounds on the postoperative patients and headed home.

Esther sat in the main room sifting through a wicker basket full of clothes that she had accepted on consignment. She pulled out a long black dress from the basket and appraised it in the natural light. "Home so soon, Franz? Have they closed both hospitals?"

"His Highness did not require my assistance today. I thought I would collect Hannah from school."

Esther expertly folded the dress. "She will be excited to see you."

Franz stepped closer. "Essie, I operated on her today."

"The diplomat's wife? *Ach so*." She laid the dress beside the basket. "How did it go?"

"As well as could be expected. Fortunately, no one questioned her identity."

"Simon will be relieved." A troubled look flitted across her face.

"What is it, Essie?"

She unfolded a gray silk scarf carefully. "It's not important."

"Has something happened between Simon and you?"

Esther studied the scarf for several seconds and then slowly lowered it. "He told me he loves me," she said softly.

"Oh, Essie, I could have told you that. Months ago, in fact."

She shrugged. "I suppose I had my suspicions, but we

had never discussed our feelings before. Simon caught me . . . unawares."

"How do you feel about him?"

She balled up the scarf and dropped it back into the basket. Her shoulders slumped. "Simon is not Karl."

"And he never will be. No one will." Franz wrapped an arm around her. "Essie, I saw how special your relationship with Karl was. What you had was rare indeed. But it's no reason to never try again."

She gazed at the floor without comment.

"Simon is a good man." Franz smiled tenderly. "I have seen how happy he makes you."

"But, Franz, I cannot even begin to—"

He held up a hand. "Imagine for a moment that your destinies were reversed and you had died before Karl. Would you have wanted him to spend the rest of his life lonely and pining?"

She folded her arms across her chest. "That is not how I spend my life, Franz."

"You are right. I apologize. But would you have wanted him to give up a second chance at love and happiness for the sake of your memory together?"

"I suppose not," she murmured.

"Trust me, Essie. Karl would feel the same. He would be overjoyed that you found someone who made you happy in his absence."

An anguished look crossed her face. "I understand what you are saying, Franz, but I still can't help feeling as though I am somehow betraying his memory."

"Oh, Essie, Karl's memory will never be threatened, no matter what happens between Simon and you. He is yours forever. Nothing will change that."

Esther didn't respond. Instead, she raised a pair of trousers to examine them but, after only a few seconds, let them fall back into the basket in a heap. She looked up at him, her eyes glistening. "I think I might . . . I might love Simon, too."

"You see." Franz smiled, pleased for his sister-in-law.

Franz left Esther to her work and headed out to meet Hannah. Walking northward in the warm sunshine, he crossed over into the International Settlement. Under blue skies, the sidewalk bustled with pedestrians again. He continued along the fashionable Seymour Road, arriving at the Shanghai Jewish School before classes had been dismissed.

With time to spare, he admired the school grounds. Across the courtyard stood the stunning neoclassical synagogue, the Ohel Rachel, where the most prosperous and established of Shanghai's Jews—the Baghdadi Sephardic families—came to worship. He considered returning with Kingsley's old camera. But as he studied the ornate building, imagining how it would look through his lens, he realized he had no interest in photographing it. To his eye, the temple was too perfect, lacking the character and dignity wrought only by time and the elements.

A bell chimed and, moments later, the school doors opened. Students of all ages, from tots to grown teens, flooded out. A few teenage boys were already lighting up smokes on the school steps. The girls were dressed in navy tunics with white blouses; the boys wore matching blazers and ties, several sporting yarmulkes.

Franz spotted Hannah before she saw him. She was walking between a girl of her height and a boy who was half a head shorter. They were all smiles and giggles. Hannah saw her father and broke free of her two friends. She shouldered through the crowd and rushed toward him.

"Papa!" She hugged him. "Why did you come? Is Tante Esther all right?"

"Esther is fine. I finished early today."

She kissed him on the cheek, her warm breath tickling his ear. "I'm glad you came."

Hand in hand, they headed back home, Hannah bubbling nonstop with details about the classroom, her teacher, and her friends. At one point, she looked up at him and asked, "Papa, will we have a Seder dinner this year?"

Franz realized that Passover was only three days away. "I think so, Hannah. Yes."

"Lotte told me we might be going to her home for Seder."

"Not this year. Your aunt has made alternate arrangements."

Hannah accepted the news with a shrug. "Today Mrs. Goldbloom taught us more about Passover and the story of Exodus."

"Did she?" The specifics of the Israelites' escape from Egyptian slavery had dimmed in Franz's memory. Lately, Hannah often referenced Jewish customs and biblical stories of which he had little or no recollection. He had attended a secular public school as one of only three Jews in his class. He found it ironic that his daughter, who was half Christian by birth, was growing up far more Jewish than he ever had.

"Mrs. Goldbloom compared the pharaoh who tried to stop the Jews from leaving Egypt to Adolf Hitler," Hannah said. "What do you think, Papa?"

"I suppose it's a fair comparison," he muttered.

She stopped walking. "In Egypt, God helped Moses free the Israelites. He sent down the ten plagues until the pharaoh had no choice but to let the Jews go. And then God parted the Red Sea to let them escape." She paused. "Papa, how come God isn't helping the Jews now?"

Franz had heard adults pose a similar question. For

him, the answer was easy, but he did not share his atheism with his daughter. Instead, he said, "Hannah, look at Shanghai. There are over twenty thousand German Jews here already."

Hannah's face lit with sudden insight. "Do you mean Shanghai is for us what the Sinai desert was for the Jews of Egypt?"

Franz had not thought of it that way, but he nodded. "Perhaps."

Her eyes went wide. "Or maybe, Papa, Shanghai *is* our Promised Land?"

Franz gently tousled Hannah's hair and laughed. "Time will tell, *liebchen.*"

His daughter abruptly switched topics to her school's upcoming track meet. Her disability prevented Hannah from running in the events, but she was ecstatic to have been chosen as one of the cheerleaders. She spent the rest of the walk speculating on how the new dress that Esther had promised to make would turn out.

As they reached their street, Hannah jerked her hand free of Franz's grip and raced toward the building. He looked over and saw Ernst Muhler and Shan Zhou at the entrance.

"Onkel Ernst!" Hannah cried as she jumped into his arms.

Cigarette in hand, the slender artist hoisted her higher with obvious effort. "Oh, puffin, if we're going to keep this greeting up, either you have to stop growing or this weakling will have to lift some weights." He lowered her. "Now let me have a look at you."

Hannah giggled as Ernst clutched his chin in his hand and squinted as he studied her as though assessing a piece of art. Ernst, who had added a Sun Yat-sen jacket to his black ensemble, clasped his hands together and shook them. "Those poor boys don't stand a chance. You get more and more glamorous with each passing day."

"Oh, Onkel Ernst, you're being silly."

"I'm an artist, Hannah. And if there's one thing I recognize, it's true beauty."

Franz shook hands with both men. "Will you come up and see Esther too?" he asked.

"We've already been," Ernst said. "We were just leaving."

"Where are you off to?" Franz asked.

Ernst subtly nodded in Hannah's direction. Franz understood. "Go on upstairs, *liebchen*," he said. "See how your aunt is coming along with your costume."

She hesitated. "But I haven't seen Onkel Ernst in so long."

"Oh, puffin, you will see me tomorrow night when I come for dinner." Ernst winked at her. "Now go tell your aunt that your father just invited us over for dinner tomorrow."

After Hannah left, Franz glanced from Shan to Ernst. The pair had become inseparable over the past year. Franz assumed they were lovers, but Ernst had never said as much, and Shan rarely spoke at all. "What is it, Ernst?" he asked.

The artist's eyes narrowed. "You remember Colonel Kubota?"

"Of course." Franz had sat through several dinner parties at the Reubens' with the colonel, but Clara had never invited Ernst back after the stir he had caused at their first dinner there. "What about him?"

"Lawrence Solomon," Ernst grumbled. "That soulless fraud who calls himself my art dealer sold Kubota one of my paintings."

"Is that not what an art dealer is supposed to do?"

Ernst grimaced. "He's not supposed to sell my work to the goddamned enemy!"

"Since when is Colonel Kubota your enemy?"

Ernst glanced at Shan, who stood as impassively as ever with a cigarette smoldering between his lips. He turned back to Franz. "Kubota and all his refinement and genteel rationalizations . . . He's no better than my Gestapo captain back in Vienna. Down deep, the Japanese are no different from the Nazis. Thugs and bullies, the lot of them. And I won't allow Kubota to use my art as part of his cultured disguise."

Franz's unease rose. "How do you intend to stop him?"

Ernst shrugged. "I am going to go and refund his money."

"And if he doesn't want a refund?"

"I will take my painting anyway!"

Shan eyed Ernst with a rare smile, but Franz's concern mushroomed. "Listen to me, Ernst. This is a mistake."

"I have built a career on mistakes." Ernst shrugged. "What is one more?"

Franz saw that his friend would not be swayed. "I'm coming with you," he said.

"Suit yourself," Ernst said. "Of course, Shan can't join me for obvious reasons. Who knows what they would do to a Chinaman on their own turf."

Franz and Ernst rode a rickshaw to the Garden Bridge and then crossed through the military checkpoints on foot. Just beyond the bridge, the Astor House Hotel—once known as the Waldorf Astoria of Shanghai—stood on the prime Broadway corner lot, fronting both the Whangpoo River and Soochow Creek. The low-rise Edwardian building had lost much of its luster: sun had

faded the walls and mortar had damaged the emboss-
ments and cracked many of the windows. A massive
Rising Sun flag flapped lazily over the entrance. Out
front, two Japanese soldiers stood rigidly on guard in
their khakis and puttees, bayoneted rifles held across
their chests.

Ernst strode straight over to the two guards. As he
neared, they closed the gap between them. "I must
see Colonel Kubota," he demanded.

The soldiers' expressions remained blank, but the
taller one shook his head and made a shooing gesture with his fingers.

Ernst put his hands on his hips. "I demand to see
Colonel Kubota!"

Both soldiers raised their rifles higher. Franz grabbed
Ernst by the arm and began to gently pull. "Ernst, this
is not working."

Ernst shrugged free of Franz's grip. He turned back
to the soldiers. "I am not going anywhere until I speak
to Colonel Kubota!" he said, raising his voice.

The shorter guard began to swing the barrel of his
rifle out toward Ernst. He stopped halfway through
the arc. The two men suddenly parted. Another soldier,
wearing a green officer's uniform, stepped out between
them. He had a weak chin and high cheekbones that
made his face look almost triangular. "I am Captain
Yamamoto," he announced in serviceable English.
"What is your meaning?"

"I have to speak to Colonel Kubota," Ernst said.

"Who are you?"

"I am Ernst Muhler. This is Dr. Franz Adler."

Yamamoto nodded. "Why do you require to see
Colonel Kubota?"

Ernst puffed out his chest. "That is between the colonel and me."

Yamamoto eyed him for a long cold moment and then turned for the entrance. "You will stay here."

They waited in front of the hostile guards for ten tense minutes before Yamamoto returned. "Come," he ordered.

Ernst and Franz followed him into the lobby of the hotel. The carpets were frayed and the textured wallpaper torn and peeling in places, but the massive chandelier that hung above the spiral staircase hinted at the building's former grandeur. Yamamoto led them upstairs to the second floor. Near the end of the hallway, he stopped and knocked on a door.

They entered a hotel suite that had been converted into a spacious office. Colonel Kubota rose from his desk and walked over to greet them. His graying hair was shorter than before, but he had kept his pencil-thin mustache. As usual, Kubota wore a civilian suit and tie. "Dr. Adler, Mr. Muhler, what a pleasant surprise," he said.

Kubota indicated the far wall, where two oils hung. The first was a rolling countryside scene, reminiscent of a Constable painting. Ernst had painted the other: a portrait of a frail, ghostly white Chinese adolescent standing below a streetlight. The prostitute leaned back unnaturally toward the post as though she were suspended from it, her feet barely touching the ground. "You see, Mr. Muhler," Kubota said. "I did find the opportunity to view your work. And I was most taken."

"That is precisely what I have come to discuss," Ernst said.

Kubota bowed. "I would be honored to. I certainly have my own theories, but I would like to hear more about your inspiration—"

"Colonel!" Ernst cut him off. "I have come to reclaim my painting. Of course, I will refund you in full and cover any additional expenses."

Kubota shook his head. "Refund, Mr. Muhler? I do not understand."

"It's quite simple, Colonel. I do not want my work hanging in your office."

Kubota eyed him quizzically but said nothing.

Franz coughed into his hand. "Colonel, Ernst is very particular about where his work is displayed. He does not want it to be linked in any way to politics or governments—"

"Nonsense, Franz!" Ernst cut him off and turned back to Kubota. "I believe the Japanese army has no business in Shanghai. Or China. And I don't want my name or my art in any way associated with its presence here."

"I see," Kubota said quietly.

Ernst reached for his wallet. "So if you will tell me how much to reimburse you, I will make arrangements to have the painting collected."

"I enjoy this painting, Mr. Muhler," Kubota said softly. "I do not intend to part with it."

Ernst folded his arms across his chest. "But it's my creation, Colonel!"

Kubota indicated the desk behind him. "If you were the carpenter who built that desk, would you have the right to reclaim it because you didn't agree with my government?"

"That is an anonymous piece of furniture." Ernst shook a finger at his own painting. "This is my art. It is a part of me. And I have the right to say who owns it and where it hangs."

"I mean no disrespect, Mr. Muhler, but I do not agree," Kubota said slowly. "I purchased this painting. So I believe I have the right to determine where it hangs."

Ernst's cheeks flushed and his eyes darkened. Franz recognized that his friend was on the verge of snapping. "The colonel is right," Franz said.

Ernst turned on Franz, mouth agape. "You are taking *his* side?"

"It's not a matter of sides, Ernst. Like it or not, the colonel owns this painting now. You cannot stop him from displaying it as he sees fit."

Glaring, Ernst looked from one man to the other. "Perhaps you're right." He nodded to himself. "But Colonel, I wonder if you will wish to continue displaying it—more to the point, I wonder if your superiors will let you—once my next exhibition opens."

Kubota frowned. "Why would that make a difference, Mr. Muhler?"

"Because of its theme."

"Which is?"

Ernst's lips broke into a vindictive smile. "The rape of Nanking."

Franz caught the gasp before it left his lips. Kubota's face blanched momentarily, but he quickly regained his composure. "Perhaps, Mr. Muhler, it would be best if I returned your painting after all. I will have my aide make arrangements with Mr. Solomon."

"That will be most satisfactory," Ernst said.

"If there is nothing else then . . ." Kubota turned for his desk but stopped after a few strides. "Mr. Muhler, I admire a man who stands on principle. It is a most honorable stance. However, we have a saying in Japanese: *I no naka no kawazu taikai wo shirazu.*"

"What does that mean?" Ernst demanded.

"'A frog in a well does not know the great sea.'" Kubota sighed again. "The winds of change are howling through the Far East. Where your paintings do or do not hang, Mr. Muhler, might soon be the least of any of our concerns."

Captain Yamamoto escorted them out in sullen silence.

Franz decided that, since he was already in Hongkew, he would check in on Edda Schwartzmann at the refugee hospital. He found her asleep from the painkillers. In the same rumpled suit as earlier and reeking of pipe tobacco, Hermann Schwartzmann hovered at his wife's bedside. His face was haggard, but he broke into a grateful smile at the sight of Franz.

Franz pulled the partitions around them. "Mr. Silberstein, the nurses tell me that your wife's recovery from surgery has been uneventful so far."

"Yes, yes," Schwartzmann said. "She even mumbled a few words to me earlier in the afternoon. She said the pain was not as bad as she had expected."

"It will still be a few days before she can eat or drink." Franz indicated the blanket covering her abdomen. "I must examine her dressings now."

Schwartzmann nodded. "Please do, Dr. Adler."

After Schwartzmann stepped out, Franz pulled down the blanket and lifted up Edda's gown. She shifted slightly but did not open her eyes. The original bandages had not soaked through with blood or bile. Satisfied, Franz covered her again without removing the dressing.

Franz called Schwartzmann back to the bedside. "All is in order," he declared. "We will change the dressing tomorrow and every day thereafter."

As Franz turned to leave, Schwartzmann called to him. "Dr. Adler?"

Franz stopped. "Yes?"

"Regardless of your opinion of me, what you said earlier was not entirely correct." Schwartzmann cleared his throat. "I am extremely aware of what you have done for us. And one day, Dr. Adler, I hope I will be able to show you the extent of our gratitude."

Though Franz did not doubt the man's sincerity, Franz could not forget who Schwartzmann worked for. "I will see you tomorrow, Mr. Silberstein."

Drained, Franz longed to go home and climb into bed. As he stepped outside, he spied Fai's black Buick pull up to the curb. Sunny climbed out of the backseat. Franz's heart beat in his throat as he waited for her on the pathway.

Sunny hesitated and then walked toward him, stopping a few feet away. She mustered a small smile. "How is Mrs. Silberstein, Dr. Adler?"

"Reasonably well, Miss Mah, all things considered."

"That is a relief. Are you leaving now?"

Her jasmine scent drifted to him. "I was planning to, yes."

They fell into an awkward silence. Finally, Sunny looked down at her shoes. "Well, I promised Mr. Silberstein I would check in on them tonight too. I had best go see them."

Franz found her closeness and her fragrance overwhelming. He stepped forward, wrapped his arms around her, and pulled her to him.

Sunny looked at him with inviting eyes. He pressed his mouth against hers. The warm softness of her lips was exhilarating. She leaned her body into his and he kissed her hungrily.

Suddenly, Sunny wriggled out of his arms. She backed up two or three steps. "No, Franz. We can't!"

He held out a hand but let it fall back to his side without speaking a word.

Sunny's eyes misted over and her voice cracked. "You were right this afternoon. Lotte . . . Esther . . . Hannah . . . If something were to happen to your family, especially your daughter, we could never forgive ourselves."

PART V

Chapter 30

DECEMBER 7, 1941, SHANGHAI

"He asked me to marry him," Sunny murmured into her teacup.

Simon leaned against the table, propping himself up by his elbows. "Well? What did you tell him?"

"That I would think about it."

Simon whistled. "You wouldn't actually go through with it, would you?"

Sunny shrugged. "I am twenty-seven years old, Simon."

"Is that any reason to get married?" He grimaced. "Look at me. I'm five years older than you. I'm not concerned."

"Age doesn't matter for men. Besides, you will marry Esther someday. We both know it."

"Yeah, Essie will be ready soon enough." He nodded happily to himself. "Anyway, how could you marry one guy when you're in love with another?"

"Oh, Simon, that was a lifetime ago," she sighed. But every detail of that evening, eighteen months earlier, still burned in her consciousness. She could feel Franz's warm breath on her cheek and his hands pressing into the small of her back. She could taste the baking soda in his toothpaste and feel the soft pressure of his lips on hers. Most of all, she remembered how her heart broke wider with each step she took away from him.

But Sunny did not regret what she had done. *What kind of life could a mixed-blood and a widowed Jewish refugee share? And how selfish would it be to risk a child's well-being for the sake of my happiness?* She kept the thoughts to herself. "Besides, none of it matters now that Franz and Lotte are engaged," she said.

Sunny also had Wen-Cheng to consider. He blamed himself for the horrific car accident that had killed his wife. Wen-Cheng had caught their driver swilling rice wine before but had let him off with only a rebuke. The young doctor was supposed to have been in the car too; only a medical emergency kept him from the dinner party and certain death. Witnesses said they saw the Huangs' car weaving across Great Western Road even before it veered head-on into the oncoming traffic.

The guilt and sorrow had overcome Wen-Cheng. Sunny, who still grieved for her father, helped to see Wen-Cheng through his loss. She brought him meals that Yang had prepared, joined him on long walks, and even twice accompanied him to the Buddhist temple to burn incense in memory of his wife. After six months, Wen-Cheng snapped out of his despair and claimed to be more in love with Sunny than ever. She no longer loved him, though, and she knew she never again would. But she doubted that alone would stop her from marrying him.

"Sunny," Simon repeated, snapping his fingers. "It was only last year. Remember? The kiss that changed your life."

"Exactly, Simon. A lifetime ago." She looked out at the empty tables around them; until recently, the café had always been full. So many Shanghailanders had

already fled the city. Most of the others had seques-
tered themselves in their homes, fearing the worst.

"Everything has changed now that the war is coming to the Pacific," he sighed.

"You say it with such certainty."

He lowered his Coca-Cola bottle. "The peace talks
between the Americans and the Japanese have gone
nowhere. It's only a matter of time."

Sunny thought of the morning three weeks before,
when she stood at the harbor with thousands of others. The Whangpoo swarmed with Japanese naval vessels, but Sunny could not peel her eyes off the Fourth
Division U.S. Marines as they silently filed aboard their
carrier ships and prepared to leave Shanghai. The crowd
was silent. Its collective sense of abandonment hung in
the air like the low-lying clouds.

"I hate to say this, Sunny, but I'm relieved," Simon
said.

She tilted her head. "Relieved that your country is
on the verge of war?"

"Compared to the alternative? Yeah." He grunted.
"The Nazis have swallowed up the rest of Europe. And
they're steamrolling the Soviets. Leningrad under siege.
Germans at the gates of Moscow. At this rate, the Russ-
kis won't last the winter." He tapped the table. "Only
the Brits and their colonies fight on. But Churchill can't
do it alone, no matter how many tanks and planes
FDR sends him. America has to join this war." He
sighed. "I don't even want to think about what will
happen to all us Jews if they don't."

Lately, Sunny had avoided listening to the wireless,
as the war news was inevitably bad, but she couldn't
tune out the endless conversations at the refugee hospital. The Jewish staff and patients spoke about almost

nothing else. They were frantic with worry over families left behind in Europe. People were beyond despair. The rate of suicide had skyrocketed in the Jewish community, where it had once been so rare. The day before, Sunny had heard that Mrs. Waldenstein, a kind older woman with asthma, had slit her wrists in her bathtub only hours after being discharged from the hospital. Apparently, she had gone home to the news of her daughter's deportation to a relocation camp. Mrs. Waldenstein had ended her suicide note with the words "There is no room left in this world for our people."

Sunny and Simon parted ways outside the restaurant, and she headed straight home. As soon as she stepped through the door, Yang hurried up to her. "Ko Lo-Shen came looking for you, Soon Yi."

Sunny stiffened. "Is something wrong with Jia-Li?"

"It's always the same with her." Yang shook her head and cited the old Chinese proverb: "*Zì xiāng máo dùn*"—she pierces her shield with her own spear.

Opium. It had to be. But her friend had been clean for three years. *Why has she relapsed now, of all times?*

Jia-Li had turned her life around in the past year. She had quit the life of prostitution, rescued by a rich client, a divorced British Standard Oil executive. The last time Sunny had seen her best friend, she was sporting an engagement ring along with a smile even more luminous than the two-carat diamond solitaire.

Sunny stepped into her father's old office. She had never intended to turn it into a memorial to Kingsley, but she kept finding excuses to not clear it out. She rooted through the shelves of medications, dusting off some labels to read them. She pocketed the bottles of atropine and cannabis, wondering if the four-year-old medicines would even still be effective. She wavered a moment and then reached for a bottle of morphine and a glass syringe.

Fai was waiting for her at the curbside. The mid-afternoon streets were eerily quiet, as though people were battening down for a storm. The old Buick rattled over the Garden Bridge and came to a stop at the Japanese guard post. Out of habit, Sunny checked for the sailor with the scarred lip. She was alarmed to spot two soldiers posted instead of the usual one.

Fai climbed out of the car and bowed deeply before them. The second guard suddenly swung his rifle in Sunny's direction. Her heart leapt into her throat as he summoned her out of the car with a waggle of his bayonet. Hand trembling, she opened the door and stepped out. The soldier's lips curled into a snarl. She threw herself forward and bowed deeply at the waist, afraid her knees might buckle.

"All okay, Missy," Fai reassured in a whisper.

The second guard shrieked in Japanese for silence.

Out of the corner of her eye, Sunny saw the first guard climb into the car. The other guard uttered a grunt to free them from their bows. Gun pointed at Fai, he marched the driver over to the back of the Buick and gestured for him to open the trunk. Fai calmly complied.

The two soldiers scoured the car. Satisfied, they turned away from it, leaving the doors and trunk open. The first soldier shooed them away with a disdainful flick of his fingers.

As soon as they sped off, Sunny asked, "What was that all about, Fai?"

Staring at the road ahead, Fai shook his head. "The dwarf bandits are planning something, Missy. It is bad. Very bad."

They drove the rest of the way in silence. Fai dropped

Sunny off in front of the narrow lane that led to the Kos' *longtang* home.

Jia-Li's mother opened the door, and Sunny was overwhelmed by the sense of déjà vu. Inside, the windows were covered, and a slightly musty smell pervaded the small flat. Sunny tried to engage Lo-Shen in pleasantries, but the stooped woman hurried her to the bedroom before fleeing to another part of the apartment.

Since Sunny's last visit, the bedroom had been furnished with a simple Chinese-style bed and nightstand, but nothing else had changed. Jia-Li, shivering in her flimsy gown, lay curled up on the bed, facing the far wall.

"What has happened, *bǎo bèi*?" Sunny asked from the doorway.

Jia-Li rolled over and struggled to sit upright. Her loose gown scrunched up, exposing one of her small breasts and the tuft of hair between her legs. Despite the room's chill, sweat dripped down Jia-Li's pale brow. "You came!" she cried.

"Of course I came," Sunny said as she moved toward the bed.

"I need something strong," Jia-Li moaned.

"How long have you been back on the pipe?"

"A few weeks. Perhaps more." The words tumbled out in a tone that matched Jia-Li's frazzled appearance. "Who knows? Who cares? I haven't smoked any for over two days. And now I have the opium sickness again. I can't go on any longer, Sunny. I can't. Not this time!"

Sunny sat down on the mattress beside her friend, ignoring the smell of vomit that intensified with each inch that she drew nearer. "This is familiar territory for us, *bǎo bèi*."

Jia-Li shook her head wildly. "This is much worse, Sunny!"

Sunny chuckled softly. "You sound like a phonograph during these fits."

"No. No. *No!*" Jia-Li cried, writhing as though overcome by tics. "It's never been like this. *Never.*"

Sunny dug into her pocket and pulled out the bottle in which she had consolidated the two types of pills. She tapped out a few tablets into her palm. "These will help."

Jia-Li batted Sunny's hand, sending the pills scuttling across the floor. "Not that useless junk, Sunny! I need opium! Heroin. Or morphine. Something real!"

"Tell me, Jia-Li," Sunny said in a calm, firm tone. "What is so different this time?"

Jia-Li gaped at her, eyes ablaze. "I have never wanted to die before!"

Sunny was stunned. "No, Jia-Li. You do not mean that. You will feel differently once the sickness has passed."

Jia-Li hurled her small frame into Sunny, almost knocking her off the edge of the bed, and buried her face in Sunny's shoulder. "Godfrey left me." She sobbed. "He's gone, Sunny. Gone!"

Sunny stroked her friend's sweat-soaked hair. "Tell me, *bǎo bèi.*"

Jia-Li shivered uncontrollably. "We were going to elope. Godfrey was going to take me to Macau. He said it was so beautiful there . . ." She gulped back a gag. "Then Standard Oil called him back to England. They told him the Far East was too unstable."

"When did this happen?" Sunny asked.

"Three weeks ago."

"Why didn't you tell me sooner?"

"I was so ashamed," Jia-Li said in a small voice.

Sunny continued to stroke her friend's hair as she felt Jia-Li's tears seep through the fabric on her shoulder. "He will come back for you."

"No, he never will," Jia-Li choked out. She pulled her head back and stared at Sunny. "Godfrey told me . . . He said I would have 'done fine' for Asia, but that I would never be suitable for a London wife."

"The selfish fool!" Sunny filled with hatred for the man whom she had never even met. "Good riddance!"

Jia-Li's face crumpled. "I'm not good enough for anyone. I'm just a burden. An aging prostitute. Why did I ever think anyone could love me?"

"I love you."

Jia-Li clutched her abdomen, racked by cramps. She began to gag again. "You are my only real friend, Sunny," she sputtered.

Sunny reached into her pocket for the bottle of morphine and the syringe. Jia-Li watched with grateful eyes as Sunny dissolved the morphine tablet in drops of water and drew up a dose. Sunny pulled the damp gown off her friend's shoulder, exposing a patch of skin, and jabbed the needle into her upper arm.

They sat on the bed together for several minutes without saying a word. Finally, Jia-Li turned to Sunny, her pupils constricted and her brow dry. "My body feels better now." She gulped. "Not my heart, though. I can't go on without him."

"You can, and you will."

Jia-Li turned back to Sunny. "How did you do it, *xiǎo hè*? How did you just walk away from love?"

Sunny lightly touched her friend's cheek. "Life goes on, Jia-Li. It does. You will see."

But even as she spoke the words, the same thought looped in her head: *You can't walk away from love. It clings to you night and day.*

Chapter 31

Franz had not slept a full night through since proposing to Lotte Weczel. But he did not hold Lotte or their engagement responsible for his insomnia. He blamed Hitler. The flood of disastrous news from Europe, where the Nazis stood poised to dominate the continent and beyond, cut into his sleep like a neighbor's howling dog.

But Franz had yet to shake the doubt that had possessed him since sliding the ring onto her finger two months earlier. Even Lotte seemed excessively reserved in accepting his proposal. Franz sensed a dutifulness on her part that matched his own.

Still, his fondness for Lotte had steadily grown. On warmer evenings, they would stroll for miles through the French Concession chatting about music, religion, architecture, and, of course, Hannah. Despite their warm companionship, they never achieved true intimacy. The only time Franz had seen Lotte lower her guard was once, in the early fall at their favorite café, when they ran into a childhood friend of hers, a Swiss national named Bernard Leudenberger.

"A pleasure, Dr. Adler," the narrow-framed banker said before turning to Lotte with a wide smile that belied his otherwise somber appearance. "Always a delight to run into you, Charlotte."

"It has been a while." Lotte fought back a grin. "How is the family, Bernard?"

"Still very Swiss. You know Father." He sighed good-naturedly. "And your aunt and uncle, are they well? Does Clara still rule Shanghai with an iron fist?"

Lotte burst out laughing. "You exaggerate, Bernard.

Clara tries to help. She is very involved with schooling for local Jewish children." She motioned to Franz but kept her focus on Bernard. "She helped Franz's daughter secure a spot at the Shanghai Jewish school."

"Of course." Bernard held her gaze for a moment. "And your music, Charlotte?"

She looked away and cleared her throat. "I only teach now, Bernard."

"That is truly a pity." Bernard looked over to Franz. "Have you ever heard her play Brahms, Dr. Adler? The sound of an angel weeping."

Franz had never seen Lotte act as relaxed or laugh so freely. He hoped that one day she would open up around him as she had with her childhood friend, but in the months since bumping into Bernard, he had not glimpsed that side of her again.

Clara Reuben, of course, was elated over Franz and Lotte's engagement. More important, Hannah was happy. Franz could not tell, though, whether she was pleased for her own sake or for his. But Lotte was not the wife he would have chosen under different circumstances. *Sunny.* A year and a half had passed since their only kiss. The world had been upended in that time span, and yet his feelings had not budged.

A few days after that kiss, he had broached the subject again as they stood on the pathway outside the hospital. But Sunny did not waver. "We cannot just give in to our emotions, Franz."

"The world is already awash in sacrifice and tragedy," he said. "How can we turn our backs on a sliver of potential happiness?"

"We must, Franz," she said softly.

The urge to touch her face smothered his objectivity. "Why must we?"

Sunny viewed him with glistening eyes. She looked

so beautiful that his chest ached. "What would happen to Lotte?" she asked.

"Down deep, Lotte is strong. She will be all right."

"And what would become of your job at the Country Hospital?"

"There are other jobs."

"But there are no other schools for Hannah, are there?" she said. "There are just too many other lives to consider, Franz."

In the eighteen months since, Sunny's words had proven prophetic. Under Clara's continued sponsorship, Hannah had thrived at the Jewish school. And Franz's job at the Country Hospital had remained secure. He might have tolerated his fate better, perhaps even been contented, had he not had to face Sunny so often at both hospitals. He was constantly reminded how much he was missing in not sharing a life with her.

With the thoughts tumbling around in his head, he gave up on sleep. Just before five o'clock, he headed outside for a stroll to try to settle his mind. Franz even considered lugging the Kodak Brownie camera along but decided against it.

Over the past year, Franz had started to enjoy photographing buildings in Shanghai, as he had once done in Vienna. On his first trip, through the French Concession, he did not snap a single shot. Despite the neighborhood's charm and grandeur, none of the architecture piqued his interest. On his next outing, he wandered through Little Vienna and found himself standing outside the heim on Ward Road. The building was the largest of Shanghai's heime, the hostels, literally "homes," that the CFA ran for the thousands of refugees who could not afford their own housing. The walls of the faded brown structure were crumbling and its windows boarded, but something about the decrepit building moved Franz. He spent a full roll of his precious film photographing the heim, and returned three more times to capture it in different lighting.

However, his camera would have been of no use in the predawn darkness.

A damp night chill still hung in the air, but Shanghai was beginning to stir. Trucks rattled down Avenue Joffre. The little old vendor down the street had opened his newspaper stand, muttering to himself as he laid out his English, French, and Russian magazines. The wind carried the scent of yeast from a nearby bakery.

Without a specific destination in mind, Franz headed east toward the water. As he approached the riverfront, he heard an unfamiliar rumbling. The ghostly glow of ships moving in the harbor's morning fog wasn't unusual, but Franz sensed something was different.

Moments after he reached the Bund, the sky above the Whangpoo lit as though someone had launched New Year's fireworks early. Gunfire crackled. The pavement below his feet vibrated from a thundering explosion.

A few hundred feet offshore, three ships raced across the water. Smoke billowed from the *Idzumo*'s stack as the Japanese flagship and a second vessel chased a river gunboat, which was trying to outrun the other ships. In the light of the shell bursts, Franz spotted a Union Jack flying from the gunboat's platform. Though hopelessly outmatched, the sailors continued to fire back at the two ships trying to run it down.

Franz hardly breathed. The sky flashed with another round of explosions and gunfire. A sulfuric smell filled his nostrils. Amid the ground-shaking booms and flashes, it took Franz a moment to digest the implication of what he was witnessing. *Japan and Britain are at war!*

Horrified, Franz watched as thick black smoke streamed from the British gunboat. Flames lapped at its side. Soon, the Japanese ships overtook the wounded vessel that, even while sinking, continued to return gunfire. Franz saw British sailors leaping from its burning hull into the murky river. The gunboat began to list to the port side, but the Japanese ships kept shelling the boat. Then they turned their machine guns on the sailors bobbing in the dark waters of the Whangpoo. Franz's pulse pounded at the heartless slaughter.

This is how they treat their enemies? Cold fear crawled over him. *Oh my God, Hannah!*

Franz wheeled and ran back toward home.

The naval battle had shaken the city awake. Several people, some half-dressed in nightwear, stumbled through the streets in bewildered anxiety.

At the entrance to his building, he almost collided with Heng Zhou, fully dressed and heading off in the opposite direction. "Where are you going, Heng?"

"To Mr. Muhler's home to find Shan!" Heng said without slowing. "They have attacked Pearl Harbor!"

"Pearl Harbor? Where is that?" Franz called after him, but Heng was already gone.

Franz rushed inside the building and raced up the stairs. He burst into the apartment to find Hannah and Esther in their nightgowns sitting on the sofa, holding hands. They stared at the wireless as though it were a movie screen. In her stiffened left hand, Hannah held Schweizer Fräulein. Franz had not seen the doll in a long time.

Over the speaker, the tinny voice of the CBS commentator crackled with emotion. "Huge black clouds of burning oil still obscure the massive naval base at Pearl Harbor. It is too early to assess the damage or to know how many lives have been lost in this unprovoked attack. What is clear is that the Japanese have drawn America into this global conflict. And they have done so with a terrible first blow . . ."

Esther turned down the volume. "Those Hawaiian Islands are American soil, Franz. The Japanese have just attacked America."

Franz hung his head. "I was just at the waterfront, Essie. I saw them sink a British ship!"

Hannah turned to her father. "Papa, will the Japanese take over all of Shanghai now?"

Franz hesitated a moment. "I think so, *liebchen*, yes."

"They are on the side of the Nazis, aren't they?" Hannah's voice cracked with worry. "What will happen to us, Papa?"

"We will be all right," he said, trying to sound convincing. "The Japanese have controlled Hongkew for over four years, and they have never bothered with the German Jews there. There is no reason to think it will be any different now."

Hannah chewed on her lip. "And my school?"

"It will work out," he muttered.

Hannah clutched her doll even tighter to her chest as she struggled to maintain her composure. Months from her twelfth birthday and on the cusp of adolescence, Hannah had sprouted in the past year. But she was still only a child. "Will we really be all right, Papa?" she asked in a small voice.

The windows shook again with the sound of artillery fire. "Everything will be . . ." But Franz's words petered out.

Esther threw an arm around Hannah and pulled her into a tight hug. "The family is together. We are survivors, Hannah. And we have survived worse than this."

Staring off at the flashes of light outside the window, Hannah said nothing.

Franz turned the volume back up on the wireless. The bleak news drifted in from halfway across the Pacific. "Pearl Harbor was not the only site of Japanese aggression," the announcer declared. "They have launched simultaneous assaults on the Wake Islands, Guam, the Philippines, Malaysia, and Thailand. The safety of the many American expatriates living in the Far East is uncertain at this time."

Esther glanced over to Franz. "Simon . . ." she murmured.

She had already lost her husband to one enemy. Franz could not fathom the depth of her worry. "There are thousands of Americans in Shanghai," he said. "Think of how the Japanese treated the Chinese in Hongkew after the original invasion."

Esther's face blanched. *"Oh, mein Gott,"* she croaked.

"Essie, I only mean that the Japanese didn't arrest them all."

"We have all seen how the Japanese treat the locals," she whispered.

"Simon will be all right," Franz insisted. "He is a survivor too."

The gunfire and explosions finally quelled after dawn broke. The Adlers maintained their vigil beside the wireless. Hoping to hear news on Shanghai, Franz fiddled with the dial, then tuned in to the most popular local English-language station. The British announcer sounded as confused and frightened as the Adlers felt. "We are told that Japanese marines are storming building after building along the Bund," the reporter spat out over the static. "The Rising Sun already flies in place of the Union Jack in front of the Hongkong and Shanghai Bank! Good Lord, the Jewel of the Bund has fallen to the enemy!"

A series of rapid knocks rattled the door. Hannah

jumped in surprise. Esther and Franz shared worried glances before Franz rose to his feet and padded to the door. "Yes? Who is it?"

"Shan Zhou."

Franz opened the door to him. Shan's face was gray. "It's Ernst," he said without stepping inside.

"What about Ernst? Is he all right?"

"He will not listen to me." Shan beckoned Franz out with a frantic wave. "You have to see for yourself. Come with me. Please."

Franz shook his head. "I cannot leave my family. Not with an invasion going on."

"The streets are safe," Shan said. "The Japanese will not enter the French Concession. Not as long as Vichy France still controls Frenchtown."

Franz saw Shan's point. Japan was unlikely to go to war with the puppet Vichy regime controlled by her ally, Germany. But Franz was not swayed. "Not now, Shan. Perhaps later."

Shan looked down at his own hands. "Ernst is going to get himself into trouble. Probably killed." He looked back up with pleading eyes. "He might listen to you."

"Ernst doesn't listen to anyone."

"Please, Dr. Adler, you must try."

"Where is he?"

"At home."

"Franz, you had better go," Esther piped up. "Hannah and I will be all right."

Franz hesitated. "You will stay and watch over them?" he asked Shan.

In response, Shan stepped inside, clasped his hands behind his back, and took up a post by the door.

Franz strode over to the couch. He hugged his sister-in-law and then embraced his daughter for a long moment, kissing her on the forehead. He freed her from his grip and stared into her eyes. "Your aunt is right, *liebchen*. We are going to be all right. Do you understand?"

She cracked a brave smile. "Yes, Papa."

Outside, for a confused moment Franz wondered if it had snowed, then realized that the streets had been papered with leaflets dropped from the sky. He scooped up a page and saw it was written in English, Chinese, and French. *Be advised,* the terse announcement read, *the Imperial Japanese Army will occupy the International Settlement at 1000 hours this eighth day of December. Any persons in uniforms of other nationalities or bearing arms will be treated as hostile. Any persons suspected of resistance will be shot on sight.*

Franz looked at his watch: 9:05. He took off in a sprint, slipping occasionally on the leaflets. He arrived within five minutes at Ernst's apartment just off Avenue Joffre. It filled the top floor of a building that housed a furrier and a Russian restaurant on the main floor.

Unshaven, Ernst wore a black housecoat and pajama bottoms. "Shan sent you," he grunted from the doorway.

"Yes." Franz stepped inside.

As usual, the smell of borscht and something less palatable from the restaurant below pervaded the loft-like space. Along one wall, easels held up various-sized canvases. Franz didn't even pay attention to the images until he had crossed half the floor. The sudden recognition froze him in mid-stride. "Ernst, you can't!" Franz instantly understood why the artist had always insisted on advance notice so that he could store his latest work out of sight.

Ernst flapped his hand toward the paintings. "Two years I've been working on nothing else. And now, a week before the debut, that coward, Lawrence Solomon, telephones to say he is canceling my show."

Franz couldn't peel his eyes off the largest of the oils. In the painting, a Chinese woman who was naked from the waist down lay on the ground with her legs splayed open. She had been impaled through the vagina by a steel standard. The pool of bright blood between her legs was the same red as that of the Rising Sun flag that hung off the standard. Eyes open and face contorted with helplessness, the staked woman held a desperate hand out to the viewer.

Several other paintings—depicting acts of murder, torture, and rape—stood on either side of the central canvas. The images never explicitly revealed the perpetrators, but Ernst conveyed them via symbols such as the Rising Sun and samurai swords.

Franz grabbed his head in his hands. "My God, Ernst! If the Japanese see these, do you have any idea what they will do?"

Hands on his hips, Ernst shook his head. "The world needs to see what they have done! If not Solomon, I will find another dealer and gallery willing to show them."

Franz gestured to the windows. "The Japanese are here now. They control *all* of Shanghai."

"So what would you have me do?" Ernst asked calmly. "Should I just abandon my convictions? Toss away my principles because it is convenient?"

"Convenient?" Franz groaned. "Are you trying to be a martyr?"

A wry smile crossed Ernst's face. "Why not? Martyrdom is invariably beneficial to an artist's reputation. Taking the very-long-term view, it would be good for my career too."

A cold rush filled Franz. He recognized that, behind the sarcasm, Ernst was not bluffing. "And Shan?"

Ernst's face creased with suspicion. "What about him?"

"Are you prepared to sacrifice him for your art also?"

"How so?"

"Do you not think that the Japanese will track down your source and muse?"

Ernst opened his mouth but said nothing. His eyes clouded with uncertainty.

Franz shook a finger at the orgy of violence portrayed on the canvases. "This is how they treated Shan's family in Nanking in 1937. What do you imagine they will do to him now, if they associate him with this . . . this embarrassment?"

Ernst paled. "I suppose I never thought about it in those terms."

"Well, you had better start."

"Perhaps it's best if I hide these paintings until—"

"Not hide, Ernst. You must destroy them!"

⌒ *Chapter 32*

"Sunny, have you heard?" Simon uttered in disbelief, even though he had predicted war only the day before.

"Yes," she breathed into the receiver.

"On our own soil, too!" Simon cried. "Those sneaky sons of bitches declared war by surprise-bombing the naval port! Our poor sailors never stood a chance. I thought the Japanese were supposed to be all about honor and dignity."

"There is no dignity in war, Simon."

"Not the way the Japs fight it." He exhaled and his tone calmed. "Sunny, are you okay?"

"I am all right. And you, Simon? Are you somewhere safe?"

"Yeah, I'm fine. Just boiling mad is all."

"Have you spoken to Esther?" Sunny asked, though she was thinking more of Franz.

"She's at home with Hannah."

Sunny sat up straighter. "Not Franz?"

"He had to go see his artist friend about something or other. But he's okay. Matter of fact, I'm heading over there right after I hang up."

"You will be careful, Simon, won't you?"

"Always am, Sun."

"It's different now," she pointed out. "They will control the whole city soon."

Simon sighed into the receiver again. "Who's going to look after our refugees now?"

"It is time to worry more about yourself, Simon."

"Nah, I always land on my feet. It's the refugees that have got me troubled. And what will become of the hospital?"

"The Japanese have controlled Hongkew for years. They have never bothered with the refugees or the hospital. Why would that change now?"

"The Marines and the Brits used to be just across the bridge in case of trouble," Simon pointed out. "The Japanese had to be on their best behavior. Who's watching them now?"

What we have seen so far is their best behavior? The night of her father's murder flashed to her mind. "Why would they care about a group of German Jews?" she asked.

"They're not Germans anymore. Hitler revoked their citizenship." Simon snorted. "Besides, the CFA is still feeding and housing almost ten thousand refugees. Even if the Japanese leave us alone, where will we come up with the dough to pay for it?"

"Why will the CFA stop paying now?"

"All our cash comes from a few established Jewish families like the Sassoons and the Kadoories *or* the Joint Distribution Committee. Those Sephardic families arc all Brits. The JDC is a Jewish relief organization based out of New York." He sighed once again. "One thing's for sure: the Japanese won't let money continue to flow in from the enemy."

Sunny saw his point. *Ten thousand mouths to feed. A hospital to stock.*

"We'll find another way," she said.

"Yeah, after all, isn't necessity supposed to be the mother of something or other good?" Simon chuckled grimly. "Once I check on Essie, I'm going to head on over to the hospital."

"I will meet you there," she said.

"No, Sunny. You stay put until things are more settled."

"I'm just another Chinese in a city teeming with them, Simon. How much worse could they treat us?" she said with far more certainty in her voice than she felt.

"At least wait for me to call and tell you the coast is clear. I hear they're marching up Nanking Road as we speak."

"Oh, no!" Sunny squeezed the receiver. "My housekeeper, Yang! She insisted on going out for supplies this morning. She was heading to Nanking Road."

"She should be okay. It's only a parade, that's all."

Sunny checked the clock. Yang had been gone for over two hours. The tiny woman was so terrified of the Japanese that she had not ventured into Hongkew once during its four years of occupation. *What if Yang panics and tries to run from them? She might make herself look guilty!*

Outside, a canopy of gray clouds darkened the sky. Only a few people scurried along the sidewalk. The ground was still dry, but the streets were littered with the aerial-dropped leaflets. The damp breeze sent a few sheets cartwheeling down the road like tumbleweeds.

The Buick was parked at the curb, but it took Sunny a moment to spot Fai, who uncharacteristically already sat behind the wheel. "Fai, please take me to Nanking Road," she said as she climbed inside.

Fai's head snapped in her direction. "Missy, the dwarf bandits are on Nanking Road!"

"So is Yang."

Without another word, Fai started the ignition. Normally, the traffic would have been bumper to bumper by this time of the morning, but the roads were so deserted that Fai could have driven into the oncoming lane without fear of hitting another car. One street before Nanking Road, they ran into a barricade formed by two military vehicles parked askew across the intersection. A Japanese soldier leveled a machine gun at their windshield, while another chopped his arm up and down, indicating for Fai to turn the car around.

Fai screeched the tires in his hurry to back away from them. As soon as he had spun the Buick around, he looked over his shoulder. "No good, Missy. We go home now."

Sunny shook her head. "Drop me off at the corner."

"Missy . . ."

Sunny shot him a look that silenced him. He eased the car over to the curb and let her out. The sky had darkened even more with the imminent threat of rain. Pamphlets swirled at her feet. Sunny steeled herself with two deep breaths and then headed for Nanking

Road. She veered off the main street and ducked down an alley until she found a path between buildings that took her out to Nanking.

She heard stomping feet and rumbling vehicles before she even reached the sidewalk. A crowd lined the street, but the parade was unlike any she had ever witnessed. The air was thick with tension. Aside from a smattering of pro-Japanese cries, the crowd was quiet. There was not a child to be seen.

Columns of armed Japanese soldiers and sailors in dress uniform trooped along the street, eight abreast, in near-perfect synchrony. Their eyes were unblinking and their faces blank. Numerous tanks and other vehicles rumbled along interspersed between them. The Rising Sun flag flew everywhere, hanging from the sides of buildings and poking out through the windows.

Sunny scanned the crowd but saw no sign of her housekeeper. Suddenly a group of marching sailors inexplicably caught her eye. She scrutinized the rows of passing men, able to make out little more than their profiles. Anxiety gripped her as she sensed something familiar about an approaching sailor, the nearest in his row. *Could it be Father's killer?*

Sunny's breath caught and her stomach plummeted. The rhythmic slapping of boots on pavement matched the pounding of her heart. The conflicting urges to lunge out at the sailor and to flee nailed her feet to the ground.

As the sailor passed before her, Sunny focused on his face. His lip bore no scar. He was only a look-alike. But it was still two or three minutes before her breathing steadied and her legs responded again.

She forced herself to concentrate on Yang. She scanned the faces of the parade observers again, without sighting her. Sunny realized her housekeeper could be anywhere, possibly even home, but she was not ready to abandon her search. She slipped out of the lineup and began walking westward, stopping every hundred feet or so to scour the crowd.

Two blocks later, she spotted Yang, planted dutifully along the parade route. The woman's gaze was frozen on the passing soldiers. Sunny touched her shoulder and Yang's head flinched as she turned with a start. Her eyes were huge and, through Yang's thin coat, Sunny could feel her housekeeper's bony frame trembling. "Everything is going to be all right, Yang," she soothed. "I am taking you home now."

Sunny led the petrified woman by her still shaking arm toward the car. As soon as Fai saw them, he yanked open the back door. Sunny guided Yang into the backseat and closed the door after her.

Fai motioned frantically toward the road. "Missy, we hurry! Go now!"

"Take Yang home, Fai," Sunny said. "I'm going to walk to the hospital."

Fai shook his head urgently. "Better if you come too. Missy, please, now . . ."

Sunny shook her head and turned away. "I will see you at home."

She wove through the alleys and side streets to the Bund. In their ever-present white armbands, the feared Kempeitai military police patrolled the major road, allowing only vehicles that sported the Rising Sun flag to pass. The symbol was everywhere. Sunny felt disoriented and heartsick at the sight of the grand European-style buildings, which she had known her entire life, flying huge Japanese flags. She even spotted several swastikas hanging from windows.

Franz, oh Franz! She knew he had to be consumed with worry for his daughter. *Are you thinking of me too?*

Sunny hurried on to the Garden Bridge. Although the soldiers were everywhere else, for the first time in four years, the bridge itself was unguarded. The sight deepened her despondency. No longer did she live on the fringe of the Japanese rule; she was trapped fully within it.

Sunny felt almost relieved to be back in Hongkew, where existence under the Japanese boot had been a way of life for so long that it felt familiar. She hailed a rickshaw and arrived at the hospital just as the clouds finally burst. Her hair was dripping wet by the time she squeezed through the front door.

The corridor was deserted. As she passed the laboratory, she saw Max Feinstein sitting on a stool, staring at the wall beyond his microscope. His face had aged decades in the past year, but Sunny had never seen him looking so downcast. "Dr. Feinstein, is everything all right?"

"Fine, yes, thank you, Sunny," he mumbled.

The abject resignation etched into his face stopped Sunny from prying further. "Are any of the other staff here today?" she asked.

Max shrugged. "I saw Berta earlier. And, of course, Dr. Adler is on the ward."

Anxious to find Franz, Sunny began to back out of the room.

"What were we thinking, Sunny?" Max muttered without looking up. "Did we really believe we could outrun Hitler? How foolish! He was bound to catch up with us."

Sunny wanted to reassure Max that the Japanese were not the Nazis and that, at least in Hongkew, nothing had changed. She could tell from his expression that her words would have no impact, but she tried anyway. "It will be all right, Dr. Feinstein. You will see."

Sunny stepped into the hallway, rounded the corner and almost slammed into Franz. "I thought I heard your voice!" he cried.

His eyes were sunken and cheeks unshaven, but his face lit with a smile that warmed her heart. "Are you all right?" she asked.

He folded his arms around her. "Everything is better now. And you?"

"Better, too." Sunny relaxed, feeling so much safer in his arms.

She leaned into the embrace. The stubble on his chin scratched her cheek. "Oh, Sunny," he breathed.

The desires stirred inside her. She wanted to feel his lips on hers again. She longed for the contact of his skin. His mouth moved closer to her lips.

Suddenly, the reality of their predicament hit her like a bucket of cold water, and she stiffened in his arms.

Franz released her and took a step back. "I'm sorry," he stammered. "I was just so relieved to see you."

"Of course, Franz. Me too. How are Esther and Hannah?"

"Frightened. Same as everyone else. But otherwise all right."

"The uncertainty is the worst," Sunny said.

"Let's hope it is the worst, anyway."

She laughed nervously. "Poor Simon is most worried about the hospital's funding."

Franz nodded. "He has a point. Everything is going to change now that—"

The front door flew open. Boots stamped against cement. Instinctively, Sunny squeezed Franz's upper arm. He stared back at her, jaw clenched and face taut. "Let me handle this, Sunny," he said grimly.

Two Japanese soldiers approached. Sunny's jaw fell

open when she saw their white armbands. *The Kempeitai!*

Franz stepped forward and gently maneuvered Sunny behind him. "May I help you?"

The nearer guard shook a finger. "Franz Adler?" he spat in heavily accented English.

Franz hesitated a moment. "Yes, I am Dr. Adler."

"You come with us!" the Kempeitai officer snapped.

"I don't understand. I have done nothing—"

The soldier grabbed Franz by the arm and jerked him forward. "*Now!*"

"Franz!" Sunny reached a hand out but missed as he lurched past.

Franz regained his footing and dug his heels into the ground. He looked frantically over his shoulder to her. "Sunny, let Esther know what is happening. But not Hannah! Tell her I had to go away on urgent business. You understand?"

The second policeman grabbed hold of Franz's other arm and began to pull also.

Sunny took a step toward him. "*Franz!*"

"*No, Sunny!* Let them take me." He stopped resisting and allowed himself to be dragged away by the soldiers. "Tell Esther! Please . . . please, my dear one."

⁓ *Chapter 33*

Rain pelted the windshield. Franz's pulse hammered in his temples as fast as the wipers. The same dread gripped him as three years before, when he had sat sandwiched between the two SS men on the ride to

Eichmann's office in Vienna. Only the stench of the Nazis' hair oil was missing.

Neither of the stone-faced Kempeitai men flanking Franz had uttered a word since dragging him from the refugee hospital. Franz's pulse sped even faster as the car turned onto Soochow Creek Road. *Please, not Bridge House!*

Bridge House stood a stone's throw from Soochow Creek, and only a few hundred yards from the Garden Bridge. Franz had passed the heavily guarded prison numerous times on his way to and from the refugee hospital. He knew the Kempeitai took suspected spies, saboteurs, and other captured enemies to Bridge House for interrogation. Rumors of round-the-clock screams, water torture, and electrocutions abounded among the Westerners. Franz had heard that, as often as not, prisoners taken to Bridge House never emerged.

Assuming his association with Ernst must have drawn the Kempeitai's attention, Franz wished again that he had never accompanied the impetuous artist to Colonel Kubota's office.

What will happen to Hannah without me?

The mental image of Hannah clutching her rag doll reminded Franz that she was still only a child—one with a subtle but visible handicap. Franz knew that, culturally, the Japanese had little tolerance for disfigurement. He had once seen soldiers chase a child beggar off the street because the boy was missing half of his arm and most of an ear.

Franz caught a glimpse of Bridge House ahead of them. The blood in his veins turned to ice. But the car didn't slow. Instead, they flew past the building and continued east toward the river. The car slid to a stop in front of the military headquarters at Astor House. The man to his left jabbed Franz in the ribs with an elbow and shoved him out of the car. The guards led him toward the entrance of Astor House, their boots drumming the pavement like an executioner's march. The sentries guarding the door parted to make way for them.

The Kempeitai men led Franz up the spiral staircase. His heart sank as they shepherded him down the hallway, stopping outside Colonel Kubota's office. The door opened, and Franz recognized the triangular face of Captain Yamamoto, Kubota's aide. The Kempeitai men backed out of the room with deep bows, leaving Franz alone in front of the desk. He stole a glance at the wall, where a bland landscape painting hung in place of Ernst's portrait.

Three uniformed men clustered behind the desk. It took Franz a moment to recognize Colonel Kubota, who had shaved off his mustache and, instead of his usual civilian suit, wore a dark green uniform and matching officer's cap. A gaunt older man in an all-white naval dress uniform stood beside Kubota. To his left, a shorter man wearing round wire-rimmed glasses, knee-high leather boots, and the tan Kempeitai uniform glared at Franz.

"Ah, Dr. Adler, it is good to see you again." Kubota smiled as though they were meeting at one of the Reubens' dinner parties.

Franz nodded nervously.

"Allow me to introduce my colleagues." Kubota motioned to the older man in the white uniform. "Vice-Admiral Iwanaka, the senior naval officer in Shanghai." He swung his hand toward the man in the glasses. "Colonel Tanaka, the Chief of Kempeitai for Shanghai." He nodded to the door. "And you will remember Captain Yamamoto from your previous visit."

Yamamoto and Iwanaka offered unsmiling bows, but Tanaka's scowl only deepened.

"I must apologize for our abrupt summons," Kubota said with a helpless shrug. "Unfortunately, we are facing an unexpected emergency."

"The artwork?" Franz blurted.

The Japanese officers shared confused glances. Kubota's face filled with sudden understanding, and he broke into a quiet chuckle. "I am afraid, Dr. Adler, that now is not the time to concern ourselves with artistic differences."

"I see," Franz said with a mix of relief and confusion.

Kubota turned to Iwanaka. "I will let the vice-admiral explain."

Iwanaka nodded sternly. "Earlier this morning, General Nogomi, the military governor of Shanghai, became unexpectedly ill." He spoke English with a slight stutter, but his pronunciation was nearly perfect and his accent not much thicker than Kubota's. "Our military doctors believe his condition is a result of a ruptured ulcer but, unfortunately, most of our field surgeons have been mobilized."

Franz's shoulders sagged with relief. "And you would like a second opinion?"

Iwanaka shook his head. "We are requesting that you operate on the general."

"Me?" Franz gasped. "You want *me* to operate on the governor?"

Kubota nodded. "As the vice-admiral explained, our most experienced surgeons are unavailable. And you have an excellent reputation."

"But I am a . . ."

"A stateless refugee!" Tanaka spoke up for the first time. His accent was thick, and his clipped nasal tone hostile. "A possible enemy of Imperial Japan."

"Come now, Colonel Tanaka," Kubota said. "We are seeking Dr. Adler's assistance."

Tanaka turned and snapped at Kubota in Japanese.

"Not only me," Kubota replied calmly in English. "Vice-Admiral Iwanaka and I agree that Dr. Adler is the correct choice. And we are the highest-ranking officers still fit for duty to make such a decision." He finished with a few Japanese words in the same even tone.

Tanaka stiffened as though insulted, but he nodded his acceptance.

"Excuse me, Colonel Kubota," Franz spoke up. "May I ask why you have not turned to your friend, Dr. Reuben?"

Kubota glanced at Iwanaka before answering. "We are informed, Dr. Adler, that you are the best surgeon for this procedure."

Franz cleared his throat. "Colonel, are you asking or . . . or telling me to operate?"

Kubota merely smiled. "We believe it would be best for everyone involved if you were to agree to help."

Tanaka's lips curled into a sneer and his dark eyes simmered. The unspoken threat was clear. Suddenly, Franz understood the purpose of the Kempeitai man's presence.

"Where is General Nogomi now?" Franz asked.

"At the Shanghai General Hospital."

"May I see him?"

"Straightaway," Kubota said.

As they were filing out the door, Tanaka caught Franz by the arm and squeezed hard. "I am responsible for security in the whole of Shanghai," he snapped.

Franz's neck and shoulders tensed again. "I understand."

"You German Jews." Tanaka nodded knowingly. "You hate Nazis."

Uncertain whether it was a question, Franz nodded.

"You would do anything to lose them the war."

Tanaka's glare intensified. "And Japan fights beside Germany."

"It's not like that, Colonel. I don't concern myself with—"

"You do what you have to so Japan loses the war too!" Tanaka tightened the grip until Franz's whole arm ached. "Is it so?"

"No, Colonel, not at all," Franz spluttered. "All I want is for my family to be safe."

Tanaka glared ferociously at him for a moment before his lips curved into a malevolent smile. "*No one*— not you, not the girl child, not the woman—is safe if the general dies."

The implication hung between them like a grenade with its pin pulled.

"I will do all I can." Franz held his hands out in front of him. "I do not know how ill the general is. Sometimes people with perforated ulcers die no matter what we do."

Tanaka released Franz's arm. "If he dies, you *and* your family . . ." He shook his head slowly before he wheeled and marched out of the room.

Franz rode with Kubota in the back of his staff car. As they drove, the colonel seemed intent on justifying the Japanese attacks on Pearl Harbor, the Philippines, and elsewhere. "We are an island nation with few natural resources," he explained. "The Americans cut off our oil supply. Starved us of our sources of steel and bauxite. It would be little different had they cut off our food and water too."

Franz nodded, too preoccupied with what awaited him at the hospital to absorb the colonel's stream of rationalizations. Franz realized he would again be forced to drag politics into the operating room. But this time would be much worse—the well-being of his whole family hinged on the fate of a patient he had never even met.

The ride to the Shanghai General Hospital, on North Soochow Road, was mercifully short. At the hospital's entrance, four soldiers stood at attention. Colonel Tanaka and two of his Kempeitai men were waiting inside. Franz spotted only a few doctors and nurses, all of whom scurried about in silent trepidation. Franz wondered how many of them were facing an ultimatum similar to his.

Kubota and Tanaka led Franz down a hallway and past two guards, who snapped rigid salutes as they stepped into the private room. A Japanese doctor hovered by the patient's bed, fiddling with the intravenous tubing that ran into the man's arm. An apple-cheeked nurse stood at the head of the bed, dabbing at the patient's brow with a damp cloth, her hand steady. She shot the Japanese officers a look of cold defiance but said nothing.

Franz had expected the worst, but the sight of General Nogomi still shocked him. Covered up to his neck with a sheet, the balding man stared glassy-eyed at the ceiling. His color matched the storming gray skies outside. For a moment, Franz thought the general might already be dead, but then one of his eyelids fluttered.

Franz almost whipped the sheet off in his hurry to examine Nogomi, but he glanced at Kubota for permission. The colonel nodded. "Please proceed, Dr. Adler."

Nogomi showed no sign of awareness as Franz peeled back the sheet and grasped for the general's wrist. The man's skin was afire, and his pulse ominously faint. Franz turned to the two senior Japanese officers. "This man is septic! Blood poisoning has already set in."

Kubota nodded gravely, but Tanaka stared hard at Franz, unwilling to accept any excuses.

Nogomi's abdomen bulged outward from his thin frame. Franz lightly touched the skin and met board-like rigidity. He laid his left middle finger flat on the belly and tapped it with the other. The hollow sound was unmistakable. Only air that had leaked out of a perforated intestine could turn a human abdomen into a snare drum.

Franz turned to Kubota. "I agree with your doctors. The general must have perforated his intestine. Probably a stomach ulcer. But someone should have operated hours ago!"

"You will do it now!" Tanaka commanded.

"The general is already overwhelmed by infection. The odds of this man even surviving surgery are—"

"*Now!*" Tanaka cried.

Franz's own pulse fluttered wildly. Tanaka's threat resonated stronger than ever. He thought of Hannah and Esther. Ernst's gut-wrenching depiction of the woman impaled on the Japanese standard flashed to mind.

"I am going to scrub for surgery." Franz lowered his head and strode for the door.

"Very well," Kubota said. "I will see that General Nogomi is transferred to the operating room immediately."

If it's not already too late for him. And for my family.

Chapter 34

Franz's hands had never shaken so violently in the operating room—not even that day he raced to excise Sunny's hemorrhaging spleen. He willed his fingers still, but the tremble persisted.

Franz scanned the room. The Japanese doctor sat perched on a stool at the head of the operating table, timidly assuming the role of anesthetist. Two English scrub nurses stood gowned and masked across the table, waiting to assist Franz. Both were wide-eyed with fear. A Kempeitai officer stood at the door as an observer. His overly long gown produced a comical effect that was grimly misleading.

Abdomen exposed but covered from the waist down with a sheet, General Nogomi lay on the operating table, his breathing shallow and halting.

Franz glanced at the Kempeitai officer, who stared back intently. Technically, the soldier was there to ensure that no one sabotaged the surgery, but Franz suspected that Colonel Tanaka had stationed him to remind everyone of the consequences of failure.

The Japanese anesthetist tentatively dripped ether onto the mask over Nogomi's face.

"Only another drop or two," Franz instructed. "The general is far too unstable for anything but the lightest dose."

The young doctor jerked the bottle upright. "Of course, Dr. Adler," he said in clear English. "Dr. Reuben felt the same way."

Franz gaped at the anesthetist. "Are you saying Dr. Reuben has already seen the patient? *When?*"

The anesthetist shrugged. "Perhaps two hours ago."

So what in God's name am I doing here?

As though reading his thoughts, the anesthetist added, "Dr. Reuben told us you were the best surgeon in Shanghai for such emergencies."

The rat-bastard!

"Scalpel!" Franz said to one of the nurses.

He grabbed the knife from her hand, jabbed the blade into the central indentation just below Nogomi's rib cage, and sliced downward in one continuous cut. The second nurse sponged at the incision's bleeding vessels but could not stem the blood flow. Franz stuck the blade back into the wound and slit the layers of muscles and tendons that formed the abdominal wall.

Air hissed out of the abdomen like a tire rupturing. The patient's belly visibly deflated. Franz snatched the retractors and tucked them into the edges of the incision, stretching its edges wide apart. One of the nurses silently freed the retractors from his grip. Franz dipped his gloved hand inside the general's belly. Warm fluid enveloped his fingers.

Sweat beaded on his forehead as Franz tried not to think about the damage the corrosive stomach acid had already inflicted. He ran his hand over the rubbery deflated loops of intestine until his fingers touched the pylorus, the base of the stomach. He had to palpate the area twice before his finger slid through a button-sized hole.

"Dr. Adler, the general's pulse . . ." the anesthetist croaked.

"What about it?" Franz said.

"It is so weak I can barely sense it."

Colonel Tanaka's threat rang in Franz's ears like gunfire. *What will they do to my Hannah?*

"Increase the fluids!" Franz snapped as he turned his attention back to the wound. The only hope was to patch Nogomi's leaking stomach as fast as humanly possible. "Needle driver and stitch!" he called out.

Franz pushed the omentum, the ligamentous layer of tissue that hung off the outside of the stomach like a thick curtain, out of the way. He craned his neck until he glimpsed the small defect in the front of the stomach. Franz poked the tip of the needle through the full thickness of the stomach wall beside the hole and ran a ring of stitches around it. He dropped the needle driver and pulled taut on both ends of the thread, closing the hole as though tightening a purse string. He poked at the stomach wall with a finger. Satisfied, he grabbed at a piece of the omentum and sewed it on top of the defect site to reinforce his repair.

Franz dropped his equipment on the tray and glanced over to the anesthetist. "Well?"

Without removing his hand from the patient's neck, the pale young man nodded. "I feel it still. Very delicate."

Franz grabbed for the syringe loaded with saline. He pointed its nose into the abdomen and sprayed the fluid. He showered the abdomen with multiple sprays, washing out as much stomach acid and bacteria as possible.

Franz turned to the anesthetist. "Please remove the ether."

The man dutifully pulled the mask from the patient's face.

Franz rushed to suture Nogomi's abdominal wall back together. As he threaded the final loop through the skin, the general flinched in pain.

"He is waking," the anesthetist announced joyously.

"And his pulse?"

"Still not good."

Even though Nogomi had survived the operation, Franz knew that the odds were still stacked against the general, and as Franz watched the nurses bandage the general's abdomen, the sting of Reuben's betrayal burned deeper. Any competent surgeon could have performed the operation. Fate, not surgical prowess, would determine Nogomi's outcome. Reuben would have known it too.

Franz found the two Japanese colonels waiting in the hallway. Tanaka appeared as hostile as ever, with shoulders squared and eyes glaring. Kubota viewed Franz expectantly. "How did the surgery proceed, Dr. Adler?" he asked.

"The general survived but . . ." Franz held out his hands. "His condition is grave."

"Now the general gets well!" Tanaka stated.

Franz shrugged. "Only time will tell, Colonel."

Tanaka grunted, but his icy stare indicated that he intended to hold Franz, not time, responsible for any unfavorable outcomes.

Franz eyed Kubota intently. "I am certain Dr. Reuben must have given you the same prognosis," he said evenly.

Embarrassment darted across Kubota's face, but he quickly regained his composure. He bowed his head. "Thank you, Dr. Adler. You have done all we could ask of you."

"May I go home to my family now?" Franz asked.

"Of course." Kubota smiled. "I will have my driver take you."

Tanaka shook a finger at Franz. "You will come back later to see the general." He scoffed. "I will have *my* men carry you here."

Outside, flecks much larger than snowflakes fell steadily from the sky. Franz let a few drift onto his palm. After a moment, he recognized them as ash from burnt paper.

As Franz rode home in the backseat of Kubota's staff car, he did not see a single pedestrian on the streets of the International Settlement. Even the beggars had disappeared. Shanghai struck Franz as surreal, as though he was experiencing it in a postapocalyptic nightmare.

Kubota's driver pulled up to Franz's building and barely slowed long enough for Franz to hop out. As soon as the car sped away, Heng Zhou materialized at the front door. His watery eyes darted around vigilantly. "Franz! What did they want from you?"

"My help."

"*Help?*" Heng grimaced. "How can you help the Japanese?"

"I had to perform surgery on one of them."

"Is that so?" Heng asked shakily.

"Are you all right, Heng?"

"I am a defeated old man," Heng sighed. "Shan is . . . Shan. He is so angry with the Japanese. I worry that he might do something rash."

"You cannot allow that, Heng!"

"I might have to solicit Mr. Muhler's assistance." Heng's shoulders slumped. "I believe he has more influence on Shan than anyone."

Franz had long suspected that Heng understood the nature of the two men's relationship, but they had never discussed the subject. "We will all keep an eye on Shan," he said. "Meantime, I must check on my family."

"Yes, please do." Heng waved distractedly. "Wish them well for me, please."

Franz opened the door to his flat to find the four most important people in his life collected in the same room. Lotte and Sunny must have come to sit vigil with Esther and Hannah after his detainment.

"Franz!" Esther cried as she leapt off her chair in surprise. "Oh, thank God."

"Yes, welcome back," Lotte added with a shy grin.

Sunny beamed with a relieved smile that meant more to him than words.

Hannah sat on the couch between Sunny and Lotte, appearing confused by the women's exuberant greeting. "Why are you back so soon, Papa? Tante Essie said you went away on special business."

"I might still have to go away, *liebchen*." Franz glanced purposefully at Esther. "But I am home for now."

"I hope you stay, Papa."

Franz's heart melted at the sight of his eleven-year-old daughter flanked by his fiancée on one side and the woman he loved on the other. "I hope so too."

"Tea?" Esther offered as she headed to the stove.

"Yes, please." He turned to Lotte and Sunny. "Is there any news?"

Lotte pointed to the radio. "We still can pick up the BBC, but there is hardly any news of Shanghai. The Japanese have blocked all transmissions from the local stations."

"Of course." Franz understood that the Japanese were obsessed with controlling communication. "And the ash falling from the sky? Do you know where that comes from?"

Lotte motioned to the ceiling. "From the tops of office buildings. People are burning all types of documents before the Japanese seize them."

Sunny turned to Franz, her expression a blend of affection and apprehension. "Do you think it likely that you will have to leave again on business?"

He held her gaze for a long moment. "I wish I knew, Sunny. The next few days will tell, but yes, I think there is every chance I will have to go."

Franz had trouble breaking off the eye contact, until he sensed Lotte's gaze upon them. He forced a smile for his fiancée. Conflicted as he felt, he realized that his focus had to be on protecting his family. An idea occurred to him. "Sunny, I wonder if I could impose on you for an enormous favor?"

"Of course," she said.

"I have to host a meeting tonight. A very private and discreet one." He lowered his voice. "Even Esther and Hannah cannot attend. I wonder if you might find space in your home for them to spend the night?"

"Papa, I want to stay here!" Hannah said.

"*Liebchen,* it will only be for a night or two," Franz said.

Picking up on his urgency, Sunny turned to Hannah with a smile. "You know what, Hannah?" She squeezed the girl's hand. "It could be fun. We will make a girls' night of it!"

Heart aching, Franz studied Sunny with silent admiration. In the wake of the Japanese takeover and Reuben's betrayal, none of Clara's threats mattered any longer.

If the general survives, then maybe, just maybe, Sunny, there will be hope for us yet.

⌒ *Chapter 35*

In the backseat of the Buick, Sunny sat on one side of Franz, and Lotte on the other. Sunny had offered the other woman a ride home, and Franz insisted on joining them. The awkwardness between the three of them that Sunny had anticipated had no chance to materialize. As soon as they had loaded into the car, Franz explained the real reason why the Kempeitai had dragged him away.

"I am sure you did all that anyone could do for the general," Sunny said. "Do you really think the Japanese would hold you responsible for his death?"

His gaze fell to his lap. "Colonel Tanaka will, yes. Without question."

"It seems so unfair," Lotte murmured. "Surely they should be grateful."

"I doubt Colonel Tanaka is capable of gratitude," Franz said.

"You think the Kempeitai would go after Esther and Hannah too?" Sunny asked.

Franz shook his head. "I am not willing to find out."

"Of course not." Only Lotte's presence prevented Sunny from reaching for his hand.

Franz turned to Lotte. "I think it would be too risky to keep Hannah and Esther at your aunt and uncle's home. The Japanese are bound to look there."

Lotte smiled tightly. "It only makes sense that they stay with Miss Mah. I just hope Hannah isn't too frightened by all the upheaval."

Fai slowed the car to a stop in front of the Reubens' building. "Franz, are you staying here with Miss Weczel?" Sunny asked.

He shook his head. "I will just see her to the door."

"We will wait." Sunny leaned past him and nodded to the other woman. "It was nice to see you again, Miss Weczel. I only wish the circumstances were happier."

"Yes, I feel the same. Good-bye, Miss Mah. Thank you for the ride and . . . and all your generous help."

Waiting for Franz to return, Sunny stared at the seatback ahead of her. Temptation finally got the better of her and she glanced over to the entrance just in time to see Franz embrace Lotte and kiss her on the cheek. Irrational jealousy racked Sunny. She turned away and checked herself in the rearview mirror to ensure that her expression showed no trace of it.

"Thank you for waiting," Franz said as he climbed back into the car.

"There is no hurry," Sunny said. "Fai and I can wait longer if you would like to go upstairs to visit with the Reubens—"

"I never want to see that man as long as I live!" Franz spat.

"Oh, I . . . I had no idea," Sunny stammered.

"I am sorry, Sunny." Franz skimmed his fingers across her cheek. "This has nothing to do with you. It's Reuben. That cowardly devil!"

She had never heard Franz speak with such vitriol. "What did Dr. Reuben do?"

"He sold me out. Not only me, my whole family!" Franz went on to explain how Reuben had offered him up as a replacement scapegoat.

"That snake!" Sunny blurted.

They lapsed into a short silence until Sunny spoke up again. "Since my father died, there is only my house-keeper and me at home. It's a waste, really. The house is too big for the two of us."

The anger drained from Franz's face. "You are terribly generous. Thank you. I hope Esther and Hannah will only have to stay with you for a short while."

"Why don't you join them? I . . ."

He cocked his head in puzzlement. "You mean to hide me in your home?"

"I suppose so." She cleared her throat. "Yes."

"I could never!" He shook his head vehemently. "I am already exposing you to far too great a risk by asking you to board Hannah. I know Tanaka's kind. He would only hunt me down. Hannah and Esther are in far greater danger in my presence. Oh, and how Tanaka would punish you." He winced. "No. Absolutely not."

"What are you going to do, Franz?"

"Nothing. You have given me the peace of mind I need by protecting my girls. The rest?" He shrugged. "Is in the hands of God."

"I thought you didn't believe in God."

He mustered a faint smile. "Can you think of a better time to start?"

They gazed at each other for a long moment without needing to fill in the silence. Finally, Sunny admitted in a near whisper, "I thought I saw *him* today, Franz."

"'Him'?" His jaw dropped. "Oh, you mean the man who . . . ?"

"Killed my father. Yes."

Franz reached over and took her hand in his. "But it wasn't him?"

She gripped his hand tightly. "Not until he marched right past me did I realize it wasn't the same man. I was so terrified, Franz."

He clutched her hand tighter. "He will not find you, Sunny."

"And what if I want to find him?"

"Sunny, it is best if you never see him again."

"I hate him more than I ever thought possible." Her voice quivered.

"Whatever happens to that creature, your father will still be gone."

She looked away but left her hand in his. The contact between them felt so right. If she let go of his hand, she knew it would only be to throw herself into his arms.

Fai pulled up to Franz's apartment building. Esther and Hannah were already waiting out front with bags packed. Reluctantly, Sunny slipped her hand free of Franz's.

Franz reached for the door handle. Before opening the door, he turned back to her, at a loss for words. She motioned to Hannah and Esther. "I will keep them safe, Franz. I promise."

He ran his fingers over her cheek again. "I know." Then he was gone.

Sunny watched him hug Esther good-bye, but she had to turn away during his long embrace with Hannah.

The girl was crying as she climbed into the car beside her. Even Esther was red-eyed. They spent the ride back to Sunny's house in subdued silence.

Yang was waiting anxiously by the door. Sunny explained that the Adlers would be staying for a while. "I will prepare the guest room," Yang said. "Girlie, Dr. Huang has telephoned three times for you. And he has visited once."

"Is Wen-Cheng all right?" Sunny asked.

"He worries so much for you, that good doctor." Yang had always held a soft spot for the handsome physician. And now that Wen-Cheng was a widower, the housekeeper had launched a relentless campaign to see Sunny marry him. The news of Wen-Cheng's proposal would have overjoyed Yang, but Sunny had yet to inform her.

"I will ring him as soon as we settle our guests," Sunny said.

Within minutes of their arrival, the phone jangled. Sunny rushed to answer it, hoping that it might be Franz.

"Where have you been, Sunny?" Wen-Cheng's tone verged on frantic.

"I had to visit the hospital and run some errands," Sunny said.

"Run errands?" Wen-Cheng croaked. "Shanghai is

being overrun by the enemy. The *Rìběn guǎzi* are everywhere. You should only leave the house for absolute emergencies!"

His patronizing tone grated. "I am home now," she said coolly.

"Let me come over, Sunny."

"You had best stay where you are."

"I should be with you at this time."

"It is not necessary, Wen-Cheng."

"I want to be there, Sunny," he said. "To comfort you. And to protect you if need be."

A few years before the same words might have melted her resistance, but now they bounced off her like a rubber ball off a wall. "I have house guests."

"*Guests?*" he sputtered. "During an invasion?"

"It's complicated, Wen-Cheng. I will explain soon. Right now, I must attend to them."

"Oh, I see," he sulked.

No, Wen-Cheng, you do not see at all.

The scents of sautéing ginger and garlic permeated the house, and soon Yang summoned Sunny, Esther, and Hannah to dinner. Despite the lack of fresh supplies, Yang had still somehow whipped up a small feast of fried rice, noodles, and vegetables. But none of them had much appetite, and most of the food went back into the icebox untouched.

After dinner, Esther and Hannah retired to the guest room. Sunny wandered into the sitting room and pulled her dog-eared copy of the *Merck Manual* off the bookshelf. She could not believe how much she missed her father's quizzes. Flipping the book open to a random page, she read the same sentence three times without absorbing a word. Giving up, she slid the book back onto the shelf.

Distracted with worry for Franz, Sunny switched on

the wireless. The local stations were all off the air, but she managed to pick up the static-filled BBC signal. Grimly, she listened to the announcer list the setbacks that the British, and their new fighting American allies, had suffered in a single day. "Japanese ground troops have established footholds in the Philippines, Indochina, and Singapore," he intoned somberly.

Esther stepped into the room. "It seems as though the Japanese have attacked the entire Pacific," she said.

Sunny switched off the wireless. "I wonder if anyone can stop them."

"Power lust has gotten the best of them. They will be turned back."

"Do you believe that, Esther?"

"I have to." Esther lowered herself into the chair opposite Sunny.

"I wonder how much things will change for us," Sunny said.

"A rumor was tearing through our building that the Japanese plan to round up all enemy citizens and dump them in prison camps." Esther frowned. "Hitler stripped us of our citizenship. I have no idea how the Japanese will view us." She tilted her head. "And you, Sunny? What is your citizenship?"

"Chinese," she sighed. "I am not too concerned, though. The Japanese could not build camps big enough to house all the Chinese in Shanghai."

Esther looked down at her knees. "But they could easily gather up all the Americans."

Sunny stroked her arm. "Simon?"

Esther nodded.

"Simon is not worried," Sunny reassured. "His only concern is how to feed and house all the refugees."

Esther looked up with a small smile. "That reckless man believes he is invincible!"

Sunny nodded. "He has a big heart."

"To use one of his favorite sayings, 'it's the size of Staten Island.'" Esther laughed. "However large that is!"

"Esther, in Vienna with you . . . and, um, your husband . . ." Sunny stammered, "I cannot imagine what it must be like for you now."

Esther's forehead furrowed. "I never dreamed I would find someone after Karl. I expected to live and die as his widow. And then this brash American comes along with all his flighty charm and impossibly big dreams. Nothing at all like Karl, really." She paused. "And yet they are so much alike in spirit. Karl would have done anything to help someone in need. Simon is the same. Maybe that is why I love him too." She laughed again. "Though I could do with a little less conversation about his precious Yankees and all those Hollywood cinema stars."

"Do you think you will marry him?" Sunny asked.

"I know I will." Esther blushed. "Sunny, can I ask that you please keep that to yourself?"

"Of course. Simon has been assuring me the same since the day he met you."

"He can wear a person down." Esther sighed good-naturedly. "And you, Sunny?"

Sunny wondered if Simon had told her about Wen-Cheng's proposal, but before she had a chance to reply, Esther added, "I know how my brother-in-law feels about you."

Sunny could not meet Esther's eyes. "Feelings are not the issue. Franz is already engaged to another woman."

"Out of obligation, not love."

"Does that really matter?"

"Absolutely!" Esther said. "Particularly now."

"What of Hannah's schooling? Will Mrs. Reuben still not hold that over Franz?"

"So what if she does?" Esther pointed to the wireless. "What sense is there in sacrificing for a future that we don't even know will come?"

Esther's words struck a chord. "Perhaps you are—"

The ringing telephone cut Sunny off. She reached for the receiver.

"Sunny, it's me!" Franz blurted. "How is everyone?"

"Fine. Hannah is already asleep." She hesitated. "Franz, how is the general?"

"Better. His fever has broken and he is no longer delirious."

Esther leaned forward in her seat, staring at Sunny.

"Do you think he will rally?" Sunny breathed.

"I cannot be sure, but I think so. I really do, Sunny."

She was so overwhelmed by relief that her voice caught in her throat.

Esther grimaced. "What is it, Sunny? Is Franz in some kind of trouble?"

Esther's response confused Sunny, until she became aware of the tears of joy streaming down her cheeks. "No, Esther. Everything is better. Much better now."

⌒ *Chapter 36*

DECEMBER 25, 1941, SHANGHAI

"Happy Christmas!" Franz said with a wry smile as he stepped into the hospital's storeroom.

Simon shook his head. "You've converted, have you, Doc?"

"All I need is another religion," Franz said with a sigh.

Simon pointed to the near-empty cupboard of

medications. "So tell me one thing that's happy about this particular Christmas."

"Well, the world didn't end with Pearl Harbor as so many people were predicting."

"Might be a bit early to say. Did you hear that Hong Kong fell to the Japs today?"

Franz nodded. "But remember all those rumors, Simon? The Japanese were going to close all the hospitals and schools. They were going to throw all the foreigners into prisons to let us starve. None of it has happened."

"Not so far. But imagine what might have happened to you and your family if the general had died." Simon scratched his head. "And don't forget, Doc, the Japanese have a couple million new prisoners in Shanghai. Bound to take them a while to figure out what the hell to do with us all. Makes me nervous how they registered everyone."

Franz saw Simon's point. The Japanese had given foreign nationals only four days to register after the takeover. The lines of Americans and British twisting around the police offices reminded Franz of the queues of Jews outside the consulates following Kristallnacht.

"Besides, Franz, things are worse. A lot worse," Simon went on. "You know what I'm talking about! The strict curfews. Banks and businesses seized. No gasoline for cars. Accounts frozen." He shook his head. "People are scrambling just to put scraps on the table."

Simon wasn't exaggerating. Esther's shrewd knack for coping with crisis, along with a learned distrust of banking institutions, had kept the Adlers' cupboards supplied with the basics, but many others in the community were not as fortunate.

Simon pointed to the storeroom's barren shelves again. "What use is it if they let us keep the hospital's doors open but don't allow us the money or supplies to run it?"

Simon's cold reason doused the last of Franz's cheerfulness. "What we need here more than anything is ether," Franz said. "We are running very low. And without anesthetic . . ."

"No more surgery, I know." Simon puffed out his cheeks. "But I've got even more pressing worries."

"Such as?"

"At the heime," Simon said. "We've already cut the meals back from three times to once a day, but I don't know how we're going to keep feeding the families. Those hungry little kids, Franz." He rolled his shoulders. "Surgery won't matter much to these folks if they're already starving to death."

"How long will the food last?"

"A few weeks at most," Simon said. "The Sephardic Jews can't help us now. Their accounts are all frozen. The JDC funds from New York have been cut off too. Our only hope now is the Russian Jews. The Soviets and Japs signed some kind of neutrality pact, so their money wasn't confiscated. I'm meeting with the Russian Jewish community leaders this afternoon."

"Let's hope they see us as brothers."

Simon grinned. "I'll make them see. Doesn't matter if you're Russian, Mexican, or even Eskimo, no Jew alive is immune to guilt." His smile faded and he looked down at his hands. "You know, Franz, there is one other group who could help us out of this jam."

"The Japanese?"

Simon nodded. "Didn't you just save the life of the highest-ranking officer in the city?"

Uneasy as the thought made him, Franz knew Simon was right. None of the other refugees would have the same access to the local Japanese leadership. "I'm off to visit General Nogomi now. Perhaps he or Colonel Kubota might be feeling a little more charitable toward us."

"Never hurts to ask, right?" Simon said.

Franz sighed. "I will find that out soon enough."

Franz headed out to the street. Several men beckoned him to their empty rickshaws. As sorry as Franz felt for the line of emaciated runners, every cent mattered, and he had no choice but to wave off their approaches.

As he walked, Franz realized that he had not set foot inside the Country Hospital in almost three weeks. The British-run facility had remained open after the Japanese takeover, albeit operating on threadbare supplies, but Franz had committed all his time and energy to the refugee hospital. Besides, the idea of seeing Reuben again, let alone working with the man, turned his stomach. Franz had avoided Lotte too, but not because of her uncle's betrayal. The guilt had kept him away, ever since he realized that he could never go through with their marriage.

Outside the Shanghai General Hospital, a junior officer was waiting to escort Franz to General Nogomi's room and past the guards posted at his door. The general was sitting upright in his bed, propped up by pillows. His color had improved, but he had lost more weight since surgery and his cheeks and jawbones protruded sharply.

Colonel Kubota sat at the bedside with a folder open in his lap. As soon as he saw Franz he snapped it shut and stood up. "Good morning, Dr. Adler."

Franz bowed to both men. The general, who spoke no English or German, viewed Franz with the same cold-eyed indifference as ever. He had never shown Franz an inkling of gratitude.

"How is the general today?" Franz asked Kubota.

Kubota and Nogomi spoke in Japanese, then the colonel turned back to Franz. "There is less pain," Kubota translated. "His appetite is improving."

"Good," Franz said. "Please tell General Nogomi I would like to examine his abdomen."

Kubota informed Nogomi, who grunted his approval.

A quick glimpse and a light palpation assured Franz the wound was healing. "In my opinion, General Nogomi could safely be discharged by the end of the week to recuperate at home."

Kubota informed Nogomi, but the general registered no response. "The general is delighted," Kubota said with a dry smile.

Franz cleared his throat. "Colonel, I was hoping to ask a favor of you both."

Kubota tilted his head and raised an eyebrow but said nothing.

"It concerns the Jewish refugees," Franz said. "The new financial restrictions are having a terrible consequence on our community, Colonel. My people are going hungry."

Franz expected Kubota to translate for Nogomi, but he didn't even look at his superior. "May I speak to you outside regarding this matter, Dr. Adler?" Kubota asked somberly.

The colonel did not say another word until they were on the street and out of earshot of the soldiers guarding the entrance. "Dr. Adler, we are most grateful for your efforts on the general's behalf."

Franz's belly tightened. "Of course, Colonel."

"May I speak frankly, Dr. Adler?"

"Yes."

"We are not in a position to offer any assistance to your community."

"Not in a position?" Franz echoed. "I do not understand, Colonel."

"Our German allies."

Franz tensed. "What of them?"

"The German consulate—and their Gestapo office here—has taken an active interest in the German Jews."

Franz fought off a shudder. "I thought you once told me your government did not share the Nazis' racial policies."

"We do not," Kubota said. "However, since December 7, our strategic collaboration with the German government has deepened substantially. We now share common enemies in England and America. As a result, we have certain diplomatic considerations."

Franz swallowed. "Is your government adopting the Nazis' policies toward Jews?"

"Not at all, Dr. Adler," Kubota said evenly. "However, we cannot afford to be seen to single out the Jews for favorable treatment over other foreign nationals."

"Colonel, unlike the Shanghailanders, most German Jews escaped here with nothing. Many rely on the charity of fellow Jews for the barest necessities. Without access to funds, our hospital will soon close. And we fear that families—little children, mothers—might starve."

Kubota's gaze fell to the ground, but he did not comment.

Franz held out his hand. "Colonel, you told me once that you respected the Jewish way of life. You have always struck me as a decent and civilized man. We need your help. Urgently."

Kubota studied the pavement. "Please give me a little time to consider the situation. Unfortunately, I can promise nothing more." He looked back up at Franz. "And please understand, Dr. Adler, we can *never* appear to favor your community with special treatment."

Franz read the message in Kubota's eyes. "You can rely on my discretion, Colonel. Thank you."

Kubota began to turn away but stopped. "Dr. Adler, I am confused."

"Regarding what?"

"The Jewish refugees are ten thousand miles away from home, living in reduced circumstances. They pose no imaginable threat to German interests and yet . . ." Kubota shook his head. "I do not understand why the Nazis are so single-minded in their concern with you."

"You do not understand?" Franz uttered a shocked laugh. "Believe me, Colonel. No one is more baffled than us Jews!"

With the cold biting at his exposed ears, Franz hurried home. The streets of the International Settlement were less crowded than before the Japanese takeover, but people had begun to emerge from their post-invasion seclusion. Several shops had reopened, some even with anemic Christmas displays in their windows. The street vendors, performers, and beggars had reappeared, though Franz doubted many pedestrians, if any, had money to spare for them.

Franz's legs were rubbery with fatigue by the time he mounted the last step up to his apartment. As soon as he opened the door, Hannah rushed happily to him. "Papa, school is reopening the day after New Year's!" she announced. "We just heard from Sara Kleinman."

"*Wunderbar, liebchen!* I worried you were going to grow lazy if you stayed home too much longer," he teased, though he knew his daughter was incapable of indolence. Hannah had insisted on helping Esther with her consignment business, which had expanded to include clothing alterations and repair. She also volunteered with her aunt in the soup kitchen at the largest of the heime, on Ward Road.

Esther popped her head out of the kitchen. "Franz, a Mr. Silberstein rang for you."

"*Silberstein?*" Franz prickled at the name. He had not seen or heard from Hermann Schwartzmann in the eighteen months since his wife had left the hospital. "What did he want?"

"To meet you. At Public Garden at three o'clock." She glanced at her watch. "That is only ten minutes, Franz."

"He did not leave a telephone number? Or mention what it concerned?"

Esther shook her head. "Only that he would wait at the benches in Public Garden for you. Franz, he made it sound urgent."

Franz wavered, wondering if the diplomat wanted to solicit another medical favor. Franz sensed that, whatever it might be about, the meeting was important, so he donned his coat and hurried for the door.

Public Garden was almost deserted. A windblown stream of pipe smoke led Franz to Hermann Schwartzmann, who sat on a bench wearing a Tyrolean hat and thick overcoat.

Schwartzmann stood and extended a gloved hand. His mustache twitched and his lips broke into a warm smile. "Good day, Dr. Adler."

"Hello, Mr. Silberstein," Franz said coolly. "How is your wife?"

"Ah, of course, you would not have heard." Schwartzmann's voice cracked. "Edda passed away last month."

After weeks of caring for Schwartzmann's wife in the hospital, Franz had grown fond of the gracious woman. "I am sorry," he said genuinely.

"Edda did so well in those months after surgery. She gained weight and she rediscovered her joie de vivre. Dr. Adler, you gave her—us, actually—a whole year together that we would have otherwise never had." Schwartzmann looked past Franz and chewed on his pipe stem. "Of course, nothing is the same without her. Especially Christmas."

"I know what it is to lose a wife, Mr. Schwartzmann," Franz said stiffly. "But I find it hard to believe that is why you wanted to see me."

Schwartzmann shook his head. "I understand that since the occupation, circumstances have grown more challenging for your people. I imagine that must be true for you personally as well."

Franz folded his arms across his chest. "We are coping."

"I meant no disrespect, Dr. Adler. I only wanted to offer my assistance."

Franz squinted at him. "You want to help the Jews?"

Embarrassed, Schwartzmann looked away. "Edda never understood the Führer's racial policies. She found them abhorrent. We both did, but I chose to turn a blind eye. And after what you did for us—" Flustered, he cleared his throat again. "Do my motives really matter so much?"

"I am not accustomed to hearing offers of assistance from officials who work for the Nazis," Franz said. "Surely, Mr. Schwartzmann, you can appreciate my wariness?"

"There is nothing official about the offer, but I do understand." Schwartzmann smiled sadly. "And it's probably best for all concerned if you continue to refer to me as Silberstein."

Franz uncrossed his arms. "Why now, Mr. Silberstein?"

"When my wife and I came to you for help, you had every reason in the world to turn your back on us. I realize you must have assumed a grave personal risk to operate at a Jewish hospital on someone who could have been considered a Nazi. I am now prepared to take a chance of my own. With Edda gone, no one else has to face the consequences of such a choice."

"What did you have in mind, Mr. Silberstein?"

Schwartzmann pulled the pipe from his lips. "What is your greatest need, Dr. Adler?"

Franz didn't even have to consider his answer. "From the refugees' point of view, what we need most is food or at least money to buy it. In terms of the hospital, we need supplies, especially medications such as ether."

"Ether, you say." Schwartzmann bit his pipe again, lost in concentration. "I might be able to secure some."

Franz nodded.

"Please give me a day or two," Schwartzmann said as he adjusted his hat. "I will contact you when I have news."

"All right," Franz said, stunned by the turn of events. "Thank you . . . Mr. Silberstein."

Schwartzmann smiled. "One day, I hope you will discover—as I did—that sometimes help comes from the most unexpected places."

"I hope I do, Mr. Silberstein. Very much so."

Schwartzmann turned from the bench and began to walk away. Without slowing, he called over his shoulder, "I left something on the bench for you."

Franz looked down and noticed a manila envelope. He picked it up, aware of the content by its weight alone. He pulled back the flap, and his heart sped at the sight of all the banknotes inside. He extracted the stack of money and fanned through it, seeing only hundred-mark bills. He had not seen so much money since he had received his father's early bequest aboard the *Conte Biancamano*.

∽ *Chapter 37*

JANUARY 3, 1942, SHANGHAI

Franz could not follow the Hebrew characters, but he dutifully held the book open in front of him and hummed along to the mournful prayer as the cantor led the congregation in song.

Six months earlier, Hannah had persuaded her father to join Esther and her at the Ohel Rachel Synagogue for a Saturday Sabbath service. While Franz had initially attended out of obligation, he soon came to look forward to the services. He enjoyed the ambience. The cavernous synagogue, with its marble pillars, massive chandeliers, high balconies, and perfect acoustics, reminded him more of a fine Viennese theater than a house of worship.

During the services, Franz's thoughts often drifted to his family. He imagined his father would have found his display of religiousness amusing. But Karl would have approved, regardless of his brother's motives. Franz did not feel much closer to finding God, but he took unexpected solace in the traditions and rituals. And he found a renewed sense of community among his fellow Jews, inspired by their unflappable faith in the face of such persecution.

The congregation had thinned considerably since the

attack on Pearl Harbor. Many wealthier Sephardic Jews, including Sir Victor Sassoon, had fled Shanghai before the Japanese takeover. Lady Leah Herdoon had the means to escape too, but the plucky old lady still sat in her usual spot in the front row of the women's section.

After the service, Franz and Simon caught up to Esther and Hannah in the temple's courtyard. They stood huddled in the cold dry air beside Lotte and the Reubens. Esther shifted from foot to foot, while Hannah stood between her aunt and Lotte and out of Clara's reach.

Samuel extended a hand to Franz. "Happy New Year, Adler!" he said. "Or at least, let's hope '42 will be better than '41!"

Franz resisted the urge to confront Reuben in front of both families but, regardless of appearances, he refused to shake the man's hand. "We can hope," Franz said with a stiff nod.

Franz conceded to himself that 1942 had begun better than how the previous year ended. With Schwartzmann's donation, Simon had restocked food in the pantries of the heime and purchased medical supplies through Shanghai's rapidly expanding black market. The morning before, Franz had arrived at the refugee hospital to find cases of medications, including ether, lying on the doorstep. He had no idea who was behind the late-night delivery—Kubota, Schwartzmann, or someone else—but he was desperately grateful for the supplies.

Clara looked from Lotte to Franz. "Now that the situation has normalized somewhat, I understand that weddings will resume again next week at the temple."

Lotte reddened. Franz bit his lip, afraid of how he might respond.

Esther crossed her arms. "I do not understand how

you can describe our circumstances as even close to normal," she said.

"I never suggested that," Clara shot back. "I was merely pointing out that the situation is less volatile than immediately following the invasion. Life goes on. Would you not agree that one needs to at least try to make the best of one's circumstances?"

Before Esther could answer, Reuben piped up, "Speaking of weddings, say, Adler, did you hear about Dr. Huang? Word is that the fool has gone and proposed to Miss Mah!"

Franz went cold. "Wen-Cheng and Sunny?"

Reuben nodded. "Can you imagine what he would be getting himself into by marrying that woman? To be led around by a rope for the rest of his days, no doubt."

Franz was too stunned to respond, but Simon grabbed him by the arm and ushered him away with a quick excuse.

"She doesn't love him, Franz," Simon said when they were out of earshot of the others.

Franz stopped dead. "You knew about this too?"

Simon dug his hands in his pockets and shrugged.

Franz squinted at Simon. "And you chose not to tell me?"

"Sunny swore me to secrecy."

Franz let the anger with Simon cover his hurt. "So instead you betrayed me!"

"Listen, Franz, Sunny hasn't said yes to him."

"But has she told him no?"

Simon shook his head slightly.

Franz's chest ached. "When did this happen?"

"Right before Pearl Harbor."

"Almost a month ago?" Franz groaned.

"I know you're upset. But after all, Doc, you're engaged, yourself."

"Only to protect my family. Sunny understands that too." Franz tapped his chest. "She never even mentioned Wen-Cheng's intentions toward her."

"Doesn't that make you think that she plans to turn him down?"

"I need a few moments to myself. Will you please accompany Hannah and Essie home?" Franz turned and trudged away without waiting for his friend's response.

As Franz wandered home alone, he began to calm down. Still, he could not shake the sting of Sunny's deception and, worse still, the sense of foolishness he felt for believing his own romantic fantasies.

As Franz neared his building, he saw Heng Zhou struggling with the sack of rice slung over his shoulder as he tried to open the front door. Franz hurried over. "Let me help you," he said.

"No." Heng stumbled back a few steps. "I need the exercise, my friend."

"Are you certain?"

"Yes, yes. Thank you, though." Stooped below the weight of his load, Heng appeared to have aged years in the past month. "It has been too long since we last had tea. I do not suppose you would have time for a cup now?"

In no hurry to face Simon and Esther, and the inevitable discussion about Sunny, Franz nodded. "A cup of tea would be very welcome, my friend."

The old man lumbered up the single flight of stairs, tottering at times. Franz wondered again where Heng managed to find rice in such quantity and how he and his mostly absent son could go through so much of it.

Inside the flat, Heng headed straight for the closet and delicately lowered the sack to the floor, then pulled the closet curtain closed. He went to the kitchen and placed a rusting kettle on top of the element. "I suppose I should consider myself fortunate," he remarked as he raised the can of jasmine tea. "I never expected to live through a second invasion."

"It is not as bad as Nanking, is it?"

"Nothing could be."

"Did Ernst ever show you his paintings of Nanking?"

Heng shook his head. "I would not have wanted to see them had he offered. Shan assures me they are painfully accurate." He pulled two cups off the shelf and spooned tea leaves into a small ceramic pot. "He is talented, your friend Ernst."

"Maybe even a genius," Franz sighed. "At the very least, he is certainly temperamental and difficult enough to be a genius."

Heng stared past Franz out the window. "He cares about my son. He is good to him. For me, that is what matters."

The kettle whistled. Heng poured the boiling water into the pot and replaced the lid. "Shall we sit?"

Heng carried the teapot while Franz took the cups over to the table. "Children have an endless capacity to surprise their parents," Heng said, lowering himself into a chair. "Have you not noticed the same in your daughter?"

"I suppose so, yes," Franz said. "Hannah's tenacity amazes me. All the setbacks and misfortunes fate throws in her path only make her that much more determined."

Heng smiled sadly. "Neither of my children turned out as I had envisioned."

"How so?"

"When Chang Jen was a little girl, she loved insects—ants, earwigs, moths, even spiders." Heng paused a moment, lost in thought. "We had to keep insect zoos in the home. Chang Jen would divert herself for hours sketching and handling them, or simply observing. I expected her to become an entomologist, a biologist, or a scientist of some kind." He chuckled to himself. "All those *ist*s, but I never dreamed fervent Communist would be her choice. Of course, there are some unavoidable analogies between Communism and the insect world. Worker bees, colonies of ants, and so forth."

"And Shan?" Franz asked.

"He was the protective one. Always keeping an eye out for his little sister and his mother. That is why what happened in Nanking was that much worse for him."

"What could he have possibly done?"

"Nothing, of course, but guilt is rarely rational." Heng rubbed his watering eyes again with a handkerchief. "I am the only one who could have made a difference. Had we left for Canada a few weeks earlier, we would still be together now."

"But the timing was so random, my friend. Surely you see that?"

Heng shrugged. "When Shan was a boy, I worried he might grow up to be a policeman or a soldier or some such dangerous profession. I never expected him to wind up as an engineer or become as . . . as sensitive as he is."

A vehicle roared down a nearby street, drawing Heng's attention. He listened for a moment before turning back to Franz. "Please do not misunderstand me. I do not mean to condemn Shan's inclination. While Chang Jen was born a Communist, Shan was destined—"

The whine of tires skidding around the corner cut Heng off in mid-sentence. He sprang from the chair and dashed for the window. Pressing his forehead against the glass, he peered out to the street below.

Heng jerked his head back as though shot at. *"Leave here, Franz. Now!"*

"What is it?"

The vehicle screeched to a halt. Boots pounded the pavement.

Heng went white. *"The Kempeitai!"* he breathed.

Franz's heart thumped in his throat.

"Go!" Heng swung his hand wildly at the door. "They've come for me! *Go, Franz!"*

"For you?"

Heng gestured wildly toward the closet. "Inside the sack! My shortwave transmitter!"

"A transmitter?"

"I have been reporting on Japanese troop movements. They must have tracked my signal." He clutched his chest. "I am a spy!"

Franz was dumbfounded.

A pane of glass shattered below, launching a chill up Franz's spine. A vision of Karl's hanging corpse flashed into his mind.

"Go, Franz!" Heng cried again.

Franz bolted for the door. As he grabbed hold of the knob, Heng called to him, "Don't let them find my son!"

"I won't!" Franz blurted. He dashed out the door and into the stairwell.

Feet thundered on the stairs below as Franz shot up the staircase and vaulted the last few steps onto the landing. He thrust open the door to his apartment, lunged inside, and slammed it shut behind him.

Across the room, Esther yelped in surprise and grabbed for Hannah, pulling the girl tightly against her. Simon gaped at him. "Franz, what the—"

Franz silenced him with a rigid forefinger to his lips. "Essie," he whispered. "Take Hannah to the bedroom. Close the door. Under the bed, both of you. *Now!"*

Eyes like saucers, Esther nodded. Hannah grabbed her aunt's hand and they hurried off together.

Banging, stomping, and shrieks leaked through the floorboards from the Zhous' apartment below. Barely breathing, Franz stood motionless and listened to the commotion. After a few minutes, the noises died away and he heard the sound of boots in the stairwell again.

Simon rushed to the window. Franz followed. With heads almost touching, they looked out to the street. A military transport truck was parked on the sidewalk between two police cars. Several Kempeitai men patrolled the street.

One officer burst out of the building, balancing coils of copper wire in his arms, along with a speaker, transmitter components, and the empty rice sack.

Two officers stepped out behind, dragging Heng roughly between them. Their prisoner hung limply in their arms. His shoes scuffed the ground as they hauled him toward the truck. Franz wondered if Heng was even conscious; for his friend's sake, he hoped not.

⌒ *Chapter 38*

Sunny knelt at the bedside as she ran her fingers up and down the wrist of the young patient, Frieda Schnepp, in search of her radial artery. The woman's skin felt like parchment paper, but Sunny finally sensed a faint pulse.

"Sunny!" Dr. Feinstein called. She glanced up to see Max standing at the foot of the bed. "I just reviewed the slide. Definitely cholera. Her stool is loaded with the bacteria."

Sunny didn't need Max's microscope to know that cholera was the culprit. Frau Schnepp, the twenty-three-year-old mother of two, had walked in on her own steam four hours earlier complaining of diarrhea and now lay in a coma from extreme dehydration. She was the hospital's third such patient in forty-eight hours, but even without the others, Sunny would have diagnosed her with cholera. Nothing else could sap someone's fluids so rapidly or completely. The oral rehydration formula had run through Schnepp as though poured through a sieve. Even after the woman had slipped into a coma, she continued to ooze odorless rice water–like fluid.

Sunny ran her fingers higher up Frau Schnepp's arm until she felt a flattened vein slide under her fingers. She pierced the skin with the needle and had to jiggle it at several angles before the tip found the vein and the first drop of blood formed at its end.

Sunny reached behind her for the rubber tubing and attached the bottle of Ringer's lactate. Two nights before, forty-eight bottles of the intravenous fluid had materialized on the hospital's doorsteps. Without the anonymous donation, Frau Schnepp would certainly have died. Even with the fluid, Sunny wondered if she could possibly hang on.

As the solution ran into the woman's arm, Sunny stood up and stretched her back. There was nothing left to do. Either the cholera or the fluid would prevail, and soon.

Sunny turned to Max. "I thought cholera didn't strike in wintertime."

He tilted his head from side to side. "Normally, no. But cholera loves water, and this has been a wet and, thanks to the Nazis of the Pacific, a particularly miserable winter."

Sunny had worked through two previous cholera outbreaks. She cringed at the memories of the victims, especially the children, who were most susceptible and often died. "Dr. Feinstein, if this takes hold in the community . . ."

Max closed his eyes and shook his head. "God help us."

Sunny glimpsed the clock again and realized Franz was already two hours late for surgery. With the supply of ether refreshed, he had scheduled two surgeries, a hernia repair and a hysterectomy, for the afternoon. She had never known Franz to be so late. Still, Sunny thought it would be easier not to see him. In the operating room, she sometimes melted at the incidental brush of their shoulders or the feel of his breath on her cheek. In bed at night, she could not stem the recurring fantasy of Franz slipping under the covers beside her. The image was enough to set her skin afire.

Sunny looked over and noticed that Frau Schnepp's intravenous bottle had run halfway through. She prepared a fresh bottle, acutely aware how rapidly a cholera outbreak would exhaust their replenished supplies.

Franz called out from behind her. "May I speak to you outside, please, Miss Mah?"

Relieved, Sunny hurried across the room and followed him out to the hallway.

Max joined them from the other direction. "Ah, Franz, have you heard about the cholera?" He gestured to Schnepp's bed. "All the cases have come from the same heim. On Ward Road."

"I know the place," Franz muttered. "Esther and Hannah volunteer in the kitchen."

Max shook his head. "Four hundred people live there. Imagine if the cholera spreads."

Franz glanced at his watch. "Listen, Max, can we discuss this after surgery?"

"I will be here." Max shrugged. "And with luck so too will poor Mrs. Schnepp."

Sunny followed Franz outside. Franz stopped half-way down the pathway leading to the street. He glanced over either shoulder and then spoke in a hushed voice. "My friend, Ernst, the artist—"

"Yes, I met him once."

"Has he come by the hospital today?"

"I haven't seen him, no."

Franz kicked at the ground and mumbled something unintelligible.

"What is it, Franz?" she asked.

"My neighbor, Heng Zhou, was just dragged away by the Kempeitai. Right before they came, he actually admitted to me that he is a spy." He exhaled. "His son, Shan, is a close friend of Ernst's. I am worried the police might have already arrested them too."

Sunny brought a hand to her cheek. "What makes you think so, Franz?"

"I went to Ernst's flat. It had been ransacked. They even ripped the walls away in places."

"Then surely the men were not home?"

"Perhaps, but I cannot find them anywhere. What if the Kempeitai already have them?"

"Or perhaps they are in hiding." Sunny laid her hand on his wrist. "I am sorry about your friends, Franz."

Franz pulled his arm free of her grip. "Our surgical patients are waiting."

His cool tone stung Sunny more than his physical withdrawal. "Yes. Yes, of course."

Franz started for the entrance, but Sunny hesitated, wondering what had suddenly changed between them.

In the operating room, Franz allowed Sunny to perform the hernia surgery with complete independence. He barely uttered a word as he held back retractors and cut sutures for her. Afterward, Franz excused himself to step outside for fresh air.

Sunny followed him back out to the pathway. "Franz, have I done something to offend you?"

"How so?"

"You seem so . . . so distant."

He eyed her, stone-faced. "Were you planning to ever tell me about Wen-Cheng's proposal?"

"Yes . . . yes, I was going to . . ." she mumbled, feeling her face heat. "Wen-Cheng proposed two days before Pearl Harbor. Everything has been so chaotic since. I have had no time to discuss it with him, let alone you."

"What is there to discuss?"

She squared her shoulders, feeling her own indignation rise. "When do you intend to marry Lotte?"

He shook his head. "I do not."

She gaped. "You . . . you are still engaged to her, surely?"

"I have made up my mind, Sunny. I intend to—" He stopped and his gaze darted over her shoulder.

Sunny looked behind her to see two men rapidly approaching. She recognized one of them as Ernst Muhler. She suspected the other man was Shan Zhou, but no one spoke a word as Franz shepherded them inside the hospital and into the staff room.

As soon as Franz closed the door, Shan stared at him with fear in his eyes. "What happened to my father, Dr. Adler?"

"They came for him. They found his radio." Franz swallowed. "I am so sorry."

Shan's face fell but he said nothing. Ernst placed an

arm around his shoulders, pulled him closer, and ran a hand tenderly over his cheek, but the young man remained unresponsive.

"They have been to your apartment too," Franz said.

Ernst nodded. "We escaped out the back just as they arrived."

"They tore it apart," Franz said. "Were they looking for another shortwave transmitter like Heng's?"

"I suspect they were looking for the rest of my paintings," Ernst sighed.

"*Paintings?*" Franz jerked his head as though slapped. "Not the Nanking series? *Scheisse,* Ernst! You swore you were going to destroy those."

Ernst held a hand out. "How could I burn my work? Only the Nazis treat art that way."

"What Nanking paintings?" Sunny asked.

Franz turned to her, his face pale with worry. "Ernst painted a series he called *The Rape of Nanking.* You can imagine how the Japanese might view such paintings."

"No, I can't," Sunny mumbled.

"Between Shan's father and Ernst's canvases . . ." Franz massaged his temples. "They're going to search everywhere for you two."

Ernst sighed heavily. "We have no right to endanger you or your hospital. We will go."

"Go where, precisely?" Franz asked.

"To the countryside," Shan spoke up in a monotone. "Free China. The villages and mountains where the Communists and Nationalists are organized."

"Is that not hundreds of miles west?" Franz asked. "How would you possibly reach it?"

Shan and Ernst glanced at each other and shared a helpless shrug. "We will fumble our way somehow," Ernst said. "We should go now, Shan."

Franz stared hard at Ernst, then broke into a small smile. "You and I have a long history of endangering each other. Why stop now?"

Ernst grinned. "I'm nothing if not consistent in my recklessness."

Franz frowned. "They're bound to come here looking for you. We have to hide you."

Sunny motioned to the door. "Why not keep them on the ward, Franz?"

Franz's brow furrowed. "You mean out in the open?"

"Yes." She smiled faintly. "With the other cholera patients."

～ *Chapter 39*

Jia-Li stubbed out her cigarette and dabbed at her lower lip, removing a flake of bloodred lipstick with her little finger. "So you are the world-famous Dr. Franz Adler?" Her accent was similar to Sunny's, but her tone was naturally flirtatious.

The three of them stood huddled in the hospital's staff room beside the cot where the night staff stole the odd hour of sleep. Jia-Li was dressed like a cinematic femme fatale in a black cocktail dress, white gloves, and a hat with attached veil. She could have passed for one of the ubiquitous poster models in Shanghai—or "beautiful girls," as they were commonly known—who advertised everything from cigarettes to motor oil.

Franz bowed his head. "Thank you for coming, Miss Ko."

"It's Jia-Li, please." She turned to Sunny and laughingly added something in Chinese.

Sunny, who had been on edge ever since Jia-Li arrived, did not offer even a wisp of a smile. Franz did not understand her uncharacteristic irritability, especially considering that her friend had come to help them.

But Jia-Li appeared indifferent to Sunny's coolness. "So you need to make two people disappear into thin air," she said.

"Not thin air," Sunny corrected. "The countryside."

Jia-Li angled her head and smiled. "Is there really a difference, *xiǎo hè*?"

Sunny rolled her eyes. "Can you help us or not?"

"*Pas de problème.*" Jia-Li snapped her fingers. She turned to Franz with another airy smile. "Do you speak French, Franz?"

"Only German and English, I am afraid."

"Pity."

"Jia-Li, please! This is serious," Sunny snapped. "Can you really get two wanted men past the Japanese sentries and out to Free China?"

Jia-Li nodded dreamily.

"But how is this possible?" Franz asked.

Jia-Li floated her hand up in the air. "My boss's boss is Du Yen Sheng. Are you familiar with the name?"

The gangster and his Green Gang were as legendary in Shanghai as the bronze lions guarding the Hongkong and Shanghai Bank. "He is the man they call 'Big Ears' Du?" Franz said.

Jia-Li exhaled as though blowing out smoke. "Only the suicidal call him that to his face," she said. "But Mr. Du is exceptionally well connected in this city."

"Even after the invasion?" Franz asked.

"War has had little effect on Du's business." Jia-Li

waved away the question. "After all, no one loves clubs, gambling, or women more than the Japanese. And not only the foot soldiers. It goes right to the top with them."

Franz shook his head. "How can he possibly smuggle two people out from under their noses?"

Jia-Li laughed again. "Trust me, my dear Dr. Adler, the Green Gang could smuggle an entire circus out of Shanghai, elephants and all."

"When can it be done?" Sunny asked.

"Tomorrow morning at three," Jia-Li said. "The boys will pick up your friends and transport them to the city's western outskirts. There they will rendezvous with members of the Chinese militia, who will guide them out to the countryside."

"Is it dangerous?" Sunny's words were clipped and quiet.

Jia-Li extracted a silver cigarette case from her handbag. She offered a smoke to the others, both of whom refused. She lit a cigarette and took a long drag before answering the question. "Nothing is without danger these days, Soon Yi. But the Japanese don't have nearly enough men to patrol the whole countryside. At night, the militia moves freely in and out of Shanghai. How do you think they plant their little bombs all over the city?"

Despite the media blackout, Franz had heard of the wave of guerrilla attacks on Japanese military installations across Shanghai.

Sunny checked her watch with concern. "It's not even six o'clock yet."

"Don't worry so much, *xiǎo hè*." Jia-Li massaged Sunny's shoulder. "By tomorrow, your problem will have disappeared like the morning mist lifting."

Sunny shrank from her friend's touch and snapped at her in Chinese.

"Of course I am high!" Jia-Li replied in English. Taking another drag of her cigarette, she turned to Franz. "Doctor, my oldest and dearest friend can't seem to comprehend that nothing aside from opium could possibly get me through another day."

"We worked so hard to wean you off the pipe this time!" Sunny's tone resonated with hurt. "You made a promise to me."

"And Godfrey promised to take me away with him." Jia-Li shrugged. "The world is built on broken promises."

Sunny stared hard at her friend for a long moment. "Not ours, Jia-Li."

Jia-Li looked away and nodded. "I had better go finalize the arrangements," she said. "Remember, the truck will pull up at the front door at three o'clock. No lights. No horns. It will not wait, so the two men had better be outside and ready."

Sunny leaned forward and hugged Jia-Li. "Thank you for this."

"You never have to thank me, *xiǎo hè*." Releasing Sunny, Jia-Li surprised Franz by folding her arms around him and kissing him lightly on either cheek. "It is a pleasure to finally meet you, Franz."

"And you as well, Jia-Li." He bowed his head. "I cannot thank you enough."

"You are most welcome, dear doctor." Jia-Li turned to Sunny and nodded in Franz's direction. Giggling, she spoke in their dialect. Sunny's face reddened, but she laughed too.

They saw Jia-Li to the front door. After she had gone, Franz turned to Sunny and asked, "What was so funny?"

Sunny blushed deeper. "Just silly girl talk. Jia-Li told me that you are not nearly as hard on the eyes as she had feared."

"Oh." But his smile faded quickly. "Sunny, can we trust the Green Gang with Shan's and Ernst's lives?"

"Jia-Li has always been true to her word." She sighed. "Except, of course, when it comes to opium."

They fell into silence for a few moments, then Sunny turned to him with a timid smile. "Earlier, Franz, on the pathway, you started to tell me about your engagement to Lotte . . ."

"I am not going to marry her, Sunny."

"Have you told Lotte?"

"No," Franz admitted.

"That is not really fair to her, is it? To keep her in limbo like that." But she sounded relieved.

"I intend to tell her soon." He bit his lip. "And you? Have you given Wen-Cheng an answer yet?"

"Not yet." She looked away and added softly, "But I'm not going to marry him, either."

Franz nodded, trying to conceal his relief and elation. The sound of vehicles thundering down the road broke the moment. The floor shook slightly. Franz craned his neck to peer out the small window to the street. Raw fear gripped him as he glimpsed two military vehicles screeching up to the curb. "I will meet them here," he said as calmly as he could. "Go make sure everyone else is in position!"

Face pale but eyes calm, Sunny nodded once and hurried off down the hallway.

Franz watched Kempeitai officers pour out of the cars. His mouth went dry as he recognized Colonel Tanaka at the head of the group.

Tanaka stormed through the door, his face already contorted into a snarl.

Franz held out his hand. "Good evening, Colonel Tanaka."

Ignoring Franz, Tanaka turned to the men behind

him and barked out orders in Japanese. One of the soldiers knocked shoulders with Franz as he raced past him into the hospital.

"Colonel, may I ask why you and your men have come?"

Tanaka jabbed a finger at Franz, stopping just short of his chest. "Your neighbor, Heng Zhou, is a Communist spy!" he spat as though Franz were somehow responsible. "His son is an enemy spy too. He lives with the painter. Your good friend!"

Franz nodded. "Herr Muhler, yes."

Tanaka squinted behind his glasses. "Where are they?"

Franz shook his head. "I have not seen them in days, Colonel. Perhaps they have already left the city?"

"No! They are in Shanghai!"

Franz took a step down the hallway. "Colonel, why don't we go inside and—"

Tanaka's hand shot out and clamped onto Franz's elbow. He jerked Franz back. "We wait for my men!"

Helpless, Franz prayed Ernst had remembered to secure his face mask snugly. Sunny had altered the artist's appearance with a near head shaving, but Franz doubted it would be disguise enough. They were gambling on the proximity of the two profoundly ill cholera victims, along with Ernst's bogus coughing fits, to deter the Kempeitai from examining him too closely. Meanwhile, Shan was in the basement dressed as a repairman and pretending to fix the boiler. Franz reassured himself that even he would not recognize Shan in his coveralls, haphazard haircut, and Coke-bottle glasses borrowed from a patient.

"We owe you nothing!" Tanaka snapped.

"Excuse me, Colonel?" Franz's voice cracked involuntarily.

"For fixing General Nogomi-san," Tanaka grunted. "We owe you nothing. Shanghai is part of Imperial Empire of Japan. All Jews are war prisoners. We tell you to operate on general, you operate!"

Franz lowered his head. "I understand."

"You understand better at Bridge House. You be there now, if not for Taisa Kubota." Tanaka used the Japanese term for Kubota's rank. "If we find your friends here, Taisa Kubota is no more protection to you."

His pulse pounding in his temples, Franz stared silently at the floor.

Another five or ten taut minutes crawled past before one of the Kempeitai officers hurried down the hallway toward them. He reported to Tanaka in a rush of Japanese. Tanaka's scowl only deepened as the man spoke. The colonel snapped his fingers and pointed outside. Without a word to Franz, Tanaka spun and stormed out of the hospital. The rest of the Kempeitai men marched after him.

As soon as the military vehicles' engines sputtered to life, Franz's shoulders sagged with relief. His legs almost gave way as he took his first full breath in minutes. He ran into Sunny in the hallway. "Well?" he demanded.

She flashed a small smile. "Your friend Ernst is quite the actor. You should have seen how far the Kempeitai men jumped back from his coughing fits."

"Sunny is not exaggerating!" Ernst cried as he caught up to them. "I was the very embodiment of contagion."

"And Shan?" Franz asked.

"They hardly spent any time in the basement," Sunny said.

Ernst tapped his chest. "Once the Japanese met Typhoid Mary here, they couldn't get out soon enough."

Sunny laughed. "Probably best to stay in costume. In case they surprise us again."

Franz headed straight to the staff room to telephone home. Esther answered on the second ring. "Is everything all right, Essie?"

"All right now," Esther said calmly.

"*Now?* What happened?"

"Colonel Tanaka and his men searched the apartment. They left quite the mess."

"And Hannah?" Franz breathed.

"Hannah was a trooper. She is fine. And Simon is here with us now."

Franz felt guilty that he had not been home to protect them.

Moments after he hung up, Ernst wandered into the room with a lit cigarette between his lips. Franz's gaze drifted involuntarily to the artist's shorn scalp. Ernst ran a hand over the stubble. "Believe me. No one misses those gorgeous blond locks more than I do."

"How is Shan managing?" Franz asked.

"Devastated."

Sympathy stirred in Franz for both the father and the son. "Poor Heng. I cannot imagine what they will do to him."

"Family means everything to Shan, and now he's lost them all." Ernst dragged heavily on his cigarette. "I spent most of the afternoon talking him out of marching himself into Bridge House to join his father."

"Time will help, surely," Franz mumbled.

"I wonder," Ernst sighed. "Shan was completely lost after his mother and sister died. Now this."

"He still has you," Franz pointed out.

"Some consolation. The poor devil." Ernst rolled his eyes. "Can you imagine, Franz? If we're extremely fortunate, in the next few days we will find ourselves a thousand miles from civilization in some backwater village that has never seen a white man." He tapped his chest again. "Let alone *this* queer one."

"You've survived the Nazis and the Japanese," Franz pointed out. "How much more challenging could a Chinese village be?"

"Not just any village. One full of Communists!" Ernst shuddered. "When I think back to my socialist friends in Vienna and all their insufferable moralizing. *Mein Gott,* the only saving grace is that I won't understand a word of their Marxist tripe in Chinese."

Franz laughed. "Now you sound more like your old self."

"I've been a fool, my friend," he sighed. "A lovesick fool. I should have listened to you eons ago."

"About?"

"Everything. Nanking was never my battle. I was swept up in Shan's passion and thirst for justice." He looked down sheepishly. "I had no right to endanger your family—the people I love—for the sake of my artistic pride."

"Those paintings were some of your best work, Ernst. Besides, what is done is done. At least we survived."

"So far." Ernst took another puff of his cigarette. "You have risked too much for my sake."

Franz grinned. "Where in this city could I possibly find another bullheaded prima donna with your flair for art and style?"

Ernst laughed. "Or any city, really."

"That morning after Kristallnacht, when you risked your life to bring us food and support when we needed it most . . ." Franz shook his head. "I will never forget that, Ernst."

"It's what friends do."

"Only the best ones."

Ernst inhaled his cigarette until it was burned down to the stub. When he spoke, his voice was thick. "You will say good-bye to Essie and Hannah for me?"

"Of course."

"In spite of it all, the little puffin has flowered here in Shanghai, hasn't she?"

Franz nodded, warming with pride.

"I'm so disappointed that I will miss your wedding," Ernst said.

"Oh, Lotte and I will not be—"

"Not her!" Ernst waved away the suggestion. "I meant to Sunny."

Franz shook his head in surprise. They had never before discussed his feelings for Sunny.

Ernst brought two fingers to his eyes. "You do not need to be an artist to recognize love when it's staring you in the face." He winked. "But of course, it does help."

Franz did not bother denying it. "There is so much I have to do first."

"But nothing nearly as important, my friend." Ernst sighed heavily. "Look where love is leading me. To a village forgotten by time, where I will have to exchange my paintbrush and my beloved gin for a tree toilet and endless Stalin speeches in Chinese." He jutted out his lower lip. "God willing, I will be picked off by a Japanese sniper before I ever arrive."

Franz chuckled. "It's only temporary, Ernst."

"One can always hope." Ernst smiled enigmatically as he extended his hand to Franz.

Chapter 40

Franz's mouth felt as though it were lined with wool, and his wrists dug into his forehead. He lifted his head off the small table and blinked the sleep out of his eyes. Gray morning light leaked in through the window. He glanced at his watch, surprised to see that it was almost eight o'clock.

He rose to his feet and was stretching his lower back just as Sunny stepped into the staff room.

"Any news from Jia-Li?" he asked hopefully.

Sunny shook her head. "No, but that is to be expected."

As promised, the truck had pulled up in front of the hospital two minutes before three o'clock that morning. If not for the three blinks from the flashlight inside the cab, Franz would never have known anyone had come for Ernst and Shan.

Sunny rubbed her eyes. Her hair was unusually tousled and her face drawn. "We do have another problem, Franz," she said gloomily.

Does this never end? "What is it, Sunny?"

"The cholera."

"Mrs. Schnepp?"

Sunny shook her head. "Mrs. Schnepp has improved, but several other cases have arrived in the past few hours."

"How many?"

"Twelve."

"*Twelve?*" he gasped.

"They've all come from the Ward Road *heim*." Sunny shook her head. "One of the patients, a four-year-old girl . . . she was already dead when her father brought her in."

"Such a shame." With deepening unease, he thought again of Hannah and Esther, who volunteered at the heim. "How much fluid do we have left?"

"The other nurses and I have mixed up several liters of oral preparation, but some patients are too ill to drink," she said. "We have thirty-one bottles of Ringer's lactate left."

"A drop in the bucket if this cholera spreads." Franz ran a hand through his matted hair. "Sunny, I will meet you on the ward once I have telephoned home."

After Sunny left, Franz picked up the receiver and dialed. It rang numerous times before Esther finally answered. "Essie, I hope I am not waking you."

"I've been up for hours, Franz," Esther said groggily. "What of Ernst and Shan?"

"They were picked up on schedule. No news since."

"I see," Esther said. "Listen, Franz, Hannah has had to go back to bed. She cannot go to school today."

"Why not?"

"Neither of us are well," she said. "Perhaps influenza."

The receiver froze in his hand. "Not diarrhea?"

"I am afraid so," Esther said, clearing her throat, embarrassed. "Hannah is vomiting, too. She is really suffering, the poor child. I think we must have eaten something—"

"Essie!" Franz's throat constricted. "Bring Hannah here to the hospital! *Straightaway!*"

"I am not sure it is a good idea, Franz. She is really in no shape to walk that far—"

"Hire a rickshaw! Damn the fare. Just get her here! *Please,* Essie!"

"Franz, what is going on? I do not—"

"You both worked in the kitchen at the Ward Road heim this week, did you not?"

"And every week for the past four months, Franz."

"Essie, did you eat there?" he asked, terrified of the answer.

"We never do. There is not nearly enough food for the residents, let alone the volunteers." Just as Franz felt his throat opening again, Esther added, "Oh, except this week. On Thursday, the cook, that young Mrs. Schnepp, made a potato soup she wanted us to try. We each had a small bowl—"

"Oh, God!" he croaked. *"Bring Hannah here straightaway!"*

Franz slammed the receiver down. He dashed out to the ward to find it overflowing with newly arrived patients. Several women lay curled up on their beds, others sat hunched over, holding buckets to their lips. Retching sounds filled the room. The stench of vomit was almost eye-watering. Berta and Liese rushed between patients, carrying flasks of rehydration fluid. It took Franz a moment to spot Sunny in the far corner, inserting an intravenous needle into a patient's arm.

"Miss Mah! *Sunny!*" he called, ignoring the woman in the nearby bed who clutched her belly and waved frantically to him with her free hand.

Sunny's head swiveled in his direction. "Yes, Dr. Adler?"

"I need two beds readied!" he cried.

Berta gaped at him. "Dr. Adler, we have no more beds."

"It's Esther and Hannah!" Franz cried. "They have it too, Sunny!"

Sunny sprang up from her crouch beside the patient and raced over to him. "Cholera?"

He nodded. "Yes."

The color drained from her face. She pointed to a stout woman who sat up in her bed worriedly watching the commotion around her. "Berta, put Mrs. Shapiro in a chair in the hallway." She swung her finger to an older woman who lay dozing in another bed. "And Mrs. Steinman can be put in the cot in the staff room."

Berta grimaced. "The staff room? *With cholera?* You cannot—"

"Dr. Adler's child is coming!" Sunny's words silenced Berta.

Franz rushed out to the street to wait for Hannah and Esther. He paced up and down. His open lab coat flapped in the icy breeze, but he was indifferent to the chill. He kept thinking of the four-year-old who had died before even reaching the hospital. Wringing his hands, he called out to the empty street, "Where are you, *liebchen*?"

Forever seemed to pass before a woman and a man, the latter carrying a child in his arms, rounded the corner. *Simon carrying Hannah?* Franz rushed toward them. After only a few strides, he realized that they were strangers.

"Herr Doktor!" the man called urgently and motioned to his staggering wife.

Franz waved toward the entrance. "Inside, my friend! They will help you there."

Five or six minutes later a rickshaw swerved around the corner. Franz darted out to meet it. He saw his daughter lying in the back huddled against Esther's shoulder, her coat pulled up and over her face.

"*Hannah!*" he cried. "Do you hear me?"

Hannah didn't stir at the sound of his voice. Esther's face scrunched in discomfort. "Franz, Hannah was mumbling only moments ago. Then she just stopped!"

Franz shot his hand inside the rickshaw and pulled the coat from Hannah's head. Her face was ashen and her eyes closed.

Time stopped.

Then Hannah's lips sputtered.

Franz scooped up his daughter. She hung limp in his arms as he ran her down the pathway toward the hospital.

Meeting Franz at the door, Sunny raced them to the ward and guided him to the waiting bed. His hands were damp from Hannah's soiled clothing as he lowered her onto the mattress. Head flopping to one side, she lay as still as her old doll, Schweizer Fräulein. Berta stripped off Hannah's coat and sopping dress, while Sunny reached for an intravenous needle.

Franz shook Hannah's shoulder again. "*Liebchen*, it's me. Papa!" Nothing. "Please, Hannah, wake up!"

Hannah's lips bubbled and she muttered something incomprehensible.

Franz stroked the loose strands of hair back from her forehead, his fingers warmed by the fever ravaging her brow.

Esther appeared at the far end of the bed, holding herself upright by the railing. Berta and Liese joined them at the bedside, but their flasks of fluid were useless to the unconscious girl. Liese laid a hand on Esther's elbow and tried to guide her to the other waiting bed, but she clung to the bed railing and weakly shrugged her off.

"Speak to me, Hannah!" Franz implored.

"Please, God!" Esther moaned. "*Please!*"

With the intravenous needle in hand, Sunny leaned forward. She tied a rubber tourniquet under Hannah's armpit and then ran her fingers up the girl's arm in search of a vein.

"Can you feel anything?" Franz demanded.

Sunny poked the needle through the skin and wiggled the tip back and forth. Hannah didn't flinch. Holding his breath, Franz stared at the hub of the needle, desperate to see a drop of blood form.

I will do anything, God. He prayed for the first time in his adult life. *Anything. Just—please—do not take her from me!*

Franz stepped around Berta to where Sunny hunched over the bedside. She looked up at him helplessly. "She's so dehydrated, Franz. Her veins have all collapsed."

Leaning forward, Franz took the needle from her hand. He burrowed the tip deeper under the skin, pivoting and angling it, but unable to pierce the flattened vein. Heartbeat drumming in his ears, he withdrew the needle and poked the skin higher above Hannah's elbow. Still no blood.

Franz yanked out the needle and jabbed Hannah's arm again. His vision clouded over as the tears welled and fell onto the child's arm.

"No, God, no!" Esther sobbed. "*Please, no!*"

Sunny jumped to her feet and ran for the door.

~ Chapter 41

The doubt engulfed Sunny as she sprinted down the hallway toward the storeroom. *Is the needle even still in Father's medical bag?*

A few weeks before, Sunny had stuffed all the medicines she could find into Kingsley's bag and taken them to the refugee hospital without even checking what other equipment had been left inside.

Sunny burst into the storeroom, swept the bag off the lower shelf, and spun back for the ward. While she ran, she rummaged blindly through the bag. A glass syringe fell and shattered on the floor but Sunny kept moving. Her anxiety soared as she dug deeper without finding it. Then her fingers touched the long skinny sheath that rested on the bottom. She dropped the bag where she stood and stepped onto the ward holding only the needle in its cloth sheath.

Hannah lay statue-still on the bed. Esther and the two nurses stood as motionless. With sweat streaming down his brow, Franz hunched over the bed jabbing the intravenous needle back and forth in his futile search for a vein.

Sunny's respiration was ragged as she reached the foot of the bed. "Liese, please get me a syringe and prime the intravenous tubing," she panted.

Her eyes skeptical, Liese turned and reached for the nearby bottle of Ringer's lactate.

Franz looked up at Sunny, his face anguished. "What more can you do?"

Holding up the sheath, Sunny extracted the enormous needle from inside. She had not laid eyes on the tool since the day, three years earlier, when her father had used it to save the life of the diabetic boy.

Sunny leaned forward and laid her free hand on Hannah's exposed shin, palpating upward until she hit the bony ridge near the knee that was the tibial tuberosity. She measured two fingers' width below and planted the tip of the huge needle against the skin. She flattened her palm over the top of the needle and pushed down. The tip easily penetrated Hannah's skin but glanced off the thick bone below and slid away.

The child remained motionless.

Feeling the sweat bead on her lip, Sunny pulled back

the needle and repositioned the tip over the initial spot. She placed her palm back on the hub of the needle, locked her elbow and leaned her entire body weight down on it. She felt the resistance of the bone against the needle and worried that it might bend the metal. Suddenly, her hand plunged forward with a gut-wrenching crack as the needle perforated the bone.

Sunny let go and the needle stood upright, anchored inside the bone marrow. "The syringe!" she called to Liese.

Sunny attached the syringe and pulled back on the plunger, comforted by the sight of the gelatinous bone marrow flowing into the glass. "The tubing, please."

Sunny hooked the tube to the end of the needle and opened the flow. Her eyes darted to the bottle of Ringer's lactate. A moment passed, and then fluid began to drip into the tubing. Sunny removed the bottle from the pole. She stretched her arm and held it as high as she could above her head, maximizing the force of gravity on the flow.

Franz's fingers flitted over Hannah's neck in search of a pulse. They finally came to rest just beneath her jaw. He blinked in obvious relief. "The fluid runs directly into the bone marrow?" he asked Sunny.

"Yes," Sunny said. "And from there into the veins. My father taught me this approach."

"Can it possibly work?" he asked, his voice husky.

"It did the last time."

"Please, God, let it also work now," Esther murmured. Still clutching the bed railing, she began to sink slowly toward the floor, her legs no longer able to hold her up.

Berta responded with remarkable speed, catching Esther by the armpits before she hit the ground. She half-dragged the fainting woman to the nearby stretcher.

Sunny's arm ached as she held the bottle high over her head. Almost half the fluid had already drained into Hannah. Without taking her eyes from the bottle, she said, "My father told me that since the needle's caliber is so wide, the fluid actually runs into the bloodstream faster through the marrow than a vein."

Franz kept his fingers glued to Hannah's neck, as though afraid that her heart would stop beating if he lost contact with the pulse. "It's a little stronger, I think," he said.

Sunny lowered her arm and secured the bottle of Ringer's lactate to a pole. "Liese, we'll need at least two more bottles."

The nurse hurried off toward the storeroom.

Franz stroked Hannah's hair. "Everything will be better now, *liebchen.*" He glanced at Sunny. "These fluids will fix you. Sunny has brought you back."

Sunny became aware of the moans and smells around her. She knew that other patients, including Esther, needed attention too, but her feet were glued to the ground. She could not leave Hannah or Franz. The bottle emptied and Sunny hung a second one. Berta brought Franz a wet cloth, and he tenderly dabbed Hannah's face and neck while murmuring constant reassurances.

Hannah's eyelids fluttered. Franz's hand froze in mid-dab. His eyes darted to Sunny. "I saw her blink too, Franz!" she said.

Franz squeezed Hannah's hand in his. "*Liebchen,* can you hear me?"

Her eyelids opened and she stared back at him glassily but said nothing.

"*Oh, Hannah!*" He kissed her brow joyously. "*Liebchen,* you are awake."

"Where am I, Papa?" she croaked.

"At the hospital." His voice faltered. "You lost so much fluid. You passed out."

"Will I get better?" she mumbled as her eyes drifted shut again.

"Yes, *liebchen*!" Franz laughed and kissed her forehead again. He looked at Sunny, his eyes brimming with gratitude. "Thanks to our wonderful, brilliant Sunny, yes, you will."

Simon burst onto the ward. Sunny had never seen him so flustered. He rushed back and forth between Hannah's and Esther's beds, repeating the same questions and tossing his hands around as though juggling imaginary balls. Eventually, Simon settled down beside Esther's bed. He peppered her with nonstop nervous chatter as he clung to her hand.

The rest of the morning passed in a blur. Patients from the same cholera-contaminated heim soon overran the small hospital. The staff had to lay down mats and blankets along the hallway to accommodate the overflow. Eventually, Max set up a triage desk outside the front door, where he turned away all but the sickest of patients. Before noon, the intravenous fluids had been depleted and the nurses could offer only oral fluids. Three other victims, including two children, died in the span of six hours. One nurse had started vomiting.

Word of the cholera outbreak spread through the refugee community. Several people showed up to volunteer. With Simon coordinating, they helped feed fluid into the weakest patients, scrub the beds, and hand-wash the sheets.

By the evening, the worst of the crisis had passed. Sunny had gone to the staff room to rest her legs for a few minutes, but she nodded off in her chair almost as soon as she sat down. She woke to the aroma of steeping tea, a welcome reprieve from the stench of disease that permeated the hospital.

Face haggard but calm, Franz sat across the small table from her. He slid a steaming cup of tea toward her. Sunny sat up. "*Hannah?* How is she?"

"Much better," he said. "She was drinking so well that I pulled the needle from her leg. She is sleeping now."

Sunny nodded with relief. "And Esther and the others?"

"Essie is all right." Franz held up his hands. "Another man died, but there was nothing to be done. We have had no new patients in the past three hours."

Sunny rubbed her eyes and then took a sip of the hot tea, realizing how parched her lips were. Franz grinned widely. "That was something this morning, Sunny. A miracle."

She took another sip. "You can thank my father."

"And I intend to. Every day of my life. But right now, I am thanking you." His eyes misted over and his voice cracked. "Sunny, if I had lost Hannah, I don't know what . . ."

"But you won't lose her, Franz." She took another sip of tea.

He stared at her for several moments. A fresh smile lit his face. "I love you, Sunny."

She shook her head. "Franz, it's not the time to say such things. You are overwrought. You are confusing gratitude with—"

He grasped her hand. "I am confusing nothing. If I live to be a hundred, I will never be able to thank you enough for saving Hannah's life. But that does not change a thing." He squeezed her hand tightly. "I have been in love with you for years. And I am tired of denying it to you and to myself."

Sunny gulped back the lump in her throat. She felt the tears welling. "And what about Lotte and Mrs. Reuben?"

"I will tell Lotte the truth." He shrugged. "As for Mrs. Reuben, her threats are meaningless now. We have just survived cholera, we can also survive Clara."

Sunny laughed as tears ran down her cheeks. "The time has come for me to be truthful with Wen-Cheng too."

Franz leaned farther forward and gently cupped a hand around her neck. He drew her head toward his and touched his lips to hers.

Her heart pounded with elation. "I love you too, Franz."

PART VI

Chapter 42

JUNE 28, 1942, SHANGHAI

Sunny swiveled from side to side to view her reflection in the full-length mirror. Her high-neck, bright red cheongsam, embroidered in silver and gold, clung smoothly to her slight curves without bunching or wrinkling. Self-conscious as she felt in the lavish gown, the touch of the silk enthralled her.

Sunny glanced over to Jia-Li. With her hair tied back and pinned with a vibrant blossom, Jia-Li looked exquisite in her simple royal blue *qipao*. "Is this dress not too much for me, *bǎo bèi*?" Sunny asked. "You would suit it so much better."

"Nonsense!" Jia-Li cried. "I have never seen a more beautiful bride, *xiǎo hè*."

Sunny's face heated and she giggled happily. She spun around on her toes. "This dress is the most generous gift I have ever received. I cannot thank you enough, Jia-Li."

"You can and you have." Jia-Li wrapped her arms around Sunny and hugged her tightly. "I am so happy for you."

Sunny filled with affection for her friend. She was proud of her. Jia-Li had rebounded from the heartache of her broken engagement. She had not touched the opium pipe in over three months. She had even fallen for another man, a soft-spoken Russian poet with wild curly hair and understanding eyes.

"I am so glad you are here with me," Sunny whispered in her friend's ear. "It means everything. I only wish Father . . ."

"Oh, *xiǎo hè*, your father—our father—is watching somewhere." Jia-Li released Sunny and straightened her friend's wedding dress. "Let's get you out there before the good doctor thinks you have changed your mind."

Sunny smiled. "I just need a moment."

Jia-Li turned for the door. "I will go and see if everyone is seated."

Sunny stole another glimpse in the mirror. The dress was as perfect as the setting. Even though the Japanese had seized the Cathay Hotel, Simon had mysteriously managed to secure the use of the hotel's tearoom for the wedding service. He refused to tell Sunny what it cost him, insisting that it was his wedding present to the couple.

Sunny held up her hand to view her gold band gleaming in the light. She was eager to move the ring from her left to right hand, which to Austrians, Franz had told her, signified a woman's transition from engaged to wed. Three months earlier, he had proposed to her on the same bench in Public Garden where they had shared their first lunch. As thrilled as she was, she tried to decline the ring, arguing that they could not afford the expense. Franz explained that it had cost him nothing, since Esther had smuggled the ring—her grandmother's wedding band—out of Vienna in her clothing. Sunny even tried to persuade Esther, who wore her mother's band, to sell the ring to fund other essentials. But Esther would not hear of it. "We have so little, Sunny. You deserve something special to mark this occasion."

The guilt for having such an extravagant wedding and valuable ring still nagged Sunny. Hardship and deprivation in Shanghai were constant under the Japanese. Paid work was scarce. Rationing of everything—rice, water, coal, medicine, and electricity—had become the rule after the conquerors had claimed most of the resources to feed their massive military machine. So many people, even among the once prosperous Shanghailanders, went hungry. Each morning, the city woke to record numbers of corpses piled on the sidewalks.

"What's done is done," Sunny reassured her reflection. "It would be far worse not to relish every moment of this."

The soft strains of a cello floated to Sunny from the ballroom. It reminded her of Lotte. Sunny had written the other woman a heartfelt letter of apology but never posted it. Even if it had cleared Japanese censors, Sunny knew it was not the right way to apologize. She had intended to do it in person but Lotte preempted her, arriving unannounced one morning only days after Sunny had accepted Franz's ring.

Sunny blushed deeply as she led Lotte into the sitting room, but nothing about the woman's demeanor suggested the least trace of hurt or betrayal. On the contrary, she exuded a sense of lightness that Sunny had never seen in her before.

"Lotte, it is so decent of you to . . . to drop in," Sunny stammered. "I was intending . . . er . . . to come see you this week."

"No need." Lotte smiled kindly. "I only wanted to express my very best wishes for Franz and you."

Sunny did not know what Franz had told Lotte

when he broke off their engagement, but her sincerity was beyond a doubt. "Lotte, I feel so badly about what happened. I—we—never intended this . . . or to hurt you in—"

Lotte reached out and squeezed Sunny's hand. "I understand what it means to be in love. Honestly, Sunny. It has worked out for the best. Franz and you were meant for each other."

"Oh, Lotte." Sunny leaned forward and wrapped her in a hug.

"I am very happy for you both." Lotte wriggled free of the embrace, appearing slightly embarrassed. "Truly, Sunny."

Jia-Li appeared at the doorway, snapping Sunny out of the memory. "Everyone is seated, *xiǎo hè*." Her friend winked. "Franz has waited long enough, don't you think?"

Sunny reached for the small bouquet of colorful peonies on the desk. The flowers lay beside her parents' wedding photo, which she had brought with her to the hotel. She lifted the frame to her lips, kissing the glass before placing it back on the desk and following Jia-Li into the hallway.

The corridor's thick carpet and textured wallpaper showed no sign of wear, but Sunny had spotted other indicators—burned-out light bulbs in the chandeliers, empty vases in the lobby, and cracked moldings—reminding her that even the grandest hotel in Shanghai was suffering under Japanese occupation.

"Are you nervous?" Jia-Li asked over her shoulder.

"No."

"And why should you be, *xiǎo hè*?" Jia-Li laughed as she thrust open the door to the tearoom.

The cello's melody grew louder. Sunny was touched

to see Lotte seated in the corner, softly playing Mouret's "Rondeau."

Franz stood at the front of the room beneath the white cloth canopy that resembled the traditional *chuppah* of a Jewish wedding. At the sight of her, he broke into a beaming smile. Sunny resisted the urge to race down the aisle to him. She waited for Jia-Li to walk several paces before she took her first deliberate step.

With only twenty-four guests present, the ballroom seemed relatively empty; a striking contrast to Esther and Simon's wedding two months earlier. Between Esther's widespread popularity and Simon's exalted status among the refugees, so many people had turned up that the synagogue couldn't hold them all. Sunny had insisted on a smaller wedding but, regardless, the guest list would never have rivaled the Lehrers'. After General Nogomi's surgery, rumors had swirled among the Jewish community that Franz was a Japanese sympathizer. Franz never complained, but Sunny sensed his hurt.

Sunny scanned the room. In the front row, Hannah, who sat between Esther and Yang, wore a light blue dress with navy trim that her aunt had sewn. Hannah had recovered quickly from her brush with death. In the past six months, she had burst into adolescence. Now as tall as Sunny, the girl had grown gangly and slightly awkward, but with her large eyes, delicate bones, and inner grace, she was destined for beauty. Turned in her seat, Hannah flashed Sunny a broad grin and welcoming wave as she began walking down the aisle.

Berta, Liese, and Max all sat together with their spouses in the fourth row. Fai and his wife sat across from them, beside Jia-Li's mother. A few seats away, Sunny's two nursing friends from the Country Hospital, Meredith Blythe and Stacy Chan, sat side by side, while a small man in a three-piece suit sat alone in the fifth row. It took Sunny a moment to recognize him as Hermann Schwartzmann.

Garbed in robes specific to their faith, two elderly officials stood at the front of the room facing Franz and Simon. Rabbi Hiltmann, the uncle of Golda, wore a yarmulke and a white prayer shawl around his neck. Sunny's eyes misted over at the sight of Reverend Anderson, the stooped octogenarian who had been her minister for her entire life.

Her heart thumping faster with each step, Sunny arrived at the edge of the canopy. Lotte's music died away. Jia-Li moved aside to take her spot beside Sunny, while Simon stood on the far side of Franz.

Franz looked younger and happier than she had ever seen him. He extended a hand to Sunny. She fought back tears as she joined him under the canopy.

Rabbi Hiltmann held his hand out to the minister. "Reverend Anderson, as this is a second-generation wedding for you," he said in heavily accented English, "please . . ."

"What the rabbi says is most true," the reverend said in a tremulous voice. "I was honored to officiate at the wedding of our beautiful bride's parents. Too many years ago for almost anyone—especially this old codger—to remember." He exhaled. "Ida and Kingsley Mah were two special souls. Idealists, they were. Brave enough to defy many naysayers for the sake of love. Tragically, their lives were cut far too short, but their happy marriage gave us the lovely Soon Yi. And I am delighted to be a part of this—as Rabbi Hiltmann pointed out—second generation of Mah weddings. How delighted her parents would be." He sighed. "Sunny and Franz also face many challenges in these particularly narrow-minded times, but I believe they are strong enough to overcome everything that lies in their path." He laughed at himself again. "Dear me, this decrepit old minister seems to be confusing a wedding ceremony for a sermon."

The rabbi clapped the other man on the shoulder. "You speak only wisdom, my friend. Please continue."

Franz squeezed Sunny's hand tighter as Anderson fumbled with his reading glasses and flipped open the service book in his hand. "Dearly beloved, we are gathered here today . . ."

Butterflies fluttered wildly in her stomach as Sunny listened to Anderson read the vows. Respectful of the Jewish tradition, he stopped before asking the pivotal questions and allowed the rabbi to catch up in Hebrew. The two spiritual leaders merged the ceremonies seamlessly, as though joint Christian and Jewish weddings were the rule rather than the exception.

Anderson turned to Sunny with a gentle smile. "Soon Yi, wilt thou have this man to be thy wedded husband to live together after God's ordinance in the Holy Estate of matrimony?"

Sunny turned to Franz and drank in his loving gaze. "I will."

"Wilt thou love him, in sickness and in health and—forsaking all others—keep thee only unto him, so long as ye both shall live?"

"I will." Her voice caught.

The reverend turned to the rabbi. Hiltmann rhythmically chanted a short prayer in Hebrew. Then in English he said, "Do you, Franz Isaac Adler, take Soon Yi Mah to be your wife?"

Franz took her other hand in his. His eyes glistened. "I do." His voice was husky.

The rabbi nodded his approval. "Do you promise to love, cherish, and protect her, whether in good fortune or in adversity, and to seek with her a life hallowed by the faith of Israel?"

"Yes, I do. Always."

The two spiritual leaders shared a look, and then the rabbi laughed. "You first, Reverend."

Anderson grinned. "I now pronounce you husband and wife."

The rabbi echoed the declaration in Hebrew.

Simon placed a cloth-covered wineglass on the floor in front of Franz. "It's all yours," he whispered. "Don't miss! It's bad luck."

Laughing, Franz stomped on the glass. Sunny's heart leapt.

The rabbi turned to Franz with an exaggerated shrug. "Well, is this not what you have been waiting for all this time, Dr. Adler? You may kiss Mrs. Adler now!"

⌐ Chapter 43

JULY 19, 1942, SHANGHAI

Franz slowly slid his arm out from under Sunny's waist. As soon as she shifted and stirred, he stopped and left his hand where it lay beneath her.

Sunny stilled. Franz was tempted to kiss her awake to make love again but decided it would be selfish after they had stayed up so late talking, laughing, and exploring each other's bodies. Besides, he loved to watch her sleep. He was contented just to stare at the nape of her neck—his favorite place to kiss—and the curve of her supple back. He considered the best angle to photograph her and realized that, for the first time since Hilde's death, he was eager to focus his lens back on a living subject.

The three weeks since their wedding had been a whirl of passion. His sexual reawakening was more gratifying and intense than even he had expected. They quickly felt at home in each other's arms.

But apart from their joy, the world around them seemed to be going to hell. The threat of internment hung over foreigners in Shanghai like a guillotine's blade. The war news was disastrous, with seemingly nonstop losses and setbacks for the Allies in Europe, North Africa, and the Pacific. Depression ran rampant among the refugees, and suicide was all too common. Yet, Franz felt blessed. Not only had his daughter returned to him from the brink of death but he was surrounded by family, deeply in love and, while most others were unemployed, still able to practice surgery.

With the surreptitious aid of Colonel Kubota and Hermann Schwartzmann, Simon had managed to keep the refugee hospital functional. Franz was still not certain whether or not Kubota was behind the late-night drop-offs, but every month new shipments of vital medical supplies had arrived. And so did Schwartzmann, with his envelopes full of cash.

Franz fought the urge to run his fingers along Sunny's perfect shoulder blades. He smiled to himself, remembering how close he had come to never discovering this bliss. He would be forever grateful to Lotte for her strength of character. He recalled the evening, almost six months earlier, when he first told Lotte the truth.

Esther and Hannah were still recovering from cholera in the hospital, leaving Franz and Lotte alone in the apartment. Hands folded on her lap and expression neutral, she listened as Franz fumbled to explain his feelings for Sunny. By the time he finished, Lotte's eyes were dry. She actually appeared relaxed. "We should probably announce the breaking off of the engagement," she said pleasantly.

"Yes." He cleared his throat. "Yes, of course."

"May I ask you a rather private question, Franz?"

"Certainly, Lotte."

"Our relationship?" Her gaze fell to her lap. "Did my aunt put you up to it?"

Franz rose to his feet. "Lotte, you are a lovely and wonderful woman. I saw that the first time we met. However, working so closely with Sunny—"

She held up her hand to stop him. "I want to hear the truth. Please, Franz."

"Your aunt did encourage me, yes," he muttered. "Of course, I was glad to—"

"And did this encouragement include any consequences?"

Uneasy, Franz stalled. "Consequences? I am not sure I understand."

"For example, did my aunt threaten your position with my uncle in any way?"

He cleared his throat. "Well, indirectly . . ."

Lotte eyed him intently. "Did Clara threaten to have Hannah removed from school?"

"I . . . I . . ." he stammered. "How could you know?"

"Because I have lived with that woman for most of my life!" Lotte spat with uncharacteristic bitterness. "I know how she thinks."

"Clara was only looking out for you. For your long-term security."

"Hardly!" Lotte scoffed. "Oh, Franz, this never had anything to do with you. Or even finding me a nice Jewish doctor."

"No? Then what?"

She exhaled softly. "For years, Clara has tried to prevent me from marrying Bernard."

"Bernard?" He frowned in thought. "The Swiss man we met in the café?"

"Yes, Bernard Leudenberger." She smiled as she spoke his name. "I should have told you long ago. Forgive me. Like you, I felt too intimidated by Clara."

"There is no need to explain." Franz chuckled. "To me, of all people."

"But I want to, Franz," Lotte said. "Bernard and I grew up on the same street with few other children our age. We were the best of friends. After my parents died, I moved in with Clara and Samuel while Bernard went off to school in Switzerland. As soon as he returned, he came for me." The color left her cheeks, and she shook her head. "When Clara heard that we were in love . . ."

"Bernard is a Gentile, isn't he?" Franz asked with sudden insight.

Lotte nodded. "Clara calls him a Nazi because he is of German origin. But it couldn't be farther from the truth. Bernard is the gentlest man I have ever met."

It all made sense to Franz. "So Clara bullied you into our relationship too?"

"Yes." Lotte swallowed. "She said I would be considered a Nazi sympathizer. That I could never attend *shul*. That I would have no friends. That I would become an outcast, without a home or a job."

"Why did you allow this, Lotte?"

She buried her face in her hands. "Bernard's family threatened to disown him too. They don't want him to marry a Jew—or a Catholic, for that matter—any more than my aunt and uncle want me to marry a goy. Bernard's father manages the Shanghai office of the Uberseebank. He could easily have his son dismissed from his job there as a currency trader. We would have nowhere to go and nothing to live on."

"Lotte, there must be something to be done. I know a German diplomat who might be able to help find work for Bernard."

She looked up at him with a small smile. "Sunny is indeed a fortunate woman."

"Perhaps not as fortunate as Bernard."

Lotte's expression stiffened. She grabbed Franz's hand, her grip cool and firm. "Do not worry about Hannah. I will not let my aunt threaten her position at the Jewish school."

"How can you stop her?"

"Clara may sit on the board, but she exaggerates her influence. I still work at the school. And I do have some say."

Lotte's words proved prophetic. When the Jewish school finally reopened in late January, no one questioned Hannah's enrollment. After the attack on Pearl Harbor, Franz never returned to his post at the Country Hospital, so the security of his job became irrelevant. Instead, the family relied on Sunny's inheritance and the occasional loan from Jia-Li. And, in the weeks and months that followed, Bernard and Lotte began to appear together in public. In the end, Clara's threats turned out to be empty.

Sunny rolled toward Franz and pulled him back to the moment with a soft kiss. "What time is it?" she murmured.

"Early." Franz kissed her back. "Go back to sleep."

She yawned, stretched, and kissed him again.

He pressed his lips harder to hers. "It's never too early, is it?"

"Never with you." She ran the tips of her fingers lightly down his bare chest.

Franz woke again to find sunlight leaking around the blinds. His watch read 8:14. The room was already warm. By late morning, it would be unbearably stuffy.

Franz rose and headed to the kitchen. Hannah had not yet risen, but Yang was already standing at the stove, steaming something in a large pot. A delicious aroma wafted through the room. "Good morning, Yang."

She nodded in her unsmiling way. Other than Sunny, only Hannah seemed to be able to dent the woman's stony exterior. Yang had beamed the day she discovered that Hannah was fluent in Shanghainese. Ever since, the two of them had spent much time chatting while the tiny woman cooked all kinds of treats for the girl.

A soft knock drew Franz's attention. He opened the door to Simon. Franz knew that Hannah would be pleased to see her uncle. As much as his daughter enjoyed living at Sunny's house, where she had her own bedroom, she missed her aunt and uncle, who now lived in their old flat on Avenue Joffre.

But Franz saw at a glance that there was nothing social about Simon's visit. His expression was dark and his eyes unusually grave. "What is it?" Franz demanded. "Is Esther all right?"

Stone-faced, Simon nodded. "I need you to come meet someone."

"Right now? Who?"

"Aaron Grodenzki." The name meant nothing to Franz. "Just come, Franz. Please."

Outside, Simon explained further. "Grodenzki showed up out of the blue. He told his story to Chaim Adelman, who sits on what's left of the CFA committee. Chaim summoned an emergency council meeting last night. Several refugees were invited. Reuben was there too."

Whether or not the Reubens were the source of the collaborator rumors concerning him, Franz knew that they had perpetuated them. He found himself shunned by former friends at the temple and excluded from meetings. Franz had tried to defend himself, but the gossip fed on itself. His marriage to a woman outside his religion and race only compounded his isolation.

Franz and Simon arrived at the small Russian café a few blocks from Franz's old apartment. Franz immediately noticed the haggard man sitting alone in the corner. He was hunched over and clasping a coffee cup in both hands. A jagged scar ran across his forehead. At first glance, Franz thought that Aaron Grodenzki was middle-aged or older but soon realized that the man was still in his twenties. Struck by Grodenzki's skeletal appearance, Franz didn't notice his mangled hands until he reached the table. Grodenzki's left hand was fingerless beyond the knuckles, and he had only a thumb and part of a forefinger on his right.

Grodenzki studied Franz with suspicion. "You were not there last night." His German was tinged with a Polish accent.

"Some people think I cooperate with the Japanese," Franz said.

"Do you?"

"Only when they threaten my family," Franz said.

Grodenzki accepted the explanation with a shrug.

"Aaron, tell Franz about the place," Simon encouraged. "Chełmno."

Grodenzki looked from Simon to Franz. "My family is from Łódź. You have heard of it?"

Franz nodded. "In central Poland?"

"Poland's third-largest city, or it used to be, anyway." Grodenzki grunted. "After Łódź fell, in September of '39, the Nazis herded us into a walled ghetto with hundreds of thousands of other Jews. The conditions . . ." He exhaled.

"I've heard," Franz said.

Grodenzki shot him a look that suggested Franz had no inkling of how awful it was. "Two and a half years, we manage to survive in this ghetto. But just after New Year's Day, the SS begins to round up the Jews. Whole families—old people, children, babies—doesn't matter to them. They tell us only they are taking us to 'relocation camps' in Germany."

A chill ran up Franz's spine as he remembered Max using the same term regarding his daughter's family.

"They take us to a little town, seventy kilometers away, called Chełmno." Still clutching his cup, Grodenzki stopped for another sip of coffee. "My family's turn came on the twentieth of January. My older brother, my little sister, and my parents." And then, as though speaking to himself, he added, "Standing in that stinking, frozen cattle car. We are—hundreds of us—jammed in too tight to sit. Even the old and sick have to stand for the entire trip. Hour after hour. At the train station, they unload us into the backs of big transport trucks and drive us into the town. Chełmno. To a big, old manor house." He grunted. "It is quite pretty, actually. But none of us are so stupid as to believe the Nazis might let us stay in a castle."

Franz glanced over to Simon, whose eyes were glued to the table.

"But there they are—the SS brutes—leading a long line of Jews into the castle," Grodenzki continued. "We know there has to be trouble because they aren't shrieking or beating us like usual. Right before we get to the doors, two Nazi guards pull my brother and me out of the lineup, along with a few other young men. We watch my parents, and my little sister, Perla, disappear inside." He paused a moment. "The Nazis drive us men—many are boys, actually—out to Waldlager.

The forest camp." Grodenzki stared out past the others and fell silent.

"Forest camp?" Franz asked with a shake of his head.

"Sonderkommando labor detachment." Grodenzki laughed bitterly. "That's what they call us slaves who work at the forest camp. Our job is to empty the trucks." Grodenzki pointed to Franz with the nubs of his left hand. "You see, inside the castle, the new arrivals—little children with their dolls, old men with canes, women carrying babies—all of them—are led down a grand hallway. Beautiful paintings hang on the wall. Soft carpets. Heated, even. At the end of the hallway, they stop in front of a desk. A Polish man tells them they must change for a doctor's medical examination and that they have to check all their valuables in at the desk. The man even writes a receipt for their possessions." He snorted with disgust. "From there, the Jews are led through a doorway, along a dark passageway, and into an empty room with plywood for walls and metal grates on the floor. When the room is full—more crowded than the cattle cars leaving Łódź—the door is slammed shut. Only when the engine turns over do people realize that they have been packed into the back of a truck."

"*Oh, mein Gott,*" Franz murmured.

"God is nowhere near Chełmno, Herr Doktor, trust me," Grodenzki said. "One of the SS men connects the truck's exhaust pipe to the only vent inside the back of the truck. And the driver runs the engine until the screams stop." He glanced from Simon to Franz. "Then the guard unhooks the exhaust pipe, and the driver heads off with his load of fresh corpses out to the forest camp. To us waiting Sonderkommandos. We carry the bodies to mass graves—pits, not graves. And we dig others while we wait for more trucks. There are SS guards at the forest camp too. They don't help unload the bodies, of course, but if anyone from the truck is still moving, they put a bullet in the back of his or her head." He shook his head. "Then the guards . . . they always laugh."

Grodenzki took one more slow sip of his coffee. "Day and night, the trucks make the four-kilometer trip between the forest camp and the castle, leaving empty and always returning full. Perhaps a thousand Jews are murdered every day. Maybe more." He shrugged. "Who knows?"

Franz brought a hand to his mouth. "And you, Aaron. How did you escape?"

"One day, my brother, Szmul, and I are sent with a bunch of others into the forest to cut trees. The Nazis are running out of space to stuff all the victims." Grodenzki rubbed his forehead with his palm. "Szmul knows we have little time left. Every two or three months the Nazis replace the Sonderkommandos with new recruits. They retire the previous ones with machine guns." He put his shortened forefinger to his temple. "So we work extra hard, sawing down as many trees as we can and moving deeper into the forest. At dusk, right before the SS come to round us up, we run. The guards don't notice us missing right away. By the time they release the dogs, it's dark and we're hiding high in a tree. The Nazis don't worry much about us. They assume the Polish winter will save them the bullets. And the cold almost did finish us off." Grodenzki held up his hands with the eight missing fingers. "Frostbite."

"Awful," Franz muttered.

"No, Doctor." He grunted. "Frostbite saved my life!"

"How is that possible?"

"Szmul and I would have died quickly if we did not stumble across a group of partisan guerrillas. Polish

Resistance fighters." Grodenzki wiggled his stubs again. "The leader takes pity on us. He feeds us and lets us sleep in their camp. He shows us maps and the best route eastward. Takes us three months, but Szmul and I reach Soviet territory. As soon as we do, Szmul is recruited—at gunpoint—into the Red Army. But me?" Grodenzki raised his hands again. "What good am I as a soldier?

"I tell everyone who will listen about Chełmno. But they don't believe me or they don't care." He nodded to himself. "I realize that I have to tell them in America. But how? Then I remember Shanghai, where my aunt and uncle live. The travel through China was even harder than behind enemy lines in Poland, but somehow I arrive here."

Simon gaped at Franz. "It's even worse than the wildest rumors, isn't it?"

Franz was too shocked to speak. He didn't doubt a word of Grodenzki's story, but despite all he had seen and heard in the past few years, he still could not digest the idea of a human slaughterhouse.

Simon's expression hardened and he tapped the tabletop with his finger. "We can't ignore this, Franz. The world needs to hear what the hell the Nazis are up to in Chełmno!"

⏤ *Chapter 44*

Franz had hardly spoken since returning home two hours earlier. Sunny had never seen him as preoccupied or as shaken. As soon as Hannah left to visit a friend, Sunny sat him down on the sofa. "Franz, tell me what happened this morning."

He rubbed his temples. "I do not want to discuss it. Not today, Sunny."

"I thought we shared everything now. Good and bad."

"Not this, Sunny." His voice faltered. "I wish to God I had never heard a word of it."

Sunny leaned forward and wrapped her arms around him. She tilted her face up and kissed him tenderly on the lips. "I can wait until you are ready to talk."

"Chełmno," he croaked.

Sunny pulled free of the embrace. "What is Chełmno?"

"A village in Poland. Or it used to be. Now it's an extermination factory." He swallowed. "I met a Polish Jew this morning. He only had two fingers . . ."

By the time Franz finished recounting Grodenzki's tale of the asphyxiation trucks, tears rolled down Sunny's cheeks. "Gassing whole families?" she sputtered. "Can this really be true?"

"The local Jewish leaders are skeptical, but I know he is telling the truth." Franz nodded to himself. "It was not his words or even his missing fingers. His eyes. They held the look of a cancer patient near the very end. His eyes were dead, Sunny."

Sunny wrapped her arms around him again. "Thank God you, Hannah, and Essie are here in Shanghai. So far away from them."

"I hope we are far enough."

Sunny insisted on accompanying Franz to the hospital. Hand in hand, they walked the sidewalk in the blistering July heat.

"Simon wants me to help him find a radio transmitter," Franz said. "So Aaron can tell Jewish leaders in America and Palestine about Chełmno."

Sunny's chest tightened with dread. "You know how the Japanese treat spies! If they caught you with a transmitter . . ."

"I can still see them dragging Heng away." Though no one had heard what had become of his neighbor, he, like everyone else, assumed the worst. "But this is worth the risk. Someone has to tell the rest of the world."

"The world is already at war with Germany. What more can be done?"

"The war is not going well for the Allies," he said. "What if they negotiate a cease-fire or a peace treaty with the Nazis?"

Sunny racked her brain for some way to talk Franz out of such high-risk espionage. "Would Churchill or Roosevelt really agree to peace with Hitler?"

"They can be replaced by leaders who might," Franz said. "Besides, think of all the countries from France to Belarus already overrun by the Nazis. Imagine how many Jews are caught in their clutches? Millions of women, children, old people . . ."

"It hurts to even think about it, Franz. But how will risking your life on a transmitter possibly help them?"

"If the Nazis see that the world knows about Chełmno, perhaps they would stop killing people. Or if the Jews themselves know what awaits them in such camps, maybe they would resist more?" He looked at her helplessly. "Sunny, I have to do something. You understand?"

She did. "I want to help too, Franz."

Franz broke into the first smile she had seen since his visit with Grodenzki. "I love you so much, Sunny Adler. Your support is all that I need."

At the refugee hospital, Max beckoned to them from inside his lab. "I went to a meeting last night," he said in lieu of a greeting. "We met a man. A Polish Jew—"

"Aaron Grodenzki," Franz said. "I spoke to him this morning."

"Grodenzki's story. The trucks and the carbon monoxide . . ." Max wrung his hands together. "You don't believe him, do you, Franz?"

Franz looked down and shrugged.

"Those Nazis are as uncivilized as they come," Max continued. "Capable of cruelty beyond belief. But a camp built for no purpose other than murder?"

"I agree that it makes no sense, Max," Franz said, choosing his words carefully.

Sunny saw how hard Max was struggling to convince himself that his daughter and her family would not meet the same fate as the Jews at Chełmno. "No doubt there are camps," Max said. "Terrible ones like Buchenwald and Dachau. But I think Grodenzki exaggerated his story in order to play upon our sympathy. We can't allow him to spread such irresponsible stories. To panic people with these rumors. If my wife heard this . . ."

Franz laid a hand on his friend's arm. "I believe him, Max."

Max's face fell and his shoulders slumped.

"Listen, my friend," Franz hurried to add. "The Nazis have always held a particular hatred for the Polish Jews. Remember Herschel Grynszpan? It does not mean they will treat German Jews the same way. Not at all."

Max shrugged off Franz's hand. "I don't believe him."

"But if it were true, would you not agree that silence might only encourage the Nazis?"

"I won't believe it!" Max's voice cracked as he groped for the handkerchief in his pocket. "I won't. I can't." Without another word, he jumped to his feet and rushed out of the lab.

From the grim faces of the staff and patients on the ward, Sunny recognized that the word of Chełmno had already spread. To distract herself, she set to work.

She was checking the temperature of a patient, a woman recovering from malaria, when she heard a commotion in the hallway. She looked up and saw Berta waving frantically to her from the doorway. Abandoning the thermometer in the patient's mouth, Sunny hurried over to her. Franz arrived from the opposite direction.

"The Japanese!" Berta whispered urgently. "They're here!"

Franz squinted. "*Here?* Why?"

"They have brought wounded soldiers," Berta said.

Franz dashed for the entrance, and Sunny followed. Two uniformed Japanese medics sporting Red Cross armbands marched down the pathway toward the door. The medics slung a wooden stretcher between them that held a sailor in a bloodied white uniform.

The medic at the rear of the stretcher called in English, "A bomb exploded at the wharf! Chinese sabotage. We have four injured sailors. Get us beds!"

"How serious are the injuries?" Franz asked.

"You are doctor?" the medic demanded.

"A surgeon, yes."

"Two are bad," the medic snapped. "You have operating room here, yes?"

They cleared four beds in a row for the wounded sailors. Sunny and Franz stood at the foot of the beds beside the English-speaking medic and assessed the casualties. Blood and debris covered the men. They reeked of burnt clothing and sulfur. Three of the four sailors had their heads bandaged. Sunny could see that the patients in the first two beds suffered far more serious injuries than the other two.

The sailor in the second bed lay still with his head and half of his face draped in heavy bandages. His blood-soaked pants were shredded over his left leg. A towel covered his leg, but from the thigh down, the limb twisted unnaturally and the foot pointed at a right angle to the rest of the leg. The medic nodded at him. "Shattered femur from a falling wall. Many cuts to his head and face."

The medic swung his finger to the first bed, where a wide-eyed sailor, as pale as the wall behind him, stared silently back. His tunic had been sliced open, exposing his chest and abdomen. He clutched a blood-soaked towel to his belly. "He has lost much blood," the medic grunted.

Franz leaned closer to the sailor. "May I?" he asked, pantomiming the act of removing the towel.

The sailor nodded warily. Franz gently peeled it back. Blood caked the man's abdomen, and more oozed out from a central hole the size of a fist. A grayish-pink loop of bowel poked out of the wound. A long shard of glass glinted under the skin. Franz lowered the towel back over the abdomen and rested the sailor's hand on top of it. He turned to the nearest nurse. "Berta, prepare the operating room."

"Certainly, Dr. Adler," she replied.

Franz motioned to Sunny as he spoke to the medic. "Mrs. Adler is an able surgeon. She will be in charge of the others while I operate on this man. All right?"

The medic glanced at her skeptically before turning to Franz with a single nod.

Franz pointed to the patient with the shattered leg. "Sunny, you might have to reset his femur while I'm in surgery."

"I will," Sunny said. "Go."

As soon as Franz left, Sunny turned to the plump nurse near her. "Irma, I will need catgut and several needles. Also, can you bring a fresh supply of bandages and plaster?"

Irma hurried off in search of the supplies.

Sunny looked at the gray-haired nurse who stood against the far wall motionless with fear. "Miriam, can you please draw me up three full syringes of morphine?"

Sunny assessed the man in the fourth bed. He was moaning the loudest. He had an obvious wrist fracture, broken ribs, and a deep laceration over his head that required multiple sutures, but his repairs would have to wait. She turned to the sailor in the third bed. Aside from cuts and nicks to his head, he had a probable pelvic fracture and multiple fragments of wood and debris embedded under the skin of his chest and back. His care would not be a priority either.

Sunny turned to the man with the misshapen leg. As she reached for the blood-stiffened towel covering his wound, she noticed that his non-bandaged left eye had opened. He stared at her groggily. As she gently pulled back the towel from his leg, she suppressed a gasp. A ragged crater the size of a soup bowl cut into his thigh. Inside the wound, Sunny saw tattered flesh, torn muscle, and fragments of bone and metal. Only the belt-tourniquet cinched above the wound stemmed the bleeding, but the leg had turned blue and mottled from lack of blood.

Sunny saw that resetting the leg would be futile. Only an amputation could save his life. As she laid the towel back down, he shifted. A grimace formed on what she could see of his lips.

"Miriam, where is that morphine?" Sunny called.

"Coming, Sunny," Miriam replied shakily.

Sunny examined the sailor's head wounds. She peeled back the bandages from his scalp to reveal three or four deep lacerations and began to remove the dressings over his face. He lay still as she worked, but she saw that his exposed eye had come into focus and was watching her more intently.

Suddenly, there was a horrible familiarity to his face. Nausea swept over her. Her hands began to tremble as she pulled off the rest of the dressing to reveal the jagged scar running between the man's upper lip and nose.

Holding the bandage limply in her hand, she gaped at the man who had murdered her father and tried to rape her. She had to resist the impulse to grab his neck and squeeze with all her might.

The sailor's right eye was swollen shut from the bruising, but his left eye stared back at her with a glint of fear.

"Sunny. Sunny!" Miriam prompted with a light shake of her shoulder.

"Yes?" Sunny said without taking her eyes off the sailor.

"Your morphine."

Sunny grabbed the three full syringes out of the nurse's hand. Each one held at least three standard doses of painkiller; enough morphine to reliably kill a patient with a narcotic overdose.

The sailor tried to lift his head off the bed, but it fell right back. Spittle flew from his lips as he muttered something unintelligible.

"What is the wait?" the medic barked. "Are you going to give him medicine or not?"

"Yes, I will," she said evenly. "He is in a great deal of pain. He will require extra doses of painkiller."

Chapter 45

Three days after the wounded Japanese sailors had been rushed to the refugee hospital, Franz hurried through his ward rounds and returned home before noon. He found Esther and Simon nestled together on the overstuffed sofa in the sitting room. Hannah sat in the chair in the corner with her cello between her legs. Sunny moved between them, a teapot in hand. Hannah pushed the cello aside and rose to greet her father.

Simon pointed at Hannah's cello. "You missed it, Franz. That girl of yours is terrific. Carnegie Hall terrific, as far as I'm concerned."

"Oh, Onkel Simon!" Hannah groaned. "I am still not good."

Esther patted Simon's wrist. "My husband is right, Hannah. Once you get past his American tendency to exaggerate, of course. Your improvement is wonderful. You must keep practicing now."

Franz mussed her hair gently. "Will you play again for me, *liebchen*?"

"Later, Papa." Hannah pulled away from him and fixed her hair. "I am off to meet Natasha now."

"Give my best to Mr. and Mrs. Lazarev," Franz said. "And have a glass of water before you leave. It's scorching hot outside."

"Oh, Papa, don't worry so much. I'm not a little girl anymore," Hannah said as she packed up her cello and hurried out of the room.

Franz watched her go, astounded by how his daughter had changed in the past year. Her limp was almost imperceptible. And he could not deny that she resembled an adolescent more than a child.

"Sunny, may I speak to you in the kitchen?" Franz asked.

"Don't blame your poor wife for our presence." Simon chuckled. "We invited ourselves over."

"It concerns a patient, Simon," Franz said. "We will only be a moment."

Franz and Sunny stepped into the kitchen and he shut the door behind them. "The man whose leg I amputated three days ago," he said, referring to the sailor with the scarred lip. "He died from his wound infection."

Sunny showed no response.

Franz folded his arms around her and pulled her into his chest. "It's over now, darling," he whispered into her ear.

"I suppose it is," she murmured into his shoulder.

"I still do not understand why you waited a day to tell me that he was the one who had killed your father."

Sunny wriggled out of his embrace. "If I had told you before the surgery, Franz, would you have still operated? Would you have tried as hard as you did to save his life?"

"Yes." He considered the question further. "Perhaps not. I can't be sure. What he did to you and your father . . . I will not lie, Sunny. I am relieved that he is dead."

"I am too," she said. "But—oh, Franz—I almost killed him with morphine. I was wrong to have ever considered it. And I worried you would be tempted to do something similar. I couldn't let you. Especially not in a hospital, of all places."

Before he could say anything, the hallway phone jangled.

Sunny walked out to answer it. A moment later, she came back to get him.

Franz picked up the receiver.

"Dr. Adler, Herr Silberstein calling," Schwartzmann

said gravely. "Sorry to disturb you, but I was hoping you might be free to meet me at the usual place."

"Of course, Mr. Silberstein. When?"

"Would in half an hour be inconvenient?"

"So soon?"

"It really is rather urgent."

"*Natürlich.*"

Back in the sitting room, with Hannah departed, Simon's expression had turned grave. "Franz, we have to talk about Grodenzki. I have a lead on a radio transmitter—"

Franz held up his hand. "Not now, Simon. I have to go meet Hermann. It sounds urgent."

Esther straightened. "Schwartzmann? What does he want?"

"I am not sure, but I think there could be trouble."

Tight gasoline rationing had kept almost every civilian car off the road, including taxis. The once-thriving rickshaw trade had withered as people saved their money for essentials such as food and coal, the prices of which had soared under occupation. Franz covered the more than two miles to Public Garden on foot. He was drenched in sweat by the time he reached the park.

Schwartzmann sat on their usual bench wearing a three-piece wool suit despite the heat. At the sight of Franz, he rose from the bench with a hand extended. "Good afternoon, Dr. Adler. I trust married life agrees with you. Is Mrs. Adler well?"

Franz shook his hand. "Very well indeed, thank you."

"*Wunderbar.* Delighted to hear it." Schwartzmann pointed with the bowl of his pipe toward the pathway that led away from the gazebo and through the garden. "It's such a lovely day. Shall we stroll?"

Franz's concern rose. They had never left the bench on previous encounters.

As they walked, Schwartzmann indicated the sparse flower beds lining the pathway. "Not quite the same as in other years, is it?"

In previous summers, the colorful peonies, daffodils, and roses were in bloom by summertime, but Public Garden, like most of Shanghai, had wilted under Japanese occupation and neglect. Schwartzmann stopped to examine a patch of dried, barren soil. "I am sorry to drag you out on such short notice, but I have news that I feel compelled to share."

"What news, Hermann?"

Schwartzmann glanced from side to side. "Have you heard of a man named Meisinger? Standartenführer Josef Meisinger?"

The SS title set Franz's heart pounding, but he could not place the name.

Schwartzmann brought his pipe to his lips. "Meisinger is the highest-ranking Gestapo officer in Tokyo. Nominally, he is the police attaché at our Tokyo embassy, responsible for Reich security in all of East Asia. Of course, his unofficial duties go far beyond that."

Franz's internal alarm sounded, but he kept his tone even. "I see."

Schwartzmann looked over his shoulder again. "Before Tokyo, Meisinger was in Warsaw. The chief of the Gestapo there." He pulled the pipe from his lips. "He . . . ah . . . developed somewhat of a reputation in Poland."

Franz swallowed. "What kind of a reputation?"

"Meisinger was known for his brutal methods. Even by SS standards. To the point that his own men gave him a rather crude nickname." Schwartzmann cleared his throat. "They call him the Butcher of Warsaw."

Franz's mouth went dry. He glanced at the lifeless soil. "Is Meisinger here in Shanghai?"

"I saw him this morning. A man hard to miss." Schwartzmann shook his head grimly. "Meisinger is not alone. He has come with a contingent of SS officers from Tokyo."

"Why?"

"The SS is nothing if not secretive. They tell us diplomats as little as possible." Schwartzmann stopped to chew on his pipe stem. "But I have heard rumors."

The park was hot and silent. In the distance, a mother and her child walked hand in hand. But for Franz, the world stood still. "What kind of rumors?"

Schwartzmann viewed him with a sympathetic smile and held his hands out helplessly.

"*Us?*" Franz gasped. "These Nazis have come to Shanghai to deal with the German Jews?"

"I hear that they refer to you as 'the escapees.'"

Franz's sweat-soaked shirt suddenly felt icy. "What do they have in mind for us?" His thoughts flashed back to the atrocities at Chełmno that Grodenzki had related three days earlier.

Schwartzmann averted his gaze. "A colleague in my office went out with one of Meisinger's aides, an old school chum. They drank too much. He returned with . . . with outlandish tales."

Afraid to ask, Franz held his breath and waited for Schwartzmann to continue.

"Apparently, Meisinger intends to present several options to the Japanese authorities here," Schwartzmann said.

"Options?"

Schwartzmann avoided Franz's eyes as he spoke. "One plan involves tugging old barges that are no longer seaworthy out to the China Sea. Another concerns an undersupplied labor camp on a remote island in the Whangpoo." His voice fell to a near whisper. "Apparently, Meisinger even brought a canister with him that contained a substance called Zyklon B."

Franz felt as though his throat was closing over. "What is Zyklon B?"

"I am told it's a form of odorless cyanide gas contained within solid pellets."

"God help us. They want to turn Shanghai into Chełmno!"

"Chełmno? I am not familiar with the place."

"I will explain later, my friend. Thanks for this."

Franz raced off without another word. He ran across the Garden Bridge and did not slow until he reached Japanese Military Headquarters at Astor House. Panting from his exertion and the heat, he called out anxiously to the group of sentries at the entrance, "I must speak to Colonel Kubota!"

A guard barked in Japanese and raised his rifle. Franz lifted his hands over his head. "Colonel Kubota or Captain Yamamoto, *please!* It is most urgent."

The soldier jabbed the bayonet at him as though trying to scare away a yapping dog.

"Colonel Kubota! I must see him!" Franz cried.

The soldier raised the rifle butt to his shoulder and sighted Franz down its barrel. The guard beside him lifted his weapon too. Franz's heart fluttered wildly, but he stood his ground.

The lobby door opened and Captain Yamamoto stepped out between the sentries. Bone straight, Yamamoto kept his arms rigidly at his side. His face was stone. "What is it, Dr. Adler?"

"I must speak to Colonel Kubota."

"The colonel is engaged."

"Please, Captain Yamamoto, it's a matter of life and death!"

Yamamoto stared back impassively. "Return here

tomorrow morning at eight o'clock. I will inform you if the colonel has time to see you."

Franz's mind raced, desperate to find a way into Kubota's office. "Captain, lives are at stake. Just as they were the day I was brought to see General Nogomi in the hospital."

Yamamoto stared hard at Franz for a long moment before he spun and marched off. "You stay here!" he called over his shoulder.

Franz waited at least ten minutes under the glare of the late-afternoon sun and the withering stares of the guards. Finally, Yamamoto emerged from the building and motioned for Franz to follow him inside.

After dismissing Yamamoto, Colonel Kubota sat down across from Franz. The lines on his usually placid face were deeper than before, and he appeared almost embarrassed to see Franz. "You wanted to speak to me, Dr. Adler?"

"I am sorry to disturb you, Colonel," Franz said. "I have just received information regarding a German delegation in Shanghai."

Kubota stared at the inkwell on his desktop but did not comment.

"Apparently this delegation is headed by a Colonel Meisinger of the SS."

"We met with them this morning," Kubota said without elaborating on who else had been present.

Franz swallowed. "I realize that you must be far too busy to involve yourself in German politics, but I am concerned that these men intend the Jewish refugees harm." Kubota's pained expression confirmed Franz's worst fear. "So it's true?"

Kubota nodded. "Colonel Meisinger argues that as long as the German Jews are free to live in Shanghai, they will always present a security risk to our forces here."

"*Security risk?*" Franz sputtered.

"'Twenty thousand potential spies and saboteurs' was how the colonel phrased it," Kubota said.

Franz struggled to control his tone. "None of us Jews are so foolish as to think that we have any power to influence the outcome of the war." He held his hands open in front of him. "We are only trying to survive. Nothing more."

Kubota stared dead ahead. "The Germans realize that we do not share their policy of anti-Semitism."

"So, instead, they are portraying us German Jews as security threats."

Kubota nodded.

Franz gripped his damp palms together. "And did they convince you?"

"Not me, no," Kubota said. "However, the security of Shanghai is not my responsibility."

"Whose responsibility is it, Colonel?"

"Civilian order and counterespionage falls under the authority of our military police, the Kempeitai."

Franz's stomach plummeted. "Colonel Tanaka?"

"I am afraid so, yes."

"And Colonel Tanaka could take actions against twenty thousand civilians on the recommendation of a few SS officers? What about his superiors in Tokyo?"

Kubota sighed. "In our system, the field command has almost complete autonomy when making decisions regarding issues of local security and order."

"What about General Nogomi?"

"The general has the ultimate authority but . . ."

Franz rose partially out of his seat. "But what, Colonel Kubota?"

"The general tends not to interfere with security matters."

Franz imagined hands on his back and felt as though

his feet were sliding off the edge of a cliff. "I have heard rumors that the SS have specific plans to exterminate German Jews, Colonel. With rickety barges or poisonous gas."

"I am not at liberty to discuss such matters, Dr. Adler."

Franz dropped back into his seat. "Please, Colonel, I beg you."

For a long silent moment, Kubota stared over Franz's head. Finally, he said, "I found their proposal most dishonorable."

"Did Colonel Tanaka approve their plan?" Franz croaked.

Kubota shrugged. "We did not give them an answer this morning."

"There must be some way to stop this," Franz said. "Colonel, please."

Kubota looked down at his desk. "General Nogomi," he muttered.

"Yes, of course, the general!" Franz nodded vehemently. "I saved his life."

Kubota looked up and studied Franz for a moment. "I'm afraid, Dr. Adler, that alone will not be enough."

⌐ *Chapter 46*

Tension permeated the sitting room. In the background, a BBC announcer somberly described the Germans' rapid advance toward the Volga River and the strategic city of Stalingrad. Normally, the Adlers, like other refugees, would have dissected every scrap of information, hoping for a hint that the Soviets were repelling the Nazis and turning the tide of the war. But after Franz's update about the SS intentions for local Jews, the Russian Front seemed desperately remote and irrelevant.

The color drained from Esther's face. Simon's jaw hung open. Sunny felt dazed, almost incapable of accepting her husband's words as fact.

Franz glanced around the room, holding Sunny's gaze the longest. He looked gray, lined, and hopeless.

"Cyanide gas, Franz?" Simon muttered.

"*Gott in Himmel,*" Esther breathed. "Did Colonel Kubota tell you when the Japanese plan to give these creatures an answer?"

Franz shook his head. "It's not his decision to make."

"But surely the colonel will arrange for you to meet General Nogomi?" Esther said.

"He said he would try."

"Try?" Simon jumped to his feet and began to pace the room. "Meantime, we can't just sit around and wait for the Japanese to decide whether or not to hand us over to the Nazis."

"Not you, Simon." Franz shook his head. "Only German Jews like Essie, Hannah, and me."

"*Not true!*" Simon cradled his arm around Esther's shoulder. "It's all of us."

"Simon is right," Sunny said quietly. "We are in this together."

Franz glanced apologetically from Simon to Sunny. "Of course we are. I am sorry."

Simon shrugged his acceptance, while Sunny showed her husband a small smile.

"What else can we do?" Esther said hopelessly.

"I know Shanghai inside and out," Sunny said. "I could find us somewhere to hide."

"But for how long, Sunny?" Esther held up her palms. "This war could last years. We can't hide forever."

Simon turned to Franz. "What about Ernst? He managed to escape to the countryside."

"We don't even know that he made it alive," Franz said. "Besides, I have Hannah to consider. Travel like that would be almost impossible for her."

Sunny's heart ached at the idea of Hannah being forced to flee into the wild countryside. Sunny had never expected to fall so quickly and completely into her role as the girl's stepmother, but she already loved Hannah as though they were blood relatives. "I agree," she said. "The countryside is no place for a twelve-year-old, especially Hannah."

"Besides, I can't just run away." Simon ran a hand roughly through his hair. "Those refugees are like family. I can't abandon them now of all times."

"Surely there are alternatives," Esther said to no one in particular.

"What else, Essie?" Franz asked.

"Why must we always be on the defensive?" Esther's soft voice resonated with indignation.

"What are you suggesting, Esther?" Sunny asked.

"The Nazis hold no more authority in Shanghai than we do," Esther said. "They have to rely on the Japanese to approve their monstrous plans."

"Right." Simon turned to Franz. "So we'd better damn well persuade the Japanese—and that General Nogomi guy you patched up—to hand the Nazis their walking papers!"

"Of course, that would be ideal, darling." Esther stroked the back of her husband's hand. "But in case we cannot persuade them, perhaps we can exert our own influence."

Simon straightened. "You're right! Why should those bastards—with their poison gas and leaky barges—feel any safer here in Shanghai than we do?"

Sunny glanced over to Simon with concern. His face had darkened and his eyes burned recklessly. Esther noticed it too. She brought a hand to her lips. "Simon, I am not suggesting violence."

"Why not?" he grumbled. "How many guards could these Nazis possibly have?"

"Simon . . ." Esther whispered.

"Some of our young refugees are real fighters." Simon motioned wildly in the air. "Several even had military experience with the old Shanghai Volunteer Corps. They're chomping at the bit for a chance to get into the action. Maybe this is it."

"You believe we could get rid of these Nazis ourselves?" Franz asked.

Simon folded his arms across his chest. "Sounds to me like it might just come down to us or them."

Sunny remembered her own ambivalence as she held a lethal dose of morphine over her father's murderer. "Violence is not the answer, Simon."

Esther nodded. "Darling, if something happens to Meisinger and his men, the Nazis will only send more men, who will be even more determined."

"The women are correct, Simon," Franz said. "And no doubt it would only strengthen the Nazis' argument with the Japanese as to the subversive risk we Jews pose."

"Maybe, maybe not," Simon said. "Either way, it might buy us more time."

Esther grabbed her husband's arm again. "Simon, it's not what I had in mind."

Her touch had a soothing effect on Simon. "What did you have in mind, sweetheart?"

Esther cleared her throat. "Perhaps Meisinger and the other brutes like to bet on horse or dog races?" she suggested. "Maybe they carouse in the nightclubs? Or better still, for our purposes, perhaps they frequent the opium dens or brothels here in Shanghai?"

Simon nodded enthusiastically. "Maybe we could catch the rats in the act."

They brainstormed for the next hour, agreeing only to reconvene in the morning after the Saturday Sabbath service to discuss further.

After Simon and Esther left, Sunny and Franz sat together on the sofa. Sunny nestled her head into Franz's shoulder, inhaling his scent.

"Sunny, I need you to do something for me," he said.

She looked up at him. "Anything."

"You must take Hannah away from here." His jaw tightened. "Away from me too."

"No, Franz. Anything but that. I will never leave you."

"Listen to me, Sunny," he said. "Ever since the Anschluss, Hannah's life has been in near-constant jeopardy. And all because of me."

She stiffened in his arms. "Franz, you can't blame yourself!"

"I can and I do. If her mother were still alive, life would be so different for Hannah . . ."

"Not only for her," Sunny said, shrugging off the slight. "You are the only parent Hannah has ever known. You have protected her from terrible circumstances, all of which have been beyond your control."

Franz would not be swayed. "In Vienna, right after Kristallnacht, I had the opportunity to send Hannah off to safety in London. But I selfishly chose to keep her with me. To drag her to Shanghai with all its dangers. I came so close to losing her to cholera. Now the Nazis want to finish the job that the bacterium could not." He shook his head. "I will never allow that to happen. Never."

She caressed his cheek. "Of course not."

"That means I have to let her go." His voice faltered. "And, aside from Essie, there is no one else in the world I would trust to take her."

Even as her eyes clouded with tears, Sunny held his stare. "I won't leave you, Franz."

"You have to." He held the back of her hand against his face. "Take her. Protect her. I am begging you, Sunny. For me. Please."

Tears streamed down her cheeks. "Jia-Li can help. I would trust her with my life. She has more connections than anyone. Yes, Jia-Li can get Hannah to safety."

"I trust Jia-Li too," Franz said. "But think of the life she leads. With gangsters and other . . . elements. I do not want Hannah immersed in that world."

"Jia-Li's mother lives a simple life in Hongkew," Sunny pointed out. "And if not Jia-Li's family, then maybe my friends Stacy and Meredith, from the Country Hospital. Or even Yang. We will find someone, I promise. Just don't make me leave you, Franz." She paused to get her voice to cooperate. "I would rather die."

"Oh, Sunny." He ran his lips along her cheek, kissing away her tears. "I can't bear the thought of losing you."

The phone rang and they both froze.

"Shall I answer it?" Sunny asked.

"I will." Franz broke free of her and rushed down the corridor to grab the receiver.

Sunny heard him say, "The sooner the better, Colonel Kubota. One hour would be fine."

Chapter 47

Even under the long shadows of early evening, the streets of Shanghai still baked. Franz sweated profusely under his best wool suit, but the humidity and temperature were only partly to blame. Outside Astor House, Captain Yamamoto stood waiting between two sentries. He escorted Franz and Simon directly to Kubota's office. The colonel rose from his seat to greet them, but Samuel Reuben remained seated in his chair.

Franz glared at the other surgeon. "What are you doing here?"

Reuben adjusted his bow tie. "Helping to find a solution to a difficult situation."

"This situation does not concern you," Franz said.

"I beg to differ, Adler," Reuben said. "If the Nazis are allowed to treat the German Jews in such a barbaric manner, it only stands to reason that they will turn on the British Jews next."

Franz turned to Kubota. "Colonel, it might be best if the general heard from as few people as possible. Simon and I have rehearsed our message—"

"See here, Adler," Reuben interrupted. "This crisis affects all of Shanghai's Jews, many of whom, I might add, have lived here for generations. This threat would not even exist at all were it not for the flood of, frankly, uninvited German refugees that we have seen over the past few years."

Simon squinted at Reuben. "Are you blaming the refugees for this?"

"Obviously, the Nazis are far more responsible." Reuben brushed a hand through the air. "Regardless, I am more than capable of speaking for the *entire* Jewish community. Arguably, *more* qualified than an American globetrotter and an Austrian who has repeatedly turned his back on his own people."

"Turned my back?" Franz gritted his teeth.

"How else would you describe it, then?" Reuben said. "Supporting your queer artist friend in his determination to publicly embarrass the Japanese? Marrying a local half-breed? Encouraging my niece to pursue a relationship with a Gentile? And, perhaps worst of all, trying to sneak a Nazi's wife into a Jewish hospital for surgery."

Gripped by fury, Franz took a step toward Reuben.

"*Gentlemen, enough!*" Kubota snapped. "This is not the time for quarrelling." He locked eyes with Franz. "I invited Dr. Reuben to join us today." He turned to Reuben. "And I have personally witnessed Dr. Adler's commitment to the Jewish refugees."

"But—" Reuben began.

"It is decided," Kubota said. "The general was most reluctant to meet with any of you. You will have only this one opportunity. You would be most foolish to squander it by arguing among yourselves."

Franz swallowed his outrage and nodded, while Reuben simply shrugged.

The four of them silently rode the elevator to the top floor. The guard posted outside Nogomi's office saluted Kubota and opened the door. The room had high ceilings, ornate wainscoting, and a central chandelier. Franz smelled lavender, but he spotted no flowers.

General Nogomi sat behind a large oak desk near a bank of windows overlooking the Whangpoo River. He glanced briefly at Kubota but said nothing. His face had filled out in the six months since Franz had last seen him. In a pressed green uniform with a row of glittering medals lining his chest, the general exuded power and authority. And he eyed Franz with an expression that verged on contempt.

Franz and Simon bowed deeply. Reuben hastily followed suit. With a crisp salute, Kubota addressed the general quietly in Japanese. Nogomi sat motionless as he listened and murmured only a few words in response.

Kubota turned back to the others. "General Nogomi will only spare a few minutes for your visit. What would you like me to tell him?"

Reuben opened his mouth to speak, but Simon nudged Reuben's ribs and motioned his head toward Franz.

Franz cleared his throat. "General, our entire community is most grateful to the Imperial Japanese Empire for its graciousness and generosity in allowing the Jewish refugees to live in peace and safety in Shanghai."

Kubota translated. The general only grunted; his stare remained as impassive as ever.

Franz bowed his head. "Moreover, we respect and recognize the full Japanese authority in Shanghai."

Nogomi spoke a few words, and then Kubota said, "Since the Nazis are the Jews' prime enemies, the general assumes that the Jews must also view the Japanese as enemies."

"Not at all, Colonel," Simon interjected.

"Indeed," Franz agreed, feeling beads of cold sweat drip down his sides. "We do not associate the Japanese with the Nazis. On the contrary, the Japanese have been as decent to us as the Nazis have been cruel."

Unmoved, Nogomi spat several words, which Kubota translated in a monotone. "The Germans say that you Jews would do whatever is required to ensure Germany—and therefore Japan—loses the war. They say that your only loyalty is to other Jews and you would betray anyone else to get ahead. That it would be dangerous to leave you free to roam the city. Colonel

Meisinger compared it to leaving foxes free to roam the henhouse."

"That is simply not so!" Reuben said indignantly.

Franz saw that they had reached a pivotal point. His hands felt sticky as he racked his brain for some way to counter Meisinger's case. He decided to use the pacifist argument that Simon and he had rehearsed. "Perhaps the general might be interested to hear how the Jews ended up so downtrodden in Germany?"

The question seemed to pique the general's curiosity.

"We Jews are law-abiding citizens." Franz chose his words meticulously, pausing to allow Kubota to translate each sentence. "We have no nation of our own. In any country where Jews live, we have always respected the customs and laws of the land. It is true that we are a close-knit community dedicated to family, scholarship and, yes, financial stability. But we have always considered ourselves loyal and productive citizens."

Franz waited for the general to comment, but he said nothing.

"Jews are peaceful people," Franz stressed. "We have no army of our own and have always relied on the laws of the land to protect us. So when the Nazis decided to blame us for all of Germany's troubles, we were easy scapegoats. We were defenseless."

Franz paused again, but Nogomi only eyed him blankly, so he continued. "We abided by every new law that banned our way of life and, eventually, our existence. We never resorted to violence, subversion, or espionage. It is not in our nature, General." He brought his hand to his chest and repeated, "We Jews are peaceful people."

Nogomi clasped his hands together. Finally, he looked at Kubota and muttered a few words.

Kubota eyed Franz. "The general wants to know

why you think it is that the Germans hate Jews so passionately."

"Not all Germans, General," Franz said. "Only the Nazis."

"Also, the Nazis hate us because we look different from them," Reuben added.

After the translation, Nogomi cracked a trace of a smile and spoke a few words.

"Different?" Kubota said. "The general says that, swastikas aside, you Jews look identical to the Nazis."

The visitors broke into tense laughter.

"Colonel," Reuben said. "Please tell the general that we know the Japanese are too honorable to hand innocent people over to the Nazis for their evil purposes."

Simon and Franz shared a concerned glance. Kubota eyed Reuben skeptically, then translated the remark. Nogomi pulled his hands from his desk and sat up straighter.

"Furthermore," Reuben persisted, evidently unaware of the new unease in the room. "Please tell the general that the rest of the world is *very* aware of how the Nazis have mistreated the Jews. If the Japanese were to abet them in their proposed criminal endeavor, the world would judge Japan very harshly indeed."

"No, Reuben!" Simon snapped.

Alarmed, Franz swiveled his head to face Kubota. "Please, Colonel, do not translate that last remark!"

Kubota glanced from Franz to Reuben. "I am inclined to agree with Dr. Adler. I am not convinced the general will respond favorably to such arguments."

"The general must hear the consequences," Reuben urged Kubota. "Trust me, my friend."

"No, Colonel," Franz insisted.

Reuben turned on him. "You have had your say, Adler! Now it is time for mine."

Nogomi addressed Kubota in a sharp tone as he wiggled a finger from Reuben to Franz. With a wary glance at the others, Kubota spoke in Japanese.

The general's eyes widened and his face flushed. He stared at the others for a tense moment. Suddenly, he pushed his chair back and jumped to his feet. He shook a finger at the door and screamed at them.

A sense of doom overcame Franz. *We have lost our only chance.*

With Nogomi still shouting, the others scuttled out of his office and hurried to the elevator. No one spoke during the agonizing ride down. As Kubota parted ways with them in the lobby, he turned to Franz glumly. "Once General Nogomi has calmed, I will approach him again," he said with little confidence.

"Thank you, Colonel," Franz murmured, realizing that Kubota's career was in as much danger as their lives.

As soon as they reached the street, Reuben hastened away from the others. "Reuben!" Franz called after him. "Do you have any idea what you have just done?"

Reuben wheeled to face him. "All I did was try to open the general's eyes. Clearly, the man is too proud to acknowledge the truth. Given time, my message will sink in with him."

"*Sink in?*" Simon echoed. "You might have just sealed our fate with your stupidity."

Reuben's face went blotchy. "You think you can just drift into Shanghai and meddle with generations of cultural balance. You Yanks! A bunch of bulls in china shops. Always thinking you know best."

The rage ran through Franz like a current. "You pompous, deceitful coward!"

"How dare you!" Reuben cried, puffing out his chest. "Deceitful? *Coward?*"

"Yes, coward," Franz growled, moving closer. "When

the general needed urgent surgery, you served me up to the Japanese because you were too scared of the consequences of failing. Then, out of jealousy, you spread poisonous rumors about my family and me."

"Why, you arrogant ingrate!" Reuben spat. "You crawled into my city and threw yourself at my feet for help. Out of the goodness of our hearts, my wife and I took pity on you and your family. We took you under our wings. And this is how you thank me?"

"No, this is!" Franz swung his fist at the center of Reuben's face, hitting his nose with a grinding crunch.

⌣ *Chapter 48*

Immediately after Franz returned from the disastrous meeting with General Nogomi, he took Sunny aside to tell her what had transpired and to inform her of his plans for Hannah. As heartbreaking as she found the idea, she could think of no safer alternative.

They sat Hannah down in the sitting room to break the news. For a moment, the girl said nothing as her eyes darted from Sunny to Franz and back. "You are sending me away?" Her face crumpled. "Why?"

Guilt racked Sunny. She wondered if her stepdaughter held her responsible for the unwelcome news.

Franz knelt in front of Hannah and took her hand in his. "*Liebchen,* this is the last thing we want. It's to protect you. We hope it will only be for a short while."

Hannah pulled her hand free of his. "Why will I be safer without you, Papa?"

Franz glanced uncertainly to Sunny, who nodded her encouragement. "She has a right to know, Franz."

"The Nazis have come to Shanghai," he said.

Hannah's eyes widened. "What do they want?"

"They are trying to persuade the Japanese to arrest us," Franz said. "All of the refugees."

"But where would they put us all?" Hannah asked.

He shook his head. "It will not be any place fit for a twelve-year-old girl."

Hannah straightened her shoulders. "I'm not a child anymore."

Franz stroked her cheek. "Of course not. But if the Japanese agree to the Nazis' demands, *liebchen,* it will be no place for any of us."

"Why don't we all go away together then?" Hannah demanded.

"You speak the language and will be able to blend in," Franz explained. "The Japanese know me. They will come for me, *liebchen.* If you stay with me, you will be arrested too."

Hannah folded her arms across her chest. "Then I will be arrested. I am not leaving you, Papa!"

Franz rose from his knees. "It's decided."

"It was the same in Vienna, Papa!" Hannah cried. "You said I had to go away or terrible things would happen. But we stayed together and it worked out for the best. It could happen again now." She extended her weaker hand. "Please, Papa, don't do this."

"It might only be for a few days, Hannah," Sunny pointed out.

"Or it might be forever," Hannah moaned.

Franz turned helplessly to Sunny. She struggled for the right words. "Hannah, darling, none of us—"

They heard a pounding at the door. *"Franz Adler!"* a voice barked.

"So soon?" Franz turned to Sunny. "You must leave with Hannah. Straightaway."

Sunny shook her head. "I will not leave you."

"They are here to take me from you!" Franz exclaimed. "You will not do either of us any good by staying in an empty home. Take care of my Hannah. Do this for me. Please!"

The door shook so hard that Sunny expected it to blow off the hinges. "*Open now!*"

Mouth dry, Sunny rushed to answer it. Two Japanese soldiers filled the doorway. Both wore the white armbands of the Kempeitai. One stormed past Sunny, and the other knocked her off balance as he followed.

Sunny regained her footing as the men reached her husband's side. "You are Adler?" the taller one demanded. Without even waiting for the answer, he grabbed Franz by the right elbow. The second man clamped his hand on Franz's left shoulder.

"I am Dr. Adler, yes," he said calmly.

"You come." The taller one jerked Franz forward.

"Where are you taking my husband?" Sunny demanded.

Ignoring Sunny, the soldiers dragged Franz toward the door.

"Leave my father alone!" Hannah cried as she rushed past Sunny. The girl grabbed the shorter soldier's arm and tried to pry it off Franz's shoulder.

The Kempeitai officer thrust his elbow into Hannah's chest. Moaning, she stumbled back and collapsed.

"*Hannah, no!*" Franz cried, and thrashed wildly in the soldiers' grip.

The shorter man rammed his fist into Franz's abdomen. Franz started to double over but the taller man held him upright, and the other one punched him again.

"*Stop it!*" Sunny screamed as she rushed toward Hannah, who lay crumpled on the floor.

Hannah struggled up to a sitting position with Sunny's help. Hannah's dry eyes burned with purpose. "We can't let them take Papa."

Sunny heard the sound of feet scuffing against the ground as the Kempeitai men dragged Franz away. "There is nothing we can do, Hannah," she said.

Franz looked over his shoulder and locked eyes with Sunny. "Promise me you will take Hannah away!" he gasped.

"Franz . . ."

"Promise me, Sunny. Please!"

Sunny's voice wouldn't cooperate, so she simply nodded.

"I love you both so much!" Franz called out as the men jerked him out the door.

Sunny helped Hannah to her feet and guided her over to the chair.

Yang emerged from the kitchen, wringing her hands. "Oh, Soon Yi, oh, little girlie, what have they done? Where have they taken the doctor?"

Sunny refused to allow herself to consider it. Instead, she focused on their escape. "Yang, put together all the food you can fit into the big market basket. We each must pack one light bag of clothing to carry."

"Where are we going, Soon Yi?" Yang asked.

Sunny wondered the same herself.

Jia-Li arrived within half an hour of Franz's arrest. While Yang packed the food in the kitchen, the childhood friends sat on the couch, holding hands and speaking in whispers.

"Franz is right," Jia-Li said. "You will do him no good by staying here and pining."

Sunny swallowed. "And you have room for the three of us?"

"What kind of question is that?" Jia-Li grimaced. "I

think, however, it is best if I take you to Mother's. My apartment is not entirely . . . my own." She dug inside her handbag and withdrew the silver cigarette case. "I have certain visitors I would not want the girl to meet."

Sunny squeezed her hand. "Your mother's apartment is perfect, *bǎo bèi*. Her neighborhood is one of the last places the Japanese would think to look for us."

Jia-Li lit her cigarette. "Not many Caucasians live there."

Sunny shrugged. "We will just have to keep Hannah inside. We can cut her hair and dye it even darker. That will help. She speaks the language almost fluently."

"I suppose." Jia-Li exhaled, forming a ring with the smoke. "Those Nazis would really drown entire families? Even the women and children?"

"I think they would, yes."

Jia-Li shook her head. "Insanity."

"Perhaps we can help prevent them."

Jia-Li's forehead furrowed. "How?"

"Do you happen to know where a group of high-ranking Nazis might stay in Shanghai?"

"The Cathay Hotel. The Japanese host all their dignitaries there." Jia-Li took another drag of her cigarette. "I have gone there myself to . . . *entertain* certain VIPs."

"Do you think we could find a man named Meisinger?"

Chapter 49

The military vehicle skidded to the curb in front of Bridge House.

As the Kempeitai officers hauled Franz toward the entrance of the feared prison, the memory of Sunny crouching over Hannah looped inside his head. *Who will take care of them now?*

Inside, the building was oppressively stuffy. A rank odor hit Franz as his captors dragged him across the floor of the foyer toward a desk, manned by a clerk with thinning greasy hair and thick glasses. "Franz Adler," the taller Kempeitai officer grunted.

The clerk whipped a form out of a drawer. "Name spelling?" he demanded in a shrill tone.

The clerk also asked his birthday, place of birth, and current address, meticulously filling in each box on the form. He reached below his desk and produced a pair of tan pants and a matching collarless shirt, which he dropped as a bundle on the desktop. "You take uniform!" the clerk pointed to a little alcove with a sagging curtain hanging halfway across it. "Bring me clothes, shoes, and valuables. I receipt you."

Just like in Chełmno. A chill racked Franz as he remembered the Nazi's ruse.

Franz changed into the stained and frayed uniform. For a moment, he considered swallowing his wedding ring. Instead, he kissed it and then wriggled it off his finger. He laid his watch, wallet, and ring on top of his folded clothes before handing them back to the clerk.

The shorter Kempeitai officer grabbed him by the scruff of his neck and dragged him toward a narrow hallway. The stench of urine and excrement worsened with every step. No natural light permeated the hallway; a single bulb burned at the far end. Franz stumbled twice as his eyes adjusted to the dimness. The second time, the officer shrieked and jabbed him in the ribs. They passed a series of wooden cages, each one seven or eight feet wide. Franz heard an occasional groan but, in the darkness and relative silence, it took him several moments to realize how many prisoners were crammed into each cell.

By the fifth cell, Franz could make out some of the faces. Women and men, Chinese and white, young and old, huddled shoulder to shoulder. No one spoke.

At the end of the corridor, they came to a smaller empty cell. Franz was jerked to a stop. He was shoved so hard that he was rammed shoulder-first into the far wall of the cage. The door slammed shut behind him.

Other than a filthy bucket, presumably meant as a toilet, which sat in the corner, the wooden cell was empty. The howls and screams of other prisoners shattered the quiet. Fear crawled over Franz. *Will I cry for mercy? Will I give them the pleasure?*

Left alone in his dark cell, and with no watch or natural light by which to judge time, he estimated that at least four or five hours passed. The unrelenting screams and cries echoed down the hallway, but after a while Franz managed to tune them out. Even his hunger and thirst barely registered.

The door to the cell suddenly sprang open, and the same two officers who had arrested Franz stormed inside. "Up! *You up!*" the taller one shouted in English.

The Kempeitai men each grabbed an arm and jerked him upright. They yanked Franz out of the cage and dragged him toward the source of the screaming. They shoved him into another dimly lit room, which was empty except for an inclined wooden bench in the center and a grubby plywood cabinet against a wall.

Franz glimpsed the filthy soiled sheet beneath the bench. He instinctively resisted as the men pushed him down onto the bench. The squatter guard punched him on the chin. His teeth rattled and pain shot up to his ear. He tasted blood. His will drained away, and Franz lay down on the backless bench.

As soon as his body touched the wood, the captors forced his hands behind his back and lashed them together with rough rope. They moved in tandem, neither speaking nor making eye contact. The shorter one grunted rhythmically as he worked. They tightened the binding until the fibers dug into Franz's wrists. Once his hands were secured, the two men roped his feet to the bench. They strapped his head to the board with a scratchy fabric.

Behind him, the door to the room opened and closed. His captors snapped salutes. Franz tried to crane his neck, but with his head bound, he could not see the person standing directly behind him.

"I knew you come to me at Bridge House sometime," Colonel Tanaka snickered.

Franz's blood ran cold at the man's voice. "Why am I here, Colonel?"

Tanaka didn't respond. Instead, he snapped commands in Japanese to the two other men. They converged on the plywood cabinet and swung open its doors. Glimpsing the contents, Franz began to hyperventilate. Whips and rods were neatly stacked on one side. A huge battery rested on the cabinet's floor, and wires attached to it dangled from pegs above. A long metallic tool, resembling hedge clippers, leaned against the far wall.

The taller guard extracted a wooden bucket and a gray towel. The shorter one lifted the longest of the bamboo rods and tapped it against his palm as though testing its flexibility. The man with the bucket disappeared. Franz heard a tap running. The soldier re-emerged moments later carrying a full and sloshing bucket. He marched up to the side of the bench, lowered the bucket to the floor, and wadded the filthy towel deep into Franz's mouth. The bitter, moldy taste made him gag.

Still out of Franz's line of sight, Tanaka said, "You want to shame us to the world. You say we do terrible things to Jews. True?"

Franz tried to open his mouth to explain that Reuben had spoken out of turn, but he only choked on the gag.

"We have been patient," Tanaka continued. "Too patient. Now you know what happens when you throw gossip and you dishonor Empire of Japan." Tanaka switched to Japanese and addressed the guards.

The taller one raised the bucket over Franz's head.

"We call this 'water cure,' Doctor," Tanaka grunted.

Franz tried to speak but the towel in his mouth swallowed his words.

"You will tell me who you tell about Colonel Meisinger!" Tanaka snapped.

Before Franz could answer, the man above him tilted the bucket and water splashed onto his face. It ran into his eyes, up his nose, and down his shirt neck. The foul-tasting water dripped down the back of his throat, despite the gag, and Franz coughed involuntarily.

Even after his hair and clothes were drenched, the soldier kept pouring. The towel swelled in his mouth, and Franz choked and sputtered. He bucked and thrashed futilely against his bindings.

"Who did you tell about Meisinger?" Tanaka said. "I want all names."

The officer with the bamboo rod whipped it down across Franz's abdomen. The searing pain only compounded Franz's breathlessness. He gagged again as he swallowed gobs of water.

"I want names!" Tanaka shouted.

The rod came whizzing down across his belly again. The pain was so intense that his eyes teared and he vomited into the gag. The water mixed with the vomit burned his throat. His head swam and his vision tunneled as though he were peering through binoculars. Franz felt detached from his own body. The sounds around him grew muffled and distant. The room steadily darkened as though someone was dimming a light switch.

Everything went black.

Franz woke to find his arms and legs still bound to the bench. Someone had pulled the towel from his mouth, and he tasted his own vomit. He smelled urine. Pain racked his belly.

"Did water cure you?" Tanaka grunted.

Franz nodded, terrified that they might stuff the towel back into his mouth.

"Who did you tell about Colonel Meisinger?" Tanaka demanded.

Franz had trouble thinking, but he realized that Tanaka must already have been aware of Simon and Reuben. "Only my friend, Simon Lehrer. Dr. Samuel Reuben already knew." He shook his head frantically. "We never meant to accuse the Japanese. We only—"

"You lie!" Tanaka screamed.

The bamboo rod sliced into Franz's abdomen again.

"No . . ." Franz gasped. "No, I don't . . . I didn't . . ."

"The China woman! Your wife! She knows too."

Fear worse than anything he had ever known seized him. "*Leave her alone!* She doesn't know anything—"

Before Franz could get his words out, the taller soldier jammed another dry towel between his lips.

Then the water splashed into his eyes and up his nose again.

⌐ *Chapter 50*

JULY 27, 1942, SHANGHAI

Sunny lay with her arm lightly draped over Hannah's side and listened to the girl's soft breathing. Five days had passed since Franz's arrest. Sunny and Hannah had spent every night since on the same mattress in the Kos' bedroom, where Jia-Li had ridden out her opium withdrawal fits. Sunny doubted she had slept more than a few hours since the Kempeitai had dragged Franz away.

She assumed that the Kempeitai had taken her husband to Bridge House, but her suspicions were not confirmed until the third day of his confinement. Sunny had made three trips to Astor House in search of Colonel Kubota, each time turned away by the hostile sentries; it wasn't until her fourth visit that she happened upon him.

Flanked by two junior soldiers, Kubota was heading toward his car as Sunny approached. Uncertain whether it was the colonel, Sunny called out to him. One of the young guards spun and pointed his rifle at her, but Kubota laid his hand on the gun barrel and pushed it down. "May I ask who is inquiring, madam?" he said with a politeness that she had never before heard from a Japanese officer.

"Soon Yi . . ." she began. "Mrs. Franz Adler."

He beckoned her with a small wave. "Come ride with me, Mrs. Adler. Please."

Sitting beside Sunny in the backseat, Kubota told her that Franz and Simon were both being held at Bridge House. "As of this morning, Dr. Adler and Mr. Lehrer were in reasonable health," he said solemnly. "Unfortunately, the same cannot be said of Dr. Reuben."

Sunny was far too concerned about Franz to ask after Reuben. "What does the Kempeitai want from my husband, Colonel?"

"The meeting with General Nogomi did not end well."

"But that wasn't Franz's fault!"

"You are correct." He lowered his head. "I am responsible."

"My husband told me that Dr. Reuben pushed the general too far."

Head still hung in shame, Kubota didn't look up. "I should have foreseen it."

"You were only trying to help." She almost reached out to touch his hand but thought better of it. "What can we do now, Colonel?"

"As difficult as this might be to hear, Mrs. Adler, all we can do now is wait."

"Waiting is one thing I am not capable of," she murmured more to herself than Kubota. "Colonel, may I see him?"

He shook his head. "That is not possible."

"Please, Colonel," she implored. "I just have to see Franz. Even if we cannot speak. If only from a distance . . ."

"They will never allow it, Mrs. Adler."

So as to not give away Hannah's whereabouts, Sunny asked the colonel to drop her off at the refugee hospital. As she was climbing out of the car, Kubota leaned toward her. "Mrs. Adler, your husband is a decent man," he said. "I am indebted to him. And I will do everything in my power to help."

"Can you, Colonel?"

"We will see." He summoned a small smile but the hopelessness in his eyes said so much more.

As Sunny lay in bed beside Hannah, remembering Kubota's words, the tears welled again. Her sobs woke the girl. "Sunny, what is it?"

"Nothing, Hannah. Go back to sleep."

"I can't," Hannah said softly. "I miss Papa too much."

Sunny stroked Hannah's warm cheek. "Me too, darling."

"Are you going to the prison again today?"

The Kempeitai men had chased Sunny away from Bridge House's entrance, but each day she loitered nearby for as long as possible. Sunny sensed Franz's proximity behind the brick walls, and that alone inspired her to soldier on. "Yes, Hannah, I will," she said.

"Can I come too?"

"I'm sorry. No. It's too dangerous."

"Please."

Sunny pulled her hand from the girl's cheek. "Hannah, I promised your father that I would protect you. I cannot allow you to leave the house right now."

"Not even to see Tante Essie?"

After Simon's arrest, Esther had refused to join Sunny and Hannah in hiding. Sunny had pleaded, but Esther insisted that, regardless of the risk, she would stay in their home on Avenue Joffre and wait for her husband's return. "No, Hannah," Sunny said firmly. "It is too risky. They might come for the refugees at any moment."

Hannah rolled away to face the wall. Sunny stared at her back, too tired to think of any way to placate her. Soon, Hannah began to snore lightly. Eventually exhaustion overcame Sunny and she drifted off.

Sunny awoke with the first light of dawn. As soon as she heard the sound of Lo-Shen's tiny bound feet shuffling in the main room, Sunny rose and tiptoed out of the bedroom. Sitting down at the small table, she accepted a cup of black tea but waved away the cold dumplings that Lo-Shen offered.

Sunny had known Jia-Li's mother her whole life and considered her family, but they had hardly ever exchanged more than a few sentences at a time. Sunny was surprised when Lo-Shen said, "I am worried for what will become of you, Soon Yi. Where will you raise the child?"

"I have no idea, *shěn shěn*," Sunny admitted.

Lo-Shen lowered her teacup to the table. "You are both welcome here as long as you like. You know that, Soon Yi?"

Sunny smiled. "I do."

"It is nice, sometimes, to have company," Lo-Shen said shyly.

"Especially family."

"Yes. Family."

The doorknob rattled and the door opened. With a summer hat pulled low over her head, Jia-Li hurried toward them. "Hello, Mother," she said with a quick bow before turning to Sunny. "We must talk, *xiǎo hè*."

Lo-Shen rose from the table. "I have laundry to begin." She padded over to the corner of the room, picked up a wicker basket, and headed out. As soon as Lo-Shen left, Jia-Li sat down and grabbed Sunny's hand in hers. "I have news," she said excitedly.

Sunny leapt up, unable to contain her sudden hopefulness. "About Franz?"

Jia-Li shook her head once, deflating Sunny's mood with the single gesture. "Where is the girl?" Jia-Li asked.

Sunny sank back into her seat. "In bed. Asleep, I hope."

Jia-Li glanced over her shoulder to confirm they were alone before she reached inside her handbag. Sunny expected to see her friend's silver cigarette case, but instead Jia-Li produced an envelope and extracted several four-by-six photographs. She laid the black-and-white images on the table and fanned them out like playing cards. Jia-Li raised an eyebrow. "Chih-Nii designed a special room for taking such photographs. Sometimes the clients request them as keepsakes. Other times, it provides . . . security."

Sunny brought her hand to her mouth as she gaped at the graphic images. In one photograph, a naked boy knelt in front of a hulking man. In another, the man's flabby buttocks faced the camera as he gripped the hunched-over boy by the hips. "The boy," Sunny muttered. "How old is he?"

"Lok is thirteen but, of course, he passes for much younger." Jia-Li shrugged. "Lok has been with us at Chih-Nii's for almost a year now. He's very popular with certain clientele."

"It's . . . it's unimaginable. That poor, poor boy."

Jia-Li tapped one photograph, a close-up of the same sweaty man who appeared in all the other shots. He had a bulbous nose, protuberant forehead, and close-set dark eyes. "Meisinger?" Sunny asked.

"Hideous, isn't he?" Jia-Li wiggled the snapshot. "I wonder what his superiors would make of this."

Sunny's disgust receded as the significance of the photographic evidence sank in. "Are these the only copies you have?"

"Our photographer took several others."

Sunny swept them into a stack and eased them back into the envelope. Gripping the envelope tightly, she rose from the table.

"Where are you going?" Jia-Li asked.

"To the Cathay Hotel."

Jia-Li's eyes widened. "You intend to confront Meisinger?"

"What else can I do?"

Jia-Li slapped a hand to her forehead. "Drop him a letter at the hotel with your demands. Include one of these photographs. That is how the Green Gang does it at Chih-Nii's."

Sunny shook her head. "I have no time for letters."

"Then I'm coming with you."

"No, *bǎo bèi*." Sunny smiled gratefully as she leaned forward and hugged her best friend. "You have done more than your share. Stay with your mother and Hannah." She touched Jia-Li's face. "For me. Please."

Sunny's hands shook as she applied her lipstick in front of the mirror. She dreaded the prospect of confronting Meisinger. She had no idea how to approach blackmail. She desperately wished there was another way.

What if he refuses? Will I panic in the heat of the moment?

"There is no choice," she assured her reflection. "You have to do this for Franz and Hannah."

She felt nauseated as she stood up and smoothed out the front of her light blue cheongsam. Tucking the photographs into her handbag, she took a deep breath and then headed for the door.

The morning sun had risen over the tall buildings that fronted the Whangpoo. Hurrying along the Bund, Sunny worried that she might already have missed Meisinger for the day.

As Sunny was crossing Nanking Road, she caught sight of a familiar face. *Ushi!* The hulking Chinese man in the black suit stood a few feet from the entrance of the Cathay Hotel with his tree-trunk arms folded across his chest.

Sunny had known Ushi for years. He was reputed to be the toughest and most intimidating bodyguard at the French Concession brothel where Jia-Li worked. Sunny also knew that behind his fearsome exterior, Ushi harbored a lifelong crush on Jia-Li. He would do anything for her.

As Sunny passed Ushi, he flashed a gap-toothed grin before resuming his fierce stare. Sunny smiled back as she silently thanked Jia-Li for sending Ushi ahead to watch over her.

Sunny had not been inside the Cathay Hotel since her wedding. Banishing the happy memories to focus on her task, she stepped through the revolving door and into the sprawling marble lobby. She glanced at the hotel's clock, which read 7:11. She walked into the restaurant and scanned it discreetly. Several Japanese men and women sat at the tables, but Sunny did not see Meisinger or any other Nazi official.

Sunny sat down at the corner table and ordered tea. She pulled out Jia-Li's envelope and chose the photograph that best captured Meisinger's face and the boy in the same shot. She turned it over and wrote in German: *Meet me alone in the hotel restaurant. Corner table. Blue dress.* She tucked the photograph into a separate envelope and addressed it to Colonel Meisinger.

Sunny asked the waiter to send over a bellhop. Moments later, a skinny Chinese youth in a white uniform and matching hat hurried over. She produced a photograph that showed only a close-up of Meisinger's sweaty face. A trace of fear crossed the bellhop's features as he recognized the man. Sunny offered him a generous tip and, warily, the bellhop agreed to take the envelope to the man's room.

Her stomach flip-flopped as she waited. After twenty agonizing minutes, she assumed that either she had missed Meisinger or he was ignoring her request. Disappointed but also relieved, she was gathering up her handbag to pay for the tea when she sensed a pair of eyes on her.

Sunny's heart slammed against her breastbone as she looked up to see Meisinger. Wearing an ill-fitting gray suit instead of a uniform, he glared from across the room, more rabid dog than high-ranking military officer. He jerked his head, looking from side to side, and then dropped his chin and marched over to her table. He stopped and stood at her side, hovering so close that she picked up a whiff of his rough alcoholic aftershave.

"Wouldn't you prefer to sit, Colonel?" Sunny's voice cracked.

With a sneer that set his ugly face further askew, Meisinger dropped heavily into the chair across from her. The waiter approached but was angrily waved away. "Who are you?" Meisinger growled in a deep baritone as he slammed his hands down on the table.

Sunny glanced at his ragged fingernails before meeting his hostile eyes. "That is not important."

"I will be the judge of that," he said through gritted teeth.

"Colonel, we have other photographs."

The veins in his temples pulsated visibly. "So what?" he hissed.

Sunny willed herself to speak calmly. "If those photographs were to find their way to Berlin and Tokyo . . ."

"I have been a policeman my whole career," he said in his clipped German. "I track people down. I am very good at my job." He exhaled his sour breath into her face and then looked down at her wedding ring. "You have children?"

Sunny thought of Hannah with a stab of fear. "No. No, I don't."

Meisinger squinted. "Listen to me, you half-Chink! *If* those photographs are not immediately destroyed, I will personally see to it that your husband and your children—and anyone else you consider family—die in front of your eyes. Perhaps I will beat them to death. Or bleed them. Or . . . or electrical shock. *Ja, ja!* Have you ever witnessed a prolonged electrocution? You will!"

Sunny's heart leapt into her throat. *He's bluffing. Don't let him turn the tables. You have the control, girl.*

"This is Shanghai, not Germany, Colonel," Sunny said evenly. "We have other photographs. Consider how your superiors in Berlin and Tokyo would react to them. It would destroy your career."

"I will kill you and your family long before that ever happens," he breathed.

Sunny pressed her palms against the table to prevent them from trembling. "I have come here with protection. Besides, whether I live or die, the photographs will still be sent. My friends holding the other copies will see to it."

His lips twitching, Meisinger glowered at Sunny for several moments without speaking. "What do you want?" he finally grunted.

"I want you to leave."

"Shanghai?"

"Yes. Immediately."

Meisinger's thick mouth curved downward and he shrugged. "All right, I will return to Tokyo today."

Sunny shook her head. "And I want you to take the rest of your SS men with you."

Meisinger didn't respond.

"And your canister of poison gas too."

His jaw dropped in surprise. His pocked skin wrinkled as though he were on the verge of laughter. "I should have known it!" he spat. "You work for the Jews! Of course you do. Who else but Jews and Chinamen would resort to such underhanded tactics?"

Emboldened by her own anger, Sunny leaned closer. "Listen to me, Colonel. We know all about your plans for the refugees—"

His face twisted again in rage. "How do you know that?"

She shook her head. "Go back to Tokyo, Colonel. Tell your superiors that the Japanese refused to cooperate. And then forget about the Jews in Shanghai. Forever. And we will forget about you."

"You think the fatherland can just forget about twenty thousand Jews who slithered out of Germany?"

"You had better persuade them to, Colonel. Otherwise the *fatherland* will learn all about your perverse interest in Chinese boys." She folded her arms across her chest. "I doubt those photographs conform to the Führer's image of an Aryan super race. And I do not think the Japanese would view them in any better light."

Meisinger's eyes iced over. "All right, you half-breed cow." He exhaled so heavily that his breath whistled. "I will do what I can to help you save those rotting Jews. But you must understand that I am not the only one involved. I can only do so much."

"Do what you have to, Colonel! If you do not, those pictures will find their way to your superiors, Tokyo, the newspapers, and anywhere else we think to send them. I promise you that."

He pushed himself up from the table, rocking the cutlery and spilling the last of Sunny's tea. He turned to go and then wheeled back to her. "One day, *Chink!* I will find you . . ."

～ Chapter 51

Franz woke up on the damp floor with the knee of another prisoner digging into his back. His right forearm throbbed so steadily that he knew his torturers must have fractured it with the rod. His tan pajama trousers were stained beyond recognition. The most pungent stench wafted off his own body now. He had lost all track of time. *Is this the sixth day or the seventh?*

Dragging himself up to sitting, Franz inadvertently kicked the woman in front of him, who grunted in pain. "I'm sorry," he croaked. But his apology served no real purpose, since the woman, like all the other prisoners stuffed in the cage, spoke only Chinese. Franz suspected that the Kempeitai had deliberately separated him from other Westerners. He thought of Simon. A few days earlier, he had heard his friend's muffled voice calling out to him from another cage. Franz had shouted back, but it had only drawn a quick beating from the guard. There had been no contact since.

Franz focused on the mental image of Sunny and Hannah. Only the memory of their smiling faces kept him going. Death no longer frightened him. On the contrary, it seemed more and more like the only possible reprieve.

"Adler!" the tall Kempeitai officer barked from the door to the cage.

Not again. Please. Not so soon.

"Up, Adler!" the man repeated as he opened the door.

Franz's legs wobbled as he climbed unsteadily to his feet. He stumbled over his cellmates' bodies and limbs as he wove his way to the door. He felt the light pressure of a woman's hand patting him surreptitiously on the back and smiled slightly: it was one of the only signs of compassion he had encountered at Bridge House. As soon as Franz stepped through the opening, the officer grabbed his right arm, launching a wave of pain through his entire right side.

Instinctively, Franz turned toward the torture chambers, but the guard yanked him in the opposite direction. Refusing to let his hopes rise, Franz hung his head and shuffled along the corridor until they emerged into the bright light of the main lobby. The guard dragged Franz over to the check-in desk.

"Adler, Franz," the guard informed the clerk, who sniffed in distaste.

Franz felt a flicker of anticipation as he watched the clerk flip through the stack of forms and pull out a sheet with his name near the top. The clerk rose and disappeared into the room behind him. A minute later, he returned with Franz's folded clothes and dropped them on the desktop. He opened an envelope and casually tapped out its contents on top of the pile.

Franz's eyes filled with tears when he saw his wedding ring. The clerk waved to the alcove behind him. "You change clothes. Leave uniform inside!"

Franz hobbled as fast as his bruised legs and feet would carry him. He pulled off the stinking soiled pajamas and left them on the floor. His own clothes had never felt more comfortable, but he had trouble doing up the buttons with his broken arm and swollen fingers, six of which were missing fingernails.

By the time he stepped back into the lobby, the tall guard was gone. Franz stood in the middle of the foyer awaiting instructions, but none came. He waited another five or six minutes and then, with trepidation, inched toward the door. None of the soldiers showed the slightest interest. His pace quickened as he slipped through the door and out to the sidewalk. The bright sunshine burned his eyes. His legs were so weak that he could walk only a block or so before he had to stop and rest. But his relief at being out of Bridge House—if only temporarily—far overshadowed any other sensation.

Franz hobbled home, stopping at each corner, sometimes having to hang on to the street signs or lampposts until his muscles and lungs would cooperate again. It took him over an hour to get home. He did not expect to find Sunny or Hannah there, but he was still crestfallen to walk into the empty house.

Franz picked up the phone in the hallway and dialed Simon and Esther's number, but their phone went unanswered. His eyes wandered to the shelf beneath the telephone, and he spotted Sunny's telephone directory. He stared at it, trying to resist the urge to look up Jia-Li's phone number.

Franz had no idea whether the Japanese had responded yet to Meisinger's proposal. For all he knew, they might have already begun rounding up the refugees. He reminded himself that the best way to keep Sunny and Hannah safe was to stay away from them. They would be far more likely to stick to their escape plans if they thought he was still imprisoned, or worse. But Franz had to know that they were all right. He grabbed for the directory and tore through the pages until he found Jia-Li's number. He dialed and let the phone ring repeatedly. He hung up and tried a second time, but without success.

Franz riffled through the phone book looking for a phone number for Jia-Li's mother. But it was hopeless. He did not even know her name.

Frustrated, Franz trudged to the bathroom and drew a warm bath. As soon as the tub was half-full, he eased his raw body into it. The sting of the hot water against his open wounds and bruises felt minor compared with what he had just experienced at Bridge House. He gingerly scrubbed every inch of skin he could reach as the bathwater turned progressively darker.

Franz had just climbed out of the tub when he heard the phone ring. Dripping a trail of water, he hobbled out to the hallway and grabbed the receiver. "Yes? *Hello?*"

"Dr. Adler, this is Mr. Silberstein," Schwartzmann said.

"Oh, hello, Hermann," Franz mumbled.

"Something is wrong, Dr. Adler?"

"Excuse me. I was expecting my wife."

"Ah, of course, I would be disappointed too." Schwartzmann laughed softly. "Frau Adler? She is well?"

"I . . . Yes. Fine."

"Oh, good. Herr Doktor, would you have time to meet this evening?"

"I am not certain I will be free."

"It is rather urgent."

Please, God, no more grim news! "I cannot promise, Herr Silberstein."

"I understand, Dr. Adler, but if your schedule does permit . . . Are you familiar with the Woo Sing Ding teahouse in the old Chinese quarters?"

"Yes, of course," Franz said.

"One of my favorite sites in the whole world," Schwartzmann said, sighing. "I will be there at eight o'clock tonight, regardless. I hope you will have a chance to join me."

Franz hung up and tried Jia-Li again. Nothing. He called Esther and Simon's home again, but they did not answer either. Frantic with worry, Franz changed into clean clothes, agonizing over each button. Tying his shoes was almost impossible.

Light-headed and dizzy, he realized that he was starving. While other prisoners devoured the buckets of rancid rice that the soldiers slammed down in the cage every morning, Franz had been unable to eat.

In the kitchen, he discovered that the cupboards were almost bare. In the pantry, he spotted a small box hidden on a back shelf. He opened it to find a package of food, carefully wrapped and sealed, that Yang had obviously prepared for him. The sweet rice ball, stuffed with vegetables, almost brought tears to his eyes. Three hard almond cakes, which Yang knew he loved, were wrapped in one of Sunny's handkerchiefs. He grabbed the package and, eating as he walked, headed for the street.

He limped the six blocks over to the "establishment," as Sunny had euphemistically referred to the brothel where Jia-Li worked. The tasteful Spanish villa was set back on the property among shade trees and blooming gardens. Franz opened the steel gate and trudged up the footpath toward the door.

Before he reached the house, a brawny giant of a man in a black suit stepped out and blocked the pathway. The Chinese guard slipped his hand menacingly into his jacket pocket. "May I help you?" he rumbled in clear English.

"Yes, I am Dr. Franz Adler. A friend of Jia-Li's."

The man nodded his blocklike head. "Do you have an appointment?"

"No."

The guard took a step forward. "Then I have to ask you to leave, sir. Now."

"Please tell Jia-Li that I have to see her. It is imperative!"

The guard puffed out his chest. "The lady only accepts appointments."

"I am not a client! My wife, Mah Soon Yi, is Jia-Li's best friend."

The man's expression suddenly softened. "You are Sunny's husband?"

"Yes. Franz Adler."

"Wait here, sir!" The guard turned, lumbered up the pathway, and disappeared into the villa.

A few minutes later, the door opened and Jia-Li burst out. She ran down the pathway toward Franz in a short red cheongsam and high heels. She threw her arms around him and hugged him tight, sending a wave of pain through his broken ribs. "I couldn't believe it when Ushi told me you were here!" she cried. "They released you!"

Jia-Li took a step back, but her spicy perfume still filled his nostrils. Her painted face creased with concern. She gestured to the bruising over his cheeks and neck. "Franz, what have they done to you?"

"I am fine," Franz said. "Where are Sunny and Hannah? Please, Jia-Li!"

"They're safe." She shrugged slightly. "But I do not know exactly where."

He held out his hand. "How can you not know?"

"They were staying with my mother, but they had to leave in a hurry. Yang found them places with families who live on the outskirts of the city. We thought it best to separate them."

Franz felt a cold rush. "Separate them? *Why?*"

Jia-Li viewed him for a second or two. "Sunny thought it safest for Hannah. Especially after she had gone to confront that SS colonel—"

"*Oh, mein Gott!* She confronted him? Meisinger?"

"Yes, two days ago." Jia-Li's powdered face broke into a small grin. "Franz, we found his weak spot."

"What do you mean?"

"The colonel likes young boys." She went on to describe how they had photographed Meisinger in flagrante delicto and how Sunny had threatened the colonel with the evidence.

"She provoked him with those?"

Jia-Li's smile widened. "Sunny convinced him to leave Shanghai!"

"She did?" Franz said, simultaneously shocked and elated. "Meisinger left Shanghai before getting an answer from the Japanese?"

"Apparently so."

"Oh, that's wonderful." A sense of pride washed over him. "How can I reach her?"

"I will get Yang to pass a message to her."

"Let Sunny know that I'm back at home. And I will wait for her there." He gently clasped her arm with his left hand. "But, Jia-Li . . ."

She tilted her head, looking suddenly tired. "Yes?"

"Tell them not to let Hannah know I am home."

"Why not, Franz?"

"Hannah must believe I am still in custody. At least until we are convinced that the Nazis are truly gone." He squeezed her arm once and let it go. "I know my daughter. She would risk everything to find me. I cannot allow that."

Jia-Li nodded. "I will tell them."

Franz hugged Jia-Li gratefully again and then headed

back to the street. Checking his watch, he realized he still had time to meet Schwartzmann by eight o'clock.

The light was fading as Franz reached the Old City and wove his way down the curved streets past storefronts, restaurants, and pagodas. He limped by the dejected Chinese merchants operating near-empty booths that, thanks to strict rationing, carried little merchandise and attracted few consumers. Several beckoned him urgently with calls and waves, but Franz shook his head and kept moving.

In the open square at the center of the market, the renowned Woo Sing Ding teahouse stood elevated on stilts above an emerald-colored pond. Franz was about to step onto the zigzag bridge that led to the teahouse when a voice called to him. He turned to see Hermann Schwartzmann standing at the edge of the pond with his pipe between his teeth and his hands buried in his pockets.

Schwartzmann studied Franz's face for a moment but did not comment on the injuries. "It would be a lovely evening to stroll Yuyuan Garden. Would you agree, Dr. Adler?"

As they walked the garden maze, the diplomat glanced over either shoulder every few minutes, appearing more on edge than Franz had ever seen him. Schwartzmann said nothing until they stepped onto a pavilion overlooking a rock pond. He stopped and waved the stem of his pipe toward Franz's face. "All that bruising, Dr. Adler? Your arm."

"I spent several days in Bridge House."

"Mmm. Of course." Schwartzmann put the pipe back into his mouth and chewed the stem worriedly. "These are not good times for your people, are they?"

"That is putting it mildly indeed." Franz exhaled.

"A terrible understatement, yes." Schwartzmann gazed down at the pond. "And I'm afraid there are still more SS men arriving in Shanghai."

Franz tensed. "I was led to believe Colonel Meisinger had left the city."

"He has, yes." Schwartzmann puffed on his pipe. "However, I have been informed that another group of SS has arrived. Their mission even more secretive than Meisinger's."

A fresh wave of dread rolled over Franz. "How can this be?" he sputtered.

Schwartzmann shook his head. "It's all rumors and innuendo. None of us at the consulate even knows who has come."

"For what purpose? After Meisinger, what more could the Nazis possibly ask of the Japanese?"

"I do not know." Schwartzmann blew out his cheeks. "I wish I could be of more assistance. I am sorry. I just thought it best to apprise you of their arrival."

Franz nodded distractedly. "I appreciate this information."

Schwartzmann glanced nervously over his shoulder again. "Dr. Adler, I really cannot stay." He dug a hand in his pocket, pulled out another fat envelope, and held it out to Franz.

It was heavier than any previous one. "I am not convinced that money can solve our current problems, but thank you, Hermann," Franz said. "It is incredibly generous of you."

Schwartzmann extended his hand and Franz met the handshake. "Good luck." The diplomat held on to Franz's hand for an extra moment before letting go. "As I said, I only wish I could be of more help."

"You have done more than most, Hermann."

Schwartzmann opened his mouth as though to speak

but seemed to change his mind. He nodded once, turned, and walked away without looking back.

Franz sat down on a wooden bench and stared into the depths of the green pond before his feet. His arm throbbed and his body ached. New and old worries congealed inside him.

Oh, Sunny, we can never win. There will always be other Nazis.

Franz slid open the envelope's flap with little enthusiasm. He pulled out the thick wad of Reichsmarks, recognizing that it represented at least twice as much as any of Schwartzmann's previous donations. As he was shoving the cash back into the envelope, he glimpsed a single folded sheet, tucked below the bills. Franz pulled out the page, opened it, and began to read.

Dear Franz,

You cannot know how much the added year of life and health you gave Edda meant to us both. I have lived off the memories of our borrowed time together since. To know how much you risked in order to help us, when you had so many legitimate reasons to turn your back, makes your actions that much more noble.

My gratitude extends beyond your fine surgical care. Before I met you, I had lost pride in my work and in myself. I once had an honorable career, striving to protect and better the lives of all Germans abroad. And then, somehow, I became a part of a dishonorable regime. I suspended my own sense of right and wrong in order to protect my career. And the short time working for the National Socialists negated all the good I had tried to accomplish in the preceding years.

After I became involved with you, assisting Germans in true need, something changed within me. I rediscovered the sense of purpose and reward that had been missing all those years. I shudder to think that I once represented Herr Hitler.

Unfortunately, my friend, this is good-bye. I have been recalled to Berlin for "immediate reassignment." Such foolish Nazi doublespeak. Diplomats are not treated in such a manner unless they have fallen under suspicion. I have no doubt that some spy or informant has uncovered my connection to the refugees. And in many senses, I am relieved.

Be assured, my friend, that I will never allow them to send me back for one of their show trials. No, I will leave on my own terms. To be perfectly blunt, life holds little luster for me without my beloved wife. And I look forward to the opportunity to be reunited with her.

I wish you and your people only the best of fortune in overcoming this latest crisis and all the other abuses and atrocities that have been foisted upon you.

My life has been enriched for knowing you,

> *Your committed friend,*
> *Hermann*

~ Chapter 52

Sunny raced to the door more excited than ever to return home. She still had trouble believing the news that Yang had delivered to her at Fai's home, but as she fumbled with the lock, she sensed Franz's presence. Bounding inside, she cried out, "Franz! *Franz!*"

Her heart almost stopped as he rounded the corner. "Oh, Sunny!"

Franz limped toward her, his right arm hanging in a

makeshift sling. Sunny launched herself into his open arm, almost toppling him. She clung to him until she felt him reposition his arm. She pulled back to assess him.

Pale and gaunt, he had a puffy black eye and swollen, scabbed lips. One cheek bore a long red mark that extended to his chin. Bruises circled his neck, evidence of the fingers that had choked him.

Eyes glistening, Sunny ran her fingers lightly over the stubble on his swollen cheek. "What have they done to you, my darling?" she gasped.

"None of it matters." He skittered kisses over her lips, cheek, and chin. "I thought I would never see you again. That was by far the worst of it."

"For me too." She pressed her lips to his.

After another long kiss, Franz loosened his grip on Sunny. "Where is Hannah?" he asked.

"With Yang at her sister's place in the north end of Hongkew. They are taking good care of her. We . . . Franz, we cut her hair, and it's black and straighter now. And you should hear her speak Shanghainese. She is so fluent!"

Franz swallowed. "I miss her terribly."

Sunny grabbed him by his uninjured hand. "I can take you there now."

His hand went limp in hers. "No. It is too dangerous for Hannah to be anywhere near me."

Sunny beamed at him. "Did you not hear, Franz?" She couldn't resist pecking him again on the lips. "We turned the tables on Meisinger! He and his henchmen are gone."

"Jia-Li told me." He mustered a tired smile. "Sunny, I am so proud of you."

She squeezed his unresponsive hand tighter. "So what is troubling you?"

"The Nazis have found Schwartzmann out." Franz

went on to explain about the diplomat's recall to Berlin and his suicidal intent. "After I read his letter, I tried to telephone. To offer Hermann a hiding place. But there is no answer. I think he might already have . . . left."

Sunny touched his lip. "Oh, poor dear Hermann."

Franz sighed. "Hermann told me that more SS have come to Shanghai."

A chill ran up Sunny's spine. "Why?"

He opened his mouth to speak but a rapping at the door stopped him. "That must be Esther and Simon."

"Simon is also free?" she asked.

"Esther telephoned me only an hour ago," Franz said as he turned for the door.

Simon and Esther rushed inside. Everyone exchanged relieved hugs before settling in the sitting room.

Black-and-blue welts covered Simon's forehead and chin. His already prominent nose was swollen and it deviated slightly to the left. But his smile had lost none of its usual sheen. "Franz, I heard you calling back to me in the cages," Simon said as he touched the bridge of his broken nose. "But the guard had already got to me with his baton. Boy, did he beat a lesson into me. You never met anyone from the Bronx so quiet as me after that!"

Their legs touching, Esther held tightly to Simon's hand. She looked from her husband to Franz. "Do you have any idea why they chose to release you now?" she asked.

Simon shrugged. "The Japs aren't much for long good-byes. They basically dumped me on the curb without a word of explanation."

"I was treated the same," Franz said.

"I wonder if it had anything to do with Meisinger's departure?" Sunny suggested.

Esther sat up straight. "Meisinger is leaving Shang-hai?"

"He has already gone." Franz nodded in Sunny's direction. "Thanks to my brilliant wife."

"And Jia-Li," Sunny pointed out.

The worry drained from Esther's face. *"Mazel tov!"* she cried. "Where would we be without you, Sunny?"

Simon patted Sunny's hand. "Our very own Judith."

"Judith?" Sunny frowned.

"The biblical heroine," Esther explained. "She saved the Israelites by assassinating the Assyrian leader, Holofernes."

Simon chuckled. "I bet you old Holofernes was a swell salt-of-the-earth kind of guy compared with Meisinger."

Franz stared at Simon, stone-faced. "Meisinger may be gone. However, another group of SS men have come to Shanghai."

Esther stiffened. "For us?" she asked in a hush.

Simon gently pulled Esther's head onto his shoulder. "This might be related to Max's telephone call," he said.

"What did Feinstein have to say?" Franz asked.

"A rumor is running wild among the refugees. Some crazy story that the Nazis are planning to send Jews still trapped in Germany over here."

Franz grimaced. "Here? To Shanghai?"

"To China, anyway," Simon said. "Max is over the moon at the prospect of being reunited with his daughter's family."

Sunny squinted at Simon. "Could it be true?"

Simon shrugged. "Max swears that the Germans are meeting individually with local Jewish leaders to explain their plan."

Franz rose from the couch. "Nazis meeting with Jews

in order to help reunite them with lost loved ones? It's simply not possible."

Simon rolled his shoulders again. "You should have heard Max go on."

The telephone rang, and Sunny hurried over to answer it. "Adler residence."

"Mrs. Adler, this is Colonel Kubota," said the somber voice on the other end of the line.

"Hello, Colonel," she said fondly, remembering the kindness he had shown her a few days before. "Have you heard that Franz has been released?"

"I am most pleased," he said with little enthusiasm. "By chance, does Dr. Adler happen to be home?"

She turned to fetch Franz, but he was already on his way to the telephone. She passed him the receiver and leaned her head close to his, trying in vain to hear both sides of the conversation.

"Thank you. I am well." Franz repositioned his sling. "Colonel, might I ask if there have been any developments in regard to the refugees?"

Franz listened a moment. Then his face suddenly blanched and his pupils dilated. "*Me?*" he murmured. "They want to meet me?"

~ Chapter 53

JULY 31, 1942, SHANGHAI

Clouds darkened the skies, but they only served to trap the heat and humidity at street level. Oblivious to the temperature, Franz stood behind Sunny at the curbside with his free arm wrapped around her waist. He said little, trying not to show how much the thought of leaving her again was tearing him apart.

Sunny looked over her shoulder at him. "What if this is some kind of trap, Franz?"

"They don't need to trap me, darling. They had me in Bridge House for a week."

"The Kempeitai had you."

"The Nazis cannot touch us without Japanese consent." His voice cracked. "I have to do everything I can to influence their decision. Including this, Sunny."

"You've only just come home." She turned and held him tightly, clinging to his bruised rib cage. Barely aware of the pain, he inhaled the fresh scent of her hair, wishing again that Hannah, Sunny, and he were almost anywhere else on earth.

Franz heard the rumbling of a car's engine. He stepped back and laid a hand on her shoulder. "Remember, Sunny, if I am not back by nightfall you must leave the house. You cannot stay here any longer."

"I remember, Franz."

"And you will check on Hannah at Yang's sister's? If you have even the slightest of doubts—"

"I will find her a more secure place."

Franz forced a smile and said, "Thank you."

As Kubota's car pulled up beside them, Sunny touched his face once. "Come home to me soon, Dr. Adler."

Franz swallowed away the lump in his throat. "Always . . . Mrs. Adler."

The driver opened the door for Kubota, who climbed out slowly. He wore the same green uniform as before, but he looked completely changed. His once rigid back stooped and his shoulders sagged. Defeat clouded his face.

Registering Franz's injuries, Kubota looked away in

embarrassment and spoke to the ground. "Mrs. Adler, I am sorry, but I cannot permit you to accompany us."

Sunny smiled tightly. "It never seems to be an option, Colonel."

Franz folded his arms around Sunny again. She buried her face in his shoulder, and he gently rocked her on the spot. He could hear her soft, muffled sobs. At a loss for reassuring words, he kissed the top of her head before releasing her.

As the car drove off, Franz stared back over his shoulder at Sunny, who stood as still as the trees lining the street. As soon as she was out of sight, he turned to Kubota. "If Meisinger has already left Shanghai, who represents the Germans now, Colonel?"

Kubota hung his head. "After the . . . incident with General Nogomi, I no longer attend to the general, nor am I privy to the details of further negotiations with the Germans."

Franz nodded. "You have done all you can to try to protect us, Colonel. Thank you."

"I fear that your gratitude is most premature, Dr. Adler."

A familiar chill crept under Franz's skin. As he thought of the meeting with General Nogomi, Samuel Reuben came to his mind again. His outrage with the surgeon had subsided, especially after hearing how poorly Reuben had fared in Bridge House. "Colonel, was Dr. Reuben released?"

Kubota nodded somberly. "Dr. Reuben was rushed to the refugee hospital. It was the nearest one with space available for him."

"What happened to him, Colonel?"

"Pneumonia." Kubota didn't look up to meet Franz's eyes. "I understand there were also spinal fractures and other injuries. Clara tells me that he is not doing well at all."

The car rolled to a stop on the Bund in front of the Cathay Hotel. Franz's stomach knotted as he stepped through the revolving door into the sumptuous, sprawling lobby. He followed Kubota to the bank of elevators. As they rode up to the fifteenth floor, Kubota said, "Dr. Adler, I will not be present for this meeting."

Franz swiveled his head in alarm. "Why not, Colonel?"

"They have requested to speak to you alone."

"Alone?" Franz gulped.

"I am afraid so."

"Fifteenth floor," the withered elevator operator announced and the doors opened.

Their feet sank silently into the plush carpet as Kubota led Franz down the hallway to the corner suite. *Is this how a condemned man feels approaching the gallows?* The memory of his brother hit him like a club. *Oh, Karl!*

At the door, Kubota glanced over to Franz with a supportive nod and then rapped three times. The door opened and a man in a dove-gray uniform bearing the unmistakable lightning-bolt insignia of the SS on his collar stepped out. Apprehension washed over Franz as he recognized the acne-scarred face of Horst Schmidt.

Ignoring Franz altogether, Schmidt saluted Kubota crisply. "Hauptscharführer Schmidt, sir."

"Colonel Kubota." He returned the salute but spoke in English. "I am escorting my friend, Dr. Adler."

Schmidt did not acknowledge Franz. "The Obersturmbannführer is expecting him."

Kubota took a last look at Franz before turning and trudging away down the corridor.

Schmidt snapped his fingers in Franz's face. "Adler! Come."

The white-carpeted, spacious suite was airy and bright, its gilded windows offering an expansive view of the Bund and the Whangpoo. Despite the room's grandeur, Franz felt as claustrophobic as he had in Bridge House.

Schmidt marched over to the set of closed doors on the far side of the room and knocked. "Adler is here, sir!" he announced.

"Send him in, please," replied a soft voice.

Schmidt pushed open the doors and jerked his head in their direction. Franz took a long breath and then stepped into the sitting room. The door closed behind him with a whoosh.

With the exception of his uniform, now gray instead of black, the man behind the desk looked exactly the same as he had in Vienna, four years earlier. *Eichmann!* The air left Franz's lungs.

Adolf Eichmann studied Franz with cool eyes before he rose unhurriedly to his feet. "Ah, Herr Doktor Adler, so good of you to come." He extended his arm, not to shake hands but to indicate the chair on the opposite side of the desk. "Please, won't you sit?"

Mouth sour with acid, Franz lowered himself into the seat. Eichmann motioned to the small bar set up in the room's corner. "Would you care for a refreshment, Dr. Adler?"

"No thank you, Lieutenant Eichmann."

"Ah, I am actually an Obersturmbannführer now." He sat back down across from Franz. "A lieutenant colonel. I can hardly believe it myself."

Franz, flooded with a mixture of disbelief, anger, and dread, simply stared at the man.

Eichmann nodded to Franz's sling. "Did you have an accident, Dr. Adler?"

"It's nothing, really."

Eichmann shrugged. "This truly is a gem of a hotel, is it not?" he went on conversationally. "I understand it was built by Sir Victor Sassoon. Do you happen to know the man?"

"Not personally, no."

"I heard that he scurried out of Shanghai before the Japanese took over. Too bad. I would have liked to meet Sir Victor. I understand he used to be *the* most influential and successful businessman in the entire city." He tapped his temple conspiratorially. "Apparently, Sir Victor was quite the ladies' man and a close friend to royalty and movie stars alike. My sources also tell me that he provided generous financial assistance to the Jewish refugees."

"I have heard the same," Franz said, wondering why Eichmann was gushing over a Jewish entrepreneur.

Eichmann leaned back in his chair. "Recent . . . ah . . . injuries aside, Dr. Adler, I understand that you have landed on your feet here in Shanghai."

Uncertain how to reply, Franz said nothing.

"Your family is well?"

Franz tensed. "Thank you, yes," he muttered.

Eichmann continued as though they were two old friends catching up. "I myself still work for the Department of Jewish Affairs. My responsibilities now extend somewhat beyond Vienna." He laughed softly. "In fact, I'm responsible for all German-occupied territories, which—as you might imagine—covers vast geography and touches millions of lives."

Franz had no idea what to make of Eichmann's feigned friendliness. He forced warmth into his voice. "You sound terribly busy, Obersturmbannführer. May I inquire as to what brings you to Shanghai?"

"You may, indeed, Dr. Adler." Eichmann smiled

thinly. "I think you are aware that a colleague of mine—a Gestapo man named Meisinger—took it upon himself to visit the city."

Franz shook his head. "He was not sent here?"

"Yes and no," Eichmann sighed. "It is true that Reichsführer Himmler did authorize his visit, but unfortunately Colonel Meisinger vastly overstepped his bounds."

"He did?"

"If I might be perfectly frank, Herr Doktor, Meisinger is an overzealous buffoon." Eichmann exhaled heavily. "He arrived here with all sorts of drastic proposals for dealing with the refugees that were never sanctioned by Berlin."

"I see," Franz said, trying to read between the lines.

"Fortunately, I happened to be in the Far East, so I can personally sort out Meisinger's mess." His voice lowered. "Although, Dr. Adler, few people are aware of my presence, and I would prefer to keep it that way."

"Of course, Obersturmbannführer."

Eichmann sat up straighter and spoke with excitement. "Putting Meisinger's idiocy aside, we, in my department, see a real opportunity here in China."

"Opportunity?" Franz almost choked on the word.

"Yes. Before the war, despite the reluctance of other countries, we were successful in facilitating the emigration of hundreds of thousands of German Jews." Eichmann said it as though the Nazis had to struggle to overcome other countries' anti-Semitic policies. "Unfortunately, with the war situation being what it is, there is nowhere for the Jews still left in the fatherland to go. You understand that they can't possibly stay in Germany. Frankly, with war rationing and the natural backlash against them, it's neither safe nor sustainable for them."

Franz viewed Eichmann speechlessly.

"In every crisis there is opportunity." Eichmann ran his finger over the brim of the perfectly polished officer's cap that sat on his desk. "For everyone involved, including you."

"Me, Obersturmbannführer? The SS is offering *me* an opportunity?"

"I believe so, yes." Eichmann offered another thin-lipped smile. "For reasons I do not fully appreciate, our Japanese allies hold you Jews in oddly high regard. They have had a long-standing plan to repopulate the occupied territory of Manchuria in northern China— the area that they call Manchukuo—with European Jews. The Japanese feel that your people's innate industriousness could help spark the economy and productivity of a region rife with natural resources."

Franz shook his head. "Obersturmbannführer, do I understand you correctly . . ."

"It's wonderfully simple, Dr. Adler." Eichmann snapped his fingers. "We have to rid ourselves of thousands of Jews. The Japanese want them. It's a matter of supply and demand."

"For Manchukuo?" Franz said, swallowing his skepticism. "So how would that affect the Jews already living in Shanghai?"

"Two ways." Eichmann wiggled his index and middle fingers. "First, we need existing Jews who are already acclimatized to China to help orient what could amount to hundreds of thousands of new arrivals. And second, to be blunt, the Führer prefers not to have . . . ah . . . scores of Jews representing the German presence in one of the most important cities in Asia. He is concerned how it reflects on the fatherland. You do understand, Herr Doktor?"

"You would relocate us refugees to Manchuria too?"

"Exactly! To settle into your own community with the rest of your brethren from Germany." Another cold-eyed smile. "You might even think of it as the Jewish homeland you people have sought for so long!"

Franz gazed down at the carpet. "Obersturmbannführer, may I inquire how you intend to transport all of these European Jews to China?"

Eichmann shrugged. "Obviously, we would have to reach an understanding with our enemies to guarantee safe passage. However, unless Churchill and Roosevelt's words of concern and outrage for the Jews are mere lip service, then I imagine they would be motivated to cooperate. It makes us all look a little more . . . humane."

Franz forced himself to look up. "When do you foresee this relocation occurring?"

"As soon as September. Around the time of Rosh Hashanah." Eichmann grinned again. "A new beginning to launch the Jewish New Year?"

Franz forced himself to slow his breathing. "Obviously, you see a role for me in this?"

Eichmann stood up and walked over to the bar in the corner. "Are you certain you will not join me in a drink, Dr. Adler?"

Franz shook his head. Eichmann uncorked a bottle of brandy and poured a little into a snifter. He warmed the glass with his palm, swirling it around, before taking a sip. "Our Japanese friends inform us that you are one of the leaders of the refugee community here."

"I doubt the other refugees view me as such," Franz muttered.

"Ah, such modesty, Dr. Adler." Eichmann nodded appreciatively. "We certainly see you in that role. And that is why you are here now. There are bound to be skeptics. We want you to help the rest of your community to recognize the opportunity here."

He wants me to spread Nazi propaganda. Franz was speechless.

"I believe that fate has presented a unique opportunity for Germans to help Jews, and vice versa. Would you not agree?"

Franz found the idea of the Nazis going to such extremes to transport Jews to safety beyond absurd.

"Well, Herr Doktor?" Eichmann prompted Franz with a wave of his glass. "What do you say?"

"Chełmno," Franz blurted.

The smile slid from Eichmann's lips. "Excuse me?"

"Are you familiar with Chełmno, Obersturmbannführer?"

Eichmann's pale eyes registered no response. "The prison camp in Poland?"

"Yes." Franz swallowed. He knew he was revealing too much, but he couldn't help himself. "I understand that it's not a prison at all but an extermination camp. A place where thousands of Jews—women and children included—are gassed every day."

"*Ach,* such rumors," Eichmann said calmly. "You are aware, Dr. Adler, that there is a full-scale war raging in Eastern Europe?"

"Yes, but—"

"The struggle is cruel and brutal. I will not mince my words. We have set up concentration camps in Poland. And, yes, executions have been carried out. But indiscriminately? Hardly." Eichmann waved the suggestion away. "Did your sources also tell you that those chosen for Chełmno come primarily from the Łódź ghetto?"

Franz nodded.

"Do you actually believe we randomly choose people to dispatch to Chełmno?" Eichmann sighed into his brandy snifter. "The town of Łódź is the center of a relentless armed resistance. We have been forced to make examples of the subversives, Communists, and others who insist upon stirring unrest. We have found it the best and quickest way to quell an uprising."

Though he knew better, Franz found himself wanting to believe Eichmann's words.

Eichmann held out his free hand to Franz. "Besides, we would always distinguish between German Jews and those miserable Poles or Slavs. We would never dream of slaughtering our own population."

Franz had a mental flashback to Kristallnacht, watching the Nazi mob beat the old Yacobsen couple to death. And he thought of his own brother, swaying lifelessly from a lamppost with graffiti scrawled across his chest. "Last time we spoke, Herr Eichmann, you informed me that no one can outrun their own destiny."

Eichmann squinted at him. "Yes. And so?"

"I do not believe you have any interest in populating Manchukuo with Jews," Franz said, aware of the risk he was taking but too angry to care.

Eichmann's eyes iced over. "Are you calling me a liar, Adler?" he growled.

Franz thought of all the pointless pain and loss Eichmann and his kind had caused. *My father. My brother!* "You are correct about destiny." His voice rose. "Hitler will not subjugate the entire world. Eventually, you will be defeated. And history will always judge you!"

"How dare you, *schweinhund! I have been more than patient with you!*" Eichmann cried as he hurled his snifter at Franz. It flew past his head and shattered against the wall, splattering the brandy.

The door burst open. Franz looked over his shoulder

and saw Schmidt standing in the doorway with a pistol in his hand. *"Was ist los, Obersturmbannführer?"*

Eichmann shook his finger at Franz and grunted, "This . . . this Jew scum is calling me a liar."

Schmidt steadied his aim, pointing at Franz's head. "There is only one way to deal with Jews, Obersturmbannführer."

Only the thought of his family stopped Franz from lunging at Schmidt. "Colonel Kubota is my friend," he said evenly.

"So what?" Eichmann snapped.

The Luger twitched in Schmidt's hand.

"Colonel Kubota is an honorable man," Franz said. "How do you suppose he will view my cold-blooded murder at the very meeting that he delivered me to?"

Uncertainty crept into Schmidt's eyes, and he glanced over to his superior for direction.

Eichmann glared at Franz with hatred beyond reason.

The room went still. Time froze.

Finally, Eichmann snorted. "There is nowhere left to run, Adler. And when the time comes, destiny and I will both be waiting."

⌒ Chapter 54

Franz and Sunny sat silently on the couch. He looked down and studied her slim perfect fingers, which were interlocked with his. The edge of the envelope in his pocket poked against his thigh, but he was not ready to hand it over to Sunny.

Franz had written the letter to Hannah as soon as he

returned home earlier in the day from the Cathay Hotel. As he wrote, he appreciated how conflicted Schwartzmann and, especially, his father must have felt as they penned missives intended for posthumous reading. He sprinkled the letter with random thoughts and advice on career, relationships, and the keys—as he saw them—to finding contentment in life. Franz finished, in the same way his father had, by stressing his incredible pride in and love for his child. Tears rolled down his cheeks as he signed the letter.

Oh, liebchen, to hold you one last time.

"You really think the refugee leaders will believe Eichmann?" Sunny asked.

"People hear what they want to," Franz sighed. "Eichmann is offering them the illusion of a new, secure life. A reunion with loved ones left behind in Germany. Think of poor Max. It might be too good to resist."

"You said he was targeting the Jewish New Year. That means we still might have a month or more to come up with a way out."

"Or maybe, in light of my outburst today, he will speed up his plans." Franz massaged his temple. "The Kempeitai could come for me any time. Colonel Kubota cannot protect me from them. He admitted as much."

Sunny sat up straighter. "Then come away with me!"

"And get you killed? Never."

Sunny pulled her hand free of his and turned on him angrily. "In only a month of marriage, we have already been separated twice. I cannot bear it again. I won't!"

"Sunny . . ." Franz reached out to her, but she leaned away from him.

"No, Franz! This is my decision, not yours. And I will stay with you whatever happens."

Franz dropped his hand to his lap. "And Hannah? Who will care for her?"

"Yang and Jia-Li will." She shook her head. "I love Hannah, but my place is here with you."

Franz felt lost. He loved Sunny too much to let her die for him. Heavyhearted, he rose from the couch. "Then I will have to leave you."

Sunny jumped to her feet. "No, Franz!"

"I have to," he murmured.

"No, you don't. We can go into hiding together."

"Eichmann, Tanaka . . ." He shook his head. "They will hunt us down."

"I know every inch of this city, Franz. They will never find us. I promise."

He cupped her chin in his hand. "I cannot let you take that chance."

She nuzzled her face against his hand. "And Hannah?"

"What about her?"

"She has no mother. She has a permanent physical disadvantage. And she has been thrown into a family of strangers and a foreign culture."

Franz released her chin. "Sunny, I think of little else."

"She needs her father, Franz."

He grimaced. "You are not suggesting that we take her on the run with us?"

"Not right away, no," Sunny said. "The war can't last forever. Circumstances change. If we can survive this storm somehow—even if it takes years—then she will get her father back. At least she will have that hope. Don't take that away from her by surrendering."

Franz felt his conviction weakening. "And what of the other refugees?"

"There is nothing left you can do for them."

"And Esther and Simon?"

She grabbed his hand. "We can take them with us!"

"Could we?"

"Of course. We cannot leave them here."

He had run out of arguments. Remembering his father's stubborn unwillingness to leave Vienna, Franz realized that he might be repeating Jakob's mistake. Sunny was not going to leave him. Their martyrdom would not mean anything to anyone. "Very well," he said.

Sunny's eyes lit and her jaw dropped. "You mean it?"

Franz smiled tenderly. "Yes, darling, I will run away with you."

She enveloped him in a huge hug and kissed his face wildly.

He pulled free of the embrace. "We must leave right away."

Sunny kissed him one more time on the lips. "I will pack a bag for us."

As Sunny rushed off, Franz limped over to the hallway telephone.

Esther answered on the third ring. "It was Eichmann," Franz said.

"*Gott in Himmel!*" Esther gasped. "Here in Shanghai? What did that creature want?"

"To offer us a Jewish homeland."

"Franz, you shouldn't joke about such things."

"I'm not." Franz summarized Eichmann's proposal. "But Essie, I am certain it's only a pretense to round us all up for some terrible purpose."

"So it's over for us then?"

"No, Essie. Not for us. We are going to leave."

"But where will you go?"

"Anywhere. We will start with Sunny's friend, Jia-Li, and go from there. You and Simon are coming too."

Esther laughed softly. "Simon will never leave the refugees."

"He will if you go, Essie."

She was quiet for a long moment. "Yes. Yes, I see."

Relief washed over him. "You mean it?"

"Yes."

"Thank God." He exhaled. "Pack lightly, Essie."

"I will." She paused. "Franz?"

"Yes?"

"I no longer have any idea what God wants or expects from our people." She paused. "But this . . . will this never end for us?"

He sighed with a small laugh. "I understood God better when I did not believe in him at all. Essie, we must hurry."

⌒

Sunny packed their clothes into a case that she could carry on her back. She prepared a separate bag with food. At one point, she disappeared into Kingsley's library and emerged with the same framed photo of her parents that she had brought to the wedding.

Franz went to the closet and dug out the photographs he had snapped the month before of the refugee hospital. They had not turned out as well as his prints of the Ward Road heim. Dissatisfied with the background lighting and slope of the roofline, he had almost destroyed the images. But, fearing the worst for the hospital's future, he felt compelled to preserve the evidence of its existence. He tucked a handful of the prints into their bag.

At the door, Sunny stopped for one final look around. "I have never lived anywhere else." She shrugged. "I know it's just wood and plaster. Nothing that cannot be replaced. But this house always kept me close to the memories of my parents, especially my father."

Franz tapped the center of her chest. "Those memories are forever safe here."

"I know, it's just that—" She stopped talking and tilted her head to listen.

Franz heard it too: the faint rumbling of a car's engine.

She grabbed his hand and jerked him toward the door. "Let's go, Franz!" she cried.

Franz stood his ground. "My feet . . . my arm . . . I can't run, Sunny."

"We can hide! The cellar!"

He shook his head. "They will not leave without me. You go, Sunny!"

She clung to his hand. "I'm not going anywhere."

Tires screeched out front. Franz knew he had run out of time. He wriggled his hand free and dug into his pocket. He pulled out the creased envelope and passed it to her. "For Hannah. Please, Sunny!"

Her eyes misted over and she nodded, clutching the envelope to her chest.

Three heavy knocks rattled the front door. She tried to stop him from answering, but he shook free of her arm and opened the door. A tall Kempeitai officer loomed in the doorway with his stocky partner hovering behind.

Franz's neck tightened. He could almost taste the foul water running down the back of his throat.

"You come with us," the officer barked, reaching out for Franz.

"I will. I will. Just one moment." He turned to Sunny. "I . . . I love you."

Her face crumpled. "Always."

The Kempeitai officers dragged him out to the military vehicle. As the car sped off, Franz shut his eyes, not wanting to know their destination.

The driver switched off the engine and Franz opened

his eyes to see the repellent sight of Bridge House. He flailed wildly as the two guards fought to pull him free of the car. One of them clamped a hand over his broken arm. Despite the pain, he kept thrashing.

The guards jerked him up by the armpits and dragged him into the building.

Inside, the guards hauled Franz past the desk and toward an elevator. Realizing they were heading away from the filthy cages, he calmed slightly and stopped resisting.

They rode the elevator to the fifth floor. The guards marched him down a hallway to an office. Inside, Colonel Tanaka sat behind a desk with the usual scowl carved into his face. He eyed Franz with contempt. "You will stop spreading dirty rumors about Imperial Empire of Japan!" he barked.

"Colonel, I have—"

"*Silence!*" Tanaka slammed his palm against his desk. "I know you speak to Germans. I know you talk to other Jews. Do not lie!"

Franz lowered his head and gazed at the floor.

"You Jews come to Shanghai with nothing. You do not belong here." Tanaka shook his head slowly. "We treat you well. We make no trouble for you."

"It is true," Franz muttered.

"How do we know you will not spy on us?" Tanaka demanded. "You will help the enemy every way possible."

Franz looked up. "Colonel, we just want to care for our families. To live." He swallowed. "Nothing else."

"We are honorable people," Tanaka went on. "Things must change."

Despair washed over Franz. His legs began to buckle. "So you do intend to hand us over to the Nazis, then?"

Tanaka's hand smashed into the desktop again. *"I tell you we are honorable people!"* he screeched. "And you spread nothing but lies, lies, lies!"

Franz fought back a gag.

Tanaka leapt from his seat and raced over to Franz. He hovered so close that Franz could smell the fish on his breath. Tanaka jabbed his finger into Franz's chest. "We send Nazis away, and you still say terrible things about us!"

Franz shook his head in confusion. "Away?"

"We are a great army. We crush all enemies. No mercy." He thrust his finger harder into Franz's chest. "But we do not kill children and women."

A glimmer of hope electrified Franz. "Colonel Tanaka, did you refuse the Nazis' request? Eichmann too? You turned them all away?"

"Do you not hear me?" Tanaka poked Franz's chest even harder. "We are honorable soldiers. We do not kill children. Do not spread such lies!"

Franz could barely keep the smile from his face. "Never. I swear! We will tell the rest of the world that you saved our lives. You will see!"

Tanaka relaxed his finger. "Hmmm," he grunted with as much satisfaction as Franz had ever heard from the man.

"Thank you, Colonel. Thank you."

Despite the pain, Franz gingerly extended his right hand to him. But Tanaka ignored the gesture. "Things will change for Jews in Shanghai," he warned. "We have to better control you. You are too free now."

As ominous as the threat might have sounded, Franz felt too blissful to care.

They're not handing us over to the Nazis! My darling Sunny and Hannah, we will all be together again!

Chapter 55

AUGUST 3, 1942, SHANGHAI

Sunny poked the needle through the skin and tightened the thread as she pulled the edges of the wound together. She glanced over to her husband, who nodded his approval.

With his right arm set in a plaster cast, Franz had assumed the role of anesthetist. He removed the ether mask from the man's face. "Time to wake the patient?"

Sunny grinned through her mask. "I should be done in another minute or two."

Franz nodded. "That was flawless surgery, Frau Doktor."

"Hardly, Dr. Adler." She beamed as she knotted another suture. "A simple abscess of the spleen. You could have done a better job using only one arm. And possibly even blindfolded."

"I could not have done it better with two good hands." He shook his head. "Besides, an able surgeon requires far more than dexterity. After all, who made the diagnosis?"

She shrugged, concealing her delight.

Samuel Reuben had originally been misdiagnosed with pneumonia. As soon as Sunny touched his rigid belly, she suspected that a ruptured spleen and abscess better explained his symptoms: fever, pain, and difficulty breathing. Franz agreed. In the operating room, the pint of pus and blood Sunny drained from under the diaphragm confirmed her diagnosis.

She tied off the last stitch and Berta cut it. "Could you please dress the wound?"

Berta giggled. "Certainly, Frau Doktor."

Franz moved for the door. "Shall we go together to inform his wife?" he asked Sunny.

They had only just stepped into the corridor when Clara Reuben pounced. She stopped inches from them. "Well?" she demanded of Franz, ignoring Sunny. "How is my husband?"

"He is in stable condition, Mrs. Reuben," Franz said. "Sunny drained a large amount of pus. There were no—"

"You let *her* perform the surgery?" Clara was aghast. "*A nurse?*"

Franz raised his arm in its cast. "How did you suppose I was going to perform it?"

"I foolishly expected a doctor to operate." Clara huffed. "On a fellow surgeon, no less!"

"Mrs. Adler is as good as any surgeon in Shanghai." Clara began to protest, but Franz waved it off. "I will not argue this with you. The procedure went as well as it possibly could have. Sunny just saved your husband's life."

Clara stared at Franz for a moment. "Very well," she sighed. "When may I see him?"

"He is still asleep from the anesthetic," Franz said. "Perhaps in another hour or two."

"This was all so unnecessary," Clara grumbled.

Franz eyed the woman coolly. "I could not agree more." Then his expression softened. He laid his good hand on Clara's shoulder. "Samuel will be all right," he reassured.

Clara's stern face crumpled. Her eyes misted over, and she suddenly appeared aged and haggard. "How can you be so sure? He is so sick," she sputtered. "I would be lost without him."

"It will take time, but Samuel will improve."

"Are you certain, Franz?" she asked tremulously.

He squeezed her shoulder once before letting go. "As certain as I can be."

"Yes. Right then." Clara gathered herself and turned to Sunny with a conciliatory expression that passed for a smile. "Well, thank you for your efforts, Mrs. Adler."

"You are most welcome, Mrs. Reuben."

They finished rounds, checked again on Reuben, and then left for the Japanese military headquarters at Astor House.

Inside Kubota's office, the walls were bare except for rectangular outlines that marked the spots where paintings had once hung. The colonel's desk was almost obscured by boxes. Kubota greeted them at the door. "Please excuse the disorder, Dr. and Mrs. Adler."

"Are you moving offices, Colonel?" Franz asked.

"No, Dr. Adler. I am being transferred."

Franz frowned. "May I ask where?"

"Tokyo."

Franz's face fell. "You are leaving Shanghai?"

"It is for the best. I had begun to mistake Shanghai for home." Before Franz could comment, Kubota asked, "And Dr. Reuben? How did his operation go?"

"Surgery went well, Colonel," Sunny spoke up. "We expect him to improve now."

Kubota nodded with obvious relief. "I am most pleased."

Franz held his hand open. "Of course, if Colonel Tanaka had not turned the Nazis away, there would be no hospital in which to perform surgery."

A rueful smile crossed Kubota's face. "I suppose not."

"Was it really Colonel Tanaka who refused the Nazis?" Franz asked.

Kubota tilted his head from side to side. "His orders may have come from higher."

"General Nogomi?"

"I believe the ultimate decision was made by the High Command in Tokyo."

Franz squinted. "Colonel, you once told me that the field commanders handled such matters themselves."

Kubota nodded. "Usually, the High Command is not burdened with local security issues."

Franz's eyes widened. "It was you! You brought it to their attention, didn't you, Colonel?"

Kubota shifted on the spot, and Sunny saw that her husband had touched a nerve. "Oh, Colonel, this is why you are being transferred, is it not?" she said.

Kubota cleared his throat. "I do not mean to be rude, Dr. and Mrs. Adler, but I really must leave you now."

Sunny bowed deeply to Kubota. "Colonel, thank you. For everything."

Kubota returned her bow and then extended his hand to Franz.

"Colonel, you are a most honorable and decent man," Franz said. "I promise you, we will never forget all you have done for us. Never."

Kubota's face flushed. "I fear that the road ahead will not necessarily be easy for any of us, but as we say in Japan: *shikata ga nai.* 'What will be cannot be helped.'" He offered a sad smile. "I wish you and your family all good fortune and good health."

They left Astor House in silence. From what Sunny understood of Japanese military culture, she expected that Kubota would be heading back to Japan in disgrace.

～

As they arrived home, a cloud of mouthwatering aromas engulfed them. Despite the meager rations, Yang was somehow preparing a feast.

"Papa!" Hannah cried as she raced out of the kitchen and into his open arms.

Three days earlier, Sunny had wept watching Franz and Hannah's tearful reunion. Each time Franz had returned home since, even from brief errands, his daughter greeted him as though he were a soldier returning from war.

Hannah freed herself from her father and wrapped Sunny in a warm hug. Sunny ran her hand through the girl's short dyed-black hair and kissed her head once. "Jia-Li is here too," Hannah exclaimed.

Sunny found her best friend on the sitting room sofa, one leg crossed over the other, and puffing from a silver cigarette holder. In a black dress and brimmed hat, Jia-Li could have passed for a Chinese Marlene Dietrich. Sunny kissed her on the cheek as she dropped onto the couch beside her. "Will you stay for dinner, *bǎo bèi*?"

Jia-Li sighed out a mouthful of smoke. "I am afraid I have to work."

Sunny was about to protest when Hannah wandered into the room and sat down on the other side of Jia-Li.

Jia-Li patted the girl's leg. "Hannah, there's a new film playing on Nanking Road. *Tarzan's Secret Treasure*. Perhaps you would like to come with me to the matinee tomorrow?"

Hannah's eyes lit. "Oh, could we?"

"Why not, beautiful?" Jia-Li laughed. "And we will take Sunny too. A real girls' outing."

Jia-Li directed the conversation to talk of the latest fashions and then local gossip. Eventually, she rose to her feet. "I'm afraid I have to leave now."

Sunny walked her to the door. "Are you sure you won't stay? Your poet, Dmitri, could join us too."

Jia-Li smiled. "I doubt Chih-Nii would appreciate my absence tonight."

Sunny squeezed her friend's hand between hers. "If ever you choose to leave that place, *bǎo bèi,* you are always welcome to come and stay here with us. Your mother too, of course."

Jia-Li laughed. "Oh, dear sweet Soon Yi, if only it were so simple."

"After all you have done for us and the risks you have taken . . ." Sunny's voice cracked. "I don't know how I can ever thank you, *bǎo bèi.*"

Jia-Li shrugged. "It's what sisters do."

Sunny kissed Jia-Li's cheek again. "You are the best friend in the world," she whispered into her ear.

Esther and Simon arrived minutes after Jia-Li's departure. Simon had somehow scrounged up a bottle of prewar Chianti and a tin of pineapple juice for Hannah. They gathered in the sitting room with their glasses, Hannah stealing the occasional sip of wine from her father's.

Franz had reset Simon's broken nose, but it was still swollen, and most of his face had turned yellowish blue from the bruising. Despite his injuries, Simon seemed more ebullient than ever. "How lucky am I?" He glanced adoringly to Esther. "And for the cherry on top, you hear the latest war news?"

"You mean the bombing of Hamburg?" Franz said.

Simon nodded enthusiastically. "The largest bombing on German soil yet."

"Women and children live in Hamburg too," Esther pointed out.

"This war is brutal on all civilians, no question," Simon said. "But the Allies desperately need some successes. And it's not only Hamburg. The Brits pushed the Germans back in North Africa at El Alamein. The tide is turning. I feel it in my bones."

Esther laughed good-naturedly. "Oh, darling, your optimism knows no bounds."

"Meantime, we are still at the whim of the Japanese," Franz sighed. "And might be so forever."

"Think of all the odds we have already beaten." Simon stood up and raised his glass. "I want to toast the Jews of Shanghai, who have more lives than your average cat."

Hannah turned to Esther, confused. "Average cat?"

"It's an old saying that cats have nine lives," Esther explained, and then looked up at her husband. "Don't tempt fate, darling."

Simon laughed as he took hold of Esther's hand and pulled her to her feet. "You got to figure that fate must be sick and tired of dumping on us Jews."

Sunny rose and tapped her glass to theirs. "To Shanghai Jews!"

Simon winked at her. "Including you, Sunny. Not entirely sure why you would want membership in our tribe, but no one deserves it more than you."

Hannah hopped to her feet. "To Sunny and the rest of the Shanghai Jews." She giggled and clinked glasses with the others.

Franz scanned the room. "I would like to make another toast. To the most precious gift in the world." He raised his glass high above his head. "To family!"

Everyone tapped glasses again. Sunny's face glowed as Franz blew her a kiss.

"Speaking of families—" Simon began.

Esther grabbed his sleeve. "Simon, not yet!"

Simon turned to her with a huge grin. "Essie, it's the perfect time."

"Time for what, Tante Essie?" Hannah asked.

Sunny's heart fluttered in anticipation. "Esther, you're not . . ."

Esther nodded shyly. "I am pregnant."

"*When?*"

"I only found out last week. When the men were still in prison."

"Congratulations! *Mazel tov!*" Sunny threw her arms around Esther and spun her around, spilling their wine.

"I am going to have a baby cousin!" Hannah cried as she joined in on the hug.

"Yes, *mazel tov* to both of you!" Franz buffeted Simon's shoulder with his good hand and then turned quizzically to Esther. "I don't understand . . ."

Esther shrugged. "Karl and I never could. And now, at thirty-six, here in Shanghai—of all places—surrounded by the enemy . . ." She grabbed Simon's free hand, bringing it to her chest. "We're going to have a baby. God help us, an American baby!"

They all laughed and hugged again.

Hannah went into the kitchen to help Yang serve dinner. Esther turned to Franz and Sunny. "I"—she glanced at Simon with a raw smile—"*We* are so happy. But is it really fair?"

"Is what fair?" Franz asked.

"To bring a baby into this place. All this terrible uncertainty." Esther frowned. "After that Kempeitai colonel warned us that things were about to change for us. What if they intend to put us in camps or ghettos like in Europe? Our security still hangs by only a thread here."

"Esther, this is a blessing," Franz said. "A wonderful new life in spite of all the misery and loss. My brother would be"—he swallowed—"Karl would be so happy for you. For all of us. I *know* it."

Simon wrapped an arm around Esther's waist and pulled her close. "Franz is right, darling. This is a blessing. The very best thing that could happen to us."

Sunny's eyes began to fill. Feeling Franz's hand around her waist, she turned and gazed at him. "A baby, Franz! Maybe, one day we . . ."

"Oh, Sunny, I hope so." His eyes misted too.

She leaned back in his arms and kissed him on the lips, dizzy from the wine and her unbridled happiness.

"For the first time in so long," Franz said, "I hope for tomorrow."

AUTHOR'S NOTE

By the early 1940s, no city better epitomized the microcosm of a world at war than Shanghai. Governed for more than a hundred years by multiple sovereignties, Shanghai had become the fifth-largest city in the world, the planet's third most powerful financial center, and home to arguably the largest and most diverse collection of expatriates, refugees, gamblers, gangsters, prostitutes, political exiles, and other colorful figures to be found anywhere.

Aside from millions of Chinese refugees, two other large communities found a haven in Shanghai: the White Russians who had fled the Soviet Union after the Bolshevik Revolution and the Jews who had escaped Nazi Germany. No other city harbored close to as many German and Austrian Jewish refugees as Shanghai.

By the late 1930s, Hitler had stripped German and Austrian Jews of their careers, homes, possessions, and even their dignity, but it would be another few years before the Nazis launched into systemic genocide. The Nazis allowed—in fact encouraged—Jewish emigration, provided Jews possessed legitimate visas. But after the Evian Conference of 1938, most refugee quotas were exhausted and the rest of the world effectively shut its borders to these desperate Jews. However, Shanghai—a city militarily divided between the Japanese and the Western powers—had almost nonexistent passport control. In the two years leading up to the launch of the Second World War, almost twenty thousand German-speaking Jews found sanctuary in the city.

The novel tells the story of war-torn Shanghai through the eyes of two characters—Dr. Franz Adler, a secular Austrian Jew, and Mah Soon Yi, a native Eurasian nurse—caught up in a whirlwind of events in a unique time and place. While my protagonists are fictional, I endeavored to stay as faithful as possible to the history, culture, and geography of Second World War Shanghai.

Escaping Europe was no guarantee of survival for this subset of Jewish Diaspora who ended up in Shanghai. Exotic and alien, the city could also be uncaring, hostile, and lethal to these refugees. However, the German Jewish culture described in this novel existed, from the shops, restaurants, theaters, and synagogues to the refugee hospital that plays such a pivotal role in the story. Most Jews in Shanghai survived the Second World War. The city continued to boast a thriving Jewish community up until the late 1940s, when Mao Zedong expelled all foreigners. But that fascinating and complex history is for another novel.

Many of the minor characters in the novel, including the Nazis and Japanese officials, are true historical figures. All the events I have dramatized, from the hostile divide before Pearl Harbor to the Nazis' murderous plans for the refugees (championed by the Gestapo colonel Josef Meisinger), are based on fact.

The only point where the story deviates from the known record concerns Adolf Eichmann's secret visit to Shanghai. However, since Eichmann played such an ignominious role in the lives of Vienna's Jews—of course, of all Europe's Jewry—I believed it vital to have him face the relatively small group of Jews who escaped his clutches.

Before I researched this novel, I was oblivious to the essential role Shanghai played in the Second World War, particularly in terms of Jewish survival. I believe it is an often-neglected piece of history that is well worth knowing. And I have tried to capture a glimmer of those refugees' very real, and yet entirely surreal, circumstances.

Turn the page for a preview of

Rising Sun, Falling Shadow

◦—∽ DANIEL KALLA

Available in September 2013 from
Tom Doherty Associates

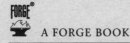
A FORGE BOOK

∽ *Chapter 1*

S oon-Yi Adler—"Sunny" to almost everyone—craved a few moments of fresh air. She still had hours to go in her shift and would be alone with the patients once Irma had changed out of uniform. The older nurse was reluctant to leave the refugee hospital, but Sunny insisted. Irma's husband had developed a fever and, like most refugees, she was terrified of malaria. The mosquitoes that carried the parasite were dormant in wintertime, but the paranoia of it lingered year-round like the stench from Soochow Creek.

Still, Sunny had to escape the ward, if only for a minute or two. The demands of running a hospital through wartime occupation—the constant shortages of food and medicine, the frequent disruption of the power and heat, and the unexpected seizures of what little supplies they had—weighed on her more heavily than ever. Especially today, when the embodiment of all her frustration and futility lay on a stretcher in the hallway draped by a fraying cotton sheet.

Sarah Fleischman had died less than fifteen minutes earlier. She was twenty-eight years old, six months younger than Sunny. The *shomer*, a male volunteer, had already arrived to sit with the body to accompany her soul while awaiting the burial, which, by Jewish law, had to be conducted within two days. Had Frau Fleischman come to the hospital only a week earlier, when the dispensary still possessed a few sulfa pills, her fate might have been so different. Without antibiotics, Sunny could do nothing but administer fluids, morphine, and hollow words of encouragement while the typhoid fever ravaged the young mother of two in front of her eyes.

The tragically familiar pea-soup odor—the hallmark of typhoid deaths—still hung in the air as a ghostly reminder of the woman's departure. Desperate to escape the smell, Sunny bolted down the hallway, yanked open the door, and stepped out into the afternoon chill. It was not yet five o'clock, but the sun—hiding behind the layer of cloud that seemed to permanently enshroud Shanghai this winter—had already begun to set.

Sunny heard men shouting in Japanese and froze halfway down the short pathway between the hospital and the street. She blanched when she spotted the source of the commotion. Four soldiers, whose white armbands marked them as members of the dreaded Kempeitai, were shoving two boys, maybe fifteen or sixteen years old, toward the abandoned building across the street. Sunny recognized the taller boy as the son of one of the Jewish women on the ward. His face was ashen with terror, but unlike his companion, he complied with the Kempeitai men silently.

The other boy's arms flailed as he desperately tried to resist the manhandling. *"Es war nur ein scherz!"* he cried before switching to English. "It was only a prank! We were not going to take it."

One of the Kempeitai men wheeled around and rammed the butt of his rifle into the boy's midsection. Crying out, the boy clasped his belly as he crumpled to his knees. Another soldier grabbed the scruff of his jacket and dragged him through the street.

"Just . . . a misunderstanding," the boy gasped as he was hauled along.

As soon as they reached the wall, the soldiers spun the boys around until they faced the road. The taller teenager's eyes locked onto Sunny's, imploring her to help. But her feet felt as though cast in clay and her tongue as if glued to the roof of her mouth. She had a flashback to a violent night four years earlier, when she had been attacked in the street by a drunken Japanese sailor—and the much greater tragedy that had followed.

Sunny hid her terror behind what she hoped was a comforting expression, the same one she had offered Sarah Fleischman in her last conscious moments. Her chest ached from the shame of her passivity, but she managed to sustain eye contact with the petrified boy.

"Stand straight!" one of the Kempeitai men barked in English.

Two of the soldiers stood shoulder to shoulder in the street ten feet in front of the boys and simultaneously raised their rifles. Dread overcame Sunny and her throat tightened.

The taller boy began to tremble. His companion raised his arms to shield his chest and face. "Please, please!" He cried out from behind his hands. "Our families were hungry. We have to eat. We are not thieves!"

The door whooshed open behind Sunny. She glanced over her shoulder to see Irma filling the doorway. The plump woman instantly appreciated what was happening and rushed toward the soldiers without hesitation.

Sunny shot out a hand out to stop her, but Irma swept past. "*Stop!*" she cried as she ran. "They are only boys! This is madness!"

One of the soldiers spun around. The muzzle of his

rifle flared twice. Sunny flinched at the crack of gun-shots, a cry lost in her throat.

Irma dropped to the pavement in midstride, as though someone had cut her legs out from beneath her.

"*Gott helfe uns!*" the shorter boy screamed.

The rifleman turned back toward the boys. Sunny covered her face, unable to watch. She could hear one of the men calling out in Japanese and, from his cadence, could tell that he was counting.

"No, no, no . . ." she muttered into her hands.

Two more shots rang in her ears and echoed along the street. A sulfuric smell drifted toward her. In the silence that followed, she kept her eyes squeezed shut, unwilling to face the inevitable.

Moments later, Sunny heard footsteps pounding the pavement as the soldiers marched off. Finally, once the worst of her trembling had subsided, Sunny opened her eyes.

Irma lay face down in the street. The two boys were slumped at the foot of the wall like a pair of discarded rag dolls.

⌐ *Chapter 2*

FEBRUARY 18, 1943

Franz Adler's black oxfords—twice resoled and polished until the leather had thinned—sank even deeper in the field's muck. The wet breeze seemed to penetrate his coat's lining, and he fought off another shiver. Franz didn't mind the cold, but the dampness was dismal. He would have gladly traded Shanghai's dreary rain for the snow that often blanketed Vienna at this time of year.

Franz's gaze drifted to the oval fence surrounding him. It outlined the track where the horses had once run, but he barely recognized the Shanghai racecourse. How different the place had looked on his previous visit, before the war. That sunny afternoon, Franz rubbed elbows with American and British Shanghailanders, along with the wealthiest of local Chinese. The city's upper crust snacked on éclairs, strawberries with cream, and chilled champagne, many betting more on a single horse race than most of the sampan families—who often spent their entire lives aboard their houseboats on the Whangpoo River—would see in a lifetime. With its vibrantly painted stands and ultrafashionable guests, especially the women in bright silk cheongsams, the track was an explosion of color in Franz's memory. But now, everything around him—the sky, the grounds, and even the people—looked gray. In his mind's eye, he framed a photograph. The scene epitomized the kind of faded glory that he loved to capture through the lens, although these days a roll of film was a rare and precious commodity that was beyond his means.

Several Shanghailanders stood near Franz, but little about the ragtag crowd hinted at its members' former standing or prosperity. Most stooped under the weight of overstuffed knapsacks. Pots and pans dangled from their packs, clanging noisily. They might have resembled a gathering of one-man bands, if not for the sense of gloom that engulfed them. The men wore red armbands imprinted with a single letter; almost all read *A* for American. A few women hovered near their husbands, their worry palpable. The Japanese were trucking the men off to the internment camp, which they insisted on referring to as "the Chapei Civic Assembly Center." No one knew when, or if, the wives would join their husbands.

Infantrymen in khaki uniforms and brimmed caps formed a loose ring around the captives. Some soldiers stood at ease, rifles slung over their shoulders, while others held their guns across the chest, at the ready. The soldier nearest to Franz tapped his finger on the weapon's trigger casing, while viewing the prisoners with unconcealed loathing.

Simon Lehrer nodded to the scowling guard. "What do you figure, Franz?" he asked in a low voice and winked. "Is that the guy to turn to for special treatment?"

Franz covered his mouth with hand and muttered, "Take care with him, Simon. With all of them."

"You know me, Franz. I'm only about self-preservation."

Franz hoped that Simon's show of bravado was intended to calm his wife, Esther, who clung to his arm. Franz's own wife, Sunny, stood on the other side of them, silently surveying the tense scene.

Simon stood out among the American prisoners. Not only was he taller than most, but his was the only smiling face. He had drifted to Shanghai five years earlier to avoid managing his family's furniture business in the Bronx but, ironically, ended up shouldering a far greater responsibility as the director of the CFA, the Committee for Assistance of European Refugees. Since the attack on Pearl Harbor, the American and British citizens who ran the CFA, including Simon, had all been deemed hostile aliens. They were, arguably, even worse off than Shanghai's twenty thousand German refugees, many of whom they had once helped to house and feed.

Another gust of wind swept over the track. Franz flipped up the collar on his tattered coat and dug his gloveless hands deeper into his pockets. Unlike the Americans, he had come to the racetrack voluntarily, and only to say good-bye to his friend. Franz was not a prisoner of war. Not yet, at least. As an Austrian Jew, he held no official nationality. The Nazis had stripped him of his citizenship—along with his academic standing, his career and his savings—years before, back in Europe. In the eyes of the Japanese, Franz was a stateless refugee: "a nothing, a no one, a nonperson," as one of his refugee colleagues often put it.

Why now? The question had been on the lips of Shanghailanders for weeks. The Japanese had originally conquered Shanghai in pieces, overrunning the Chinese-controlled neighborhoods five years earlier and then seizing the International Settlement—the European enclave—on the same day that their bombs decimated Pearl Harbor. They had frozen bank accounts, appropriated assets, and rationed everything from rice to heating oil but had allowed most Allied citizens to live relatively freely for over a year. Some speculated that the sudden roundup was in retaliation for the internment of Japanese citizens abroad, while others saw it as sign that the Japanese were running scared after a series of military setbacks at Guadalcanal and in New Guinea. The rumor mill ran rampant among Shanghailanders still awaiting internment. Stories of food shortages, lice, and beatings inside the prison camps electrified the ever-shrinking Shanghailander community.

Esther wrapped Simon's arm in both of hers. Her pregnant belly was visible through her wool coat, though her face appeared thinner than ever. With her deep-set eyes and stoic gaze, she was usually the epitome of poise, so it was unsettling to see her now on the verge of panic.

Franz understood her anxiety only too well. Esther

had once been married to his younger brother, Karl. Four years earlier, on the night of Kristallnacht, Franz had found her crouched in the alley behind her husband's office building, bleeding from her lacerated arm. Out front, Karl's body dangled from the lamppost where a Nazi mob had hanged him. Now, seven months into a precious unexpected pregnancy, Esther was facing the prospect of losing a second husband.

She tugged at Simon's arm. *"Ich will mit dir kommen,"* she implored in a thick voice. "Let me come with you. Please, Simon."

"To have our baby born in a prison camp?" He patted her belly. "Never, Essie. It's better this way."

Esther clasped his hand against her abdomen. "She needs her father."

"Soon, Essie." Simon stroked her cheek. "Meantime, his aunt and uncle will have to look out for the little fella."

"Of course we will," Sunny spoke up. "After all, Essie and the baby will stay with us until your release."

"I'm still not convinced that is necessary," Esther murmured.

Sunny laid her hand on Esther's shoulder. "Necessary or not, you are family."

"There is more than enough room for you and the baby," Franz said. "We want you with us, Essie."

"It will give me a whole lot of piece mind, too." Simon grinned. "After all, what Jewish parent wouldn't want his kid living with a couple of doctors?"

"Besides," Sunny added with a small laugh. "Hannah has already decided for you. You do realize that she intends to be the baby's amah?"

Franz bit back a smile. His daughter would be a teenager in two months. Despite her mild left-sided weakness—a consequence of her difficult birth, which had also claimed her mother's life—Hannah had adapted to life in Shanghai better than rest of her family. She spoke Mandarin and Shanghainese fluently. And ever since Hannah had learned of her aunt's pregnancy, she had been preparing for the new arrival as though the baby would be her own.

Esther nodded in gratitude, but her expression showed little relief. She continued to speak softly in German, so as not to be overheard by the guards or other prisoners. "Simon, these camps . . . the rumors . . . How will you manage?"

"I'll be fine." Simon winked. "You'll see. I will be the one on the inside with all the cigarettes and chocolates. Silk stockings, too, if you need those."

Esther was unappeased. "The last time the Japanese took you away . . ."

Simon winced. Franz shared his friend's revulsion. The previous summer, the feared Kempeitai had arrested both of them on suspicion of spreading a rumor among the refugee community that the local Japanese government was complicit in an SS plan to exterminate Shanghai's Jews—a plan that, thankfully, had never come to fruition. Those six days of interrogation and torture at Bridge House still haunted Franz. Some nights, he would wake in a cold sweat, still able to taste the moldy towel that had been stuffed in his mouth and the foul water that had trickled down his throat, choking him.

Simon shook his head. "This time is different, Essie. We're being interned, not arrested."

"How does anyone really know?"

Simon cupped her face in his hands. "We'll be one happy family—all three of us—in no time. Trust me, Essie."

"I do, darling." Esther switched to English. "I am

being selfish. I will miss you so much. I so want you to be here when . . ." She glanced down at her belly.

Simon tapped his chest. "They can't keep us apart."

"No. Never." Esther showed her first smile of the day. "Besides, this is not so bad as the catastrophe that befell your precious Yankees."

"You got a point there." Simon laughed. He had sulked for days when the radio broke the news that his beloved Bronx Bombers had lost the 1942 World Series to the St. Louis Cardinals.

One of the Japanese officers lifted a bullhorn to his mouth and shrieked, "All American men line here for transport you to Civic Assembly Center. All now! All others to go immediately."

The soldiers advanced toward the prisoners with their rifles leveled. Sunny hugged Simon and kissed him on the cheek. "We will bring you supplies as soon as we can."

Simon grinned. "I would never say no to more of Yang's treats, that's for sure. Kosher or not, I love your housekeeper's rice balls!"

Franz stepped forward. Lost for words, he simply clapped Simon's shoulder and shook his hand.

"I give the Nazis and the Japs six months, tops," Simon said, though Franz doubted his friend believed that fantasy any more than he did.

Sunny reached for Franz's hand and guided him back a few more steps, allowing Simon and Esther a moment of privacy.

Even after the other prisoners had fallen into line, Esther and Simon stood with their foreheads touching, exchanging whispered words. A Japanese soldier hurried over and jabbed Simon in the back with the butt of his rifle. After regaining his balance, Simon kissed

Esther on the lips, then turned and headed for the end of the line without a look back.

~

Sunny, Esther, and Franz trudged down Bubbling Well Road in somber silence. Tall neoclassical and art deco buildings loomed overhead, including the city's tallest skyscraper, the Park Hotel. Rickshaws and pedicabs rushed down the four-lane road. Until recently, roaring American automobiles and coughing trucks had lined the thoroughfare, but the Japanese, in their need to stockpile fuel, had since prohibited the use of nonmilitary vehicles in the city.

They reached the main road, named Avenue Edward VII on the north side and Avenue Foche on the south. Until Pearl Harbor, it had formed an informal border between two separately administered entities within the city: the International Settlement and the French Concession, known by most as simply "Frenchtown." The sovereign distinction was long gone. Still, it was hard to ignore the sudden shift in architectural style from the prim and proper British rigor that dominated the International Settlement to the more laissez-faire approach of Frenchtown.

"Why don't you come home with us, Essie?" Sunny asked. "We can collect your belongings later."

"No, thank you," Esther murmured. "I need a little time to organize my home first."

Franz suspected that she also needed private time to grieve. His heart ached for Essie. After more than a decade as a widower, he could not stomach the idea of being forcibly separated from Sunny again. Their eighteen-month marriage had been the bright spot in an otherwise dark and difficult few years. During the week he had been held captive in Bridge House, the idea that he might never see her again was harder to endure than the physical torture.

Franz had met Sunny on his first visit to the refugee hospital. She was the only volunteer nurse who was neither German nor Jewish. After years of unofficial apprenticeship at the side of her father, a prominent local physician, Sunny was as knowledgeable as any doctor. Franz offered to mentor her in surgical technique, and within a few years, she was performing at the level of a junior surgeon or better. He had been struck from their first encounter by her delicate Eurasian features: her teardrop-shaped eyes, sloping cheekbones, and glowing alabaster skin. But it was her poise, compassion, and empathy—the way she could read his mood in a glance and know exactly when to offer him a reassuring smile— that had stolen his heart.

Franz and Sunny walked Esther home through the damp littered streets of Frenchtown, passing luckless merchants and skeletal beggars but, like most others in the street, had nothing to offer them. Eventually, they reached Avenue Joffre in the heart of Little Russia: a neighborhood populated with White Russians who had fled to Shanghai after the Russian Civil War. Since Japan and the Soviet Union had signed a neutrality pact, the Russians—including a large Jewish contingent— fared better than most, but even Little Russia had suffered in the face of constant rationing, inflation, and shortages. The broken windows, backed-up gutters, and stench of stale garbage reaffirmed for Franz that Shanghai was a shell of her former self, little more than a ruin in the making.

A girl rushed down the street toward them. Even before Franz could make out her features, he recognized his daughter by her gait, which was slightly lopsided as she ran. He opened his arms to greet her, but Hannah stopped short and thrust a sheet of paper out to him.

"Papa, have you seen this?" she panted.

Franz took the page from her. "No, *liebchen*."

"What is it, Hannah?" Sunny asked.

"A proclamation! The Japanese have posted them all over."

Sunny and Esther crowded in while Franz read the English words aloud: "Proclamation concerning restriction of residence and business of stateless refugees." The hairs on his neck stood up. "Due to military necessity, places of residence and business of stateless refugees in the Shanghai area shall hereafter be restricted to the under mentioned area."

"They mean the German and Austrian Jews, Papa," Hannah murmured. "Us!"

Franz locked eyes with his daughter. He considered telling her that everything was going to be fine, but he realized she would see right through the lie. All he could muster was a meek "Yes, Hanna-*chen*."

The proclamation went on to declare that all stateless refugees had until the eighteenth of May to sell their homes and businesses and relocate to a narrow area within Hongkew, one of the most crowded boroughs in the city. It concluded with an ominous threat—"Persons who violate the proclamation or obstruct its reinforcement shall be liable to severe punishment"—and was signed by the military governor.

Sunny squeezed his hand until her nails dug into his skin. Franz knew that she must have been thinking about her parents' house—the only home she had ever known—but all she said was, "Three months, Franz."

Before he could reply, Esther's gaze darted frantically from Sunny to Franz. "A *ghetto!* Just like the Nazis created in Poland. Like Warsaw and Lodz."

All the local Jews had heard horror stories of the ghettos in Eastern Europe. "Essie, you cannot jump to . . ."

Esther's anguished expression silenced him. "My baby . . . born in a ghetto. His father gone. *Mein Gott,* what next?"

Forge

Award-winning authors
Compelling stories

. . . .

Please join us at the website
below for more information
about this author and other great
Forge selections, and to sign up for
our monthly newsletter!